Witches' Brew

Witches' Brew

Edited by
YVONNE JOCKS

BERKLEY BOOKS, NEW YORK

B

A Berkley Book
Published by The Berkley Publishing Group
A division of Penguin Putnam Inc.
375 Hudson Street
New York, New York 10014

Copyright © 2002 by Yvonne Jocks and Tekno Books.
Cover design by Jill Boltin.

Complete acknowledgments of credits and permissions can be found on pages 325–26.

PRINTING HISTORY
Berkley trade paperback edition / October 2002

Visit our website at
www.penguinputnam.com

Library of Congress Cataloging-in-Publication Data

Witches' brew / edited by Yvonne Jocks.
p. cm.
ISBN 0-425-18609-1
1. Witchcraft—Literary collections. 2. Witches—Literary collections. 3. American literature.
4. English literature. I. Jocks, Yvonne.

PS509.W57 W58 2002
810.8'037—dc21

2002071279

PRINTED IN THE UNITED STATES OF AMERICA

10 9 8 7 6 5 4 3 2 1

This collection is dedicated to all the great authors, whether or not they've found the popularity and critical acclaim they deserve, who understand the true magic of writing. To all the incredible teachers—particularly standouts like my teachers Ms. Albuquerque in Arizona (2nd grade), Mrs. Johnson in Louisiana (5th grade), and Mrs. Shirley Cooper in Texas (high school)—who teach us to appreciate that magic. And finally, thanks to Denise and the fabulous Ginjer Buchanan, who made this book happen.

CONTENTS

Witchcraft As Empowerment

The Nature Witch

Introduction

Yvonne Jocks

They call to us.

Who can remember a time when witches didn't fascinate? Magic users sweep through children's stories as old as "Hansel and Gretel" and as current as the Harry Potter series, filling movie screens from *Snow White and the Seven Dwarfs* to *The Little Mermaid*. They beckon to teenagers from television shows like *Sabrina, the Teenage Witch, Charmed,* and *Buffy the Vampire Slayer,* and from movies like *The Craft* and *The Blair Witch Project*. Even adults hear the call of witches, since before *Bewitched* to well after *Practical Magic*.

They captivate us.

Some of us seek witches' powers in the New Age shelves of our local bookstores, or at crystal- and incense-laden metaphysical shops. Others warn against witches' popularity . . . and perhaps try to remember their grandmother's instructions for warding off the evil eye. Still others find amusement in the prevalence of such pure make-believe. But are witches mere make-believe anymore?

Were they ever?

Much of that depends on what you think of when you think of that one word: *witch*.

Modern practitioners point to the Anglo-Saxon word *wicce,* meaning a wise person, one who can bend or shape. To such followers of Wicca, one of the fastest growing religions in the country, a witch is someone who worships a Goddess along with (or even instead of) a God, and who practices positive, nature-oriented magic. Make-believe? Hardly. Wiccans and neopagans have precedents in literature as ancient as the Akkadian epic *Gilgamesh*, in which a priestess tames the beast-man Enkidu into a proper companion to the king. They recognize themselves in Irish epics, which are full of goddesses, prophetesses, and druids, and in King Arthur's misunderstood half sister, Morgan le Fay.

But what of the tragic *Medea* of Euripides, whose sorcery first wins and then destroys Jason of the Argonauts? What of the witch Circe, who seduces Homer's Odysseus, or Queen Dido, who turns to the black arts after her desertion by Virgil's Aeneas? For modern-day Wiccans, whose only rule is "Harm none," these witch stories offer less representation.

Others see a witch as a powerful woman, usually one who uses her magic for ill. Dido, Circe, and Medea fit more comfortably into this definition. So do the classic Wyrd Sisters of Shakespeare's *Macbeth*, horror-movie witches, even fairy-tale antagonists. She is the cackling hag who lives alone and whose ugliness, like Medusa's, carries a horrid power. She is the untamed seductress whose siren song, like the Lorelei's, can lead man to his death. . . .

She is, frankly, the personification of feminine power, unshackled by patriarchal control. There have always been powerful women who threaten the status quo and are thus accused of witchcraft, from Joan of Arc to Susan B. Anthony. Make-believe? True, these women had powers hinging less on eye of newt than on recognizing their own strengths. But as far as metaphors go, the "evil witch" archetype does the job. How many relatively modern stories about witches still show the heroines giving up their powers to marry? How many of the older stories call well-behaved, nurturing magic users mere "fairies" or "fairy godmothers," be they from Shakespeare's *Midsummer Night's Dream* or any standard version of *Cinderella*? In Disney's *Sleeping Beauty,* the sweet but bumbling Flora, Fauna, and Merryweather are fairies. But the scorned Maleficent— "Now you deal with me, oh prince, and all the powers of Hell!"

By popular opinion, *she's* a witch.

And in this, Maleficent invokes a third definition of the witch: a person, male or female, who gains supernatural power through dealing with demons or the devil. Easily the most frightening of all, this is the sort of witchcraft claimed by Anton LaVey and Aleister Crowley, the kind described in horrifying detail by H. P. Lovecraft. Such so-called "witches" create a public-relations nightmare for the aforementioned Wiccans, and have historically added fuel to the fires that burned powerful women like Joan of Arc. Whether or not a Faustian conspiracy exists, much less wields supernatural power, remains hotly debated in arenas from daytime talk shows to Christian newsletters to occasional episodes of *The X-Files.* But make-believe or not, the consequences of such fear mongering have proven all too real. Thus comes the suspense, the danger of witchcraft—be it danger to us, or to the more innocent among the witches.

Witches enthrall us. And we let them. Their legacy of magical possibilities, of feminine power, even of dark conspiracy pervades our society and grips our imagination. Good or evil, fascinating or terrifying, holding powers we can barely comprehend, and yet somehow accessible, witches call to us.

A popular Wiccan bumper sticker states that "We Are Everywhere," and it's true.

They are everywhere.

Witches are in all cultures. They are from all times. And from the Puritanism of Nathaniel Hawthorne to the Wicca of Doreen Valiente, writers have never been able to resist the tingle down the spine, the air of mystery, and the call to power that is central in a really good witch's tale.

So here, gathered for your enjoyment, are some of the best stories featuring witches. Running the gamut from ancient to modern, and from positive magic to dark thrillers, these selections will keep you up at night, make you think, and . . . just perhaps . . . make you wonder how much of the magic is real.

It's a witches' brew, indeed, of the best in fiction about witches.

Maybe it will cast its spell over you.

Yvonne Jocks
Summer 2001

Something Wicked This Way Comes:
The Wicked Witch

Modern-day Wiccans hate being confused with devil wor-shippers, and why not? It's misleading, it's fear inducing, and it's downright insulting.

But the idea of the demonic witch has made for some darned good horror stories, all the same.

From William Shakespeare's famous scene from *Macbeth* to Cotton Mather's disturbing accounts of one of the Salem Witch Trials, here are some tales about the most frightening and fictitious type of witch—the witch who has attained his or her powers from dealing with the Dark Side.

Read on.
And watch out.

Macbeth, Act IV, Scene I

William Shakespeare

One of the most famous authors in the world wrote three of the most famous witches ever. The chant of these so-called Wyrd Sisters is often misquoted ("Bubble, bubble, toil and trouble") but always powerful. Could they be behind the supposed curse of "The Scottish Play?"

Act IV, Scene I

A dark Cave. In the middle, a Caldron Boiling.

[Thunder. Enter the three Witches.]

FIRST WITCH
Thrice the brinded cat hath mew'd.

SECOND WITCH
Thrice; and once the hedge-pig whin'd.

THIRD WITCH
Harpier cries:—'tis time, 'tis time.

FIRST WITCH
Round about the caldron go;
In the poison'd entrails throw.—
Toad, that under cold stone,
Days and nights has thirty-one
Swelter'd venom sleeping got,
Boil thou first i' the charmed pot!

ALL
Double, double, toil and trouble;
Fire, burn; and caldron, bubble.

SECOND WITCH
Fillet of a fenny snake,
In the caldron boil and bake;
Eye of newt, and toe of frog,
Wool of bat, and tongue of dog,
Adder's fork, and blind-worm's sting,
Lizard's leg, and howlet's wing,—
For a charm of powerful trouble,
Like a hell-broth boil and bubble.

ALL
Double, double, toil and trouble;
Fire, burn; and caldron, bubble.

THIRD WITCH
Scale of dragon, tooth of wolf,
Witch's mummy, maw and gulf
Of the ravin'd salt-sea shark,
Root of hemlock digg'd i' the dark,
Liver of blaspheming Jew,
Gall of goat, and slips of yew
Sliver'd in the moon's eclipse,
Nose of Turk, and Tartar's lips,
Finger of birth-strangl'd babe
Ditch-deliver'd by a drab,—
Make the gruel thick and slab:
Add thereto a tiger's chaudron.
For the ingredients of our caldron.

ALL
Double, double, toil and trouble;
Fire, burn; and caldron, bubble.

SECOND WITCH
Cool it with a baboon's blood,
Then the charm is firm and good.

[Enter Hecate.]

HECATE
O, well done! I commend your pains;
And everyone shall share i' the gains.
And now about the cauldron sing,
Like elves and fairies in a ring,
Enchanting all that you put in.

[Song.]

Black spirits and white, red spirits and gray;
Mingle, mingle, mingle, you that mingle may.

[Exit Hecate.]

SECOND WITCH
By the pricking of my thumbs,
Something wicked this way comes:—
Open, locks, whoever knocks!

[Enter Macbeth.]

MACBETH
How now, you secret, black, and midnight hags!
What is't you do?

ALL
A deed without a name . . .

The Leather Funnel

Sir Arthur Conan Doyle

Oh, sure, we all remember Doyle's Sherlock Holmes. But let's not forget that Sir Arthur Conan Doyle was also a strong believer in nineteenth-century spiritualism, particularly magic and fairies. "The Leather Funnel" takes a darker look at the world of magic: Although the word witch *is never used, the term* poisoner *is commonly interchanged with* witch *(including in the biblical warning that one shalt not suffer a poisoner to live); the collector appears to be a male witch; and the similarity in Inquisition techniques smacks of the Burning Times. So is it a reach?*

M Y friend, Lionel Dacre, lived in the Avenue de Wagram, Paris. His house was that small one, with the iron railings and grass plot in front of it, on the left-hand side as you pass down from the Arc de Triomphe. I fancy that it had been there long before the avenue was constructed, for the grey tiles were stained with lichens, and the walls were mildewed and discoloured with age. It looked a small house from the street, five windows in front, if I remember right, but it deepened into a single long chamber at the back. It was here that Dacre had that singular library of occult literature, and the fantastic curiosities which served as a hobby for himself, and an amusement for his friends. A wealthy man of refined and eccentric tastes, he had spent much of his life and fortune in gathering together what was said to be a unique private collection of Talmudic, cabalistic, and magical works, many of them of great rarity and value. His tastes leaned toward the marvellous and the monstrous, and I have heard that his experiments in the direction of the unknown have passed all the bounds of civilization and of decorum. To his English friends he never alluded to such matters, and took the tone of the student and virtuoso; but a Frenchman whose tastes were of the same nature has assured me that the worst excesses of the black mass have been perpetrated in that large and lofty hall, which is lined with the shelves of his books, and the cases of his museum.

Dacre's appearance was enough to show that his deep interest in these psychic matters was intellectual rather than spiritual. There was no trace of asceticism upon his heavy face, but there was much mental force in his huge, dome-like skull, which curved upward from amongst his thinning locks, like a snowpeak above its fringe of fir trees. His knowledge was greater than his wisdom, and his powers were far superior to his character. The small bright eyes, buried deeply in his fleshy face, twinkled with intelligence and an unabated curiosity of life, but they were the eyes of a sensualist and an egotist. Enough of the man, for he is dead now, poor devil, dead at the very time that he had made sure that he had at last discovered the elixir of life. It is not with his complex character that I have to deal, but with the very strange and inexplicable incident which had its rise in my visit to him in the early spring of the year '82.

I had known Dacre in England, for my researches in the Assyrian Room of the British Museum had been conducted at the time when he was endeavouring to establish a mystic and esoteric meaning in the Babylonian tablets, and this community of interests had brought us together. Chance remarks had led to daily conversation, and that to something verging upon friendship. I had promised him that on my next visit to Paris I would call upon him. At the time when I was able to fulfil my compact I was living in a cottage at Fontainebleau, and as the evening trains were inconvenient, he asked me to spend the night in his house.

"I have only that one spare couch," said he, pointing to a broad sofa in his large salon; "I hope that you will manage to be comfortable there."

It was a singular bedroom, with its high walls of brown volumes, but there could be no more agreeable furniture to a bookworm like myself, and there is no scent so pleasant to my nostrils as that faint, subtle reek which comes from an ancient book. I assured him that I could desire no more charming chamber, and no more congenial surroundings.

"If the fittings are neither convenient nor conventional, they are at least costly," said he, looking round at his shelves. "I have expended nearly a quarter of a million of money upon these objects which surround you. Books, weapons, gems, carvings, tapestries, images—there is hardly a thing here which has not its history, and it is generally one worth telling."

He was seated as he spoke at one side of the open fire-place, and I at the other. His reading-table was on his right, and the strong lamp above it ringed it with a very vivid circle of golden light. A half-rolled palimpsest lay in the centre, and around it were many quaint articles of bric-a-brac. One of these was a large funnel, such as is used for filling wine casks. It appeared to be made of black wood, and to be rimmed with discoloured brass.

"That is a curious thing," I remarked. "What is the history of that?"

"Ah!" said he, "it is the very question which I have had occasion to ask myself. I would give a good deal to know. Take it in your hands and examine it."

I did so, and found that what I had imagined to be wood was in reality leather, though age had dried it into an extreme hardness. It was a large funnel, and might hold a quart when full. The brass rim encircled the wide end, but the narrow was also tipped with metal.

"What do you make of it?" asked Dacre.

"I should imagine that it belonged to some vintner or maltster in the Middle Ages," said I. "I have seen in England leathern drinking flagons of the seventeenth century—'black jacks' as they were called—which were of the same colour and hardness as this filler."

"I dare say the date would be about the same," said Dacre, "and, no doubt, also, it was used for filling a vessel with liquid. If my suspicions are correct, however, it was a queer vintner who used it, and a very singular cask which was filled. Do you observe nothing strange at the spout end of the funnel?"

As I held it to the light I observed that at a spot some five inches above the brass tip the narrow neck of the leather funnel was all haggled and scored, as if someone had notched it round with a blunt knife. Only at that point was there any roughening of the dead black surface.

"Someone has tried to cut off the neck."

"Would you call it a cut?"

"It is torn and lacerated. It must have taken some strength to leave these marks on such tough material, whatever the instrument may have been. But what do you think of it? I can tell that you know more than you say."

Dacre smiled, and his little eyes twinkled with knowledge.

"Have you included the psychology of dreams among your learned studies?" he asked.

"I did not even know that there was such a psychology."

"My dear sir, that shelf above the gem case is filled with volumes, from Albertus Magnus onward, which deal with no other subject. It is a science in itself."

"A science of charlatans."

"The charlatan is always the pioneer. From the astrologer came the astronomer, from the alchemist the chemist, from the mesmerist the experimental psychologist. The quack of yesterday is the professor of to-morrow. Even such subtle and elusive things as dreams will in time be reduced to system and order. When that time comes the researches of our friends on the bookshelf yonder will no longer be the amusement of the mystic, but the foundations of a science."

"Supposing that is so, what has the science of dreams to do with a large, black, brass-rimmed funnel?"

"I will tell you. You know that I have an agent who is always on the look-out for rarities and curiosities for my collection. Some days ago he heard of a dealer upon one of the Quais who had acquired some old rubbish found in a cupboard in an ancient house at the back of the Rue Mathurin, in the Quartier Latin. The dining-room of this old house is decorated with a coat of arms, chevrons, and bars rouge upon a field argent, which prove, upon inquiry, to be the shield of Nicholas de la Reynie, a high official of King Louis XIV. There can be no doubt that the other articles in the cupboard date back to the early days of that king. The inference is, therefore, that they were all the property of this Nicholas de la Reynie, who was, as I understand, the gentleman specially concerned with the maintenance and execution of the Draconic laws of that epoch."

"What then?"

"I would ask you now to take the funnel into your hands once more and to examine the upper brass rim. Can you make out any lettering upon it?"

There were certainly some scratches upon it, almost obliterated by time. The general effect was of several letters, the last of which bore some resemblance to a *B*.

"You make it a B?"

"Yes, I do."

"So do I. In fact, I have no doubt whatever that it is a B."

"But the nobleman you mentioned would have had R for his initial."

"Exactly! That's the beauty of it. He owned this curious object, and yet he had someone else's initials upon it. Why did he do this?"

"I can't imagine; can you?"

"Well, I might, perhaps, guess. Do you observe something drawn a little farther along the rim?"

"I should say it was a crown."

"It is undoubtedly a crown; but if you examine it in a good light, you will convince yourself that it is not an ordinary crown. It is a heraldic crown—a badge of rank, and it consists of an alternation of four pearls and strawberry leaves, the proper badge of a marquis. We may infer, therefore, that the person whose initials end in B was entitled to wear that coronet."

"Then this common leather filler belonged to a marquis?"

Dacre gave a peculiar smile.

"Or to some member of the family of a marquis," said he. "So much we have clearly gathered from this engraved rim."

"But what has all this to do with dreams?" I do not know whether it was from a look upon Dacre's face, or from some subtle suggestion in his manner, but a feeling of repulsion, of unreasoning horror, came upon me as I looked at the gnarled old lump of leather.

"I have more than once received important information through my dreams," said my companion in the didactic manner which he loved to affect. "I make it a rule now when I am in doubt upon any material point to place the article in question beside me as I sleep, and to hope for some enlightenment. The process does not appear to me to be very obscure, though it has not yet received the blessing of orthodox science. According to my theory, any object which has been intimately associated with any supreme paroxysm of human emotion, whether it be joy or pain, will retain a certain atmosphere or association which it is capable of communicating to a sensitive mind. By a sensitive mind I do not mean an abnormal one, but such a trained and educated mind as you or I possess."

"You mean, for example, that if I slept beside that old sword upon the wall, I might dream of some bloody incident in which that very sword took part?"

"An excellent example, for, as a matter of fact, that sword was used in that fashion by me, and I saw in my sleep the death of its owner, who perished in a brisk skirmish, which I have been unable to identify, but which occurred at the time of the wars of the Frondists. If you think of it, some of our popular observances show that the fact has already been recognized by our ancestors, although we, in our wisdom, have classed it among superstitions."

"For example?"

"Well, the placing of the bride's cake beneath the pillow in order that the sleeper may have pleasant dreams. That is one of several instances which you will find set forth in a small brochure which I am myself writing upon the subject. But to come back to the point, I slept one night with this funnel beside me, and I had a dream which certainly throws a curious light upon its use and origin."

"What did you dream?"

"I dreamed—" He paused, and an intent look of interest came over his massive face. "By Jove, that's well thought of," said he. "This really will be an exceedingly interesting experiment. You are yourself a psychic subject—with nerves which respond readily to any impression."

"I have never tested myself in that direction."

"Then we shall test you tonight. Might I ask you as a very great favour, when you occupy that couch tonight, to sleep with this old funnel placed by the side of your pillow?"

The request seemed to me a grotesque one; but I have myself, in my complex nature, a hunger after all which is bizarre and fantastic. I had not the faintest belief in Dacre's theory, nor any hopes for success in such an experiment; yet it amused me that the experiment should be made. Dacre, with great gravity, drew a small stand to the head of my settee, and placed the funnel upon it. Then, after a short conversation, he wished me good night and left me.

I sat for some little time smoking by the smouldering fire, and turning over in my mind the curious incident which had occurred, and the strange experience which might lie before me. Sceptical as I was, there was something impressive in the assurance of Dacre's manner, and my extraordinary surroundings, the huge room with the strange and often sinister objects which were hung round it, struck solemnity into my soul. Finally I undressed, and turning out the lamp, I lay down. After long tossing I fell asleep. Let me try to describe as accurately as I can the scene which came to me in my dreams. It stands out now in my memory more clearly than anything which I have seen with my waking eyes. There was a room which bore the appearance of a vault. Four spandrels from the corners ran up to join a sharp, cup-shaped roof. The architecture was rough, but very strong. It was evidently part of a great building.

Three men in black, with curious, top-heavy, black velvet hats, sat in a line upon a red-carpeted dais. Their faces were very solemn and sad. On the left stood two long-gowned men with port-folios in their hands, which seemed to be stuffed with papers. Upon the right, looking toward me, was a small woman with blonde hair and singular, light-blue eyes— the eyes of a child. She was past her first youth, but could not yet be called middle-aged. Her figure was inclined to stoutness and her bearing was proud and confident. Her face was pale, but serene. It was a curious face, comely and yet feline, with a subtle suggestion of cruelty about the straight, strong little mouth and chubby jaw. She was draped in some sort of loose, white gown. Beside her stood a thin, eager priest, who whispered in her ear, and continually raised a crucifix before her eyes. She turned her head and looked fixedly past the crucifix at the three men in black, who were, I felt, her judges.

As I gazed the three men stood up and said something, but I could distinguish no words, though I was aware that it was the central one who was speaking. They then swept out of the room, followed by the two men with the papers. At the same instant several rough-looking fellows in stout jerkins came bustling in and removed first the red carpet, and then the boards which formed the dais, so as to entirely clear the room. When this screen was removed I saw some singular articles of furniture behind it. One looked like a bed with wooden rollers at each end, and a winch handle to regulate its length. Another was a wooden horse. There were several other curious objects, and a number of swinging cords which played over pulleys. It was not unlike a modern gymnasium.

When the room had been cleared there appeared a new figure upon the scene. This was a tall, thin person clad in black, with a gaunt and austere face. The aspect of the man made me shudder. His clothes were all shining with grease and mottled with stains. He bore himself with a slow and impressive dignity, as if he took command of all things from the instant of his entrance. In spite of his rude appearance and sordid dress, it was now his business, his room, his to command. He carried a coil of light ropes over his left forearm. The lady looked him up and down with a searching glance, but her expression was unchanged. It was confident—even defiant. But it was very different with the priest. His face was ghastly white, and I saw the moisture glisten and run on his high, sloping forehead. He threw up his hands in prayer and he stooped continually to mutter frantic words in the lady's ear.

The man in black now advanced, and taking one of the cords from his left arm, he bound the woman's hands together. She held them meekly toward him as he did so. Then he took her arm with a rough grip and led her toward the wooden horse, which was little higher than her waist. On to this she was lifted and laid, with her back upon it, and her face to the ceiling, while the priest, quivering with horror, had rushed out of the room. The woman's lips were moving rapidly, and though I could hear nothing I knew that she was praying. Her feet hung down on either side of the horse, and I saw that the rough varlets in attendance had fastened cords to her ankles and secured the other ends to iron rings in the stone floor.

My heart sank within me as I saw these ominous preparations, and yet I was held by the fascination of horror, and I could not take my eyes from the strange spectacle. A man had entered the room with a bucket of water in either hand. Another followed with a third bucket. They were laid beside the wooden horse. The second man had a wooden dipper—a bowl with a straight handle—in his other hand. This he gave to the man in black. At the same moment one of the varlets approached with a dark object in his hand, which even in my dream filled me with a vague feeling of familiarity. It was a leathern filler. With horrible energy he thrust it— but I could stand no more. My hair stood on end with horror. I writhed, I struggled, I broke through the bonds of sleep, and I burst with a shriek into my own life, and found myself lying shivering with terror in the huge library, with the moonlight flooding through the window and throwing strange silver and black traceries upon the opposite wall. Oh, what a blessed relief to feel that I was back in the nineteenth century—back out of that mediaeval vault into a world where men had human hearts within their bosoms. I sat up on my couch, trembling in every limb, my mind divided between thankfulness and horror. To think that such things were ever done—that they could be done without God striking the villains dead. Was it all a fantasy, or did it really stand for something which had happened in the black, cruel days of the world's history? I sank my throbbing head upon my shaking hands. And then, suddenly, my heart seemed to stand still in my bosom, and I could not even scream, so great was my terror. Something was advancing toward me through the darkness of the room.

It is a horror coming upon a horror which breaks a man's spirit. I could not reason, I could not pray; I could only sit like a frozen image, and glare at the dark figure which was coming down the great room. And then it moved out into the white lane of moonlight, and I breathed once more. It was Dacre, and his face showed that he was as frightened as myself.

"Was that you? For God's sake, what's the matter?" he asked in a husky voice.

"Oh, Dacre, I am glad to see you! I have been down into hell. It was dreadful."

"Then it was you who screamed?"

"I dare say it was."

"It rang through the house. The servants are all terrified." He struck a match and lit the lamp. "I think we may get the fire to burn up again," he added, throwing some logs upon the embers. "Good God, my dear chap, how white you are! You look as if you had seen a ghost."

"So I have—several ghosts."

"The leather funnel has acted, then?"

"I wouldn't sleep near the infernal thing again for all the money you could offer me."

Dacre chuckled.

"I expected that you would have a lively night of it," said he. "You took it out of me in return, for that scream of yours wasn't a very pleasant sound at two in the morning. I suppose from what you say that you have seen the whole dreadful business."

"What dreadful business?"

"The torture of the water—the 'Extraordinary Question,' as it was called in the genial days of 'Le Rol Soleil.' Did you stand it out to the end?"

"No, thank God, I awoke before it really began."

"Ah! it is just as well for you. I held out till the third bucket. Well, it is an old story, and they are all in their graves now, anyhow, so what does it matter how they got there? I suppose that you have no idea what it was that you have seen?"

"The torture of some criminal. She must have been a terrible male-factor indeed if her crimes are in proportion to her penalty."

"Well, we have that small consolation," said Dacre, wrapping his dressing-gown round him and crouching closer to the fire. "They *were* in proportion to her penalty. That is to say, if I am correct in the lady's identity."

"How could you possibly know her identity?"

For answer Dacre took down an old vellum-covered volume from the shelf.

"Just listen to this," said he; "it is in the French of the seventeenth century, but I will give a rough translation as I go. You will judge for yourself whether I have solved the riddle or not.

" 'The prisoner was brought before the Grand Chambers and Tour-nelles of Parliament, sitting as a court of justice, charged with the murder of Master Dreux d'Aubray, her father, and of her two brothers, MM. d'Aubray, one being civil lieutenant, and the other a counsellor of Parliament. In person it seemed hard to believe that she had really done such wicked deeds, for she was of a mild appearance, and of short stature, with a fair skin and blue eyes. Yet the Court, having found her guilty, condemned her to the ordinary and to the extraordinary question in order that she might be forced to name her accomplices, after which she should be carried in a cart to the Place de Greve, there to have her head cut off, her body being afterwards burned and her ashes scattered to the winds.'

"The date of this entry is July 16, 1676."

"It is interesting," said I, "but not convincing. How do you prove the two women to be the same?"

"I am coming to that. The narrative goes on to tell of the woman's behaviour when questioned. 'When the executioner approached her she recognized him by the cords which he held in his hands, and she at once held out her own hands to him, looking at him from head to foot without uttering a word.' How's that?"

"Yes, it was so."

" 'She gazed without wincing upon the wooden horse and rings which had twisted so many limbs and caused so many shrieks of agony. When her eyes fell upon the three pails of water, which were all ready for her, she said with a smile, "All that water must have been brought here for the purpose of drowning me, Monsieur. You have no idea, I trust, of making a person of my small stature swallow it all.' Shall I read the details of the torture?"

"No, for Heaven's sake, don't."

"Here is a sentence which must surely show you that what is here recorded is the very scene which you have gazed upon tonight: 'The good Abbe Pirot, unable to contemplate the agonies which were suffered by his penitent, had hurried from the room.' Does that convince you?"

"It does entirely. There can be no question that it is indeed the same event. But who, then, is this lady whose appearance was so attractive and whose end was so horrible?"

For answer Dacre came across to me, and placed the small lamp upon the table which stood by my bed. Lifting up the ill-omened filler, he turned the brass rim so that the light fell full upon it. Seen in this way the engraving seemed clearer than on the night before.

"We have already agreed that this is the badge of a marquis or of a marquise," said he. "We have also settled that the last letter is B."

"It is undoubtedly so."

"I now suggest to you that the other letters from left to right are, M, M, a small d, A, a small d, and then the final B."

"Yes, I am sure that you are right. I can make out the two small d's quite plainly."

"What I have read to you tonight," said Dacre, "is the official record of the trial of Marie Madeleine d'Aubray, Marquise de Brinvilliers, one of the most famous poisoners and murderers of all time."

I sat in silence, overwhelmed at the extraordinary nature of the incident, and at the completeness of the proof with which Dacre had exposed its real meaning. In a vague way I remembered some details of the woman's career, her unbridled debauchery, the cold-blooded and protracted torture of her sick father, the murder of her brothers for motives of petty gain. I recollected also that the bravery of her end had done something to atone for the horror of her life, and that all Paris had sympathized with her last moments, and blessed her as a martyr within a few days of the time when they had cursed her as a murderess. One objection, and one only, occurred to my mind.

"How came her initials and her badge of rank upon the filler? Surely they did not carry their mediaeval homage to the nobility to the point of decorating instruments of torture with their titles?"

"I was puzzled with the same point," said Dacre, "but it admits of a simple explanation. The case excited extraordinary interest at the time, and nothing could be more natural than that La Reynie, the head of the police, should retain this filler as a grim souvenir. It was not often that a marchioness of France underwent the extraordinary question. That he should engrave her initials upon it for the information of others was surely a very ordinary proceeding upon his part."

"And this?" I asked, pointing to the marks upon the leathern neck.

"She was a cruel tigress," said Dacre, as he turned away. "I think it is evident that like other tigresses her teeth were both strong and sharp."

Witches' Hollow

H. P. LOVECRAFT

H. P. Lovecraft is one of the most famous authors of horror fiction,
best known for his works of the Cthulhu Mythos, grimoires like the
fictitious **Necronomicon,** *and spooky New England towns.*
"Witches' Hollow," completed by August Derleth, shows you why.

DISTRICT School Number Seven stood on the very edge of that wild
country which lies west of Arkham. It stood in a little grove of trees,
chiefly oaks and elms with one or two maples; in one direction the road
led to Arkham, in the other it dwindled away into the wild, wooded
country which always looms darkly on that western horizon. It presented
a warmly attractive appearance to me when first I saw it on my arrival
as the new teacher early in September, 1920, though it had no distin-
guishing architectural feature and was in every respect the replica of
thousands of country schools scattered throughout New England, a compact, conservative building painted white, so that it shone forth from
among the trees in the midst of which it stood.

It was an old building at that time, and no doubt has since been
abandoned or torn down. The school district has now been consolidated,
but at that time it supported this school in somewhat niggardly a manner,
skimping and saving on every necessity. Its standard readers, when I came
there to teach, were still *McGuffey's Eclectic Readers,* in editions published before the turn of the century. My charges added up to twenty-
seven. There were Allens and Whateleys and Perkinses, Dunlocks and
Abbotts and Talbots—and there was Andrew Potter.

I cannot now recall the precise circumstances of my especial notice
of Andrew Potter. He was a large boy for his age, very dark of mien,
with haunting eyes and a shock of tousselled black hair. His eyes brooded

upon me with a kind of different quality which at first challenged me but ultimately left me strangely uneasy. He was in the fifth grade, and it did not take me long to discover that he could very easily advance into the seventh or eighth, but made no effort to do so. He seemed to have only a casual tolerance for his schoolmates, and for their part, they respected him, but not out of affection so much as what struck me soon as fear. Very soon thereafter, I began to understand that this strange lad held for me the same kind of amused tolerance that he held for his schoolmates.

Perhaps it was inevitable that the challenge of this pupil should lead me to watch him as surreptitiously as I could, and as the circumstances of teaching a one-room school permitted. As a result, I became aware of a vaguely disquieting fact; from time to time, Andrew Potter responded to some stimulus beyond the apprehension of my senses, reacting precisely as if someone had called to him, sitting up, growing alert, and wearing the air of someone listening to sounds beyond my own hearing, in the same attitude assumed by animals hearing sounds beyond the pitch-levels of the human ear.

My curiosity quickened by this time, I took the first opportunity to ask about him. One of the eighth-grade boys, Wilbur Dunlock, was in the habit on occasion of staying after school and helping with the cursory cleaning that the room needed.

'Wilbur,' I said to him late one afternoon. 'I notice you don't seem to pay much attention to Andrew Potter, none of you. Why?'

He looked at me, a little distrustfully, and pondered his answer before he shrugged and replied, 'He's not like us.'

'In what way?'

He shook his head. 'He don't care if we let him play with us or not. He don't want to.'

He seemed reluctant to talk, but by dint of repeated questions I drew from him certain spare information. The Potters lived deep in the hills to the west along an all but abandoned branch of the main road that led through the hills. Their farm stood in a little valley locally known as Witches' Hollow which Wilbur described as 'a bad place.' There were only four of them—Andrew, an older sister, and their parents. They did not 'mix' with other people of the district, not even with the Dunlocks, who were their nearest neighbours, living but half a mile from the school itself, and thus, perhaps, four miles from Witches' Hollow, with woods separating the two farms.

More than this he could not—or would not—say.

About a week later, I asked Andrew Potter to remain after school. He offered no objection, appearing to take my request as a matter of course. As soon as the other children had gone, he came up to my desk and stood there waiting, his dark eyes fixed expectantly on me, and just the shadow of a smile on his full lips.

'I've been studying your grades, Andrew,' I said, 'and it seems to me that with only a little effort you could skip into the sixth—perhaps even the seventh—grade. Wouldn't you like to make that effort?'

He shrugged.

'What do you intend to do when you get out of school?'

He shrugged again.

'Are you going to high school in Arkham?'

He considered me with eyes that seemed suddenly piercing in their keenness, all lethargy gone. 'Mr. Williams, I'm here because there's a law says I have to be,' he answered. 'There's no law says I have to go to high school.'

'But aren't you interested?' I pressed him.

'What I'm interested in doesn't matter. It's what my folks want that counts.'

'Well, I'm going to talk to them.' I decided on the moment. 'Come along. I'll take you home.'

For a moment something like alarm sprang into his expression, but in seconds it diminished and gave way to that air of watchful lethargy so typical of him. He shrugged and stood waiting while I slipped my books and papers into the schoolbag I habitually carried. Then he walked doc- ilely to the car with me and got in, looking at me with a smile that could only be described as superior.

We rode through the woods in silence, which suited the mood that came upon me as soon as we had entered the hills, for the trees pressed close upon the road, and the deeper we went, the darker grew the wood, perhaps as much because of the lateness of that October day as because of the thickening of the trees. From relatively open glades, we plunged into an ancient wood, and when at last we turned down the side road— little more than a lane—to which Andrew silently pointed, I found that I was driving through a growth of very old and strangely deformed trees. I had to proceed with caution; the road was so little used that underbrush crowded upon it from both sides, and, oddly, I recognized little of it, for all my studies in botany, though once I thought I saw saxifrage, curiously mutated. I drove abruptly, without warning, into the yard before the Potter house.

The sun was now lost behind the wall of trees, and the house stood on a kind of twilight. Beyond it stretched a few fields, strung out up the valley; in one, there were cornshocks, in another stubble, in yet another pumpkins. The house itself was forbidding, low to the ground, with half a second storey, gambrel-roofed, with shuttered windows, and the out-buildings stood gaunt and stark, looking as if they had never been used. The entire farm looked deserted; the only sign of life was in a few chickens that scratched at the earth behind the house.

Had it not been that the lane along which we had travelled ended here, I would have doubted that we had reached the Potter house. Andrew flashed a glance at me, as if he sought some expression on my face to convey to him what I thought. Then he jumped lightly from the car, leaving me to follow.

He went into the house ahead of me. I heard him announce me.

'Brought the teacher. Mr. Williams.'

There was no answer.

Then abruptly I was in the room, lit only by an old-fashioned kerosene lamp, and there were the other three Potters—the father, a tall, stoop-shouldered man, grizzled and greying, who could not have been more than forty but looked much, much older, not so much physically as psychically—the mother, an almost obscenely fat woman—and the girl, slender, tall, and with that same air of watchful waiting that I had noticed in Andrew.

Andrew made the brief introductions, and the four of them stood or sat, waiting upon what I had to say, and somewhat uncomfortably suggesting in their attitudes that I say it and get out.

'I wanted to talk to you about Andrew,' I said. 'He shows great promise, and he could be moved up a grade or two if he'd study a little more.'

My words were not welcomed.

'I believe he's smart enough for eighth grade,' I went on, and stopped.

'If he 'uz in eighth grade,' said his father, 'he's be havin' to go to high school 'fore he 'uz old enough to git outa goin' to school. That's the law. They told me.'

I could not help thinking of what Wilbur Dunlock had told me of the reclusiveness of the Potters, and as I listened to the elder Potter, and thought of what I had heard, I was suddenly aware of a kind of tension among them, and a subtle alteration in their attitude. The moment the father stopped talking, there was a singular harmony of attitude—all four of them seemed to be listening to some inner voice, and I doubt that they heard my protest at all.

'You can't expect a boy as smart as Andrew just to come back here,' I said.

'Here's good enough,' said old Potter. 'Besides, he's ours. And don't ye go talkin' 'bout us now, Mr. Williams.'

He spoke with so latently menacing an undercurrent in his voice that I was taken aback. At the same time I was increasingly aware of a miasma of hostility, not proceeding so much from any one or all four of them, as from the house and its setting themselves.

'Thank you,' I said. 'I'll be going.'

I turned and went out, Andrew at my heels.

Outside, Andrew said softly, 'You shouldn't be talking about us, Mr. Williams. Pa gets mad when he finds out. You talked to Wilbur Dunlock.'

I was arrested at getting into the car. With one foot on the running board, I turned. 'Did he say so?' I asked.

He shook his head. 'You did, Mr. Williams,' he said, and backed away. 'It's not what he thinks, but what he might do.'

Before I could speak again, he had darted into the house.

For a moment I stood undecided. But my decision was made for me. Suddenly, in the twilight, the house seemed to burgeon with menace, and all the surrounding woods seemed to stand waiting but to bend upon me. Indeed, I was aware of a rustling, like the whispering of wind, in all the wood, though no wind stirred, and from the house itself came a malevolence like the blow of a fist. I got into the car and drove away, with that impression of malignance at my back like the hot breath of a ravaging pursuer.

I reached my room in Arkham at last, badly shaken. Seen in retrospect, I had undergone an unsettling psychic experience; there was no other explanation for it. I had the unavoidable conviction that, however blindly, I had thrust myself in far deeper waters than I knew, and the very unexpectedness of the experience made it the more chilling. I could not eat for the wonder of what went on in that house in Witches' Hollow, of what it was that bound the family together, chaining them to that place, preventing a promising lad like Andrew Potter even from the most fleeting wish to leave that dark valley and go out into a brighter world.

I lay for most of that night, sleepless, filled with a nameless dread for which all explanation eluded me, and when I slept at last my sleep was filled with hideously disturbing dreams, in which beings far beyond my mundane imagination held the stage, and cataclysmic events of the utmost terror and horror took place. And when I rose next morning, I felt that somehow I had touched upon a world totally alien to my kind.

I reached the school early that morning, but Wilbur Dunlock was there before me. His eyes met mine with sad reproach. I could not imagine what had happened to disturb this usually friendly pupil.

'You shouldn't a told Andrew Potter we talked about him,' he said with a kind of unhappy resignation.

'I didn't, Wilbur.'

'I know I didn't. So you must have,' he said. And then, 'Six of our cows got killed last night, and the shed where they were was crushed down on 'em.'

I was momentarily too startled to reply. 'A sudden windstorm,' I began, but he cut me off.

'Weren't no wind last night, Mr. Williams. And the cows were *smashed*.'

'You surely cannot think that the Potters had anything to do with this, Wilbur,' I cried.

He gave me a weary look—the look of one who *knows*, meeting the glance of one who should know but cannot understand, and said nothing more.

This was even more upsetting than my experience of the previous evening. He at least was convinced that there was a connection between our conversation about the Potter family and the Dunlocks' loss of half a dozen cows. And he was convinced with so deep a conviction that I knew without trying that nothing I could say would shake it.

When Andrew Potter came in, I looked in vain for any sign that anything out of the ordinary had taken place since last I had seen him.

Somehow I got through that day. Immediately after the close of the school session, I hastened into Arkham and went to the office of the *Arkham Gazette*, the editor of which had been kind enough, as a member of the local District Board of Education, to find my room for me. He was an elderly man, almost seventy, and might presumably know what I wanted to find out.

My appearance must have conveyed something of my agitation, for when I walked into his office, his eyebrows lifted, and he said, 'What's got your dander up, Mr. Williams?'

I made some attempt to dissemble, since I could put my hand upon nothing tangible, and, viewed in the cold light of day, what I might have said would have sounded almost hysterical to an impartial listener. I said only, 'I'd like to know something about a Potter family that lives in Witches' Hollow, west of the school.'

He gave me an enigmatic glance. 'Never heard of old Wizard Potter?' he asked. And, before I could answer, he went on, 'No, of course, you're from Brattleboro. We could hardly expect Vermonters to know about what goes on in the Massachusetts back country. He lived there first. An old man when I first knew him. And these Potters were distant relatives, lived in Upper Michigan, inherited the property, and came to live there when Wizard Potter died.'

'But what do you know about them?' I persisted.

'Nothing but what everybody else knows,' he said. 'When they came, they were nice friendly people. Now they talk to nobody, seldom come out—and there's all that talk about missing animals from the farms in the district. The people tie that all up.'

Thus begun, I questioned him at length.

I listened to a bewildering enigma of half-told tales, hints, legends, and lore utterly beyond my comprehension. What seemed to be incontrovertible was a distant cousinship between Wizard Potter and one Wizard Whateley of nearby Dunwich—'a bad lot,' the editor called him; the solitary way of life of old Wizard Potter, and the incredible length of time he had lived; the fact that people generally shunned Witches' Hollow. What seemed to be sheer fantasy was the superstitious lore—that Wizard Potter had 'called something down from the sky, and it lived with him or in him until he died';—that a late traveller, found in a dying state along the main road, had gasped out something about 'that thing with the feelers—slimy, rubbery thing with the suckers on its feelers' that came out of the woods and attacked him—and a good deal more of the same kind of lore.

When he finished, the editor scribbled a note to the librarian at Miskatonic University in Arkham, and handed it to me. 'Tell him to let you look at that book. You may learn something.' He shrugged. 'And you may not. Young people now-days take the world with a lot of salt.'

I went supperless to pursue my search for the special knowledge I felt I needed, if I were to save Andrew Potter for a better life. For it was this rather than the satisfaction of my curiosity that impelled me. I made my way to the library of Miskatonic University, looked up the librarian, and handed him the editor's note.

The old man gave me a sharp look, said, 'Wait here, Mr. Williams,' and went off with a ring of keys. So the book, whatever it was, was kept under lock and key.

I waited for what seemed an interminable time. I was now beginning to feel some hunger, and to question my unseemly haste—and yet I felt that there was little time to be lost, though I could not define the catastrophe I hoped to avert. Finally the librarian came, bearing an ancient tome, and brought it around to a table within his range of vision. The book's title was in Latin—*Necronomicon*—though its author was evidently an Arabian, *Abdul Alhazred,* and its text was in somewhat archaic English.

I began to read with interest which soon turned to complete bewilderment. The book evidently concerned ancient, alien races, invaders of earth, great mythical beings called Ancient Ones and Elder Gods, with outlandish names like Cthulhu and Hastur, Shub-Niggurath and Azathoth, Dagon and Ithaqua and Wendigo and Cthugha, all involved in some kind of plan to dominate earth and served by some of its peoples— the Tcho-Tcho, and the Deep Ones, and the like. It was a book filled with cabbalistic lore, incantations, and what purported to be an account of a great interplanetary battle between the Elder Gods and the Ancient Ones and of the survival of cults and servitors in isolated and remote places on our planet as well as on sister planets. What this rigmarole had to do with my immediate problem, with the ingrown and strange Potter family and their longing for solitude and their anti-social way of life, was completely beyond me.

How long I would have gone on reading, I do not know. I was interrupted presently by the awareness of being studied by a stranger, who stood not far from me with his eyes moving from the book I was busy reading to me. Having caught my eye, he made so bold as to come over to my side.

'Forgive me,' he said, 'but what in this book interests a country school teacher?'

'I wonder now myself,' I said.

He introduced himself as Professor Martin Keane. 'I may say, sir,' he added, 'that I know this book practically by heart.'

'A farrago of superstition.'

'Do you think so?'

'Emphatically.'

'You have lost the quality of wonder, Mr. Williams. Tell me, if you will, what brought you to this book—'

I hesitated, but Professor Keane's personality was persuasive and inspired confidence.

'Let us walk, if you don't mind,' I said.

He nodded.

I returned the book to the librarian, and joined my new-found friend. Haltingly, as clearly as I could, I told him about Andrew Potter, the house in Witches' Hollow, my strange psychic experience—even the curious coincidence of Dunlock's cows. To all this he listened without interruption, indeed, with a singular absorption. I explained at last that my motive in looking into the background of Witches' Hollow was solely to do something for my pupil.

'A little research,' he said, 'would have informed you that many strange events have taken place in such remote places as Dunwich and Innsmouth—even Arkham and Witches' Hollow,' he said when I finished. 'Look around you at these ancient houses with their shuttered rooms and ill-lit fanlights. How many strange events have taken place under those gambrel roofs! We shall never know. But let us put aside the question of belief! One may not need to see the embodiment of evil to believe in it, Mr. Williams. I should like to be of some small service to the boy in this matter. May I?'

'By all means!'

'It may be perilous—to you as well as to him.'

'I am not concerned about myself.'

'But I assure you, it cannot be any more perilous to the boy than his present position. Even death for him is less perilous.'

'You speak in riddles, Professor.'

'Let it be better so, Mr. Williams. But come—we are at my residence. Pray come in.'

We went into one of those ancient houses of which Professor Keane had spoken. I walked into the musty past, for the rooms were filled with books and all manner of antiquities. My host took me into what was evidently his sitting-room, swept a chair clear of books, and invited me to wait while he busied himself on the second floor.

He was not, however, gone very long—not even long enough for me to assimilate the curious atmosphere of the room in which I waited. When he came back he carried what I saw at once were objects of stone, roughly in the shape of five-pointed stars. He put five of them into my hands.

'Tomorrow after school—if the Potter boy is there—you must contrive to touch him with one of these, and keep it fixed upon him,' said my host. 'There are two other conditions. You must keep one of these at least on your person at all times, and you must keep all thought of the stone and what you are about to do out of your mind. These beings have a telepathic sense—an ability to read your thoughts.'

Startled, I recalled Andrew's charging me with having talked about them with Wilbur Dunlock.

'Should I not know what these are?' I asked.

'If you can abate your doubts for the time being,' my host answered with a grim smile. 'These stones are among the thousands bearing the Seal of R'lyeh which closed the prisons of the Ancient Ones. They are the seals of the Elder Gods.'

'Professor Keane, the age of superstition is past,' I protested.

'Mr. Williams—the wonder of life and its mysteries is never past,' he retorted. 'If the stone has no meaning, it has no power. If it has no power, it cannot affect young Potter. And it cannot protect you.'

'From what?'

'From the power behind the malignance you felt at the house in Witches' Hollow,' he answered. 'Or was this too superstition?' He smiled. 'You need not answer. I know your answer. If something happens when you put the stone upon the boy, he cannot be allowed to go back home. You must bring him here to me. Are you agreed?'

'Agreed,' I answered.

That next day was interminable, not only because of the imminence of crisis, but because it was extremely difficult to keep my mind blank before the inquiring gaze of Andrew Potter. Moreover, I was conscious as never before of the wall of pulsing malignance at my back, emanating from the wild country there, a tangible menace hidden in a pocket of the dark hills. But the hours passed, however slowly, and just before dismissal I asked Andrew Potter to wait after the others had gone.

And again he assented with that casual air tantamount almost to insolence, so that I was compelled to ask myself whether he were worth 'saving' as I thought of saving him in the depths of my mind.

But I persevered. I had hidden the stone in my car, and, once the others were gone, I asked Andrew to step outside with me.

At this point I felt both helpless and absurd. I, a college graduate, about to attempt what for me seemed inevitably the kind of mumbo-jumbo that belonged to the African wilderness. And for a few moments, as I walked stiffly from the school house toward the car I almost flagged, almost simply invited Andrew to get into the car to be driven home.

But I did not. I reached the car with Andrew at my heels, reached in, seized a stone to slip into my own pocket, seized another, and turned with lightning rapidity to press the stone to Andrew's forehead.

Whatever I expected to happen, it was not what took place.

For, at the touch of the stone, an expression of the utmost horror shone in Andrew Potter's eyes; in a trice, this gave way to poignant anguish; a great cry of terror burst from his lips. He flung his arms wide, scattering his books, wheeled as far as he could with my hold upon him, shuddered, and would have fallen, had I not caught him and lowered him, foaming at the mouth, to the ground. And then I was conscious of a great, cold wind which whirled about us and was gone, bending the grasses and the flowers, rippling the edge of the wood, and tearing away the leaves at the outer band of trees.

Driven by my own terror, I lifted Andrew Potter into the car, laid the stone on his chest, and drove as fast as I could into Arkham, seven miles away. Professor Keane was waiting, no whit surprised at my coming. And he had expected that I would bring Andrew Potter, for he had made a bed ready for him, and together we put him into it, after which Keane administered a sedative.

Then he turned to me. 'Now then, there's no time to be lost. They'll come to look for him—the girl probably first. We must get back to the school house at once.'

But now the full meaning and horror of what had happened to Andrew Potter had dawned upon me, and I was so shaken that it was necessary for Keane to push me from the room and half drag me out of the house. And again, as I set down these words so long after the terrible events of that night, I find myself trembling with that apprehension and fear which seize hold of a man who comes for the first time face to face with the vast unknown and knows how puny and meaningless he is against that cosmic immensity. I knew in that moment that what I had read in that forbidden book at the Miskatonic Library was not a farrago of superstition, but the key to a hitherto unsuspected revelation perhaps far, far older than mankind in the universe. I did not dare to think of what Wizard Potter had called down from the sky.

I hardly heard Professor Keane's words as he urged me to discard my emotional reaction and think of what had happened in scientific, more clinical fashion. After all, I had now accomplished my objective—Andrew Potter was saved. But to insure it, he must be made free of the others, who would surely follow him and find him. I thought only of what waiting horror that quartet of country people from Michigan had walked into when they came to take up possession of the solitary farm in Witches' Hollow.

I drove blindly back to the school. There, at Professor Keane's behest, I put on the lights and sat with the door open to the warm night, while he concealed himself behind the building to wait upon their coming. I had to steel myself in order to blank out my mind and take up that vigil.

On the edge of night, the girl came . . .

And after she had undergone the same experience as her brother, and lay beside the desk, the star-shaped stone on her breast, their father showed up in the doorway. All was darkness now, and he carried a gun. He had no need to ask what had happened; he *knew*. He stood wordless, pointed to his daughter and the stone on her breast, and raised his gun. His inference was plain—if I did not remove the stone, he meant to shoot. Evidently this was the contingency the professor expected, for he came upon Potter from the rear and touched him with the stone.

Afterwards we waited for two hours—in vain, for Mrs. Potter.

'She isn't coming,' said Professor Keane at last. 'She harbours the seat of its intelligence—I had thought it would be the man. Very well—we have no choice—we must go to Witches' Hollow. These two can be left here.'

We drove through the darkness, making no attempt at secrecy, for the professor said the 'thing' in the house in the Hollow 'knew' we were coming but could not reach us past the talisman of the stone. We went through that close pressing forest, down the narrow lane where the queer undergrowth seemed to reach out toward us in the glow of the head lights, into the Potter yard.

The house stood dark save for a wan glow of lamplight in one room.

Professor Keane leaped from the car with his little bag of star-shaped stones, and went around sealing the house—with a stone at each of the two doors, and one at each of the windows, through one of which we could see the woman sitting at the kitchen table—stolid, watchful, *aware,* no longer dissembling, looking unlike that tittering woman I had seen in this house not long ago, but rather like some great sentient beast at bay.

When he had finished, my companion went around to the front and, by means of brush collected from the yard and piled against the door, set fire to the house heedless of my protests.

Then he went back to the window to watch the woman, explaining that only fire could destroy the elemental force, but that he hoped, still, to save Mrs. Potter. 'Perhaps you'd better not watch, Williams.'

I did not heed him. Would that I had—and so spared myself the dreams that invade my sleep even yet! I stood at the window behind him and watched what went on in that room—for the smell of smoke was now permeating the house. Mrs. Potter—or what animated her gross body—started up, went awkwardly to the back door, retreated, to the window, retreated from it, and came back to the centre of the room, between the table and the wood stove, not yet fired against the coming cold. There she fell to the floor, heaving and writhing.

The room filled slowly with smoke, hazing about the yellow lamp, making the room indistinct—but not indistinct enough to conceal completely what went on in the course of that terrible struggle on the floor, where Mrs. Potter threshed about as if in mortal convulsion and slowly, half visibly, something or other took shape—an incredible amorphous mass, only half glimpsed in the smoke, tentacled, shimmering, with a cold intelligence and a physical coldness that I could feel through the window. The thing rose like a cloud above the now motionless body of Mrs. Potter, and then fell upon the stove and drained into it like vapour!

'The stove!' cried Professor Keane, and fell back.

Above us, out of the chimney, came a spreading blackness, like smoke, gathering itself briefly there. Then it hurtled like a lightning bolt aloft, into the stars, in the direction of the Hyades, back to that place from which old Wizard Potter had called it into himself, away from where it had lain in wait for the Potters to come from Upper Michigan and afford it new host on the face of earth.

We managed to get Mrs. Potter out of the house, much shrunken now, but alive.

On the remainder of that night's events there is no need to to dwell— how the professor waited until fire had consumed the house to collect his store of star-shaped stones, of the reuniting of the Potter family—freed from the curse of Witches' Hollow and determined never to return to that haunted valley—of Andrew, who, when we came to waken him, was talking in his sleep of 'great winds that fought and tore' and a 'place by the Lake of Hali where they live in glory forever.'

What it was that old Wizard Potter had called down from the stars, I lacked the courage to ask, but I knew that it touched upon secrets better left unknown to the races of men, secrets I would never have become aware of had I not chanced to take District School Number Seven, and had among my pupils the strange boy who was Andrew Potter.

The Sorcerers

W. B. YEATS

William Butler Yeats was not only an accomplished Irish poet and playwright—he was a Ceremonial Magician. One of the first of H. P. Blavatsky's Theosophical Society, then of Hermetic Order of the Golden Dawn (a society most famous, unfortunately, for helping Aleister Crowley's rise to fame), Yeats incorporated themes of fairies and, yes, magic in many of his works—including this one.

IN Ireland we hear but little of the darker powers,* and come across any who have seen them even more rarely, for the imagination of the people dwells rather upon the fantastic and capricious, and fantasy and caprice would lose the freedom which is their breath of life, were they to unite them either with evil or with good. And yet the wise are of opinion that wherever man is, the dark powers who would feed his rapacities are there, too, no less than the bright beings who store their honey in the cells of his heart, and the twilight beings who flit hither and thither, and that they encompass him with a passionate and melancholy multitude. They hold, too, that he who by long desire or through accident of birth possesses the power of piercing into their hidden abode can see them there, those who were once men or women full of a terrible vehemence, and those who have never lived upon the earth, moving slowly and with a subtler malice. The dark powers cling about us, it is said, day and night, like bats upon an old tree; and that we do not hear more of them is merely because the darker kinds of magic have been but little practised.

---

*I know better now. We have the dark powers much more than I thought, but not as much as the Scottish, and yet I think the imagination of the people does dwell chiefly upon the fantastic and capricious.

I have indeed come across very few persons in Ireland who try to communicate with evil powers, and the few I have met keep their purpose and practice wholly hidden from those among whom they live. They are mainly small clerks and the like, and meet for the purpose of their art in a room hung with black hangings. They would not admit me into this room, but finding me not altogether ignorant of the arcane science, showed gladly elsewhere what they would do. "Come to us," said their leader, a clerk in a large flour-mill, "and we will show you spirits who will talk to you face to face, and in shapes as solid and heavy as our own."

I had been talking of the power of communicating in states of trance with the angelical and faery beings,—the children of the day and of the twilight—and he had been contending that we should only believe in what we can see and feel when in our ordinary everyday state of mind. "Yes," I said, "I will come to you," or some such words; "but I will not permit myself to become entranced, and will therefore know whether these shapes you talk of are any the more to be touched and felt by the ordinary senses than are those I talk of." I was not denying the power of other beings to take upon themselves a clothing of mortal substance, but only that simple invocations, such as he spoke of, seemed unlikely to do more than cast the mind into trance, and thereby bring it into the presence of the powers of day, twilight, and darkness.

"But," he said, "we have seen them move the furniture hither and thither, and they go at our bidding, and help or harm people who know nothing of them." I am not giving the exact words, but as accurately as I can the substance of our talk.

On the night arranged I turned up about eight, and found the leader sitting alone in almost total darkness in a small back room. He was dressed in a black gown, like an inquisitor's dress in an old drawing, that left nothing of him visible except his eyes, which peered out through two small round holes. Upon the table in front of him was a brass dish of burning herbs, a large bowl, a skull covered with painted symbols, two crossed daggers, and certain implements shaped like quern stones, which were used to control the elemental powers in some fashion I did not discover. I also put on a black gown, and remember that it did not fit perfectly, and that it interfered with my movements considerably. The sorcerer then took a black cock out of a basket, and cut its throat with one of the daggers, letting the blood fall into the large bowl. He opened a book and began an invocation, which was certainly not English, and had a deep guttural sound. Before he had finished, another of the sorcerers, a man of about twenty-five, came in, and having put on a black gown also, seated himself at my left hand. I had the invoker directly in front of me, and soon began to find his eyes, which glittered through the small holes in his hood, affecting me in a curious way. I struggled hard against their influence, and my head began to ache. The invocation continued, and nothing happened for the first few minutes. Then the invoker got up and extinguished the light in the hall, so that no glimmer might come through the slit under the door. There was now no light except from the herbs on the brass dish, and no sound except from the deep guttural murmur of the invocation.

Presently the man at my left swayed himself about, and cried out, "O god! O god!" I asked him what ailed him, but he did not know he had spoken. A moment after he said he could see a great serpent moving about the room, and became considerably excited. I saw nothing with any definite shape, but thought that black clouds were forming about me. I felt I must fall into a trance if I did not struggle against it, and that the influence which was causing this trance was out of harmony with itself, in other words, evil. After a struggle I got rid of the black clouds, and was able to observe with my ordinary senses again. The two sorcerers now began to see black and white columns moving about the room, and finally a man in a monk's habit, and they became greatly puzzled because I did not see these things also, for to them they were as solid as the table before them. The invoker appeared to be gradually increasing in power, and I began to feel as if a tide of darkness was pouring from him and concentrating itself about me; and now, too, I noticed that the man on my left hand had passed into a death-like trance. With a last great effort I drove off the black clouds; but feeling them to be the only shapes I should see without passing into a trance, and having no great love for them, I asked for lights, and after the needful exorcism returned to the ordinary world.

I said to the more powerful of the two sorcerers—"What would happen if one of your spirits had overpowered me?" "You would go out of this room," he answered, "with his character added to your own." I asked about the origin of his sorcery, but got little of importance, except that he had learned it from his father. He would not tell me more, for he had, it appeared, taken a vow of secrecy.

For some days I could not get over the feeling of having a number of deformed and grotesque figures lingering about me. The Bright Powers are always beautiful and desirable, and the Dim Powers are now beautiful, now quaintly grotesque, but the Dark Powers express their unbalanced natures in shapes of ugliness and horror.

The Horned Women

LADY WILDE

Yes, that would be Oscar Wilde's mother. The Oscar Wilde—that playwright and champion of alternative lifestyles. Lady Wilde, a respected author and superb hostess, often wrote of Irish legends and magic, as in this intriguing look at some Irish witches.

A rich woman sat up late one night carding and preparing wool, while all the family and servants were asleep. Suddenly a knock was given at the door, and a voice called—"Open! open!"

"Who is there?" said the woman of the house.

"I am the Witch of the One Horn," was answered.

The mistress, supposing that one of her neighbours had called and required assistance, opened the door, and a woman entered, having in her hand a pair of wool carders, and bearing a horn on her forehead, as if growing there. She sat down by the fire in silence, and began to card the wool with violent haste. Suddenly she paused and said aloud: "Where are the women? They delay too long."

Then a second knock came to the door, and a voice called as before—"Open! open!"

The mistress felt herself constrained to rise and open to the call, and immediately a second witch entered, having two horns on her forehead, and in her hand a wheel for spinning the wool.

"Give me place," she said; "I am the Witch of the Two Horns," and she began to spin as quick as lightning.

And so the knocks went on, and the call was heard, and the witches entered, until at last twelve women sat round the fire—the first with one horn, the last with twelve horns. And they carded the thread, and turned their spinning wheels, and wound and wove, all singing together an ancient rhyme, but no word did they speak to the mistress of the house. Strange to hear, and frightful to look upon were these twelve women, with their horns and their wheels; and the mistress felt near to death, and she tried to rise that she might call for help, but she could not move, nor could she utter a word or a cry, for the spell of the witches was upon her.

Then one of them called to her in Irish and said—

"Rise, woman, and make us a cake."

Then the mistress searched for a vessel to bring water from the well that she might mix the meal and make the cake, but she could find none. And they said to her—

"Take a sieve and bring water in it."

And she took the sieve and went to the well; but the water poured from it, and she could fetch none for the cake, and she sat down by the well and wept. Then a voice came by her and said—

"Take yellow clay and moss and bind them together and plaster the sieve so that it will hold."

This she did, and the sieve held the water for the cake. And the voice said again—

"Return, and when thou comest to the north angle of the house, cry aloud three times and say, 'The mountain of the Fenian women and the sky over it is all on fire.' "

And she did so.

When the witches inside heard the call, a great and terrible cry broke from their lips and they rushed forth with wild lamentations and shrieks, and fled away to Slieve-namon, where was their chief abode. But the Spirit of the Well bade the mistress of the house to enter and prepare her home against the enchantments of the witches if they returned again.

And first, to break their spells, she sprinkled the water in which she had washed her child's feet (the feet-water) outside the door on the threshold; secondly, she took the cake which the witches had made in her absence, of meal mixed with the blood drawn from the sleeping family. And she broke the cake in bits, and placed a bit in the mouth of each sleeper, and they were restored; and she took the cloth they had woven and placed it half in and half out of the chest with the padlock; and lastly, she secured the door with a great crossbeam fastened in the jambs, so that they could not enter. And having done these things she waited.

Not long were the witches in coming back, and they raged and called for vengeance.

"Open! open!" they screamed. "Open, feet-water!"

"I cannot," said the feet-water, "I am scattered on the ground and my path is down to the Lough."

"Open, open, wood and tree and beam!" they cried to the door.

"I cannot," said the door, "for the beam is fixed in the jambs and I have no power to move."

"Open, open, cake that we have made and mingled with blood," they cried again.

"I cannot," said the cake, "for I am broken and bruised, and my blood is on the lips of the sleeping children."

Then the witches rushed through the air with great cries, and fled back to Slieve-namon, uttering strange curses on the Spirit of the Well, who had wished their ruin; but the woman and the house were left in peace, and a mantle dropped by one of the witches in her flight was kept hung up by the mistress as a sign of the night's awful contest; and this mantle was in possession of the same family from generation to generation for five hundred years after.

April in Paris

URSULA K. LE GUIN

Le Guin's famous Earthsea Trilogy has been popular for several decades, but her career all started with this 1962 tale of Paris, academia, time travel, and some not-so-dark practitioners of black magic.

PROFESSOR Barry Pennywither sat in a cold, shadowy garret and stared at the table in front of him, on which lay a book and a breadcrust. The bread had been his dinner, the book had been his lifework. Both were dry. Dr. Pennywither sighed, and then shivered. Though the lower-floor apartments of the old house were quite elegant, the heat was turned off on April 1st, come what may; it was now April 2nd, and sleeting. If Dr. Pennywither raised his head a little he could see from his window the two square towers of Notre Dame de Paris, vague and soaring in the dusk, almost near enough to touch: for the Island of Saint-Louis, where he lived, is like a little barge being towed downstream behind the Island of the City, where Notre Dame stands. But he did not raise his head. He was too cold.

The great towers sank into darkness. Dr. Pennywither sank into gloom. He stared with loathing at his book. It had won him a year in Paris—publish or perish, said the Dean of Faculties, and he had published, and been rewarded with a year's leave from teaching, without pay. Munson College could not afford to pay unteaching teachers. So on his scraped-up savings he had come back to Paris, to live again as a student in a garret, to read fifteenth-century manuscripts at the Library, to see the chestnuts flower along the avenues. But it hadn't worked. He was forty, too old for lonely garrets. The sleet would blight the budding chestnut flowers. And he was sick of his work. Who cared about his theory, the Pennywither Theory, concerning the mysterious disappearance of the poet François Villon in 1463? Nobody. For after all his Theory about poor Villon, the greatest juvenile delinquent of all time, was only a theory and could never be proved, not across the gulf of five hundred years. Nothing could be proved. And besides, what did it matter if Villon died on Montfaucon gallows or (as Pennywither thought) in a Lyons brothel on the way to Italy? Nobody cared. Nobody else loved Villon enough. Nobody loved Dr. Pennywither, either; not even Dr. Pennywither. Why should he? An unsocial, unmarried, underpaid pedant, sitting here alone in an unheated attic in an unrestored tenement trying to write another unreadable book. "I'm unrealistic," he said aloud with another sigh and another shiver. He got up and took the blanket off his bed, wrapped himself in it, sat down thus bundled at the table, and tried to light a Gauloise Bleue. His lighter snapped vainly. He sighed once more, got up, fetched a can of vile-smelling French lighter fluid, sat down, rewrapped his cocoon, filled the lighter, and snapped it. The fluid had spilled around a good bit. The lighter lit, so did Dr. Pennywither, from the wrists down. "Oh hell!" he cried, blue flames leaping from his knuckles, and jumped up batting his arms wildly, shouting "Hell!" and raging against Destiny. Nothing ever went right. What was the use? It was then 8:12 on the night of April 2nd, 1961.

A man sat hunched at a table in a cold, high room. Through the window behind him the two square towers of Notre Dame loomed in the Spring dusk. In front of him on the table lay a hunk of cheese and a huge, iron-latched, handwritten book. The book was called (in Latin) *On the Primacy of the Element Fire over the Other Three Elements*. Its author stared at it with loathing. Nearby on a small iron stove a small alembic simmered. Jehan Lenoir mechanically inched his chair nearer the stove now and then, for warmth, but his thoughts were on deeper problems. "Hell!" he said finally (in Late Mediaeval French), slammed the book shut, and got up. What if his theory was wrong? What if water were the primal element? How could you prove these things? There must be some way—some method—so that one could be sure, absolutely sure, of one single fact! But each fact led into others, a monstrous tangle, and the Authorities conflicted, and anyway no one would read his book, not even the wretched pedants at the Sorbonne. They smelled heresy. What was the use? What good this life spent in poverty and alone, when he had learned nothing, merely guessed and theorized? He strode about the garret, raging, and then stood still. "All right!" he said to Destiny. "Very good! You've given me nothing, so I'll take what I want!" He went to one of the stacks of books that covered most of the floor-space, yanked out a bottom volume (scarring the leather and bruising his knuckles when the overlying folios avalanched), slapped it on the table and began to study one page of it. Then, still with a set cold look of rebellion, he got things ready: sulfur, silver, chalk. . . . Though the room was dusty and littered, his little workbench was neatly and handily arranged. He was soon ready. Then he paused. "This is ridiculous," he muttered, glancing out the window into the darkness where now one could only guess at the two square towers. A watchman passed below calling out the hour, eight o'clock of a cold clear night. It was so still he could hear the lapping of the Seine. He shrugged, frowned, took up the chalk and drew a neat pentagram on the floor near his table, then took up the book and began to read in a clear but self-conscious voice: "Haere, haere, audi me . . ." It was a long spell, and mostly nonsense. His voice sank. He stood bored and embarrassed. He hurried through the last words, shut the book, and then fell backwards against the door, gap-mouthed, staring at the enormous, shapeless figure that stood within the pentagram, lit only by the blue flicker of its waving, fiery claws.

BARRY Pennywither finally got control of himself and put out the fire by burying his hands in the folds of the blanket wrapped around him. Unburned but upset, he sat down again. He looked at his book. Then he stared at it. It was no longer thin and gray and titled *The Last Years of Villon: an Investigation of Possibilities.* It was thick and brown and titled *Incantatoria Magna.* On his table? A priceless manuscript dating from 1407 of which the only extant undamaged copy was in the Ambrosian Library in Milan? He lookly slowly around. His mouth dropped slowly open. He observed a stove, a chemist's workbench, two or three dozen heaps of unbelievable leatherbound books, the window, the door. His window, his door. But crouching against his door was a little creature, black and shapeless, from which came a dry rattling sound.

Barry Pennywither was not a very brave man, but he was rational. He thought he had lost his mind, and so he said quite steadily, "Are you the Devil?"

The creature shuddered and rattled.

Experimentally, with a glance at invisible Notre Dame, the professor made the sign of the Cross.

At this the creature twitched; not a flinch, a twitch. Then it said something, feebly, but in perfectly good English—no, in perfectly good French—no, in rather odd French: "Mais vous estes de Dieu," it said.

Barry got up and peered at it. "Who are you?" he demanded, and it lifted up a quite human face and answered meekly, "Jehan Lenoir."

"What are you doing in my room?"

There was a pause. Lenoir got up from his knees and stood straight, all five foot two of him. "This is *my* room," he said at last, though very politely.

Barry looked around at the books and alembics. There was another pause. "Then how did I get here?"

"I brought you."

"Are you a doctor?"

Lenoir nodded, with pride. His whole air had changed. "Yes, I'm a doctor," he said. "Yes, I brought you here. If Nature will yield me no knowledge, then I can conquer Nature herself, I can work a miracle! To the Devil with science, then. I was a scientist—" he glared at Barry. "No longer! They call me a fool, a heretic, well by God I'm worse! I'm a sorcerer, a black magician, Jehan the Black! Magic works, does it? Then science is a waste of time. Ha!" he said, but he did not really look triumphant. "I wish it hadn't worked," he said more quietly, pacing up and down between folios.

"So do I," said the guest.

"Who are you?" Lenoir looked up challengingly at Barry, though there was nearly a foot difference in their heights.

"Barry A. Pennywither, I'm a professor of French at Munson College, Indiana, on leave in Paris to pursue my studies of Late Mediaeval Fr—" He stopped. He had just realized what kind of accent Lenoir had. "What year is this? What century? Please, Dr. Lenoir—" The Frenchman looked confused. The meanings of words change, as well as their pronunciations. "Who rules this country?" Barry shouted.

Lenoir gave a shrug, a French shrug (some things never change), "Louis is king," he said. "Louis the Eleventh. The dirty old spider."

They stood staring at each other like wooden Indians for some time. Lenoir spoke first. "Then you're a man?"

"Yes. Look, Lenoir, I think you—your spell—you must have muffed it a bit."

"Evidently," said the alchemist. "Are you French?"

"No."

"Are you English?" Lenoir glared. "Are you a filthy Goddam?"

"No. No. I'm from America. I'm from the—from your future. From the twentieth century A.D." Barry blushed. It sounded silly, and he was a modest man. But he knew this was no illusion. The room he stood in, his room, was new. Not five centuries old. Unswept, but new. And the copy of Albertus Magnus by his knee was new, bound in soft supple calfskin, the gold lettering gleaming. And there stood Lenoir in his black gown, not in costume, at home. . . .

"Please sit down, sir," Lenoir was saying. And he added, with the fine though absent courtesy of the poor scholar, "Are you tired from the journey? I have bread and cheese, if you'll honor me by sharing it."

They sat at the table munching bread and cheese. At first Lenoir tried to explain why he had tried black magic. "I was fed up," he said. "Fed up! I've slaved in solitude since I was twenty, for what? For knowledge. To learn some of Nature's secrets. They are not to be learned." He drove his knife half an inch into the table, and Barry jumped. Lenoir was a thin little fellow, but evidently a passionate one. It was a fine face, though pale and lean: intelligent, alert, vivid. Barry was reminded of the face of a famous atomic physicist, seen in newspaper pictures up until 1953. Somehow this likeness prompted him to say, "Some are, Lenoir; we've learned a good bit, here and there. . . ."

"What?" said the alchemist, skeptical but curious.

"Well, I'm no scientist—"

"Can you make gold?" He grinned as he asked.

"No, I don't think so, but they do make diamonds."

"How?"

"Carbon—coal, you know—under great heat and pressure, I believe. Coal and diamond are both carbon, you know, the same element."

"Element?"

"Now as I say, I'm no—"

"Which is the primal element?" Lenoir shouted, his eyes fiery, the knife poised in his hand.

"There are about a hundred elements," Barry said coldly, hiding his alarm.

Two hours later, having squeezed out of Barry every dribble of the remnants of his college chemistry course, Lenoir rushed out into the night and reappeared shortly with a bottle. "O my master," he cried, "to think I offered you only bread and cheese!" It was a pleasant burgundy, vintage 1477, a good year. After they had drunk a glass together Lenoir said, "If somehow I could repay you . . ."

"You can. Do you know the name of the poet François Villon?"

"Yes," Lenoir said with some surprise, "but he wrote only French trash, you know, not in Latin."

"Do you know how or when he died?"

"Oh, yes; hanged at Montfaucon here in '64 or '65, with a crew of no-goods like himself. Why?"

Two hours later the bottle was dry, their throats were dry, and the watchman had called three o'clock of a cold clear morning. "Jehan, I'm worn out," Barry said, "you'd better send me back." The alchemist was too polite, too grateful, and perhaps also too tired to argue. Barry stood stiffly inside the pentagram, a tall bony figure muffled in a brown blanket, smoking a Gauloise Bleue. "Adieu," Lenoir said sadly. "Au revoir," Barry replied. Lenoir began to read the spell backwards. The candle flickered, his voice softened. "Me audi, haere, haere," he read, sighed, and looked up. The pentagram was empty. The candle flickered. "But I learned so little!" Lenoir cried out to the empty room. Then he beat the open book with his fists and said, "And a friend like that—a real friend—" He smoked one of the cigarettes Barry had left him—he had taken to tobacco at once. He slept, sitting at his table, for a couple of hours. When he woke he brooded a while, relit his candle, smoked the other cigarette, then opened the *Incantatoria* and began to read aloud: "Haere, haere . . ."

"Oh, thank God," Barry said, stepping quickly out of the pentagram and grasping Lenoir's hand. "Listen, I got back there—this room, this same room, Jehan! but old, horribly old, and empty, you weren't there—I thought, my God, what have I done? I'd sell my soul to get back there, to him—What can I do with what I've learned? Who'll believe it? How can I prove it? And who the devil could I tell it to anyhow? Who cares? I couldn't sleep, I sat and cried for an hour—"

"Will you stay?"

"Yes. Look, I brought these—in case you did invoke me." Sheepishly he exhibited eight packs of Gauloises, several books, and a gold watch. "It might fetch a price," he explained. "I knew paper francs wouldn't do much good."

At sight of the printed books Lenoir's eyes gleamed with curiosity, but he stood still. "My friend," he said, "you said you'd sell your soul . . . you know . . . so would I. Yet we haven't. How—after all—how did this happen? That we're both men. No devils. No pacts in blood. Two men who've lived in this room . . ."

"I don't know," said Barry. "We'll think that out later. Can I stay with you, Jehan?"

"Consider this your home," Lenoir said with a gracious gesture around the room, the stacks of books, the alembics, the candle growing pale. Outside the window, gray on gray, rose up the two great towers of Notre Dame. It was the dawn of April 3rd.

After breakfast (bread crusts and cheese rinds) they went out and climbed the south tower. The cathedral looked the same as always, though cleaner than in 1961, but the view was rather a shock to Barry. He looked down upon a little town. Two small islands covered with houses; on the right bank more houses crowded inside a fortified wall; on the left bank a few streets twisting around the college; and that was all. Pigeons chortled on the sun-warmed stone between gargoyles. Lenoir, who had seen the view before, was carving the date (in Roman numerals) on a parapet. "Let's celebrate," he said. "Let's go out into the country. I haven't been out of the city for two years. Let's go clear over there—" he pointed to a misty green hill on which a few huts and a windmill were just visible—"to Montmartre, eh? There are some good bars there, I'm told."

Their life soon settled into an easy routine. At first Barry was a little nervous in the crowded streets, but, in a spare black gown of Lenoir's, he was not noticed as outlandish except for his height. He was probably the tallest man in fifteenth-century France. Living standards were low and lice were unavoidable, but Barry had never valued comfort much; the only thing he really missed was coffee at breakfast. When they had bought a bed and a razor—Barry had forgotten his—and introduced him to the landlord as M. Barrie, a cousin of Lenoir's from the Auvergne, their housekeeping arrangements were complete. Barry's watch brought a tremendous price, four gold pieces, enough to live on for a year. They sold it as a wondrous new timepiece from Illyria, and the buyer, a Court chamberlain looking for a nice present to give the king, looked at the inscription—Hamilton Bros., New Haven, 1881—and nodded sagely. Unfortunately he was shut up in one of King Louis's cages for naughty courtiers at Tours before he had presented his gift, and the watch may still be there behind some brick in the ruins of Plessis; but this did not affect the two scholars. Mornings they wandered about sightseeing the Bastille and the churches, or visiting various minor poets in whom Barry was interested; after lunch they discussed electricity, the atomic theory, physiology, and other matters in which Lenoir was interested, and performed minor chemical and anatomical experiments, usually unsuccessfully; after supper they merely talked. Endless, easy talks that ranged over the centuries but always ended here, in the shadowy room with its window open to the Spring night, in their friendship. After two weeks they might have known each other all their lives. They were perfectly happy. They knew they would do nothing with what they had learned from each other. In 1961 how could Barry ever prove his knowledge of old Paris, in 1482 how could Lenoir ever prove the validity of the scientific method? It did not bother them. They had never really expected to be listened to. They had merely wanted to learn.

So they were happy for the first time in their lives; so happy, in fact, that certain desires always before subjugated to the desire for knowledge, began to awaken. "I don't suppose," Barry said one night across the table, "that you ever thought much about marrying?"

"Well, no," his friend answered, doubtfully. "That is, I'm in minor orders . . . and it seemed irrelevant. . . ."

"And expensive. Besides, in my time, no self-respecting woman would want to share my kind of life. American women are so damned poised and efficient and glamorous, terrifying creatures. . . ."

"And women here are little and dark, like beetles, with bad teeth," Lenoir said morosely.

They said no more about women that night. But the next night they did; and the next; and on the next, celebrating the successful dissection of the main nervous system of a pregnant frog, they drank two bottles of Montrachet '74 and got soused. "Let's invoke a woman, Jehan," Barry said in a lascivious bass, grinning like a gargoyle.

"What if I raised a devil this time?"

"Is there really much difference?"

They laughed wildly, and drew a pentagram. "Haere, haere," Lenoir began; when he got the hiccups, Barry took over. He read the last words. There was a rush of cold, marshy-smelling air, and in the pentagram stood a wild-eyed being with long black hair, stark naked, screaming.

"Woman, by God," said Barry.

"Is it?"

It was. "Here, take my cloak," Barry said, for the poor thing now stood gawping and shivering. He put the cloak over her shoulders. Mechanically she pulled it round her, muttering, "Gratias ago, domine."

"Latin!" Lenoir shouted. "A woman speaking Latin?" It took him longer to get over that shock than it did Bota to get over hers. She was, it seemed, a slave in the household of the Sub-Prefect of North Gaul, who lived on the smaller island of the muddy island town called Lutetia. She spoke Latin with a thick Celtic brogue, and did not even know who was emperor in Rome in her day. A real barbarian, Lenoir said with scorn. So she was, an ignorant, taciturn, humble barbarian with tangled hair, white skin, and clear gray eyes. She had been waked from a sound sleep. When they convinced her that she was not dreaming, she evidently assumed that this was some prank of her foreign and all-powerful master the Sub-Prefect, and accepted the situation without further question. "Am I to serve you, my masters?" she inquired timidly but without sullenness, looking from one to the other.

"Not me," Lenoir growled, and added in French to Barry, "Go on; I'll sleep in the store-room." He departed.

Bota looked up at Barry. No Gauls, and few Romans, were so magnificently tall; no Gauls and no Romans ever spoke so kindly. "Your lamp" (it was a candle, but she had never seen a candle) "is nearly burnt out," she said. "Shall I blow it out?"

FOR an additional two sols a year the landlord let them use the store-room as a second bedroom, and Lenoir now slept alone again in the main room of the garret. He observed his friend's idyll with a brooding, un-jealous interest. The professor and the slave-girl loved each other with delight and tenderness. Their pleasure overlapped Lenoir in waves of protective joy. Bota had led a brutal life, treated always as a woman but never as a human. In one short week she bloomed, she came alive, evincing beneath her gentle passiveness a cheerful, clever nature. "You're turning out a regular Parisienne," he heard Barry accuse her one night (the attic walls were thin). She replied, "If you knew what it is for me not to be always defending myself, always afraid, always alone . . ."

Lenoir sat up on his cot and brooded. About midnight, when all was quiet, he rose and noiselessly prepared the pinches of sulfur and silver, drew the pentagram, opened the book. Very softly he read the spell. His face was apprehensive.

In the pentagram appeared a small white dog. It cowered and hung its tail, then came shyly forward, sniffed Lenoir's hand, looked up at him with liquid eyes and gave a modest, pleading whine. A lost puppy. . . . Lenoir stroked it. It licked his hands and jumped all over him, wild with relief. On its white leather collar was a silver plaque engraved, "Jolie. Dupont, 36 rue de Seine, Paris VIe."

Jolie went to sleep, after gnawing a crust, curled up under Lenoir's chair. And the alchemist opened the book again and read, still softly, but this time without self-consciousness, without fear, knowing what would happen.

EMERGING from his store-room-bedroom-honeymoon in the morning, Barry stopped short in the doorway. Lenoir was sitting up in bed, petting a white puppy, and deep in conversation with the person sitting on the foot of the bed, a tall red-haired woman dressed in silver. The puppy barked. Lenoir said, "Good morning!" The woman smiled wondrously.

"Jumping Jesus," Barry muttered (in English). Then he said, "Good morning. When are you from?" The effect was Rita Hayworth, sublimated—Hayworth plus the Mona Lisa, perhaps?

"From Altair, about seven thousand years from now," she said, smiling still more wondrously. Her French accent was worse than that of a football-scholarship freshman. "I'm an archaeologist. I was excavating the ruins of Paris III. I'm sorry I speak the language so badly; of course we know it only from inscriptions."

"From Altair? The star? But you're human—I think—"

"Our planet was colonized from Earth about four thousand years ago—that is, three thousand years from now." She laughed, most wondrously, and glanced at Lenoir. "Jehan explained it all to me, but I still get confused."

"It was a dangerous thing to try it again, Jehan!" Barry accused him. "We've been awfully lucky, you know."

"No," said the Frenchman. "Not lucky."

"But after all it's black magic you're playing with—Listen—I don't know your name, madame."

"Kislk," she said.

"Listen, Kislk," Barry said without even a stumble, "your science must be fantastically advanced—is there any magic? Does it exist? Can the laws of Nature really be broken, as we seem to be doing?"

"I've never seen nor heard of an authenticated case of magic."

"Then what goes on?" Barry roared. "Why does that stupid old spell work for Jehan, for us, that one spell, and here, nowhere else, for nobody else, in five—no, eight—no, fifteen thousand years of recorded history? Why? Why? And where did that damn puppy come from?"

"The puppy was lost," Lenoir said, his dark face grave. "Somewhere near this house, on the Ile Saint-Louis."

"And I was sorting potsherds," Kislk said, also gravely, "in a house-site, Island 2, Pit 4, Section D. A lovely Spring day, and I hated it. Loathed it. The day, the work, the people around me." Again she looked at the gaunt little alchemist, a long, quiet look. "I tried to explain it to Jehan last night. We have improved the race, you see. We're all very tall, healthy, and beautiful. No fillings in our teeth. All skulls from Early America have fillings in the teeth. . . . Some of us are brown, some white, some gold-skinned. But all beautiful, and healthy, and well-adjusted, and aggressive, and successful. Our professions and degree of success are pre-planned for us in the State Pre-School Homes. But there's an occasional genetic flaw. Me, for instance. I was trained as an archaeologist because the Teachers saw that I really didn't like people, live people. People bored me. All like me on the outside, all alien to me on the inside. When everything's alike, which place is home? . . . But now I've seen an unhygienic room with insufficient heating. Now I've seen a cathedral not in ruins. Now I've met a living man who's shorter than me, with bad teeth and a short temper. Now I'm home, I'm where I can be myself, I'm no longer alone!"

"Alone," Lenoir said gently to Barry. "Loneliness, eh? Loneliness is the spell, loneliness is stronger. . . . Really it doesn't seem unnatural."

Bota was peering round the doorway, her face flushed between the black tangles of her hair. She smiled shyly and said a polite Latin good-morning to the newcomer.

"Kislk doesn't know Latin," Lenoir said with immense satisfaction. "We must teach Bota some French. French is the language of love, anyway, eh? Come along, let's go out and buy some bread. I'm hungry."

Kislk hid her silver tunic under the useful and anonymous cloak, while Lenoir pulled on his moth-eaten black gown. Bota combed her hair, while Barry thoughtfully scratched a louse-bite on his neck. Then they set forth to get breakfast. The alchemist and the interstellar archaeologist went first, speaking French; the Gaulish slave and the professor from Indiana followed, speaking Latin, and holding hands. The narrow streets were crowded, bright with sunshine. Above them Notre Dame reared its two square towers against the sky. Beside them the Seine rippled softly. It was April in Paris, and on the banks of the river the chestnuts were in bloom.

Can the Double Murder?

H. P. BLAVATSKY

Madame Helena P. Blavatsky, mystic and fiction writer, cofounded the famous Theosophical Society in New York City in 1875. Famous witch Sybil Leek would later claim to have been guided by this Russian-born mystic's spirit. Unfortunately, Hitler's Nazi party may also have been so influenced—at least by her theories. Whether Blavatsky's spirit would have approved is highly uncertain, but we do know that the Nazis adopted—and some would say corrupted—her favorite occult symbol: the swastika.

To the Editor of *The Sun*.

Sir,—One morning in 1867 Eastern Europe was startled by news of the most horrifying description. Michael Obrenovitch, reigning Prince of Serbia, his aunt, the Princess Catherine or Katinka, and her daughter had been murdered in broad daylight, near Belgrade, in their own garden, assassin or assassins remaining unknown. The Prince had received several bullet-shots, and stabs, and his body was actually butchered; the Princess was killed on the spot, her head smashed, and her young daughter, though still alive, was not expected to survive. The circumstances are too recent to have been forgotten, but in that part of the world, at the time, the case created a delirium of excitement.

In the Austrian dominions and in those under the doubtful protectorate of Turkey, from Bucharest down to Trieste, no high family felt secure. In those half-Oriental countries every Montecchi has its Capuleti, and it was rumoured that the bloody deed was perpetrated by the Prince Kara-Gueorguevitch, or "Tzerno-Gueorgey," as he is usually called in those parts. Several persons innocent of the act were, as is usual in such cases imprisoned, and the real murderers escaped justice. A young relative of the victim, greatly beloved by his people, a mere child, taken for the purpose from a school in Paris, was brought over in ceremony to Belgrade and proclaimed Hospodar of Serbia. In the turmoil of political excitement the tragedy of Belgrade was forgotten by all but an old Serbian matron who had been attached to the Obrenovitch family, and who, like Rachel, would not be comforted for the death of her children. After the proclamation of the young Obrenovitch, nephew of the murdered man, she had sold out her property and disappeared; but not before taking a solemn vow on the tombs of the victims to avenge their deaths.

The writer of this truthful narrative had passed a few days at Belgrade, about three months before the horrid deed was perpetrated, and knew the Princess Katinka. She was a kind, gentle, and lazy creature at home; abroad she seemed a Parisienne in manners and education. As nearly all the personages who will figure in this true story are still living, it is but decent that I should withhold their names, and give only initials.

The old Serbian lady seldom left her house, going but to see the Princess occasionally. Crouched on a pile of pillows and carpeting, clad in the picturesque national dress, she looked like the Cumaean sibyl in her days of calm repose. Strange stories were whispered about her Occult knowledge, and thrilling accounts circulated sometimes among the guests assembled round the fireside of the modest inn. Our fat landlord's maiden aunt's cousin had been troubled for some time past by a wandering vampire, and had been bled nearly to death by the nocturnal visitor, and while the efforts and exorcisms of the parish pope had been of no avail, the victim was luckily delivered by Gospoja P——, who had put to flight the disturbing ghost by merely shaking her fist at him, and shaming him in his own language. It was in Belgrade that I learned for the first time this highly interesting fact in philology, namely, that spooks have a language of their own. The old lady, whom I will call Gospoja P——, was generally attended by another personage destined to be the principal actress in our tale of horror. It was a young gipsy girl from some part of Roumania, about fourteen years of age. Where she was born, and who she was, she seemed to know as little as anyone else. I was told she had been brought one day by a party of strolling gipsies, and left in the yard of the old lady, from which moment she became an inmate of the house. She was nicknamed "the sleeping girl," as she was said to be gifted with the faculty of apparently dropping asleep wherever she stood, and speaking her dreams aloud. The girl's heathen name was Frosya.

About eighteen months after the news of the murder had reached Italy, where I was at the time, I travelled over the Banat in a small waggon of my own, hiring a horse whenever I needed one. I met on my way an old Frenchman, a scientist, travelling alone after my own fashion, but with the difference that while he was a pedestrian, I dominated the road from the eminence of a throne of dry hay in a jolting waggon. I discovered him one fine morning slumbering in a wilderness of shrubs and flowers, and had nearly passed over him, absorbed as I was in the contemplation of the surrounding glorious scenery. The acquaintance was soon made, no great ceremony of mutual introduction being needed. I had heard his name mentioned in circles interested in mesmerism, and knew him to be a powerful adept of the school of Dupotet.

"I have found," he remarked, in the course of the conversation after I had made him share my seat of hay, "one of the most wonderful subjects in this lovely Thebaide. I have an appointment to-night with the family. They are seeking to unravel the mystery of a murder by means of the clairvoyance of the girl . . . she is wonderful!"

"Who is she?" I asked.

"A Roumanian gipsy. She was brought up, it appears, in the family of the Serbian reigning Prince, who reigns no more, for he was very mysteriously mur—Halloo, take care! Diable, you will upset us over the precipice!" he hurriedly exclaimed, unceremoniously snatching from me the reins, and giving the horse a violent pull.

"You do not mean Prince Obrenovitch?" I asked aghast.

"Yes, I do; and him precisely. To-night I have to be there, hoping to close a series of seances by finally developing a most marvellous manifestation of the hidden power of the human spirit; and you may come with me. I will introduce you; and besides, you can help me as an interpreter, for they do not speak French."

As I was pretty sure that if the somnambule was Frosya, the rest of the family must be Gospoja P——, I readily accepted. At sunset we were at the foot of the mountain, leading to the old castle, as the Frenchman called the place. It fully deserved the poetical name given it. There was a rought bench in the depths of one of the shadowy retreats, and as we stopped at the entrance of this poetical place, and the Frenchman was gallantly busying himself with my horse on the suspicious-looking bridge which led across the water to the entrance gate, I saw a tall figure slowly rise from the bench and come towards us.

It was my old friend Gospoja P——, looking more pale and more mysterious than ever. She exhibited no surprise at seeing me, but simply greeting me after the Serbian fashion, with a triple kiss on both cheeks, she took hold of my hand and led me straight to the nest of ivy. Half reclining on a small carpet spread on the tall grass, with her back leaning against the wall, I recognized our Frosya. She was dressed in the national costume of the Wallachian women, a sort of gauze turban intermingled with various gilt medals and bands on her head, white shirt with opened sleeves, and petticoats of variegated colours. Her face looked deadly pale, her eyes were closed, and her countenance presented that stony, sphinx-like look which characterizes in such a peculiar way the entranced clair-voyant somnambule. If it were not for the heaving motion of her chest and bosom, ornamented by rows of medals and bead necklaces which feebly tinkled at every breath, one might have thought her dead, so lifeless and corpse-like was her face. The Frenchman informed me that he had sent her to sleep just as we were approaching the house, and that she now was as he had left her the previous night; he then began busying himself with the sujet, as he called Frosya. Paying no further attention to us, he shook her by the hand, and then making a few rapid passes stretched out her arm and stiffened it. The arm, as rigid as iron, remained in that position. He then closed all her fingers but one—the middle fin-ger—which he caused to point at the evening star, which twinkled in the deep blue sky. Then he turned round and went over from right to left, throwing on some of his fluids here, again discharging them at another place; busying himself with his invisible but potent fluids, like a painter with his brush when giving the last touches to a picture.

The old lady, who had silently watched him, with her chin in her hand the while, put her thin, skeleton-looking hands on his arm and arrested it, as he was preparing himself to begin the regular mesmeric passes.

"Wait," she whispered, "till the star is set and the ninth hour com-pleted. The Vourdalaki are hovering round; they may spoil the influence."

"What does she say?" enquired the mesmerizer, annoyed at her in-terference.

I explained to him that the old lady feared the pernicious influences of the Vourdalaki.

"Vourdalaki! What's that—the Vourdalaki?" exclaimed the Frenchman. "Let us be satisfied with Christian spirits, if they honour us to-night with a visit, and lose no time for the Vourdalaki!"

I glanced at the Gospoja. She had become deathly pale and her brow was sternly knitted over her flashing black eyes.

"Tell him not to jest at this hour of the night!" she cried. "He does not know the country. Even this holy church may fail to protect us once the Vourdalaki are roused. What's this?" pushing with her foot a bundle of herbs the botanizing mesmerizer had laid near on the grass. She bent over the collection and anxiously examined the contents of the bundle, after which she flung the whole into the water.

"It must not be left here," she firmly added; "these are the St. John's plants, and they might attract the wandering ones."

Meanwhile the night had come, and the moon illuminated the landscape with a pale, ghostly light. The nights in the Banat are nearly as beautiful as in the East, and the Frenchman had to go on with his experiments in the open air, as the priest of the church had prohibited such in the tower, which was used as the parsonage, for fear of filling the holy precincts with the heretical devils of the mesmerizer, which, the priest remarked, he would be unable to exorcise on account of their being foreigners.

The old gentleman had thrown off his travelling blouse, rolled up his shirt sleeves, and now, striking a theatrical attitude, began a regular process of mesmerization.

Under his quivering fingers the odile fluid actually seemed to flash in the twilight. Frosya was placed with her figure facing the moon, and every motion of the entranced girl was discernible as in daylight. In a few minutes large drops of perspiration appeared on her brow, and slowly rolled down her pale face, glittering in the moonbeams. Then she moved uneasily about and began chanting a low melody, to the words of which the Gospoja, anxiously bent over the unconscious girl, was listening with avidity and trying to catch every syllable. With her thin finger on her lips, her eyes nearly starting from their sockets, her frame motionless, the old lady seemed herself transfixed into a statue of attention. The group was a remarkable one, and I regretted that I was not a painter. What followed was a scene worthy to figure in *Macbeth*. At one side she, the slender girl, pale and corpse-like, writhing under the invisible fluid of him who for the hour was her omnipotent master; at the other the old matron, who, burning with her unquenched fire of revenge, stood waiting for the long-expected name of the Prince's murderer to be at last pronounced. The Frenchman himself seemed transfigured, his grey hair standing on end; his bulky, clumsy form seemed to have grown in a few minutes. All theatrical pretence was now gone; there remained but the mesmerizer, aware of his responsibility, unconscious himself of the possible results, studying and anxiously expecting. Suddenly Frosya, as if lifted by some supernatural force, rose from her reclining posture and stood erect before us, again motionless and still, waiting for the magnetic fluid to direct her. The Frenchman, silently taking the old lady's hand, placed it in that of the somnambulist, and ordered her to put herself en rapport with the Gospoja.

"What seest thou, my daughter?" softly murmured the Serbian lady. "Can your spirit seek out the murderers?"

"Search and behold!" sternly commanded the mesmerizer, fixing his gaze upon the face of the subject.

"I am on my way—I go," faintly whispered Frosya, her voice seeming not to come from herself, but from the surrounding atmosphere.

At this moment something so strange took place that I doubt my ability to describe it. A luminous vapour appeared, closely surrounding the girl's body. At first about an inch in thickness, it gradually expanded, and, gathering itself, suddenly seemed to break off from the body altogether and condense itself into a kind of semisolid vapour, which very soon assumed the likeness of the somnambule herself. Flickering about the surface of the earth the form vacillated for two or three seconds, then glided noiselessly towards the river. It disappeared like a mist, dissolved in the moonbeams, which seemed to absorb it altogether.

I had followed the scene with an intense attention. The mysterious operation, known in the East as the evocation of the scin-lecca, was taking place before my own eyes. To doubt was impossible, and Dupotet was right in saying that mesmerism is the conscious Magic of the ancients, and Spiritualism the unconscious effect of the same Magic upon certain organisms.

As soon as the vaporous double had smoked itself through the pores of the girl, Gospoja had, by a rapid motion of the hand which was left free, drawn from under her pelisse something which looked to us suspiciously like a small stiletto, and placed it as rapidly in the girl's bosom. The action was so quick that the mesmerizer, absorbed in his work, had not remarked it, as he afterwards told me. A few minutes elapsed in a dead silence. We seemed a group of petrified persons. Suddenly a thrilling and transpiercing cry burst from the entranced girl's lips, she bent forward, and snatching the stiletto from her bosom, plunged it furiously round her, in the air, as if pursuing imaginary foes. Her mouth foamed, and incoherent, wild exclamations broke from her lips, among which discordant sounds I discerned, several times two familiar Christian names of men. The mesmerizer was so terrified that he lost all control over himself, and instead of withdrawing the fluid he loaded the girl with it still more.

"Take care," exclaimed I. "Stop! You will kill her, or she will kill you!"

But the Frenchman had unwittingly raised subtle potencies of Nature over which he had no control. Furiously turning round, the girl struck at him a blow which would have killed him had he not avoided it by jumping aside, receiving but a severe scratch on the right arm. The poor man was panic-stricken; climbing with an extraordinary agility, for a man of his bulky form, on the wall over her, he fixed himself on it astride, and gathering the remnants of his will power, sent in her direction a series of passes. At the second, the girl dropped the weapon and remained motionless.

"What are you about?" hoarsely shouted the mesmerizer in French, seated like some monstrous night-goblin on the wall. "Answer me, I command you!"

"I did . . . but what she . . . whom you ordered me to obey . . . commanded me to do," answered the girl in French, to my amazement.

"What did the old witch command you?" irreverently asked he.

"To find them . . . who murdered . . . kill them . . . I did so . . . and they are no more . . . Avenged! . . . Avenged! They are . . ."

An exclamation of triumph, a loud shout of infernal joy, rang loud in the air, and awakening the dogs of the neighbouring villages a responsive howl of barking began from that moment, like a ceaseless echo of the Gospoja's cry:

"I am avenged! I feel it; I know it. My warning heart tells me that the fiends are no more." She fell panting on the ground, dragging down, in her fall, the girl, who allowed herself to be pulled down as if she were a bag of wool.

"I hope my subject did no further mischief to-night. She is a dangerous as well as a very wonderful subject," said the Frenchman.

We parted. Three days after that I was at T——, and as I was sitting in the dining-room of a restaurant, waiting for my lunch, I happened to pick up a newspaper, and the first lines I read ran thus:

Vienna, 186–. Two Mysterious Deaths.

Last evening, at 9:45, as P—— was about to retire, two of the gentlemen-in-waiting suddenly exhibited great terror, as though they had seen a dreadful apparition. They screamed, staggered, and ran about the room, holding up their hands as if to ward off the blows of an unseen weapon. They paid no attention to the eager questions of the Prince and suite, but presently fell writhing upon the floor, and expired in great agony. Their bodies exhibited no appearance of apoplexy, nor any external marks of wounds, but, wonderful to relate, there were numerous dark spots and long marks upon the skin, as though they were stabs and slashes made without puncturing the cuticle.

The autopsy revealed the fact that beneath each of these mysterious discolourations there was a deposit of coagulated blood. The greatest excitement prevails, and the faculty are unable to solve the mystery.

Bridget Bishop

Cotton Mather

Until his death, Cotton Mather defended the 1692 Salem Witch Trials and their use of "spectral evidence"—he's famous for saying that it's better to kill innocent people as witches than to let even one true witch go unpunished. His serious account in "Bridget Bishop," from Wonders of the Invisible World *(first published 1693), reveals the almost unspoken sexual nature of some of this spectral evidence, which more people think points to wish fulfillment on the part of the "victims" than guilt on the part of the accused witch.*

I shall no longer detain my reader from his expected entertainment in a brief account of the trials which have passed upon some of the malefactors lately executed at Salem for the witchcrafts whereof they stood convicted. For my own part, I was not present at any of them, nor ever had I any personal prejudice at the persons thus brought upon the stage, much less at the surviving relations of those persons, with and for whom I would be as hearty a mourner as any man living in the world. The Lord comfort them!

The Trial of Bridget Bishop, alias Oliver, at the Court of Oyer and Terminer, held at Salem, June 2, 1692.

I. She was indicted for bewitching of several persons in the neighborhood, the indictment being drawn up according to the form in such cases as usual. And pleading "Not Guilty," there were brought in several per-

sons who had long undergone many kinds of miseries which were pre-
ternaturally inflicted and generally ascribed unto an horrible witchcraft.
There was little occasion to prove the witchcraft, it being evident and
notorious to all beholders. Now to fix the witchcraft on the prisoner at
the bar, the first thing used was the testimony of the bewitched, whereof
several testified that the shape of the prisoner did oftentimes very grievously pinch them, choke them, bite them, and afflict them, urging them
to write their names in a book, which the said specter called, ours. One
of them did further testify that it was the shape of this prisoner, with
another, which one day took her from her wheel and, carrying her to the
riverside, threatened there to drown her if she did not sign the book
mentioned, which yet she refused. Others of them did also testify that
the said shape did in her threats brag to them that she had been the death
of sundry persons then by her named, that she had ridden a man then
likewise named. Another testified the apparition of ghosts unto the specter of Bishop, crying out, "You murdered us!" About the truth whereof,
there was in the matter of fact but too much suspicion.

II. It was testified that at the examination of the prisoner before the
magistrates, the bewitched were extremely tortured. If she did but cast
her eyes on them, they were presently struck down, and this in such a
manner as there could be no collusion in the business. But upon the touch
of her hand upon them, when they lay in their swoons, they would immediately revive, and not upon the touch of any one's else. Moreover,
upon some special actions of her body, as the shaking of her head or the
turning of her eyes, they presently and painfully fell into the like postures.
And many of the like accidents now fell out, while she was at the bar,
one at the same time testifying that she said she could not be troubled to
see the afflicted thus tormented.

III. There was testimony likewise brought in that a man striking once
at the place where a bewitched person said the shape of this Bishop stood,
the bewitched cried out that he had tore her coat in the place then particularly specified, and the woman's coat was found to be torn in that
very place.

IV. One Deliverance Hobbs, who had confessed her being a witch,
was now tormented by the specters for her confession. And she now
testified that this Bishop tempted her to sign the book again and to deny
what she had confessed. She affirmed that it was the shape of this prisoner
which whipped her with iron rods to compel her thereunto. And she

affirmed that this Bishop was at a general meeting of the witches in a field at Salem-Village and there partook of a diabolical sacrament in bread and wine then administered.

V. To render it further unquestionable that the prisoner at the bar was the person truly charged in this witchcraft, there were produced many evidences of other witchcrafts, by her perpetrated. For instance, John Cook testified that about five or six years ago, one morning about sunrise, he was in his chamber assaulted by the shape of this prisoner, which looked on him, grinned at him, and very much hurt him with a blow on the side of the head, and that on the same day, about noon, the same shape walked in the room where he was, and an apple strangely flew out of his hand, into the lap of his mother, six or eight feet from him.

VI. Samuel Gray testified that about fourteen years ago he waked on a night and saw the room where he lay full of light, and that he then saw plainly a woman between the cradle and the bedside, which looked upon him. He rose, and it vanished, though he found the doors all fast. Looking out at the entrydoor, he saw the same woman, in the same garb again, and said, "In God's name, what do you come for?" He went to bed and had the same woman again assaulting him. The child in the cradle gave a great screech, and the woman disappeared. It was long before the child could be quieted, and though it were a very likely thriving child, yet from this time it pined away and after divers months, died in a sad condition. He knew not Bishop, nor her name; but when he saw her after this he knew by her countenance, and apparel, and all circumstances, that it was the apparition of this Bishop which had thus troubled him.

VII. John Bly and his wife testified that he bought a sow of Edward Bishop, the husband of the prisoner, and was to pay the price agreed, unto another person. This prisoner, being angry that she was thus hindered from fingering the money, quarrelled with Bly. Soon after which, the sow was taken with strange fits, jumping, leaping, and knocking her head against the fence; she seemed blind and deaf and would neither eat nor be sucked, whereupon a neighbor said she believed the creature was overlooked, and sundry other circumstances concurred, which made the deponents believe that Bishop had bewitched it.

VIII. Richard Coman testified that eight years ago, as he lay awake in his bed with a light burning in the room, he was annoyed with the apparition of this Bishop and of two more that were strangers to him, who came and oppressed him so that he could neither stir himself nor wake any one else, and that he was the night after, molested again in the like manner, the said Bishop taking him by the throat and pulling him almost out of the bed. His kinsman offered for this cause to lodge with him; and that night, as they were awake, discoursing together, this Co-man was once more visited by the guests which had formerly been so troublesome, his kinsman being at the same time struck speechless and unable to move hand or foot. He had laid his sword by him, which these unhappy specters did strive much to wrest from him, only he held too fast for them. He then grew able to call the people of his house, but although they heard him, yet they had not power to speak or stir until at last, one of the people crying out, "What's the matter?" the specters all vanished.

IX. Samuel Shattock testified that in the year 1680, this Bridget Bishop often came to his house upon such frivolous and foolish errands that they suspected she came indeed with a purpose of mischief. Presently, whereupon, his eldest child, which was of as promising health and sense as any child of its age, began to droop exceedingly, and the oftener that Bishop came to the house, the worse grew the child. As the child would be standing at the door, he would be thrown and bruised against the stones by an invisible hand and in like sort knock his face against the sides of the house and bruise it after a miserable manner. After this, Bishop would bring him things to dye, whereof he could not imagine any use; and when she paid him a piece of money, the purse and money were unaccountably conveyed out of a locked box and never seen more. The child was immediately, hereupon, taken with terrible fits, whereof his friends thought he would have died. Indeed he did almost nothing but cry and sleep for several months together, and at length his understanding was utterly taken away. Among other symptoms of an enchantment upon him, one was that there was a board in the garden, whereon he would walk, and all the invitations in the world could never fetch him off. About seventeen or eighteen years after, there came a stranger to Shattock's house who, seeing the child, said, "This poor child is bewitched; and you have a neighbor living not far off who is a witch." He added, "Your neighbor has had a falling out with your wife; and she said, in her heart, your wife is a proud woman, and she would bring down her pride in this child." He then remembered that Bishop had parted from his wife in muttering and menacing terms, a little before the child was taken ill. The abovesaid stranger would needs carry the bewitched boy with him to Bishop's house, on pretense of buying a pot of cider. The woman entertained him in a furious manner and flew also upon the boy, scratching his face till the blood came and saying, "Thou rogue, what dost thou bring this fellow here to plague me?" Now it seems the man had said, before he went, that he would fetch blood of her. Ever after the boy was followed with grievous fits which the doctors themselves generally ascribed unto witchcraft, and wherein he would be thrown still into the fire or the water, if he were not constantly looked after; and it was verily believed that Bishop was the cause of it.

X. John Louder testified that upon some little controversy with Bishop about her fowls, going well to bed, he did awake in the night by moonlight and did see clearly the likeness of this woman grievously oppressing him, in which miserable condition she held him, unable to help himself, till near day. He told Bishop of this, but she denied it and threatened him very much. Quickly after this, being at home on a Lord's day with the doors shut about him, he saw a black pig approach him, at which he going to kick, it vanished away. Immediately after, sitting down, he saw a black thing jump in at the window and come and stand before him. The body was like that of a monkey, the feet like a cock's, but the face much like a man's. He being so extremely affrighted that he could not speak, this monster spoke to him and said, "I am a messenger sent unto you, for I understand that you are in some trouble of mind, and if you will be ruled by me, you shall want for nothing in this world." Whereupon he endeavored to clap his hands upon it; but he could feel no substance; and it jumped out of the window again but immediately came in by the porch, though the doors were shut, and said, "You had better take my counsel!" He then struck at it with a stick but struck only the ground-sill and broke the stick; the arm with which he struck was presently disenabled, and it [the black thing] vanished away. He presently went out at the back door and spied this Bishop, in her orchard, going towards her house; but he had not power to set one foot forward unto her. Whereupon, returning into the house, he was immediately accosted by the monster he had seen before, which goblin was now going to fly at him, whereat he cried out, "The whole armor of God be between me and you!" So it sprang back and flew over the apple tree, shaking many apples off the tree in its flying over. At its leap, it flung dirt with its feet against the stomach of the man, whereon he was then struck dumb and so continued for three days together. Upon the producing of this testimony, Bishop denied that she knew this deponent; yet their two orchards joined; and they had often had their little quarrels for some years together.

XI. William Stacy testified that receiving money of this Bishop, for work done by him, he was gone but a matter of three rods from her and looking for his money, found it unaccountably gone from him. Some time after, Bishop asked him whether his father would grind her grist for her? He demanded why? She replied, "Because folks count me a witch." He answered, "No question but he will grind it for you." Being then gone about six rods from her, with a small load in his cart, suddenly the off-wheel slumped and sank down into a hole, upon plain ground, so that the deponent was forced to get help for the recovering of the wheel, but stepping back to look for the hole, which might give him this disaster, there was none at all to be found. Some time after, he was waked in the night, but it seemed as light as day, and he perfectly saw the shape of this Bishop in the room, troubling of him; but upon her going out, all was dark again. He charged Bishop afterwards with it; and she denied it not, but was very angry. Quickly after, this deponent having been threatened by Bishop, as he was in a dark night going to the barn, he was very suddenly taken or lifted from the ground and thrown against a stone wall; after that he was again hoisted up and thrown down a bank at the end of his house. After this, again passing by this Bishop, his horse with a small load, striving to draw, all his gears flew to pieces, and the cart fell down; and this deponent going then to lift a bag of corn, of about two bushels, could not budge it with all his might.

Many other pranks of this Bishop's this deponent was ready to testify. He also testified that he verily believed the said Bishop was the instrument of his daughter Priscilla's death, of which suspicion, pregnant reasons were assigned.

XII. To crown all, John Bly and William Bly testified that being employed by Bridget Bishop to help take down the cellar wall of the old house wherein she formerly lived, they did in holes of the said old wall find several poppets made up of rags and hog's bristles, with headless pins in them, the points being outward, whereof she could give no account to the court that was reasonable or tolerable.

XIII. One thing that made against the prisoner was her being evidently convicted of gross lying in the court, several times, while she was making her plea; but besides this, a jury of women found a preternatural teat upon her body; but upon a second search, within three or four hours, there was no such thing to be seen. There was also an account of other people whom this woman had afflicted; and there might have been many more if they had been inquired for, but there was no need of them.

XIV. There was one very strange thing more, with which the court was newly entertained. As this woman was under a guard, passing by the great and spacious meeting house of Salem, she gave a look towards the house, and immediately a demon invisibly entering the meeting house tore down a part of it, so that though there was no person to be seen there, yet the people, at the noise, running in, found a board which was strongly fastened with several nails, transported unto another quarter of the house.

A Third Curiosity

If a drop of innocent blood should be shed in the prosecution of the witchcrafts among us, how unhappy are we! For which cause, I cannot express myself in better terms than those of a most worthy person who lives near the present center of these things. "The mind of God in these matters, is to be carefully looked into, with due circumspection, that Satan deceive us not with his devices, who transforms himself into an angel of light and may pretend justice and yet intend mischief." But on the other side, if the storm of justice do now fall only on the heads of those guilty witches and wretches which have defiled our land, how happy!

The execution of some that have lately died has been immediately attended with a strange deliverance of some that had lain for many years in a most sad condition, under they knew not whose evil hands. As I am abundantly satisfied that many of the self murders committed here have been the effects of a cruel and bloody witchcraft. . . . Thus it has been admirable unto me to see how a devilish witchcraft, sending devils upon them, has driven many poor people to despair and persecuted their minds with such buzzes of atheism and blasphemy as have made them even run distracted with terrors. And some, long bowed down under such a spirit of infirmity, have been marvelously recovered upon the death of the witches.

A Witch Trial at Mount Holly

BEN FRANKLIN

Statesman, inventor, diplomat, ladies' man—Ben Franklin was, above all else, one funny writer. Unlike Cotton Mather's tale, the end of Franklin's "A Witch Trial at Mount Holly" (Pennsylvania Gazette, Oct. 22, 1730), recognizes and mocks the prurient interests of some of those devil-fearing Puritans.

BURLINGTON, Oct. 12. Saturday last at Mount-Holly, about 8 Miles from this Place, near 300 People were gathered together to see an Experiment or two tried on some Persons accused of Witchcraft. It seems the Accused had been charged with making their Neighbours Sheep dance in an uncommon Manner, and with causing Hogs to speak, and sing Psalms, &c. to the great Terror and Amazement of the King's good and peaceable Subjects in this Province; and the Accusers being very positive that if the Accused were weighed in Scales against a Bible, the Bible would prove too heavy for them; or that, if they were bound and put into the River, they would swim; the said Accused desirous to make their Innocence appear, voluntarily offered to undergo the said Trials, if 2 of the most violent of their Accusers would be tried with them. Accordingly the Time and Place was agreed on, and advertised about the Country; The Accusers were 1 Man and 1 Woman; and the Accused the same. The Parties being met, and the People got together, a grand Consultation was held, before they proceeded to Trial; in which it was agreed to use the Scales first; and a Committee of Men were appointed to search the Men, and a Committee of Women to search the Women, to see if they had any Thing of Weight about them, particularly Pins. After the Scrutiny was over, a huge great Bible belonging to the Justice of the Place was provided, and a Lane through the Populace was made from the Justice's

House to the Scales, which were fixed on a Gallows erected for that Purpose opposite to the House, that the Justice's Wife and the rest of the Ladies might see the Trial, without coming amongst the Mob; and after the Manner of Moorfields, a large Ring was also made. Then came out of the House a grave tall Man carrying the Holy Writ before the supposed Wizard, &c. (as solemnly as the Sword-bearer of London before the Lord Mayor) the Wizard was first put in the Scale, and over him was read a Chapter out of the Books of Moses, and then the Bible was put in the other Scale, (which being kept down before) was immediately let go; but to the great Surprize of the Spectators, Flesh and Bones came down plump, and outweighed that great good Book by abundance. After the same Manner, the others were served, and their Lumps of Mortality severally were too heavy for Moses and all the Prophets and Apostles. This being over, the Accusers and the rest of the Mob, not satisfied with this Experiment, would have the Trial by Water; accordingly a most solemn Procession was made to the Mill-pond; where both Accused and Accusers being stripp'd (saving only to the Women their Shifts) were bound Hand and Foot, and severally placed in the Water, lengthways, from the Side of a Barge or Flat, having for Security only a Rope about the Middle of each, which was held by some in the Flat. The Accuser Man being thin and spare, with some Difficulty began to sink at last; but the rest every one of them swam very light upon the Water. A Sailor in the Flat jump'd out upon the Back of the Man accused, thinking to drive him down to the Bottom, but the Person bound, without any Help, came up some time before the other. The Woman Accuser, being told that she did not sink, would be duck'd a second Time; when she swam again as light as before. Upon which she declared, That she believed the Accused had bewitched her to make her so light, and that she would be duck'd again a Hundred Times, but she would duck the Devil out of her. The accused Man, being surpriz'd at his own Swimming, was not so confident of his Innocence as before, but said, *If I am a Witch, it is more than I know.* The more thinking Part of the Spectators were of Opinion, that any Person so bound and plac'd in the Water (unless they were mere Skin and Bones) would swim till their Breath was gone, and their Lungs fill'd with Water. But it being the general Belief of the Populace, that the Women's Shifts, and the Garters with which they were bound help'd to support them; it is said they are to be tried again the next warm Weather, naked.

General Andrew Jackson and the Bell Witch

M. V. INGRAM

Supposedly the legendary Bell Witch of Tennessee inspired the movie
The Blair Witch Project. And you've heard of that, right? This is
an "eyewitness" account written in 1893—sadly before the age of
handheld video cameras. . . .

GRANDFATHER Fort told me the story of Gen. Jackson's visit to the witch, which was quite amusing to me. The crowds that gathered at Bell's, many coming a long distance, were so large that the house would not accommodate the company. Mr. Bell would not accept any pay for entertaining, and the imposition on the family, being a constant thing, was so apparent, that parties were made up and went prepared for camping out. So Gen. Jackson's party came from Nashville with a wagon loaded with a tent, provisions, etc., bent on a good time and much fun investigating the witch. The men were riding on horseback and were following along in the rear of the wagon as they approached near the place, discussing the matter and planning how they were going to do up the witch, if it made an exhibition of such pranks as they had heard of. Just then, within a short distance of the house, traveling over a smooth level piece of road, the wagon halted and stuck fast. The driver popped his whip, whooped and shouted to the team, and the horses pulled with all of their might, but could not move the wagon an inch. It was dead stuck as if welded to the earth. Gen. Jackson commanded all men to dismount and put their shoulders to the wheels and give the wagon a push. The order was promptly obeyed. The driver laid on the lash and the horses and men did their best, making repeated efforts, but all in vain; it was no go. The wheels were then taken off, one at a time, and examined and found to be all right, revolving easily on the axles. Another trial was made to get away, the driver whipping up the team while the men pushed at the wheels, and still it was no go. All stood off looking at the wagon in serious meditation, for they were "stuck." Gen. Jackson after a few moments thought, realizing that they were in a fix, threw up his hands exclaiming, "By the eternal, boys, it is the witch." Then came the sound of a sharp metallic voice from the bushes, saying, "All right, General, let the wagon move on, I will see you again tonight." The men in bewildered astonishment looked in every direction to see if they could discover from whence came the strange voice, but could find no explanation to the mystery. Gen. Jackson exclaimed again, "By the eternal, boys, this is worse than fighting the British." The horses then started unexpectedly of their own accord, and the wagon rolled along as light and smoothly as ever. Jackson's party was in no good frame of mind for camping out that night, notwithstanding one of the party was a professional "witch layer," and boasted much of his power over evil spirits, and was taken along purposely to deal with Kate, as they called the witch. The whole party went to the house for quarters and comfort, and Mr. Bell, recognizing the distinguished character of the leader of the party, was lavishing in courtesies and entertainment. But Gen. Jackson was out with the boys for fun—"witch hunting"—and was one of them for the time. They were expecting Kate to put in an appearance according to promise, and they chose to sit in a room by the light of a tallow candle waiting for the witch. The witch layer had a big flint lock army or horse pistol, loaded with a silver bullet, which he held steady in hand, keeping a close lookout for Kate. He was a brawny man, with long hair, high cheek bones, hawk-bill nose and fiery eyes. He talked much, entertaining the company with details of his adventures, and exhibitions of undaunted courage and success in overcoming witches. He exhibited the tip of a black cat's tail, about two inches, telling how he shot the cat with a silver bullet while sitting on a bewitched woman's coffin, and by stroking that cat's tail on his nose it would flash a light on a witch the darkest night that ever come; the light, however, was not visible to any one but a magician. The party was highly entertained by the vain stories of this dolt. They flattered his vanity and encouraged his conceit, laughed at his stories, and called him sage, Apollo, oracle, wiseacre, etc. Yet there was an expectancy in the minds of all left from the wagon experience, which made the mage's stories go well, and all kept wide awake till a late hour, when they became weary and drowsy, and rather tired of hearing the warlock detail his exploits. Old Hickory was the first one to let off tension. He commenced yawning and twisting in his chair. Leaning over he whispered to the man nearest him, "Sam, I'll bet that fellow is an arrant coward. By the eternals, I do wish the thing would come, I want to see him run." The General did not have long to wait. Presently perfect quiet reigned, and then was heard a noise like dainty footsteps prancing over the floor, and quickly following, the same metallic voice heard in the bushes rang out from one corner of the room, exclaiming, "All right, General, I am on hand ready for business." And then addressing the witch layer, "Now, Mr. Smarty, here I am, shoot." The seer stroked his nose with the cat's tail, leveled his pistol, and pulled the trigger, but it failed to fire. "Try again," exclaimed the witch, which he did with the same result. "Now it's my turn; look out, you old coward, hypocrite, fraud. I'll teach you a lesson." The next thing a sound was heard like that of boxing with the open hand, whack, whack, and the oracle tumbled over like lightning had struck him, but he quickly recovered his feet and went capering around the room like a frightened steer, running over every one in his way, yelling, "Oh my nose, my nose, the devil has got me. Oh lordy, he's got me by the nose." Suddenly, as if by its own accord, the door flew open and the witch layer dashed out, and made a bee line for the lane at full speed, yelling every jump. Everybody rushed out under the excitement, expecting the man would be killed, but as far as they could hear up the lane, he was still running and yelling, "Oh Lordy." Jackson, they say, dropped down on the ground and rolled over and over, laughing. "By the eternal, boys, I never saw so much fun in all my life. This beats fighting the British." Presently the witch was on hand and joined in the laugh. "Lord Jesus," it exclaimed, "How the old devil did run and beg; I'll bet he won't come here again with his old horse pistol to shoot me. I guess that's fun enough for to-night, General, and you can go to bed now. I will come to-morrow night and show you another rascal in this crowd." Old Hickory was anxious to stay a week, but his party had enough of that thing. No one knew whose turn would come next, and no inducements could keep them. They spent the next night in Springfield, and returned to Nashville, the following day. . . .

That's Witch with a "W":
Witchcraft As
Em-POWER-ment

⟡

You've got to admit, it's a lovely image. Wiggling your nose or snapping your fingers and having power at your command—and often without that pesky "selling your soul" business that the demonic witch has to worry about. This is not to say that the Empowered-Female kind of witch can't be frightening . . . in fact, she often is, when it's a man telling the story! Just check out Harlan Ellison's "Goddess in the Ice," or Anton Chekov's "The Witch."

In fact, very often the way these woman witches show their power is over men, like in Louisa May Alcott's "A Pair of Eyes," or P. N. Elrod's "The Tea Room Beasts," or Emily Brontë's "The Night," or Louise Erdrich's powerful "Fleur."

Maybe it's just a lovely image for women, at that!

The Night

EMILY BRONTË

*Was eighteenth-century romantic novelist Emily Brontë, sister of
Charlotte and Anne, a witch? Not likely. But her love of nature,
both in her classic* Wuthering Heights *and in her poetry, approaches
worship. And her relations of passion come as close to magic as anything you're likely to find. In "The Night," we see affirmation that
love might be the most powerful, and perhaps most deadly, of all
spells.*

The night is darkening round me,
The wild winds coldly blow;
But a tyrant spell has bound me
And I cannot, cannot go.

The giant trees are bending
Their bare boughs weighed with snow,
And the storm is fast descending
And yet I cannot go.

Clouds beyond clouds above me,
Wastes beyond wastes below;
But nothing drear can move me;
I will not, cannot go.

Snatcher

DEAN KOONTZ

Is it any wonder that Dean R. Koontz is one of the world's bestselling authors of horror and suspense? "Snatcher" gives us a particularly eerie tale of the perils involved when young men prey on seemingly helpless old women.

BILLY Neeks had a flexible philosophy regarding property rights. He believed in the proletarian ideal of shared wealth—as long as the wealth belonged to someone else. If it was *his* property, Billy was ready to defend it to the death. It was a good, workable philosophy for a thief, which Billy was.

Billy Neeks's occupation was echoed by his grooming: he looked slippery. His thick black hair was slicked back with enough scented oil to fill a crankcase. His coarse skin was perpetually pinguid, as if he suffered continuously from malaria. He moved cat-quick on well-lubricated joints, and his hands had the buttery grace of a magician's hands. His eyes looked like twin pools of Texas crude, wet and black and deep—and utterly untouched by human warmth or feeling. If the route to Hell were an inclined ramp requiring some hideous grease to facilitate descent, Billy Neeks would be the Devil's choice to pass eternity in the application of that noxious, oleaginous substance.

In action, Billy could bump into an unsuspecting woman, separate her from her purse, and be ten yards away and moving fast by the time she realized she had been victimized. Single-strap purses, double-strap purses, clutch purses, purses carried over the shoulder, purses carried in the hand—all meant easy money to Billy Neeks. Whether his target was cautious or careless was of no consequence. Virtually no precautions could foil him.

That Wednesday in April, pretending to be drunk, he jostled a well-dressed elderly woman on Broad Street, just past Bartram's Department Store. As she recoiled in disgust from that oily contact, Billy slipped her purse off her shoulder, down her arm, and into the plastic shopping bag he carried. He had reeled away from her and had taken six or eight steps in an exaggerated stagger before she realized that the collision had not been as purposeless as it had seemed. Even as the victim shrieked "police," Billy had begun to run, and by the time she added, "help, police, help," Billy was nearly out of earshot.

He raced through a series of alleyways, dodged around garbage cans and dumpsters, leaped across the splayed legs of a sleeping wino. He sprinted across a parking lot, fled into another alley.

Blocks from Bartram's, Billy slowed to a walk, breathing only slightly harder than usual, grinning. When he stepped out onto 46th Street, he saw a young mother carrying a baby and a shopping bag *and* a purse, and she looked so defenseless that Billy could not resist the opportunity, so he flicked open his switchblade and, in a wink, cut the straps on her bag, a stylish blue leather number. Then he dashed off again, across the street, where drivers braked sharply and blew their horns at him, into another network of alleys, all familiar to him, and as he ran he giggled. His giggle was neither shrill nor engaging but more like the sound of ointment squirting from a tube.

When he slid on spilled garbage—orange peels, rotting lettuce, mounds of molding and soggy bread—he was not tripped up or even slowed down. The disgusting spill seemed to facilitate his flight, and he came out of the slide moving faster than he had gone into it.

He slowed to a normal pace when he reached Prospect Boulevard. The switchblade was in his pocket again. Both stolen purses were concealed in the plastic shopping bag. He projected what he thought was an air of nonchalance, and although his calculated expression of innocence was actually a dismal failure, it was the best he could do.

He walked to his car, which he had parked at a meter along Prospect. The Pontiac, unwashed for at least two years, left oil drippings wherever it went, just as a wolf in the wilds marked its territory with dribbles of urine. Billy put the stolen purses in the trunk of the car and drove away from that part of the city, toward other prowling grounds in other neighborhoods.

Of the several reasons for his success as a purse snatcher, mobility was perhaps most important. Many snatchers were kids looking for a few fast bucks, young hoods without wheels, but Billy Neeks was twenty-five, no kid, and possessed of reliable transportation. He usually robbed two or three women in one neighborhood and then quickly moved on to another territory, where no one was looking for him and where more business waited to be done.

To him, this was not small-time thievery committed either by impulse or out of desperation. Instead, Billy saw it as a business and he was a businessman, and like other businessmen he planned his work carefully, weighed the risks and benefits of any endeavor, and acted only as a result of careful responsible analysis.

Other snatchers—amateurs and punks, every one of them—paused on the street or in an alleyway, hastily searching purses for valuables, risking arrest by their inadvisable delays, at the very least creating a host of additional witnesses to their crimes. Billy, on the other hand, stashed the purses in the trunk of his car to be retrieved later for more leisurely inspection in the privacy of his home.

He prided himself on his methodicalness and caution.

That cloudy and humid Wednesday in late April, he crossed and re-crossed the city, briefly visiting three widely separated districts and snatching six purses in addition to those he had taken from the elderly woman outside Bartram's and from the young mother on 46th Street. The last of the eight also came from an old woman, and at first he thought it was going to be an easy hit, and then he thought it was going to get messy, and finally it just turned out weird.

When Billy spotted her, she was coming out of a butcher's shop on Westend Avenue, clutching a package of meat to her breast. She was *old*. Her brittle white hair stirred in the spring breeze, and Billy had the curious notion that he could hear those dry hairs rustling against one another. A crumpled-parchment face, slumped shoulders, pale withered hands, and shuffling step combined to convey the impression not only of extreme age but of frailty and vulnerability, which was what drew Billy Neeks as if he were an iron filing and she a magnet. Her purse was big, almost a satchel, and the weight of it—in addition to the package of meat—seemed to bother her, for she was struggling the straps farther up on her shoulder and wincing in pain, as if suffering from a flare-up of arthritis.

Though it was spring, she was dressed in black: black shoes, black stockings, black skirt, dark gray blouse, even a heavy black cardigan sweater unsuited to the mild day.

Billy looked up and down the street, saw no one else nearby, and quickly made his move. He did his drunk trick, staggering, jostling the old biddy. But as he pulled the purse down her arm, she dropped the package of meat, seized the bag with both hands, and for a moment they were locked in an unexpectedly fierce struggle. Ancient as she was, she possessed surprising strength. He tugged at the purse, wrenched and twisted it, desperately attempted to rock her backward off her feet, but she stood her ground and held on with the tenacity of a deeply rooted tree resisting a storm wind.

He said, "Give it up, you old bitch, or I'll bust your face."

And then a strange thing happened:

She seemed to *change* before Billy's eyes. In a blink she no longer appeared frail but steely, no longer weak but darkly energized. Her bony and arthritic hands suddenly locked like the dangerous talons of a powerful bird of prey. That singular face—pale yet jaundiced, nearly fleshless, all wrinkles and sharp pointy lines—was still ancient, but it no longer seemed quite *human* to Billy Neeks. And her eyes. My God, her eyes. At first glance, Billy saw only the watery, myopic gaze of a doddering crone, but abruptly they were eyes of tremendous power, eyes of fire and ice simultaneously boiling his blood and freezing his heart, eyes that saw into him and through him, not the eyes of a helpless old woman but those of a murderous beast that had the desire and ability to devour him alive.

He gasped in fear, and he almost let go of the purse, almost ran, but in another blink she was transformed into a defenseless old woman again, and abruptly she capitulated. Like pop-beads, the swollen knuckles of her twisted hands seemed to come apart, and her finger joints went slack. She lost her grip, releasing the purse with a small cry of despair.

Emitting a menacing snarl that served not only to frighten the old woman but to chase away Billy's own irrational terror, he shoved her backward, into a curbside trash container, and bolted past her, the satchel-size purse under his arm. He glanced back after several steps, half expecting to see that she had fully assumed the form of a great dark bird of prey, flying at him, eyes aflame, teeth bared, talon-hands spread and hooked to tear him to bits. But she was clutching at the trash container to keep her balance, as age-broken and helpless as she had been when he had first seen her.

The only odd thing: she was looking after him with a smile. No mistaking it. A wide, stained-tooth smile. Almost a lunatic grin.

Senile old fool, Billy thought. Had to be senile if she found anything funny about having her purse snatched.

He could not imagine why he had ever been afraid of her.

He ran, dodging from one alleyway to another, down side streets, across a sun-splashed parking lot, and along a shadowy service passage between two tenements, onto a street far removed from the scene of his latest theft. At a stroll, he returned to his parked car and put the old woman's black purse and one other in the trunk with the six taken elsewhere in the city. At last, a hard day's work behind him, he drove home, looking forward to counting his take, having a few beers, and watching some TV.

Once, stopped at a red traffic light, Billy thought he heard something moving in the car's trunk. There were a few hollow thumps and a brief but curious scraping noise. However, when he cocked his head and listened closer he heard nothing more, and he decided that the noise had only been the pile of stolen purses shifting under their own weight.

BILLY Neeks lived in a ramshackle four-room bungalow between a vacant lot and a transmission shop, two blocks from the river. The place had belonged to his mother and had been clean and in good repair when she had lived there. Two years ago, Billy had convinced her to transfer ownership to him "for tax reasons," then had shipped her off to a nursing home to be cared for at the expense of the state. He supposed she was still there—he didn't know for sure because he never visited.

That evening in April, Billy arranged the eight purses side by side in two rows on the kitchen table and stared at them for a while in sweet anticipation of the treasure hunt to come. He popped the tab on a Budweiser. He tore open a bag of Doritos. He pulled up a chair, sat down, and sighed contentedly.

Finally, he opened the purse he had taken off the woman outside Bartram's, and began to calculate his "earnings." She had looked well-to-do, and the contents of her wallet did not disappoint Billy Neeks: $309 in folding money, plus another $4.10 in change. She also carried a stack of credit cards, which Billy would fence through Jake Barcelli, the pawnshop owner who would also give him a few bucks for the other worthwhile items he found in the purses. In the first bag, those fenceable items included a gold-plated Tiffany pen, matching gold-plated Tiffany compact and lipstick tube, and a fine though not extraordinarily expensive opal ring.

The young mother's purse contained only $11.42 and nothing else of value, which Billy had expected, but that meager profit did not diminish the thrill he got from going through the contents of the bag. He looked upon snatching as a business, yes, and thought of himself as a businessman, but he also took considerable pleasure simply from perusing and *touching* his victims' belongings. The violation of a woman's personal property was a violation of her, too, and when his quick hands explored the young mother's purse, it was almost as if he were exploring her body. Sometimes, Billy took unfenceable items—cheap compacts, inexpensive tubes of lipstick, eyeglasses—and put them on the floor and stomped them, because crushing them beneath his heel was somehow almost like crushing the woman herself. Easy money made his work worthwhile, but he was equally motivated by the tremendous sense of power he got from the job; it stimulated him, it really did, stimulated and satisfied.

By the time he had gone slowly through seven of the eight purses, savoring their contents, it was 7:15 in the evening, and he was euphoric. He breathed fast and, occasionally, shuddered ecstatically. His oily hair looked oilier than usual, for it was damp with sweat and hung in clumps and tangles. Fine beads of perspiration glimmered on his face. During his exploration of the purses, he had knocked the open bag of Doritos off the kitchen table but had not noticed. He had opened a second beer, but he never tasted it; now it stood forgotten. His world had shrunk to the dimensions of a woman's purse.

He had saved the crazy old woman's bag for last because he had a hunch that it was going to provide the greatest treasure of the day.

The old hag's purse was big, almost a satchel, made of supple black leather, with long straps, and with a single main compartment that closed with a zipper. He pulled it in front of him and stared at it for a moment, letting his anticipation build.

He remembered how the crone had resisted him, holding fast to the bag until he thought he might have to flick open his switchblade and cut her. He had cut a few women before, not many but enough to know he *liked* cutting them.

That was the problem. Billy was smart enough to realize that, liking knifeplay so much, he must deny himself the pleasure of cutting people, resorting to violence only when absolutely necessary, for if he used the knife too often, he would be unable to stop using it, would be compelled to use it, and then he would be lost. The police expended no energy in the search for mere purse snatchers, but they would be a lot more aggressive and relentless in pursuit of a slasher.

Still, he had not cut anyone for several months, and by such admirable self-control, he had earned the right to have some fun. He would have taken great pleasure in separating the old woman's withered meat from her bones. And now he wondered why he had not ripped her up the moment she had given him trouble.

He had virtually forgotten how she had briefly terrified him, how she had looked less human than avian, how her hands had seemed to metamorphose into wicked talons, and how her eyes had blazed. Deeply confirmed in his macho self-image, he had no capacity for any memory that had the potential for humiliation.

With a growing certainty that he was about to find a surprising treasure, he put his hands on the purse and lightly squeezed. It was crammed full, straining at the seams, and Billy told himself that the forms he felt through the leather were wads of money, banded stacks of hundred-dollar bills, and his heart began to thump with excitement.

He pulled open the zipper, looked in, and frowned.

It was dark inside the purse.

Billy peered closer.

Impossibly dark.

Squinting, he could see nothing in there at all, not a wallet or a compact or a comb or a packet of Kleenex, not even the lining of the purse itself, only a flawless and very deep darkness, as if he were peering into a well. *Deep* was the word, all right, for he had a sense that he was staring down into unplumbable and mysterious depths, as if the bottom of the purse were not just a few inches away but thousands of feet down—even farther—countless miles below him. Suddenly he realized that the glow from the overhead kitchen fluorescents fell into the open purse but illuminated nothing; the bag seemed to swallow every ray of light and digest it.

Billy Neeks's warm sweat of quasi-erotic pleasure abruptly turned icy-cold, and his skin dimpled with gooseflesh. He knew he should pull the zipper shut, cautiously carry the purse blocks away from his own house, and dispose of it in someone else's trash bin. But he saw his right hand slipping toward the gaping maw of the bag. When he tried to pull it back, he could not, as if it were a stranger's hand over which he had no control. His fingers disappeared into the darkness, and the rest of the hand followed. He shook his head—no, no, no—but still he could not stop himself, he was *compelled* to reach into the bag, and now his hand was in to the wrist, and he felt nothing in there, nothing but a terrible cold that made his teeth chatter, and still he reached in, down, until his arm was shoved all the way in to the elbow, and he should have felt the bottom of the purse long before that, but there was just vast emptiness in there, so he reached down farther, until he was in almost to his shoulder, feeling around with splayed fingers, searching in that impossible void for something, anything.

That was when something found *him*.

Down deep in the bag, something brushed his hand.

Billy jerked in surprise.

Something bit him.

Billy screamed and finally found the will to resist the siren call of the darkness within the purse. He tore his hand out, leaped to his feet, knocking over his chair. He stared in terror at the bloody punctures on the meaty portion of his palm. Tooth marks. Five small holes, neat and round, welling blood.

He stood for a moment, numb with shock, then let out a wail and grabbed for the zipper on the bag to close it. Even as Billy's blood-slick fingers touched the pull-tab, the creature came out of the bag, up from a lightless place, and Billy snatched his hand back in terror.

It was a small beast, only about a foot tall, not too big to crawl out through the open mouth of the purse. It was gnarly and dark, like a man in form—two arms, two legs—but not like a man in any other way at all. If its tissues had not once been inanimate lumps of stinking sewage, then they had been some sludge of mysterious though equally noxious origins. Its muscles and sinews appeared to be formed from human waste, all tangled up with human hair and decaying human entrails and desiccated human veins. Its feet were twice as large as they should have been and terminated in razor-edged black claws that put as much fear into

Billy Neeks as his own switchblade had put into others. A hooked and pointed spur curved up from the back of each heel. The arms were proportionately as long as those of an ape, with six or maybe seven fingers—Billy could not be sure how many because the thing kept working its hands ceaselessly as it crawled out of the purse and stood up on the table—and each finger ended in an ebony claw.

As the creature rose to its feet and emitted a fierce hiss, Billy stumbled backward until he came up against the refrigerator. Over the sink was a window, locked and covered with filthy curtains. The door to the dining room was on the other side of the kitchen table. To get to the door that opened onto the back porch, he would have to go past the table. He was effectively trapped.

The thing's head was asymmetrical, lumpy, pocked, as if crudely modeled by a sculptor with an imperfect sense of human form, modeled in sewage and scraps of rotten tissue as was its body. A pair of eyes were set high on that portion of the face that would have been the forehead, with a second pair below them. Two more eyes, making six in all, were located at the sides of the skull, where ears should have been, and all of these organs of vision were entirely white, without iris or pupil, so you might have thought the beast was blinded by cataracts, though it was not. It could see; most definitely, it could see, for it was looking straight at Billy.

The thing reeked—a stench reminiscent of rotten eggs.

Trembling violently, making strangled sounds of fear, Billy reached to one side with his bitten right hand, pulled open a drawer in the cabinet next to the refrigerator. Never taking his eyes off the thing that had come out of the purse, he fumbled for the knives he knew were there, found them, and extracted the butcher's knife.

On the table, the six-eyed denizen of a nightmare opened its ragged mouth, revealing rows of pointed yellow teeth. It hissed again and, to Billy's astonishment, it spoke in a thin, whispery voice that managed to be simultaneously soft yet shrill yet gravelly: *"Billy? Billy Neeks?"*

"Oh, my God," Billy said.

"Is that you, Billy?" the beast inquired.

I'm dreaming this, Billy thought.

"No dream," the beast whispered.

It's from Hell (Billy thought), a demon straight up from Hell.

"Give the man a big cigar."

Twisting its deformed mouth into what might have been a grin, the demon kicked the open can of beer off the table and let out a hideous dry sound halfway between a snarl and a giggle.

Suddenly lunging forward and swinging the big butcher knife as if it were a mighty samurai sword, Billy took a whack at the creature, intending to lop off its head or chop it in half. The blade connected with its disgusting flesh, sank less than an inch into its darkly glistening torso, above its knobby hips, but would not go any deeper, certainly not all the way through. Billy felt as if he had taken a hack at a slab of steel, for the aborted power of the blow coursed back through the handle of the knife and shivered painfully through his hands and arms like the vibrations that would have rebounded upon him if he had grabbed a crowbar and, with all his strength, slammed it into a solid iron post.

In that same instant, one of the creature's hands moved flash-quick, slashed Billy, revealing two of his knuckle bones.

With a cry of surprise and pain, Billy let go of the weapon. He staggered back against the refrigerator, holding his gouged hand.

The creature on the table stood unfazed, the knife embedded in its side, neither bleeding nor exhibiting any signs of pain. With its small black gnarled hands, the beast gripped the handle and pulled the sharp instrument from its own flesh. Turning all six scintillant, milky eyes on Billy, it raised the knife, which was nearly as big as the beast itself, and snapped it in two, throwing the blade in one direction and the handle in another.

"*Come to get you, Billy,*" it said.

Billy ran.

He had to go around the table, past the creature, too close, but he did not care, did not hesitate, because his only alternative was to stand at the refrigerator and be torn to bits. Dashing out of the kitchen into the bungalow's little dining room, he heard a thump behind him as the demon leaped off the table. Worse: he heard the *clack-tick-clack* of its chitinous feet and horny claws as it scrambled across the linoleum, hurrying after him.

As a purse snatcher, Billy had to keep in shape and had to be able to run deer-fast. Now, his conditioning was the only advantage he had.

Was it possible to outrun the devil?

He bounded out of the dining room, jumped across a footstool in the living room, and fled toward the front door. His bungalow was somewhat isolated, between an empty lot and a transmission repair shop that was closed at this hour of the evening. However, there were a couple of small houses across the street and, at the corner, a 7-Eleven Market that was usually busy and he figured he would be safe if he could join up with other people, even strangers. He sensed that the demon would not want to be seen by anyone else.

Expecting the beast to leap on him and sink its teeth into his neck at any moment, Billy tore open the front door and almost plunged out of the house—then stopped abruptly when he saw what lay outside. Nothing. No front walk. No lawn, no trees. No street. No other houses across the way, no 7-Eleven on the corner. Nothing, nothing. No light whatsoever. The night beyond the house was unnaturally dark, as utterly lightless as the bottom of a mine shaft—or as the inside of the old woman's purse from which the beast had clambered. Although it should have been a warm late-April evening, the velvet-black night was icy, bone-numbingly cold, just as the inside of the big black leather purse had been.

Billy stood on the threshold, swaying, breathless, with his heart trying to jackhammer its way out of his chest, and he was seized by the mad idea that his entire bungalow was now *inside* the crazy old woman's purse. Which made no sense. The bottomless purse was back there in the kitchen, on the table. The purse could not be inside the house at the same time that the house was inside the purse. Could it?

He felt dizzy, confused, nauseous.

He had always known everything worth knowing. Or thought he did. Now he knew better.

He did not dare venture out of the bungalow, into the unremitting blackness. He sensed no haven within that coaly gloom. And he knew instinctively that, if he took one step into the frigid darkness, he would not be able to turn back. One step, and he would fall into the same terrible void that he had felt within the hag's purse: down, down, forever down.

The stench of rotten eggs grew overwhelming.

The beast was behind him.

Whimpering wordlessly, Billy Neeks turned from the horrifying emptiness beyond his house, looked back into the living room where the demon was waiting for him, and cried out when he saw that it had grown bigger than it had been a moment ago. Much bigger. Three feet tall instead of one. Broader in the shoulders. More muscular arms. Thicker legs.

Bigger hands and longer claws. The repulsive creature was not as close as he had expected, not on top of him, but standing in the middle of the living room, watching him, grinning, taunting him merely by choosing not to end the confrontation quickly.

The disparity between the warm air in the house and the freezing air outside seemed to cause a draft that sucked at the door, pulling it shut behind Billy. It closed with a bang.

Hissing, the demon took a step forward. When it moved, Billy could hear its gnarly skeleton and oozing flesh work one against the other like the parts of a grease-clogged machine in ill repair.

He backed away from it, heading around the room toward the short hall that led to the bedroom.

The repugnant apparition followed, casting a hellish shadow that seemed somehow even more grotesque than it should have been, as if the shadow were thrown not by the monster's malformed body but by its more hideously malformed soul. Perhaps aware that its shadow was wrong, perhaps unwilling to consider the meaning of its shadow, the beast purposefully knocked over a floorlamp as it stalked Billy, and in the influx of shadows, it proceeded more confidently and more eagerly, as if shadows eased its way.

At the entrance to the hallway, Billy stopped edging sideways, bolted flat-out for his bedroom, reached it, and slammed the door behind him. He twisted the latch with no illusions of having found sanctuary. The creature would smash through that flimsy barrier with no difficulty, Billy only hoped to reach the nightstand drawer, where he kept a Smith & Wesson .357 Magnum, and indeed he got it with plenty of time to spare.

The gun seemed considerably smaller than he remembered it. Too small. He told himself it seemed inadequate only because the enemy was so formidable. He told himself the weapon would prove plenty big enough when he pulled the trigger. But it still seemed small. Virtually a toy.

With the loaded .357 held in both hands and aimed at the door, he wondered if he should fire through the barrier or wait until the beast burst inside.

The demon resolved the issue by *exploding* through the locked door in a shower of wooden shards, splinters, and mangled hinges.

It was bigger still, more than six feet tall, bigger than Billy, a gigantic and loathsome creature that, more than ever, appeared to be constructed of feces, wads of mucus, tendons of tangled hair, fungus, and the putrescent bits and pieces of several cadavers. Redolent of rotten eggs, with its multiplicitous white eyes now as radiant as incandescent bulbs, it lurched inexorably toward Billy, not even hesitating when he pulled the trigger of the .357 and pumped six rounds into it.

What had that old crone been, for God's sake? No ordinary senior citizen paying a visit to her butcher's shop. No way. What kind of woman carried such a strange purse and kept such a thing as this at her command? A witch? A witch? Of course, a witch.

At last, backed into a corner, with the creature looming over him, the empty gun still clutched in his left hand, the scratches and the bites burning in his right hand, Billy really *knew* for the first time in his life what it meant to be a defenseless victim. When the hulking, unnamable entity put its massive, saber-clawed hands upon him—one on his shoulder, the other on his chest—Billy peed in his pants and was at once reduced to the pitiable condition of a weak, helpless child.

He was sure the demon was going to tear him apart, crack his spine, decapitate him, and suck the marrow out of his bones, but instead it lowered its malformed face to his throat and put its gummy lips against his throbbing carotid artery. For one wild moment, Billy thought it was kissing him. Then he felt his cold tongue lick his throat from collarbone to jaw line, up and down, again and again, an obscene sensation the purpose of which he did not understand. Abruptly he was stung, a short sharp prick that was followed by sudden and complete paralysis.

The creature lifted its head and studied his face. Its breath stank worse than the sulfurous odor exuded by its repellent flesh. Unable to close his eyes, in the grip of a paralysis so complete that he could not even blink, Billy stared into the demon's maw and saw its moon-white, prickled tongue writhing like a fat worm.

The beast stepped back. Unsupported, Billy dropped limply to the floor. Though he strained, he could not move a single finger.

Grabbing a handful of Billy's well-oiled hair, the beast began to drag him out of the bedroom. He could not resist. He could not even protest, for his voice was as frozen as the rest of him.

He could see nothing but what moved past his fixed gaze, for he could neither turn his head nor roll his eyes. He had glimpses of furniture past which he was dragged, and of course he could see the walls and the ceiling above, over which eerie shadows cavorted. When inadvertently rolled onto his stomach, he felt no pain in his cruelly twisted hair, and thereafter he could see only the floor in front of his face and the demon's clawed black feet as it trod heavily toward the kitchen, where the chase had begun.

Billy's vision blurred, cleared, blurred again, and for a moment he thought his failing sight was related to his paralysis. But then he understood that copious but unfelt tears were pouring from his eyes and, doubtless scalding, were streaming down his face. In all his mean and hateful life, he had no memory of having wept before.

He knew what was going to happen to him.

In his racing, fear-swollen heart, he *knew*.

The stinking, oozing beast dragged him rudely through the dining room, banging him against the table and chairs. It took him into the kitchen, pulling him through spilled beer, over a carpet of scattered Doritos. The thing plucked the old woman's black purse from the table and stood it on the floor, within Billy's view. The unzipped mouth of the bag yawned wide.

The demon was noticeably smaller now, at least in its legs and torso and head, although the arm—with which it held fast to Billy—remained enormous and powerful. With horror and amazement, but not with much surprise, Billy watched the creature crawl into the purse, shrinking as it went. Then it pulled him in after it.

He did not feel himself shrinking, but he must have grown smaller in order to fit through the mouth of the purse. Still paralyzed and still being held by his hair, Billy looked back under his own arm and saw the kitchen light beyond the mouth of the purse, saw his own hips balanced on the edge of the bag above him, tried to resist, saw his thighs coming in, then his knees, the bag was swallowing him, oh God, he could do nothing about it, the bag was swallowing him, and now only his feet were still outside, and he tried to dig his toes in, tried to resist, but could not.

Billy Neeks had never believed in the existence of the soul, but now he knew beyond doubt that he possessed one—and that it had just been claimed.

His feet were in the purse now. All of him was inside the purse.

Still looking back under his arm as he was dragged down by his hair, Billy stared desperately at the oval of light above and behind him. It was growing smaller, smaller, not because the zipper was being closed up there, but because the hateful beast was dragging him a long way down into the bag, which made the open end appear to dwindle the same way the mouth of a turnpike tunnel dwindled in the rear-view mirror as you drove toward the other end.

The other end.

Billy could not bear to think about what might be waiting for him at the other end, at the bottom of the purse and beyond it.

He wished that he could go mad. Madness would be a welcome escape from the horror and fear that filled him. Madness would provide sweet relief. But evidently part of his fate was that he should remain totally sane and *acutely* aware.

The light above had shrunk to the size of a small, pale, oblate moon riding high in a night sky.

It was like being born, Billy realized—except that, this time, he was being born out of light and into darkness, instead of the other way around.

The albescent moonform above shrank to the size of a small and distant star. The star winked out.

In the perfect blackness, many strange voices hissed a welcome to Billy Neeks.

THAT night in late-April, the bungalow was filled with distant, echoey screams of terror from so far away that, though carrying through every room of the small house, they did not reach the quiet street beyond the walls and did not draw any attention from nearby residents. The screams continued for a few hours, faded gradually, and were replaced by licking-gnawing-chewing sounds of satisfied consumption.

Then silence.

Silence held dominion for many hours, until the middle of the following afternoon, when the stillness was broken by the sound of an opening door and footsteps.

"Ah," the old woman said happily as she stepped through the kitchen door and saw her purse standing open on the floor. With arthritic slowness, she bent, picked up the bag, and stared into it for a moment.

Then, smiling, she pulled the zipper shut.

The Tea Room Beasts

P. N. ELROD

*Yes, this author does write great vampire stories—but that's clearly
not all she does! "The Tea Room Beasts" is one of the best magical
revenge stories you'll find, and it has fun with the Woman Power
theme that weaves through so many stories of witchcraft.*

ELLEN stared in disbelief at yet another letter from her future ex-husband. She wanted to tear the thing to shreds and make its threat
go away, but it would have to go into the growing legal folder she'd
begun since he'd filed for divorce. When she was calm enough, Ellen
called her lawyer. Marissa had gotten *her* copy of the letter that morning.

"I'm afraid there's nothing we can do," Marissa said in a cheerfully
sympathetic, but ultimately unhelpful, tone. "His name's on the owner-ship papers, so he has rights to half your business. And then there's com-munity property, you know."

"He doesn't *need* my tea room. This is pure greed and spite." Ten
years ago it had been necessary to have her brand-new husband Randall
in on the contract. The idea had been if anything happened to her, he
could inherit without any trouble. Ten years ago Ellen had been utterly
besotted with him, quite blind to his faults. Everyone had faults, but
nothing that enough love couldn't cure, and she had oceans of love for
him.

Except that she'd finally, unbelievably, run out. He'd sucked her dry,
then mocked the remaining husk. Gradually the abuses, mental and phys-ical, the daily, sometimes hourly fights, had done it. She used to forgive,
supplied him with excuses so he wouldn't leave her, and he was so sweet
afterwards with his apologies. Each fight was always going to be their
last, after all. Later, in therapy, she'd learned the ins and outs of things

called "co-dependency," "enabling," and "battered wife syndrome" and could have kicked herself for being so naive, but that would have been self-destructive, which was also a no-no.

"But what can I do?" she demanded of Marissa. "He'll sell his half or insist I sell to him or the bank at a loss or something. He knows I don't have the money to fight him on this."

Marissa made comforting noises, but the papers, signed ten years ago in a fit of cupid-inspired sentiment, were ironclad.

Sick in heart, Ellen hung up and considered her options. Even if she burned the place down he'd take half the insurance—after finding a way of proving arson and throwing her in jail. He had all the money; he had all the power. He had the whole town on his side, for God's sake.

Randall had apparently planned his divorce strategy long in advance. As a lawyer himself, he knew just how to do it. He'd hidden his own money very well and signed his major properties over to an old and trusted friend to hold for him until after the settlement. Community property laws would not benefit her, only him. He only wanted her little tea room just to heap more insult onto injury.

She discovered he'd been spreading rumors about her through the small seaside town she had called home. Bit by bit, Ellen learned to her shock that she was a rapacious man-eater who had betrayed her marriage vows to poor, long-suffering Randall again and again. People she'd thought of as friends were now too busy to speak to her, though they were more than happy to gossip. Everyone was firmly on injured Randall's side, especially all his old cronies in the legal system. She suspected her own lawyer was on his side as well, with only the high fees keeping Marissa on the case.

Ellen quit her tiny office and went out front to look with new eyes on the little tea room she had made for herself. Randall couldn't want it for the money, for business wasn't that good. In fact, it was terribly marginal. She ran the place as a labor of love. It had always been her one joyful escape from her 'til-death-us-do-part tormentor.

She thought glumly of selling the fixtures and fittings, then lying about the amount of money she got for them, but those would not net her much of anything. Her cozy little refuge with its cucumber sandwiches, consignment souvenirs, and occasional antique sales was worth more open than closed. *Maybe I could paint a line down the middle and give him the less profitable half.*

"Maybe I could strangle him."

She hadn't meant to speak aloud. She'd wanted to scream it. Wonderfully violent images came to her: Randall squirming on a roasting spit, Randall plummeting into a bottomless gorge, Randall being audited by the IRS . . .

But no, he'd get away with it. He'd stolen ten of her best years, would steal or control her tea room haven, and leave her scratching for pennies. He'd laugh his head off. Look at how he'd originally served her notice— the divorce papers had been in the gift box he'd presented to her on their tenth anniversary. How he'd hooted at the shattered look on her face as she ran screaming to the bedroom to weep over this last violation of trust.

How could she have ever fallen in love with such a cruel *bastard?*

The answer to that would have to wait. Well-to-do women, craving her shop's quaint, ladies-only charm, were beginning to wander in for lunch. They deliberated over what to eat and what to drink and debated hotly over the shortcomings of their neighbors. Ellen knew from the looks sometimes directed her way that she was one of the topics, but she endured with a brave smile and made sure everyone got free refills so they would keep coming back.

Thanks to Randall's propaganda campaign, Ellen had no one to whom she could truly confide her troubles. She felt the isolation keenly in the crowded room, yet almost savored it. This might be the last time she would ever be here. The thought of losing it made even the bitterness a precious thing.

She stared bleakly at the shop she'd built up. It wasn't much, but her devotion to its success shone from every corner. She had found the right location, had decorated it, made the gourmet delectables, and smiled at the customers with the sincerity of fulfillment. Randall had visited it perhaps twice during their marriage, and until now had dismissed all her work. It was rightfully *hers*. How *dare* he take it away?

"Because he's a bastard."

Ellen jumped as though she'd gotten a static shock, for someone had spoken her own answer aloud. She found herself eye-to-eye with another forty-ish, slightly plump woman, a total stranger.

"I beg your pardon?" said Ellen.

The woman had large sad eyes, no . . . they were more compassionate than sad. She possessed an air of having seen a lot of life's sorrows, not unlike Ellen's therapist, but in less trendy clothes.

"My name is Phylis," said the woman. "I apologize for intruding, but your thoughts were so loud I couldn't help but hear you."

"My thoughts?"

"About that man who's trying to take this sweet place away from you—oh, there I go again. I'm sorry. I'd like a pot of jasmine tea and one of those really large chocolate eclairs, please."

The switch threw Ellen slightly off balance, but she had presence of mind to ring up the sale.

"Oh, that's awful what he's doing to you," said Phylis.

"*What?*"

Phylis grimaced. "Drat, did it again. I should shut it off, but when I get low blood sugar it takes more concentration than I can spare. On the other hand, maybe I'm supposed to be here and eavesdropping on your mind. I'll be at that nice little corner booth. I love the flower picture you have there."

Dazed, Ellen took the money and hurried to fill the order. *The woman's a crazy, but looks harmless.*

Phylis smiled benignly from the booth. Ellen wondered if there was a distance limit for telepathy. *Why am I even believing in this?* And inside she shrugged and answered, *Why not? You need the distraction. A little lunacy can't hurt.*

She delivered the tray herself, turning cash register duty over to her part-time helper.

"Are you a witch?" Ellen asked, half-jokingly. Her shop was near the local college and some of the students there wore pentacles. Ellen had overheard things from them about spells and ceremonies, but fobbed it off as nothing more than youthful experimentation.

Phylis snickered. "Oh, no, that takes *years* of study, I don't have the discipline for it, I just dabble a little for myself. Nothing weighty."

"You're serious?"

"Hardly ever, if I can help it."

Ellen smiled in spite of herself.

"You need to talk, don't you?" Phylis motioned to the opposite side of the booth, inviting her to sit.

"I pay my therapist for that. No need to burden you with my problems."

"Oh, my dear, I'm a very good listener, I never judge, and I never repeat what I'm told."

Ellen found herself fighting tears. How she wanted to *talk* to someone, anyone. Even a stranger who would be gone as soon as she finished her meal.

"I'll stick around," Phylis promised. "I'm an artist, you know. I'm in town for awhile to paint some of the sights and enjoy the quiet. You deal with this lunch rush, then we'll sit down like we're old friends, and you can tell me all about it."

Ellen did just that. While her part-timer cleaned up, Ellen quietly poured her heart out to Phylis, who nodded and *tsked* as needed and handed over bushels of paper napkins for nose-blowing and tear-wiping.

"You have every right to be angry and afraid with *that* man," said Phylis, shaking her head. "I had one like him myself. Any little thing would set him off into screaming and hitting me, then he'd say he was sorry and make it up in some nice way to get me back. I finally wised up that I'd married a two-year-old. Divorce was the best thing that ever happened to me."

"Why does he hate me so?" It was the one question Ellen could not answer. She had been a *good* wife, always loving, always forgiving. Too much so, it seemed.

"Oh, it has nothing to do with you, *he's* the one with the problem. He's a sadist and still trying to hurt you, but it's time to change things in your favor. I think I might be able to help you keep your shop, but the solution may be a bit Draconian."

Ellen's heart sank. "How much will it cost?"

Phylis blinked. "Cost?"

"Half my bank account or my immortal soul?"

Phylis giggled. "Sorry, I don't need either one. I'm helping you for my own selfish purposes. I *like* this place, it's got lovely energy. I don't want to see it shut down. If I can help you save it, I will."

"Is it some sort of witchcraft?" Ellen whispered the last word.

"Well, it does involve a spell, but that's pretty much like saying a prayer."

Ellen liked the sound of that. "What will you do?"

"It's what *we* will do. Nothing harmful to us, though. Have you a quiet place where we won't be disturbed?"

"I've a storage room in the back."

"Great. Let's start now while I'm still full of righteous anger."

In the back room Phylis lighted four of the shop's decorative candles, placing them on a small table. She linked hands with Ellen across the table. Phylis shut her eyes and hummed a bit to herself, then asked for help to be sent to restore Ellen's "balance." Ellen felt nothing happening, but she didn't know what to expect. Her experience with magic was limited to TV shows. No special effects took place for her.

What if . . . what if *Randall* had sent this woman? How awful, how humiliating. If some newspaper person with a camera burst in on them just now—

Ellen shook her hands free.

"I wish you hadn't done that," Phylis said, chagrined.

"I'm sorry, this is just—I mean, it's—"

"Silly? I think not." Phylis pointed.

In spite of her sudden flash of distrust Ellen turned to look and saw . . .

Them.

She stifled a shriek of abject horror and flung herself backwards, upsetting the table and candles.

"Oh, dear. You shouldn't have done that," said Phylis, ducking out of the way.

"Eeeee!" screamed Ellen. She fled to the broom closet and shut herself in.

"Now don't be like that, you'll hurt their feelings," chided Phylis.

"What. Are. Those. *Things?!?*" Ellen shoved a folding chair under the doorknob and hoped it would hold.

"I think they're elementals. I know they look a little strange, but they can really be quite helpful if you give them half a chance."

"Strange?! They're awful! I can't stand them! Make them go away!"

"But you broke the circle I made. We're sort of stuck with them for the time being."

One of the creatures, the goat-sized, slimy one with a lower jaw better suited to a gorilla, appeared in the closet next to Ellen. Though it was pitch dark within, she could see its glowing blue eyes and skin. It showed a mouthful of needle teeth and reached for her with a web-fingered appendage.

Ellen screamed and clawed her way out, nearly running Phylis over. Phylis caught her and held her in place, showing surprising strength. "Calm down! They won't hurt you! They're here to *help* you."

Ellen gulped back her panic. The slimy one ambled from the closet, walking *through* a stack of plastic crates, and rejoined its companions. It sat on its haunches and began licking its front paws just like a cat. The others, both bipedal in contrast, squatted down and stared at her. She hoped they weren't hungry.

"Not for food as you know it," said Phylis, picking up the thought. "They live off energy. You're giving them a feast with all the fear you're projecting. That's why Water went after you. Like a pet begging for scraps at the table."

"W-w-water?"

"Yes, it looks like you are in *real* need; we've got a fine assortment: Water, Earth, and Fire. Wonder what happened to Air?"

One of the plastic crates jumped from the stack and crashed to the floor. Ellen jumped. She heard the whoosh of a strong gust of wind, but felt nothing.

Phylis clapped her hands. "Good, there you are. Would you please make yourself more visible to us? That's better, thank you. This is much more than I expected. I think you had something to do with that, Ellen. I'll bet you have some latent powers in your genes that gave the spell some extra oomph. You could be a natural witch, you know. That would explain all the positive energy you put into the tea room. It could be a subconscious thing."

Ellen barely heard her, staring. Air was only slightly less repulsive than the other three, but only because its outlines were very vague. Ellen shivered, but tried to quell her fear. She didn't want those monstrosities coming any closer for snacks. "W-w-what do we do with them?"

"Well, they're here to do things for us, nearly any kind of thing that involves working with the four elements. We send them back when we're done. Simple as that."

"Send them now!"

"Oh, I'm too tired for now. Look, as long as they're here, let's have some fun."

But Ellen was in no mood for recreational activities. Regaining some measure of inner control, she demanded an explanation from Phylis about the creatures. Phylis was forthcoming with confusing information about different planes and dimensions, interlaced with reassurances that however ugly the things might be, they were harmless.

"At least to us. Now if we sent them to visit your husband, that's another matter . . ."

Ellen paused and considered. "They'd scare him half to death."

"They can do more than that, I'm sure. Don't you want to get him off your back?"

"Yes! But won't it return onto me in some way?" Ellen had overheard enough conversations between the pentacle-adorned students to under-stand that revenge magic wasn't a wise or constructive thing to attempt.

"Not if it involves a restoration of your balance. He would be getting repaid what he dished out to you over the years. From what you said I think he deserves whatever he gets. Don't you?"

Ellen bit her lip, staring at three—four—of the absolutely ugliest things she'd ever seen or ever hoped to see. Then she measured them against her ten years of isolated, secret abuse and the prospect of a poverty-stricken future. Should there *be* consequences to her for siccing these monsters on Randall . . . well, they'd be *worth* it.

"Okay," she said. "How do we start?"

ELLEN left her part-timer in charge and went off with Phylis, elementals invisibly in tow. "You're sure they're still here?"

"Oh, yes. No one will see them but us, and we'll only see them when we want to. I had to make them understand that."

"Why are they so ugly?"

"I'm not sure, it's atypical as I understand things. Take Water, for example—it should be quite nice-looking. I'm thinking that these turned up looking just this bad because whatever purpose is ahead required them to be like this. Isn't it wonderful how the universe provides? They're smart like dogs and loyal, too. I think this bunch really likes you."

Ellen found herself strangely touched. She loved dogs, but, along with a child, Randall forbade her to have one, citing his allergies as the reason. He'd used his allergies to squirm out of everything from the joys of a pet to mowing the lawn or even going to the movies. She felt herself getting steamed again for those wasted years of isolation.

"Take it easy," Phylis warned. "You can feed them on a nice roast of anger *after* the job is done."

She and Phylis walked to the town marina, only a few blocks from the tea room. Randall kept his forty-foot boat there. Somehow his aller-gies were very forgiving of sea air. Ellen had only ever seen the boat from the dock. Randall had convinced her she would break something on it or fall overboard. He also maintained that he needed a "private space" to call his own. "You have your hen parties at that shop, I have my boat," he'd sniffed.

And she'd swallowed it, telling herself that he knew best, and besides, she was too busy with business to go on weekend fishing trips with him. Too late she came to learn his "trips" always involved other women. She suspected her lawyer might even be one of them. He had suspended philandering for the time being. He was smart enough to play the injured husband role to the hilt right now.

"What a nice big boat," said Phylis.

"It cost more than our house—his house, I mean." Both boat and house would eventually return to Randall, once the divorce was settled. The same went for his hidden savings.

"Oh, that bastard! He didn't tell you how much he made a year?"

Ellen was getting quite used to Phylis picking up her thoughts. "Not a penny. I earned what I could with the shop, shared that with him because he said he needed it, and all the time he was—oh, I could *kill* him!"

"Yes, betrayal is an awful thing. My ex did it to me, all perfectly legal, too. That's why I turned to my dabbling. I was looking for a way to get some of my life back. What a day it was when one of my little spells activated my mind-reading."

"Really? I thought people were born with those abilities."

"I suppose they are. I think I always had the gift, but it got smothered by my upbringing and life in general. Then one day it was like taking out some ear plugs. It was scary at first, but I've learned to trust and control it. Maybe that's what drew me into your tea room, I must have sensed a kindred vibration in its energy today. Come on, let's go save your place."

They walked down a short pier to the boat. It looked huge to Ellen, magnificent.

I helped pay for it and never once enjoyed it.

"You're sure your name isn't on the ownership papers?" asked Phylis.

"He made a point of throwing that in my face."

"That's good, then no one can point an accusing finger at you."

"Accusing me of what?"

"Hm, well, whatever you'd like. Our little friends here are very versatile. Air could blow him off course, Water could make a nasty whirlpool to suck him under, or they could work together as a really violent squall."

Ellen considered these new possibilities, feeling the stretching of her world as an almost physical pleasure. "I wouldn't want to hurt other people who might be out sailing."

"Yes, all right. I'm sure we can find some way to avoid dragging them in. Why don't you test Water out? Look at it, all raring to go."

Water had indeed jumped things, going visible to them and slipping into the normal water next to the pier. It darted around the pilings like an otter. A goat-sized otter with really huge, sharp teeth. Water grinned, made happy gurgling noises, and kicked up little waves. It was quite endearing, really.

"Er, ah, Water?" Ellen felt a little foolish at her diffidence, but the elemental instantly came when called, looking up attentively. "Would you—" What did she want? "—would you please do something appropriate to that boat there, if you're able, that is."

Water certainly proved able. Flashing its needle teeth in a joyous grin, it vanished under the pier. After a moment, Ellen heard a deep rolling wash of sound. The whole of the bay seemed to vibrate from it. Then a great watery fist rose thirty feet from the sea and smashed down on Randall's beautiful boat. The craft rocked drunkenly under the assault. The spray of impact soaked Ellen and Phylis, but Ellen didn't care, and Phylis was cheering.

"Oh, look at it *go!* I bet it'll cost a fortune to have that cleaned!"

The boat's deck was not only awash with water, but with greasy, muddy flotsam dredged up from the bottom. The once-pristine superstructure and fittings were alive with flopping fish, misplaced crabs, shells, foul-smelling seaweed, and waterlogged garbage. People from other boats nearby came out to stare.

"We should get out of here before someone recognizes me," said Ellen.

"Yes, you're right, but what fun! Come along, Water, oh, there's a *good* elemental. Who's the dear little creature, then? Who's Mommie's little sweetie?" Water scampered soggily ahead, playing a chasing game with the other three. "That was a wonderful start, Ellen. Have you any ideas of how to use the rest now?"

Ellen did, and began forming solid plans, much better than her roasting-Randall-on-a-spit fantasies, because she actually could implement them. Or rather her newfound friends could.

From that point forward Randall began to suffer where it hurt the most: his bank account. The following day, after he was advised of the damage to his precious boat and had had time to fully appreciate the wreckage, other disasters overtook him. Ellen was safe in her tea room serving lunch to a dozen witnesses to her whereabouts when Randall's house mysteriously caught fire. A freak wind kept the flames from traveling to any other homes, yet seemed to whip the blaze into an all-consuming frenzy. When the fire trucks arrived, the water hydrants refused to live up to their potential. Water pressure was down to a mere trickle for some reason. This lasted only until the house was reduced to a few charred sticks.

Ellen lost nothing in it. Randall had been careful to box up all her things when he'd thrown her out. She soon learned from gossip that her future ex-husband was stunned, devastated, and gripped in the horrors of utter shock. For every hour of his anguish, Ellen felt months of her own pain falling away from her soul.

Payback was a *wonderful* thing.

Randall retreated to his boat to live on, dead fish and all. He lost work time from his law office. His partners were not amused. What made things worse was that each day he came home to a renewal of the smelly, filthy mess. Neighbors at the marina told tales of freak waterspouts and strange high waves.

His car was her next target. While Ellen had made do with a wheezing, stuttering wreck that she'd driven since before their marriage, Randall had that year's top-of-the-line Lexus. "Have to let my clients know I can win for them," he'd told her. She'd never been allowed to drive any of his new cars, and only rarely got to ride in them.

Again, she was safe serving another tasty lunch to her regulars when a sinkhole opened up in the street in front of her tea room just as Randall was driving past to the marina. The front end of the Lexus plowed into the four-foot-deep, eight-foot-wide hole at forty miles an hour, stopping the car dead with a noisy and expensive-sounding crunch. All the air bags deployed. Randall was badly bruised by their unnatural force.

Phylis went to the hospital to check on him, returning with a juicy report.

"He's in a neck brace for at least a week," she said. "And he had some kind of mishap when he tried to take his contact lenses out that scratched his corneas. The doctors had to blindfold and sedate him so he wouldn't claw his eyes out from the agony."

Ellen rocked with laughter and didn't feel a bit guilty. Hadn't he given her a daily dose of pain for a decade? She still had the visible scars, but began to lose her shame of them.

Randall tried to bring a suit against the city to replace his totaled car and pay for his hospital stay. He cited shoddy paving as the cause of his mishap, but even his old friend the judge could not rule against a sinkhole in the earth, which was determined to be an "act of God." Odd, perhaps, for this part of the world, but a perfectly normal geologic occurrence.

And one not covered by Randall's insurance.

Ellen rejoiced. She and Phylis celebrated by going to a Mel Gibson film that night and pigging out on chocolate eclairs and satisfaction.

The elementals were now Ellen's fourfold joys. She'd grown very fond of them, and no longer saw them as ugly, but found them endearing, like the little alien from the Spielberg movie. She cooed and told them they were marvelous and fed them servings of Randall's frazzled feelings. In turn they adored her and Phylis.

"Don't you have anything you want them to do for you?" she'd asked Phylis.

"No, I took care of my ex years ago."

"You used elementals against him?"

"Just one. I wasn't too practiced with summonings back then. All I got was a dear little air elemental. It wasn't very large or powerful, but it was enough."

"What did it do?"

"Well, it's still being done. My ex is in the hospital a lot, suffering from a strange shortness of breath. The doctors are unable to explain it. His lungs are perfectly healthy, but he just can't seem to breathe in enough air. They think he's crazy by now. He's spent a fortune in therapy."

"Oh, Phylis, that's absolutely wicked! I wish I'd thought of that!"

"The condition comes and goes at the worst times, too. I don't think he's had sex in the last eight years. A fair payback for all the times he was in the mood and I wasn't."

Ellen screamed with delight and made a mental note about it and continued with her fun.

But one day Phylis rushed into the tea room, wearing a worried look. She dragged Ellen to the back and shut the door. "You got trouble," she blurted. "I was taking the kids for an outing in the park across from the courthouse . . ."

Early on they had begun to refer to the elementals as "the kids."

". . . and Randall walked past me! He knows you and I are friends."

"So?"

"So the sight of me sparked off a line of thought with him. It was so loud he might as well have had a bullhorn."

"What was he thinking?"

"It's awful! He's planning to kill you!"

"*What?*"

"He was positively *gloating* about it. I saw everything! He's going out on his boat, then he'll sneak back and make it look like an interrupted robbery. Oh, I've run up against some terrible people, but this one is *diseased!*"

Ellen grabbed the edge of a plastic crate to steady herself, suddenly sick. "B-but why should he? There's no reason."

"I think it's to do with your tea room. He's not going to risk getting only half. He must want it all."

"Have you any proof?"

"I wish I did."

In response to her emotional surge the four elementals swept through the closed door and surrounded her, leaning in close to feed. Impulsively seeking comfort, she reached down to pet them. They fawned even closer, though her hands passed right through them.

"This is too much." Ellen shook off the choking feeling that threatened to take her over. She used to get it all the time, but not lately. She'd almost forgotten what it felt like. *I am not going to go back to it, either!*

"I think this was inevitable," said Phylis. "He's been deprived of all his other resources, of course he'd look on the shop as his last hope of restoring his funds."

"Yes, I'd thought of that. But to take this direction . . . it's wicked."

"Oh, Ellen, we've got to do something! You've got to leave town."

"No! I won't run from him!" Ellen thought fast, and a wonderful, terrible plan blossomed. She almost shivered away from it. Almost. She knew all too well that Randall was absolutely capable of any crime if he thought he could get away with it. But not this time. She regarded the kids—her saviors—fondly. "You little dears. It's been playtime until now, with just a few little snacks. How would you like a *real* banquet?"

They gurgled, growled, rumbled, and wheezed eagerly.

"Who's Mommie's little sweeties? Hmm?"

ELLEN was on lookout duty by the front door of the tea room, waiting for Randall to drive by. It was only lunchtime, but he always cheated on Fridays, leaving his office early to get to his boat. He finally appeared, in a much less spectacular used Hyundai, the only thing he could get since the insurance company was still investigating the burning of the house. They were not yet ready to dismiss arson as the cause of the blaze, and there was a problem with the house being in his old friend's name.

Randall saw her and slowed as she stepped outside. They got a good look at each other. Ellen showed no expression. Randall, uncharacteristically, broke into a wide smile and waved, a man without a care in the world.

That decided her. His satisfied grin, rife with confidence, was her proof of his intentions. Had he still been worried over his future, he'd have sneered.

Phylis came to stand next to her. She went sheet-white. "Oh, God. It's tonight. He's going to break into your flat with a crowbar and . . ."

"It's all right." Ellen softly called the kids over. "See the car? See the man inside? Go *get* him!" she whispered.

They surged joyfully past, chasing the vehicle down the street like a mismatched wolf pack seeking easy quarry.

"How I wish I could watch."

"There might be a way," said Phylis. "I've been reading a lot lately about scrying. Have you a black bowl?"

They made do with a large blue mixing bowl, setting it on the little table in the back room, and filling it with bottled spring water. While the part-timer coped with the rush, Ellen and Phylis lighted candles, placing them carefully so none of their light reflected in the water.

"Now a deep breath," said Phylis. "Concentrate on Randall and let the image come to you."

Ellen breathed deep and waited. She didn't expect much, staring into the dark depths of the still water, then to her surprise an image did indeed surface. It was faint, just a blink, but she saw it like a still photograph: Randall, still in his business suit, climbing aboard his boat.

"Oh! Did you see that?"

"Yes! I didn't think it'd work this well. It must be you boosting the power again. Keep looking!"

Ellen was strongly reminded of a slide show. But this version of vacation pictures was vastly more riveting. More little images came to her in the water. She found she could hold on to them for longer periods, and suddenly one of them showed movement, like a film projector finally grinding to life.

"Are you getting that, too?" she asked Phylis.

"Practice makes perfect. This is *fun!*"

They watched steadily as the afternoon wore away. Randall at the wheel, Randall knocking back a number of beers, Randall taking a leak into the bay.

"What a pig," said Phylis.

"I know. He always left the seat up, too."

"Not anymore."

The kids stayed close to him, invisible to his eyes. Air made its presence known by shifting the wind. Randall jumped and cursed as his own pee was blown onto his Armani-clad legs.

"I *heard* him!" Ellen exclaimed. "Oh, I *love* this!"

Randall went below to wash and change pants. Water followed and saw to his thorough soaking when something went wrong with the faucet pressure. At the same time the toilet backed up.

"I hope you have something for Fire and Earth to do," said Phylis.

"It's coming."

The boat cut farther out into the bay toward open sea. Randall was an experienced sailor and gave a tumble of boulders marking the mouth of the bay a wide berth.

Air and Water had other ideas, though. A sudden blast of wind struck the side of the boat, accompanied by an equally unexpected wave. Two stories tall. Both had a devastating effect on the craft and its captain. The boat heeled drunkenly over, riding the water tipsily toward the rocks. Despite Randall's frantic efforts at hauling the wheel around he was helpless against the forces of nature.

Or supernature, Ellen silently added. Phylis, picking up the thought, giggled. *What a shame about the boat, though.*

Smashing brutally into the rocks, the forty-footer creaked and groaned like a live thing caught in a trap. Ellen could hear Randall's yells and cursing, a too familiar sound, always directed at her, now directed at the elements.

If he only knew.

As though in response to her thought, all four elementals became visible. To Randall.

Ellen could hear his terrified screams. My, but he was loud. He had every right to be. She recalled her initial shock at seeing them, and they'd been friendly toward her. No such restraints now. All of them did their best to induce the most fear in him, which wasn't too difficult with their looks.

Water finally swept him overboard, then threw him up high so Air could catch him in a miniature tornado. As Randall whirled around in exquisite slow motion, Fire busily dealt with the boat's fuel tanks.

Ellen heard the deep whump as the hapless craft blew into a thousand pieces, the fireball rising over the bay like a vast orange and black flower.

"Gosh!" said Phylis. "That's something right out of a James Bond film. You go, girl!"

Air flung Randall toward land. He fell into a spongy area just past the outcrop of boulders. The ground there wasn't *normally* spongy, but that was Earth's doing. Randall had just begun to feebly move when he was sucked down. Water and Earth had worked together to make a wonderfully soupy quicksand.

"Oh!" said Phylis. "That's great! They did it in a Tarzan movie!"

"That's where I got the idea. Come on!"

Ellen led the way to the rear door of her establishment, which opened to a wide, unpaved alley lined with a high fence. None of the neighbors would see. She soon felt a quivering beneath her feet. Moments later Earth opened up, and Randall's torso emerged like an exotic plant. A very muddy one. He slumped over with a groan, gasping for air.

"Ew!" said Ellen. "What a stink! Earth must have dragged him through the sewer lines."

"I didn't know Earth could do that," said Phylis.

"Neither did I, but they've all been getting very strong over the last few weeks."

"Nothing like a steady diet."

"Ellen?" Randall croaked. He stared up, bleary and blinking. "Ellen, help me!"

"Why should I?" she asked, astonished.

"For God's sake, help me!"

"Not this or any other time. You brought this on yourself. You were going to kill me tonight, weren't you?"

Randall's jaw dropped, and he made no reply. His terrified gaze shifted to the elementals that were gathering about him. They *had* grown. "Get me out of here!"

"Apologize."

"What?"

"I want to hear you say you're sorry for—"

Randall was a man quick to assess the fantastic situation and judge his best course of action. He began babbling a series of profound apologies about everything. None were too specific, but all were music to Ellen's ears. When he ran out of breath and began begging for help again, she held up her hand.

"Enough. I know you only said all that to save yourself and you don't mean a word, but it was good to hear all the same. You're a pathetic bully, Randall, and I'm going to do the next woman in your life a favor and make sure she never meets you." At a word from her, Earth sucked Randall under again. The last she heard from him was his abruptly smothered scream as the ground knitted up solidly over his head. The remaining three "kids" swirled up, laughing in their own way, and shot off, heading toward the bay again.

Ellen felt grimly amused and decidedly *free*. "I hope he can hold his breath until Earth takes him out the other side again," she remarked.

"Why is that?" asked Phylis.

"So they find water in his lungs instead of soil. It should look like a natural drowning as a result of the boat accident."

"Ellen, are you *sure?* You can still stop them."

"I'm sure. This is self-defense, pure and simple."

"True. The things I saw in his mind, what he was going to do . . . ."

"Well, try to forget it." Ellen straightened, doing a mental dusting off. "I suppose we'd better clean up the scrying stuff."

Phylis gladly seized the change of subject. "Yes. Wouldn't want to leave that lying around."

"Then afterwards I'd love to have a look at some of your reading materials. I think I must have a talent for this kind of thing."

"You should explore it, that's how I came to be an artist."

"I have an idea . . ."

Phylis caught the thought and grinned. "About helping others?"

"Lots of women come into my shop with problems. You'd be able to tell which ones were in real need, and then together we could help them. With our four little friends, that is."

"Count me in."

"Besides, I really love the little dears. I'd hate to send them back."

"Oh, no, not when there's so much *more* for them to do!"

"But tomorrow," Ellen said firmly. "Tonight there's going to be a Mel Gibson marathon at the rerun house . . ."

"Great! Let's see if there's any eclairs left!"

The Witch's Ballad

Doreen Valiente

One of the founders of modern neopaganism, Doreen Valiente ini-tiated the famous Gerald B. Gardner into witchcraft! (If you know witch history, that's big.) Her "Charge of the Goddess" is one of the most used works in Wiccan circulation. Our book includes two of her poems from her classic 1978 contribution to the craft, **Witchcraft for Tomorrow.**

Oh, I have been beyond the town,
Where nightshade black and mandrake grow,
And I have heard and I have seen
What righteous folk would fear to know!

For I have heard, at still midnight,
Upon the hilltop far, forlorn,
With note that echoed through the dark,
The winding of the heathen horn.

And I have seen the fire aglow,
And glinting from the magic sword,
And with the inner eye beheld
The Hornéd One, the Sabbat's lord.

We drank the wine, and broke the bread,
And ate it in the Old One's name.
We linked our hands to make the ring,
And laughed and leaped the Sabbat game.

Oh, little do the townsfolk reck,
When dull they lie within their bed!
Beyond the streets, beneath the stars,
A merry round the witches tread!

And round and round the circle spun,
Until the gates swung wide ajar,
That bar the boundaries of earth
From faery realms that shine afar.

Oh, I have been and I have seen
In magic worlds of Otherwhere.
For all this world may praise or blame,
For ban or blessing nought I care.

For I have been beyond the town,
Where meadowsweet and roses grow,
And there such music did I hear
As worldly-righteous never know.

Feathertop

NATHANIEL HAWTHORNE

Ironic, how many of the "wicked witch" stories seem to stem from the Colonial Puritans. At least Nathaniel Hawthorne was several generations removed from the Salem Witch Trials, at which his ancestor, Judge John Hathorne, sat in judgment. Nathaniel's most famous piece on witches is the eerie "Young Goodman Brown," but our selection, "Feathertop," has more fun with the topic—and, some say, helped create a template for the Scarecrow in Frank L. Baum's Wonderful Wizard of Oz.

"DICKON," cried Mother Rigby, "a coal for my pipe!"

The pipe was in the old dame's mouth when she said these words. She had thrust it there after filling it with tobacco, but without stooping to light it at the hearth, where indeed there was no appearance of a fire having been kindled that morning. Forthwith, however, as soon as the order was given, there was an intense red glow out of the bowl of the pipe, and a whiff of smoke from Mother Rigby's lips. Whence the coal came, and how brought thither by an invisible hand, I have never been able to discover.

"Good!" quoth Mother Rigby, with a nod of her head. "Thank ye, Dickon! And now for making this scarecrow. Be within call, Dickon, in case I need you again."

The good woman had risen thus early (for as yet it was scarcely sunrise) in order to set about making a scarecrow, which she intended to put in the middle of her corn-patch. It was now the latter week of May, and the crows and blackbirds had already discovered the little, green, rolled-up leaf of the Indian corn just peeping out of the soil. She was determined, therefore, to contrive as lifelike a scarecrow as ever was seen, and to finish it immediately, from top to toe, so that it should begin its sentinel's duty that very morning. Now Mother Rigby (as everybody must have heard) was one of the most cunning and potent witches in New England, and might, with very little trouble, have made a scarecrow ugly enough to frighten the minister himself. But on this occasion, as she had awakened in an uncommonly pleasant humor, and was further dulcified by her pipe of tobacco, she resolved to produce something fine, beautiful, and splendid, rather than hideous and horrible.

"I don't want to set up a hobgoblin in my own corn-patch, and almost at my own doorstep," said Mother Rigby to herself, puffing out a whiff of smoke; "I could do it if I pleased, but I'm tired of doing marvellous things, and so I'll keep within the bounds of every-day business just for variety's sake. Besides, there is no use in scaring the little children for a mile roundabout, though 't is true I'm a witch."

It was settled, therefore, in her own mind, that the scarecrow should represent a fine gentleman of the period, so far as the materials at hand would allow. Perhaps it may be as well to enumerate the chief of the articles that went to the composition of this figure.

The most important item of all, probably, although it made so little show, was a certain broomstick, on which Mother Rigby had taken many an airy gallop at midnight, and which now served the scarecrow by way of a spinal column, or, as the unlearned phrase it, a backbone. One of its arms was a disabled flail which used to be wielded by Goodman Rigby, before his spouse worried him out of this troublesome world; the other, if I mistake not, was composed of the pudding stick and a broken rung of a chair, tied loosely together at the elbow. As for its legs, the right was a hoe handle, and the left an undistinguished and miscellaneous stick from the woodpile. Its lungs, stomach, and other affairs of that kind were nothing better than a meal bag stuffed with straw. Thus we have made out the skeleton and entire corporosity of the scarecrow, with the exception of its head; and this was admirably supplied by a somewhat withered and shrivelled pumpkin, in which Mother Rigby cut two holes for the eyes, and a slit for the mouth, leaving a bluish-colored knob in the middle to pass for a nose. It was really quite a respectable face.

"I've seen worse ones on human shoulders, at any rate," said Mother Rigby. "And many a fine gentleman has a pumpkin head, as well as my scarecrow."

But the clothes, in this case, were to be the making of the man. So the good old woman took down from a peg an ancient plum-colored coat of London make, and with relics of embroidery on its seams, cuffs, pocket-flaps, and button-holes, but lamentably worn and faded, patched at the elbows, tattered at the skirts, and threadbare all over. On the left breast was a round hole, whence either a star of nobility had been rent away, or else the hot heart of some former wearer had scorched it through and through. The neighbors said that this rich garment belonged to the Black Man's wardrobe, and that he kept it at Mother Rigby's cottage for the convenience of slipping it on whenever he wished to make a grand appearance at the governor's table. To match the coat there was a velvet waistcoat of very ample size, and formerly embroidered with foliage that had been as brightly golden as the maple leaves in October, but which had now quite vanished out of the substance of the velvet. Next came a pair of scarlet breeches, once worn by the French governor of Louisbourg, and the knees of which had touched the lower step of the throne of Louis le Grand. The Frenchman had given these smallclothes to an Indian powwow, who parted with them to the old witch for a gill of strong waters, at one of their dances in the forest. Furthermore, Mother Rigby produced a pair of silk stockings and put them on the figure's legs, where they showed as unsubstantial as a dream, with the wooden reality of the two sticks making itself miserably apparent through the holes. Lastly, she put her dead husband's wig on the bare scalp of the pumpkin, and surmounted the whole with a dusty three-cornered hat, in which was stuck the longest tail feather of a rooster.

Then the old dame stood the figure up in a corner of her cottage and chuckled to behold its yellow semblance of a visage, with its nobby little nose thrust into the air. It had a strangely self-satisfied aspect, and seemed to say, "Come look at me!"

"And you are well worth looking at, that's a fact!" quoth Mother Rigby, in admiration at her own handiwork. "I've made many a puppet since I've been a witch, but methinks this is the finest of them all. 'Tis almost too good for a scarecrow. And, by the by, I'll just fill a fresh pipe of tobacco and then take him out to the corn-patch."

While filling her pipe the old woman continued to gaze with almost motherly affection at the figure in the corner. To say the truth, whether it were chance, or skill, or downright witchcraft, there was something wonderfully human in this ridiculous shape, bedizened with its tattered finery; and as for the countenance, it appeared to shrivel its yellow surface into a grin—a funny kind of expression betwixt scorn and merriment, as if it understood itself to be a jest at mankind. The more Mother Rigby looked the better she was pleased.

"Dickon," cried she sharply, "another coal for my pipe!"

Hardly had she spoken, than, just as before, there was a red-glowing coal on the top of the tobacco. She drew in a long whiff and puffed it forth again into the bar of morning sunshine which struggled through the one dusty pane of her cottage window. Mother Rigby always liked to flavor her pipe with a coal of fire from the particular chimney corner whence this had been brought. But where that chimney corner might be, or who brought the coal from it,—further than that the invisible messenger seemed to respond to the name of Dickon,—I cannot tell.

"That puppet yonder," thought Mother Rigby, still with her eyes fixed on the scarecrow, "is too good a piece of work to stand all summer in a corn-patch, frightening away the crows and blackbirds. He's capable of better things. Why, I've danced with a worse one, when partners happened to be scarce, at our witch meetings in the forest! What if I should let him take his chance among the other men of straw and empty fellows who go bustling about the world?"

The old witch took three or four more whiffs of her pipe and smiled.

"He'll meet plenty of his brethren at every street corner!" continued she. "Well; I didn't mean to dabble in witchcraft to-day, further than the lighting of my pipe, but a witch I am, and a witch I'm likely to be, and there's no use trying to shirk it. I'll make a man of my scarecrow, were it only for the joke's sake!"

While muttering these words, Mother Rigby took the pipe from her own mouth and thrust it into the crevice which represented the same feature in the pumpkin visage of the scarecrow.

"Puff, darling, puff!" said she. "Puff away, my fine fellow! your life depends on it!"

This was a strange exhortation, undoubtedly, to be addressed to a mere thing of sticks, straw, and old clothes, with nothing better than a shrivelled pumpkin for a head,—as we know to have been the scarecrow's case. Nevertheless, as we must carefully hold in remembrance, Mother Rigby was a witch of singular power and dexterity; and, keeping this fact duly before our minds, we shall see nothing beyond credibility in the remarkable incidents of our story. Indeed, the great difficulty will be at once got over, if we can only bring ourselves to believe that, as soon as the old dame bade him puff, there came a whiff of smoke from the scarecrow's mouth. It was the very feeblest of whiffs, to be sure; but it was followed by another and another, each more decided than the preceding one.

"Puff away, my pet! puff away, my pretty one!" Mother Rigby kept repeating, with her pleasantest smile. "It is the breath of life to ye; and that you may take my word for."

Beyond all question the pipe was bewitched. There must have been a spell either in the tobacco or in the fiercely-glowing coal that so mysteriously burned on top of it, or in the pungently aromatic smoke which exhaled from the kindled weed. The figure, after a few doubtful attempts, at length blew forth a volley of smoke extending all the way from the obscure corner into the bar of sunshine. There it eddied and melted away among the motes of dust. It seemed a convulsive effort; for the two or three next whiffs were fainter, although the coal still glowed and threw a gleam over the scarecrow's visage. The old witch clapped her skinny hands together, and smiled encouragingly upon her handiwork. She saw that the charm worked well. The shrivelled, yellow face, which heretofore had been no face at all, had already a thin, fantastic haze, as it were of human likeness, shifting to and fro across it; sometimes vanishing entirely, but growing more perceptible than ever with the next whiff from the pipe. The whole figure, in like manner, assumed a show of life, such as we impart to ill-defined shapes among the clouds, and half deceive ourselves with the pastime of our own fancy.

If we must needs pry closely into the matter, it may be doubted whether there was any real change, after all, in the sordid, worn-out, worthless, and ill-jointed substance of the scarecrow; but merely a spectral illusion, and a cunning effect of light and shade so colored and contrived as to delude the eyes of most men. The miracles of witchcraft seem always to have had a very shallow subtlety; and, at least, if the above explanation do not hit the truth of the process, I can suggest no better.

"Well puffed, my pretty lad!" still cried old Mother Rigby. "Come, another good stout whiff, and let it be with might and main. Puff for thy life, I tell thee! Puff out of the very bottom of thy heart, if any heart thou hast, or any bottom to it! Well done, again! Thou didst suck in that mouthful as if for the pure love of it."

And then the witch beckoned to the scarecrow, throwing so much magnetic potency into her gesture that it seemed as if it must inevitably be obeyed, like the mystic call of the loadstone when it summons the iron.

"Why lurkest thou in the corner, lazy one?" said she. "Step forth! Thou hast the world before thee!"

Upon my word, if the legend were not one which I heard on my grandmother's knee, and which had established its place among things credible before my childish judgment could analyze its probability, I question whether I should have the face to tell it now.

In obedience to Mother Rigby's word, and extending its arm as if to reach her outstretched hand, the figure made a step forward—a kind of hitch and jerk, however, rather than a step—then tottered and almost lost its balance. What could the witch expect? It was nothing, after all, but a scarecrow stuck upon two sticks. But the strong-willed old beldam scowled, and beckoned, and flung the energy of her purpose so forcibly at this poor combination of rotten wood, and musty straw, and ragged garments, that it was compelled to show itself a man, in spite of the reality of things. So it stepped into the bar of sunshine. There it stood— poor devil of a contrivance that it was!—with only the thinnest vesture of human similitude about it, through which was evident the stiff, rickety, incongruous, faded, tattered, good-for-nothing patchwork of its substance, ready to sink in a heap upon the floor, as conscious of its own unworthiness to be erect. Shall I confess the truth? At its present point of vivification, the scarecrow reminds me of some of the lukewarm and abortive characters, composed of heterogeneous materials, used for the thousandth time, and never worth using, with which romance writers (and myself, no doubt, among the rest) have so over-peopled the world of fiction.

But the fierce old hag began to get angry and show a glimpse of her diabolic nature (like a snake's head, peeping with a hiss out of her bosom), at this pusillanimous behavior of the thing which she had taken the trouble to put together.

"Puff away, wretch!" cried she, wrathfully. "Puff, puff, puff, thou thing of straw and emptiness! thou rag or two! thou meal bag! thou pumpkin head! thou nothing! Where shall I find a name vile enough to call thee by? Puff, I say, and suck in thy fantastic life along with the smoke! else I snatch the pipe from thy mouth and hurl thee where that red coal came from."

Thus threatened, the unhappy scarecrow had nothing for it but to puff away for dear life. As need was, therefore, it applied itself lustily to the pipe, and sent forth such abundant volleys of tobacco smoke that the small cottage kitchen became all vaporous. The one sunbeam struggled mistily through, and could but imperfectly define the image of the cracked and dusty window pane on the opposite wall. Mother Rigby, meanwhile, with one brown arm akimbo and the other stretched towards the figure, loomed grimly amid the obscurity with such port and expression as when she was wont to heave a ponderous nightmare on her victims and stand at the bedside to enjoy their agony. In fear and trembling did this poor scarecrow puff. But its efforts, it must be acknowledged, served an excellent purpose; for, with each successive whiff, the figure lost more and more of its dizzy and perplexing tenuity and seemed to take denser substance. Its very garments, moreover, partook of the magical change, and shone with the gloss of novelty and glistened with the skilfully embroidered gold that had long ago been rent away. And, half revealed among the smoke, a yellow visage bent its lustreless eyes on Mother Rigby.

At last the old witch clinched her fist and shook it at the figure. Not that she was positively angry, but merely acting on the principle—perhaps untrue, or not the only truth, though as high a one as Mother Rigby could be expected to attain—that feeble and torpid natures, being inca-pable of better inspiration, must be stirred up by fear. But here was the crisis. Should she fail in what she now sought to effect, it was her ruthless purpose to scatter the miserable simulacre into its original elements.

"Thou hast a man's aspect," said she, sternly. "Have also the echo and mockery of a voice! I bid thee speak!"

The scarecrow gasped, struggled, and at length emitted a murmur, which was so incorporated with its smoky breath that you could scarcely tell whether is were indeed a voice or only a whiff of tobacco. Some narrators of this legend hold the opinion that Mother Rigby's conjura-tions and the fierceness of her will had compelled a familiar spirit into the figure, and that the voice was his.

"Mother," mumbled the poor stifled voice, "be not so awful with me! I would fain speak; but being without wits, what can I say?"

"Thou canst speak, darling, canst thou?" cried Mother Rigby, relax-ing her grim countenance into a smile. "And what shalt thou say, quotha! Say, indeed! Art thou of the brotherhood of the empty skull, and de-mandest of me what thou shalt say? Thou shalt say a thousand things, and saying them a thousand times over, thou shalt still have said nothing! Be not afraid, I tell thee! When thou comest into the world (whither I purpose sending thee forthwith) thou shalt not lack the wherewithal to talk. Talk! Why, thou shall babble like a mill-stream, if thou wilt. Thou hast brains enough for that, I trow!"

"At your service, mother," responded the figure.

"And that was well said, my pretty one," answered Mother Rigby. "Then thou speakest like thyself, and meant nothing. Thou shalt have a hundred such set phrases, and five hundred to the boot of them. And now, darling, I have taken so much pains with thee and thou art so beautiful, that, by my troth, I love thee better than any witch's puppet in the world; and I've made them of all sorts—clay, wax, straw, sticks, night fog, morning mist, sea foam, and chimney smoke. But thou art the very best. So give heed to what I say."

"Yes, kind mother," said the figure, "with all my heart!"

"With all thy heart!" cried the old witch, setting her hands to her sides and laughing loudly. "Thou hast such a pretty way of speaking.

With all thy heart! And thou didst put thy hand to the left side of thy waistcoat as if thou really hadst one!"

So now, in high good humor with this fantastic contrivance of hers, Mother Rigby told the scarecrow that it must go and play its part in the great world, where not one man in a hundred, she affirmed, was gifted with more real substance than itself. And, that he might hold up his head with the best of them, she endowed him, on the spot, with an unreckonable amount of wealth. It consisted partly of a gold mine in Eldorado, and of ten thousand shares in a broken bubble, and of half a million acres of vineyard at the North Pole, and of a castle in the air, and a chateau in Spain, together with all the rents and income therefrom accruing. She further made over to him the cargo of a certain ship, laden with salt of Cadiz, which she herself, by her necromantic arts, had caused to founder, ten years before, in the deepest part of mid-ocean. If the salt were not dissolved, and could be brought to market, it would fetch a pretty penny among the fishermen. That he might not lack ready money, she gave him a copper farthing of Birmingham manufacture, being all the coin she had about her, and likewise a great deal of brass, which she applied to his forehead, thus making it yellower than ever.

"With that brass alone," quoth Mother Rigby, "thou canst pay thy way all over the earth. Kiss me, pretty darling! I have done my best for thee."

Furthermore, that the adventurer might lack no possible advantage towards a fair start in life, this excellent old dame gave him a token by which he was to introduce himself to a certain magistrate, member of the council, merchant, and elder of the church (the four capacities constituting but one man), who stood at the head of society in the neighboring metropolis. The token was neither more nor less than a single word, which Mother Rigby whispered to the scarecrow, and which the scarecrow was to whisper to the merchant.

"Gouty as the old fellow is, he'll run thy errands for thee, when once thou hast given him that word in his ear," said the old witch. "Mother Rigby knows the worshipful Justice Gookin, and the worshipful Justice knows Mother Rigby!"

Here the witch thrust her wrinkled face close to the puppet's, chuckling irrepressibly, and fidgeting all through her system, with delight at the idea which she meant to communicate.

"The worshipful Master Gookin," whispered she, "hath a comely maiden to his daughter. And hark ye, my pet! Thou hast a fair outside, and a pretty wit enough of thine own. Yea, a pretty wit enough! Thou wilt think better of it when thou hast seen more of other people's wits. Now, with thy outside and thy inside, thou art the very man to win a young girl's heart. Never doubt it! I tell thee it shall be so. Put but a bold face on the matter, sigh, smile, flourish thy hat, thrust forth thy leg like a dancing-master, put thy right hand to the left side of thy waistcoat, and pretty Polly Gookin is thine own!"

All this while the new creature had been sucking in and exhaling the vapory fragrance of his pipe, and seemed now to continue this occupation as much for the enjoyment it afforded as because it was an essential condition of his existence. It was wonderful to see how exceedingly like a human being it behaved. Its eyes (for it appeared to possess a pair) were bent on Mother Rigby, and at suitable junctures it nodded or shook its head. Neither did it lack words proper for the occasion: "Really! Indeed! Pray tell me! Is it possible! Upon my word! By no means! Oh! Ah! Hem!" and other such weighty utterances as imply attention, inquiry, acquiescence, or dissent on the part of the auditor. Even had you stood by and seen the scarecrow made, you could scarcely have resisted the conviction that it perfectly understood the cunning counsels which the old witch poured into its counterfeit of an ear. The more earnestly it applied its lips to the pipe, the more distinctly was its human likeness stamped among visible realities, the more sagacious grew its expression, the more lifelike its gestures and movements, and the more intelligibly audible its voice. Its garments, too, glistened so much the brighter with an illusory magnificence. The very pipe, in which burned the spell of all this wonderwork, ceased to appear as a smoke-blackened earthen stump, and became a meerschaum, with painted bowl and amber mouthpiece.

It might be apprehended, however, that as the life of the illusion seemed identical with the vapor of the pipe, it would terminate simultaneously with the reduction of the tobacco to ashes. But the beldam foresaw the difficulty.

"Hold thou the pipe, my precious one," said she, "while I fill it for thee again."

It was sorrowful to behold how the fine gentleman began to fade back into a scarecrow while Mother Rigby shook the ashes out of the pipe and proceeded to replenish it from her tobacco-box.

"Dickon," cried she, in her high, sharp tone, "another coal for this pipe!"

No sooner said than the intensely red speck of fire was glowing within the pipe-bowl; and the scarecrow, without waiting for the witch's bidding, applied the tube to his lips and drew in a few short, convulsive whiffs, which soon, however, became regular and equable.

"Now, mine own heart's darling," quoth Mother Rigby, "whatever may happen to thee, thou must stick to thy pipe. Thy life is in it; and that, at least, thou knowest well, if thou knowest nought besides. Stick to thy pipe, I say! Smoke, puff, blow thy cloud; and tell the people, if any question be made, that it is for thy health, and that so the physician orders thee to do. And, sweet one, when thou shalt find thy pipe getting low, go apart into some corner, and (first filling thyself with smoke) cry sharply, 'Dickon, a fresh pipe of tobacco!' and, 'Dickon, another coal for my pipe!' and have it into thy pretty mouth as speedily as may be. Else, instead of a gallant gentleman in a gold-laced coat, thou wilt be but a jumble of sticks and tattered clothes, and a bag of straw, and a withered pumpkin! Now depart, my treasure, and good luck go with thee!"

"Never fear, mother!" said the figure, in a stout voice, and sending forth a courageous whiff of smoke, "I will thrive, if an honest man and a gentleman may!"

"Oh, thou wilt be the death of me!" cried the old witch, convulsed with laughter. "That was well said. If an honest man and a gentleman may! Thou playest thy part to perfection. Get along with thee for a smart fellow; and I will wager on thy head, as a man of pith and substance, with a brain and what they call a heart, and all else that a man should have, against any other thing on two legs. I hold myself a better witch than yesterday, for thy sake. Did not I make thee? And I defy any witch in New England to make such another! Here; take my staff along with thee!"

The staff, though it was but a plain oaken stick, immediately took the aspect of a gold-headed cane.

"That gold head has as much sense in it as thine own," said Mother Rigby, "and it will guide thee straight to worshipful Master Gookin's door. Get thee gone, my pretty pet, my darling, my precious one, my treasure; and if any ask thy name, it is Feathertop. For thou hast a feather in thy hat, and I have thrust a handful of feathers into the hollow of thy head, and thy wig, too, is of the fashion they call Feathertop,—so be Feathertop thy name!"

And, issuing from the cottage, Feathertop strode manfully towards town. Mother Rigby stood at the threshold, well pleased to see how the sunbeams glistened on him, as if all his magnificence were real, and how diligently and lovingly he smoked his pipe, and how handsomely he walked, in spite of a little stiffness of his legs. She watched him until out of sight, and threw a witch benediction after her darling, when a turn of the road snatched him from her view.

Betimes in the forenoon, when the principal street of the neighboring town was just at its acme of life and bustle, a stranger of very distinguished figure was seen on the sidewalk. His port as well as his garments betokened nothing short of nobility. He wore a richly embroidered plum-colored coat, a waistcoat of costly velvet, magnificently adorned with golden foliage, a pair of splendid scarlet breeches, and the finest and glossiest of white silk stockings. His head was covered with a peruke, so daintily powdered and adjusted that it would have been sacrilege to disorder it with a hat; which, therefore (and it was a gold-laced hat, set off with a snowy feather), he carried beneath his arm. On the breast of his coat glistened a star. He managed his gold-headed cane with an airy grace, peculiar to the fine gentlemen of the period; and, to give the highest possible finish to his equipment, he had lace ruffles at his wrist, of a most ethereal delicacy, sufficiently avouching how idle and aristocratic must be the hands which they half concealed.

It was a remarkable point in the accoutrement of this brilliant personage that he held in his left hand a fantastic kind of a pipe, with an exquisitely painted bowl and an amber mouthpiece. This he applied to his lips as often as every five or six paces, and inhaled a deep whiff of smoke, which, after being retained a moment in his lungs, might be seen to eddy gracefully from his mouth and nostrils.

As may well be supposed, the street was all astir to find out the stranger's name.

"It is some great nobleman, beyond question," said one of the towns-people. "Do you see the star at his breast?"

"Nay; it is too bright to be seen," said another. "Yes; he must needs be a nobleman, as you say. But by what conveyance, think you, can his lordship have voyaged or travelled hither? There has been no vessel from the old country for a month past; and if he have arrived overland from the southward, pray where are his attendants and equipage?"

"He needs no equipage to set off his rank," remarked a third. "If he came among us in rags, nobility would shine through a hole in his elbow. I never saw such dignity of aspect. He has the old Norman blood in his veins, I warrant him."

"I rather take him to be a Dutchman, or one of your high Germans," said another citizen. "The men of those countries have always the pipe at their mouths."

"And so has a Turk," answered his companion. "But, in my judg-ment, this stranger hath been bred at the French court, and hath there learned politeness and grace of manner, which none understand so well as the nobility of France. That gait, now! A vulgar spectator might deem it stiff—he might call it a hitch and jerk—but, to my eye, it hath an unspeakable majesty, and must have been acquired by constant obser-vation of the deportment of the Grand Monarque. The stranger's char-acter and office are evident enough. He is a French ambassador, come to treat with our rulers about the cession of Canada."

"More probably a Spaniard," said another, "and hence his yellow complexion; or, most likely, he is from the Havana, or from some port on the Spanish main, and comes to make investigation about the piracies which our government is thought to connive at. Those settlers in Peru and Mexico have skins as yellow as the gold which they dig out of their mines."

"Yellow or not," cried a lady, "he is a beautiful man!—so tall, so slender! such a fine, noble face, with so well-shaped a nose, and all that delicacy of expression about the mouth! And, bless me, how bright his star is! It positively shoots out flames!"

"So do your eyes, fair lady," said the stranger, with a bow and a flourish of his pipe; for he was just passing at the instant. "Upon my honor, they have quite dazzled me."

"Was ever so original and exquisite a compliment?" murmured the lady, in an ecstasy of delight.

Amid the general admiration excited by the stranger's appearance, there were only two dissenting voices. One was that of an impertinent cur, which, after snuffing at the heels of the glistening figure, put its tail between its legs and skulked into its master's back yard, vociferating an execrable howl. The other dissentient was a young child, who squalled at the fullest stretch of his lungs, and babbled some unintelligible nonsense about a pumpkin.

Feathertop meanwhile pursued his way along the street. Except for the few complimentary words to the lady, and now and then a slight inclination of the head in requital of the profound reverences of the bystanders, he seemed wholly absorbed in his pipe. There needed no other proof of his rank and consequence than the perfect equanimity with which he comported himself, while the curiosity and admiration of the town swelled almost into clamor around him. With a crowd gathering behind his footsteps, he finally reached the mansion-house of the worshipful Justice Gookin, entered the gate, ascended the steps of the front door, and knocked. In the interim, before his summons was answered, the stranger was observed to shake the ashes out of his pipe.

"What did he say in that sharp voice?" inquired one of the spectators.

"Nay, I know not," answered his friend. "But the sun dazzles my eyes strangely. How dim and faded his lordship looks all of a sudden! Bless my wits, what is the matter with me?"

"The wonder is," said the other, "that his pipe, which was out only an instant ago, should be all alight again, and with the reddest coal I ever saw. There is something mysterious about this stranger. What a whiff of smoke was that! Dim and faded did you call him? Why, as he turns about the star on his breast is all ablaze."

"It is, indeed," said his companion; "and it will go near to dazzle pretty Polly Gookin, whom I see peeping at it out of the chamber window."

The door being now opened, Feathertop turned to the crowd, made a stately bend of his body like a great man acknowledging the reverence of the meaner sort, and vanished into the house. There was a mysterious kind of a smile, if it might not better be called a grin or grimace, upon his visage; but, of all the throng that beheld him, not an individual appears to have possessed insight enough to detect the illusive character of the stranger except a little child and a cur dog.

Our legend here loses somewhat of its continuity, and, passing over the preliminary explanation between Feathertop and the merchant, goes in quest of the pretty Polly Gookin. She was a damsel of a soft, round figure, with light hair and blue eyes, and a fair, rosy face, which seemed neither very shrewd nor very simple. This young lady had caught a glimpse of the glistening stranger while standing at the threshold, and had forthwith put on a laced cap, a string of beads, her finest kerchief, and her stiffest damask petticoat in preparation for the interview. Hurrying from her chamber to the parlor, she had ever since been viewing herself in the large looking-glass and practising pretty airs—now a smile, now a ceremonious dignity of aspect, and now a softer smile than the former, kissing her hand likewise, tossing her head, and managing her fan; while within the mirror an unsubstantial little maid repeated every gesture and did all the foolish things that Polly did, but without making her ashamed of them. In short, it was the fault of pretty Polly's ability rather than her will if she failed to be as complete an artifice as the illustrious Feathertop himself; and, when she thus tampered with her own simplicity, the witch's phantom might well hope to win her.

No sooner did Polly hear her father's gouty footsteps approaching the parlor door, accompanied with the stiff clatter of Feathertop's high-heeled shoes, than she seated herself bolt upright and innocently began warbling a song.

"Polly! daughter Polly!" cried the old merchant. "Come hither, child."

Master Gookin's aspect, as he opened the door, was doubtful and troubled.

"This gentleman," continued he, presenting the stranger, "is the Chevalier Feathertop,—nay, I beg his pardon, my Lord Feathertop,—who hath brought me a token of remembrance from an ancient friend of mine. Pay your duty to his lordship, child, and honor him as his quality deserves."

After these few words of introduction, the worshipful magistrate immediately quitted the room. But, even in that brief moment, had the fair Polly glanced aside at her father instead of devoting herself wholly to the brilliant guest, she might have taken warning of some mischief nigh at hand. The old man was nervous, fidgety, and very pale. Purposing a smile of courtesy, he had deformed his face with a sort of galvanic grin, which, when Feathertop's back was turned, he exchanged for a scowl, at the same time shaking his fist and stamping his gouty foot—an incivility which brought its retribution along with it. The truth appears to have been that Mother Rigby's word of introduction, whatever it might be, had operated far more on the rich merchant's fears than on his good will. Moreover, being a man of wonderfully acute observation, he had noticed that these painted figures on the bowl of Feathertop's pipe were in motion. Looking more closely, he became convinced that these figures were a party of little demons, each duly provided with horns and a tail, and dancing hand in hand, with gestures of diabolical merriment, round the circumference of the pipe bowl. As if to confirm his suspicions, while Master Gookin ushered his guest along a dusky passage from his private room to the parlor, the star on Feathertop's breast had scintillated actual flames, and threw a flickering gleam upon the wall, the ceiling, and the floor.

With such sinister prognostics manifesting themselves on all hands, it is not to be marvelled at that the merchant should have felt that he was committing his daughter to a very questionable acquaintance. He cursed, in his secret soul, the insinuating elegance of Feathertop's manners, as this brilliant personage bowed, smiled, put his hand on his heart, inhaled a long whiff from his pipe, and enriched the atmosphere with the smoky vapor of a fragrant and visible sigh. Gladly would poor Master Gookin have thrust his dangerous guest into the street; but there was a constraint and terror within him. This respectable old gentleman, we fear, at an earlier period of life, had given some pledge or other to the evil principle, and perhaps was now to redeem it by the sacrifice of his daughter.

It so happened that the parlor door was partly of glass, shaded by a silken curtain, the folds of which hung a little awry. So strong was the merchant's interest in witnessing what was to ensue between the fair Polly and the gallant Feathertop that, after quitting the room, he could by no means refrain from peeping through the crevice of the curtain.

But there was nothing very miraculous to be seen; nothing—except the trifles previously noticed—to confirm the idea of a supernatural peril environing the pretty Polly. The stranger it is true was evidently a thorough and practised man of the world, systematic and self-possessed, and therefore the sort of a person to whom a parent ought not to confide a simple, young girl without due watchfulness for the result. The worthy magistrate, who had been conversant with all degrees and qualities of mankind, could not but perceive every motion and gesture of the distinguished Feathertop came in its proper place; nothing had been left rude or native in him; a well-digested conventionalism had incorporated itself thoroughly with his substance and transformed him into a work of art. Perhaps it was this peculiarity that invested him with a species of ghastliness and awe. It is the effect of anything completely and consummately artificial, in human shape, that the person impresses us as an unreality and as having hardly pith enough to cast a shadow upon the floor. As regarded Feathertop, all this resulted in a wild, extravagant, and fantastical impression, as if his life and being were akin to the smoke that curled upward from his pipe.

But pretty Polly Gookin felt not thus. The pair were now promenading the room: Feathertop with his dainty stride and no less dainty grimace; the girl with a native maidenly grace, just touched, not spoiled, by a slightly affected manner, which seemed caught from the perfect artifice of her companion. The longer the interview continued, the more charmed was pretty Polly, until, within the first quarter of an hour (as the old magistrate noted by his watch), she was evidently beginning to be in love. Nor need it have been witchcraft that subdued her in such a hurry; the poor child's heart, it may be, was so very fervent that it melted her with its own warmth as reflected from the hollow semblance of a lover. No matter what Feathertop said, his words found depth and reverberation in her ear; no matter what he did, his action was heroic to her eye. And by this time it is to be supposed there was a blush on Polly's cheek, a tender smile about her mouth, and a liquid softness in her glance; while the star kept coruscating on Feathertop's breast, and the little demons careered with more frantic merriment than ever about the circumference of his pipe bowl. O pretty Polly Gookin, why should these imps rejoice so madly that a silly maiden's heart was about to be given to a shadow! Is it so unusual a misfortune, so rare a triumph?

By and by Feathertop paused, and throwing himself into an imposing attitude, seemed to summon the fair girl to survey his figure and resist him longer if she could. His star, his embroidery, his buckles glowed at that instant with unutterable splendor; the picturesque hues of his attire took a richer depth of coloring; there was a gleam and polish over his whole presence betokening the perfect witchery of well-ordered manners. The maiden raised her eyes and suffered them to linger upon her companion with a bashful and admiring gaze. Then, as if desirous of judging what value her own simple comeliness might have side by side with so much brilliancy, she cast a glance towards the full-length looking-glass in front of which they happened to be standing. It was one of the truest plates in the world and incapable of flattery. No sooner did the images therein reflected meet Polly's eye than she shrieked, shrank from the stranger's side, gazed at him for a moment in the wildest dismay, and sank insensible upon the floor. Feathertop likewise had looked towards the mirror, and there beheld, not the glittering mockery of his outside show, but a picture of the sordid patchwork of his real composition, stripped of all witchcraft.

The wretched simulacrum! We almost pity him. He threw up his arms with an expression of despair that went further than any of his previous manifestations towards vindicating his claims to be reckoned human; for, perchance the only time since this so often empty and deceptive life of mortals began its course, an illusion had seen and fully recognized itself.

Mother Rigby was seated by her kitchen hearth in the twilight of this eventful day, and had just shaken the ashes out of a new pipe, when she heard a hurried tramp along the road. Yet it did not seem so much the tramp of human footsteps as the clatter of sticks or the rattling of dry bones.

"Ha!" thought the old witch, "what step is that? Whose skeleton is out of its grave now, I wonder?"

A figure burst headlong into the cottage door. It was Feathertop! His pipe was still alight; the star still flamed upon his breast; the embroidery still glowed upon his garments; nor had he lost, in any degree or manner that could be estimated, the aspect that assimilated him with our mortal brotherhood. But yet, in some indescribable way (as is the case with all that has deluded us when once found out), the poor reality was felt beneath the cunning artifice.

"What has gone wrong?" demanded the witch. "Did yonder sniffling hypocrite thrust my darling from his door? The villain! I'll set twenty fiends to torment him till he offer thee his daughter on his bended knees!"

"No, mother," said Feathertop despondingly; "it was not that."

"Did the girl scorn my precious one?" asked Mother Rigby, her fierce eyes glowing like two coals of Tophet. "I'll cover her face with pimples! Her nose shall be as red as the coal in thy pipe! Her front teeth shall drop out! In a week hence she shall not be worth thy having!"

"Let her alone, mother," answered poor Feathertop; "the girl was half won; and methinks a kiss from her sweet lips might have made me altogether human. But," he added, after a brief pause and then a howl of self-contempt, "I've seen myself, mother! I've seen myself for the wretched, ragged, empty thing I am! I'll exist no longer!"

Snatching the pipe from his mouth, he flung it with all his might against the chimney, and at the same instant sank upon the floor, a medley of straw and tattered garments, with some sticks protruding from the heap, and a shrivelled pumpkin in the midst. The eyeholes were now lustreless; but the rudely-carved gap, that just before had been a mouth, still seemed to twist itself into a despairing grin, and was so far human.

"Poor fellow!" quoth Mother Rigby, with a rueful glance at the relics of her ill-fated contrivance. "My poor, dear, pretty Feathertop! There are thousands upon thousands of coxcombs and charlatans in the world, made up of just such a jumble of worn-out, forgotten, and good-for-nothing trash as he was! Yet they live in fair repute, and never see themselves for what they are. And why should my poor puppet be the only one to know himself and perish for it?"

While thus muttering, the witch had filled a fresh pipe of tobacco, and held the stem between her fingers, as doubtful whether to thrust it into her own mouth or Feathertop's.

"Poor Feathertop!" she continued. "I could easily give him another chance and send him forth again to-morrow. But no; his feelings are too tender, his sensibilities too deep. He seems to have too much heart to bustle for his own advantage in such an empty and heartless world. Well! well! I'll make a scarecrow of him after all. 'Tis an innocent and useful vocation, and will suit my darling well; and, if each of his human brethren had as fit a one, 't would be the better for mankind; and as for this pipe of tobacco, I need it more than he."

So saying, Mother Rigby put the stem between her lips. "Dickon!" cried she, in her high, sharp tone, "another coal for my pipe!"

The Witch's Steed

AMBROSE BIERCE

Ambrose Bierce's satirical The Devil's Dictionary *is one of the funniest works to come out of the nineteenth century. "The Witch's Steed," from his work* Can Such Things Be?, *shows that women can wield more than one kind of power.*

A broomstick which had long served a witch as a steed complained of the nature of its employment, which it thought degrading.

"Very well," said the Witch. "I will give you work in which you will be associated with intellect—you will come into contact with brains. I shall present you to a housewife."

"What!" said the Broomstick, "do you consider the hands of a housewife intellectual?"

"I referred," said the Witch, "to the head of her good man."

The Goddess in the Ice

Harlan Ellison

The incredibly prolific Harlan Ellison, winner of multiple Hugo, Nebula, Locus, and Poe awards (among others), is plenty powerful without any need of magic. His "Goddess in the Ice" works on several witchy levels. That Ilira was an ancient goddess condemned by priests echoes feminist themes from such works as Merlin Stone's **When God Was a Woman**—*and what she does with her powers clearly reflects the perceived danger of such women!*

JUST before nightfall the storm caught them, 3500 feet up the *massif* of the glacier, far above the timberline but still four days' climb below the summit. As the wind rose, and below them they could hear the shock-crack of ice-formations shattering away from the glacier wall, they came upon the woman frozen in the ice.

Rennels was the first over the crevasse, and as he turned sidewise, bracing himself to make the towline taut, he looked across the ledge to the niche in the snow.

She was milky-white through the ice-block, but he had no doubt from the first that it was a woman, her eyes closed, hands at her sides, frozen solid into a silver-blue block of glacial ice.

He found himself unable to turn away. Even as he stared dumbfounded at an impossibility, he was accepting it—because it was undeniably before him—and racing through theories of quick-freezing, glacial upheavals, historical precedent that would account for this incredible find.

There was the shriek of an animal in the distance, and he came back from total involvement with the still figure in the ice to realize that Scotti and Kirth were yelling up through the rising wind at him.

Quickly, he wound the nylon line tighter about himself, looped it over an outcropping of rock that was deeply coated with ice, for a slippage-lever, and began pulling the towline heavily.

In a few minutes Scotti's florid face came up over the far edge of the ledge, and then the puffy body, and then he was standing across the crevasse, hauling up Kirth. When the two of them were on the ledge, Rennels motioned them to leap the crevasse.

And when they were all together, staring at the woman, finally, Scotti said something of awe and wonder. But the howling gale caught the words and threw them away into the deepening gloom.

Kirth drew their faces close to his, and shouted, "We can't stay on this ledge! The storm! It'll blow us off! Find some shelter."

They split up and followed the ledge around the face of the *massif*, and Rennels found a deep cave that ran back for perhaps seventy feet. They met again in front of the woman and he told them. But strangely, none of them moved for the shelter. Instead, they each unshipped an icepick and began hacking at the ice that enclosed the woman.

Finally, they chipped out a block of ice six feet high and, pushing and shoving, worked it around the ledge and into the cave.

Kirth lit the survival lamps from his pack and Scotti hung a tarp across the mouth of the cave. Rennels set up the portable heater, and in the shadowy interior of the glacier they settled down, all of them.

Scotti. Kirth. Rennels . . . and the woman.

ALL but one of the lamps had been extinguished. Shadows lay like broken bodies across the rough walls. Scotti was slugged down deeply in his thermal sleeping-bag, apparently asleep. Kirth sat with his back to the wall, pulling on a cup of black coffee.

Rennels was hidden in the darkness.

He was watching the woman.

The ice had thawed slightly, and now she could be seen clearly.

Rennels was hypnotized by her beauty.

The single garment she wore resembled a light yellow chiton; it draped across her breasts, exposing one shoulder and an exquisitely formed arm. It fell in pleats to her feet. It was almost Roman in design, but Rennels had had his degree in archaeology, and he recognized it as Phoenician. There was no way of unraveling the mystery of how a Phoenician woman had come to be frozen in a glacier somewhere near the top of the world.

But it was not that mystery that held him.

It was her face.

The features were indescribably beautiful. The body would have made Helen of Troy jealous.

Rennels stared without blinking.

And in the corner, Scotti watched, from his sleeping-bag, feigning sleep. And Kirth watched, breathing deeply.

But it was to Rennels that the vision came first.

As he studied her in the ice, everything seemed to grow gray and distant, and he was somehow separating from his body, standing and looking down at himself there in the shadows. Then he turned, and went toward the ice-block, into and through it.

And the woman was waiting for him.

She opened her eyes, which were green and deep and seemed to swirl with a languid smoke of sensuality. She raised her arms to him, and the chiton pulled tightly across her breasts. Rennels came to her, and she touched him lightly on the side of the face.

It was a touch of the wind.

"Who are you?" he asked, with wonder.

"Ilira," she said. Her voice was not sound, but something deeper, more omnipresent, entering his mind and expanding, filling him with a sense of her being.

"How—"

"How did I come here?"

He nodded. She smiled a soft, sad smile. And he saw that she had a charming overbite that just faintly pressed the full roundness of her lower lip.

"The Priests of the temple. I was found to be blasphemous in my worships. I was a Goddess of the temple. So they condemned me to eternal sleep in the ice lands. But now you've come to me."

It seemed all so right, so simple, so direct. He had freed her, and now she was his. He moved closer to her, and she slipped her cool arms about his neck, drawing his face to hers. Around them the mist grew up and flooded the world, covering them in a soft gray blanket.

He could feel the length of her, down his body, and he realized with an electric shock that he was about to make love to a woman whose race had died thousands of years before . . . a woman who must be part witch . . . a woman whose lovemaking would be informed by the strange practices and passions of a pagan world.

But she did not give him time to wonder.

Her sleep in the ice might have been a second, or an eternity, so starved for his body did she seem.

RENNELS came back to himself lying on the stone floor. He had fainted. Had it been a dream? Some kind of snow vision that days up here had induced? No, there was a languor in his body that he knew was real. And yet a hunger, greater than any he had ever known.

And a message:

The other two will want me. If you want me, you will have to win me, free me, to have me.

In his sleeping-bag, Scotti was just coming awake, his breath ragged in his throat. On the far side of the cave Kirth was wedged into the rocks, his eyes glazed.

Each had had the dream. Each had enjoyed the favors of the Goddess.

Rennels paused only a second as the knowledge flooded in on him—that both Kirth and Scotti had known her body—and he lunged for his icepick . . .

Suddenly, each of them had a weapon.

Kirth with the skinning knife, Scotti with a piton, and Rennels swinging the icepick with such violence that he caught Scotti rising from the sleeping-bag and imbedded the point in his left temple. Scotti screamed with pain and died as Kirth panicked and tried to escape from the mad slashings and whirlings of Rennels's weapon. He plunged toward the mouth of the cave, smacked against the block of ice with the woman still asleep in its center, and caromed off, entangling himself in the tarpaulin that kept out the storm.

Rennels lurched forward and sank the icepick in his back, but Kirth did not die. He fumbled around the tarp and stood on the ledge, the night wind screaming curses at him.

Rennels threw aside the tarp and hurled himself at the wounded man. Kirth was rocked by the assault and with a flailing of arms and legs plunged face-forward off the ledge, his terrifying scream mingling and then disappearing into the blinding snow and the night.

Rennels stood alone on the ledge, hearing the crashing, rolling sound of thunder that was Kirth plunging to his doom. Then he went back inside. To Ilira.

He stood silently, watching her sleep, for a very long time. Then he began chipping away the ice-block carefully.

Toward morning she was divested of her ice garment, and as the relative warmth of the cave reached her, Rennels witnessed the miracle of the woman's rebirth.

For thousands of years she had been a prisoner of the ice, put there by the Phoenician wizards who had known the dark arts of Lemuria and Mu and Atlantis, of Stygia and Egypt before it was Egypt.

And as Rennels stood waiting, she came awake, her eyes opening with almond-shaped beauty to see him as he now was.

Then she came to him and enfolded him.

In an instant, it was reality for Rennels again. The scent and sense of her overpowering him. But he had only that one last moment of sensual delight to ponder, for in the next instant Ilira was standing alone as the shower of pale silver sand that had been Rennels sifted down over her arms and dusted the stone floor of the cave.

Then she turned and went out into the night.

Ten thousand years before, they had stopped her, the Priests who had known what she was. But now was another time, a later time, and she would complete her destiny. It did not matter what governments or cultures ruled the world. Ilira would subjugate them to her will.

For her weapon was herself. And there was no man born of man-and-woman who could say no to the terrors and passions of her body.

She disappeared into the storm. The storm that inexplicably blew around and over her, but did not touch her.

In the cave, the pale silver sands tossed and roiled and finally were dispersed, leaving behind nothing.

Figure of the Witch

ERICA JONG

The Mother Goddess theme in Erica Jong's witch poems is never more apparent than in the unflinching "Figure of the Witch."

Witch-woman,
tall, slender,
Circe at her loom
or murderous Medea,
Joan at her tree,
listening to voices
in the rustling of the leaves,
like the rustling of the flames
which ignited
her deciduous life . . .

Witch-woman,
burning goddess,
every woman bears
within her soul
the figure of the witch,
the face of the witch,
beautiful & hideous,
hidden as the lips
of her cunt,
open as her open eyes,
which see the fire
without screaming

as she & the tree, her mother,
are joined again,
seared,
united,
married as a forest
marries air,
only by its burning,
only by its rising
in Demeter's flaming hands,
only by its leaping

heavenward

in a single
green
flame.

Fleur

Louise Erdrich

Louise Erdrich, a member of the Turtle Mountain Band of Chippewa, shows her storytelling power in this tale of a young woman's magical revenge.

THE first time she drowned in the cold and glassy waters of Lake Turcot, Fleur Pillager was only a girl. Two men saw the boat tip, saw her struggle in the waves. They rowed over to the place she went down, and jumped in. When they dragged her over the gunwales, she was cold to the touch and stiff, so they slapped her face, shook her by the heels, worked her arms back and forth, and pounded her back until she coughed up lake water. She shivered all over like a dog, then took a breath. But it wasn't long afterward that those two men disappeared. The first wandered off, and the other, Jean Hat, got himself run over by a cart.

It went to show, my grandma said. It figured to her, all right. By saving Fleur Pillager, those two men had lost themselves.

The next time she fell in the lake, Fleur Pillager was twenty years old and no one touched her. She washed onshore, her skin a dull dead gray, but when George Many Women bent to look closer, he saw her chest move. Then her eyes spun open, sharp black riprock, and she looked at him. "You'll take my place," she hissed. Everybody scattered and left her there, so no one knows how she dragged herself home. Soon after that we noticed Many Women changed, grew afraid, wouldn't leave his house, and would not be forced to go near water. For his caution, he lived until the day that his sons brought him a new tin bathtub. Then the first time he used the tub he slipped, got knocked out, and breathed water while his wife stood in the other room frying breakfast.

Men stayed clear of Fleur Pillager after the second drowning. Even though she was good-looking, nobody dared to court her because it was clear that Misshepeshu, the waterman, the monster, wanted her for himself. He's a devil, that one, love-hungry with desire and maddened for the touch of young girls, the strong and daring especially, the ones like Fleur.

Our mothers warn us that we'll think he's handsome, for he appears with green eyes, copper skin, a mouth tender as a child's. But if you fall into his arms, he sprouts horns, fangs, claws, fins. His feet are joined as one and his skin, brass scales, rings to the touch. You're fascinated, cannot move. He casts a shell necklace at your feet, weeps gleaming chips that harden into mica on your breasts. He holds you under. Then he takes the body of a lion or a fat brown worm. He's made of gold. He's made of beach moss. He's a thing of dry foam, a thing of death by drowning, the death a Chippewa cannot survive.

Unless you are Fleur Pillager. We all knew she couldn't swim. After the first time, we thought she'd never go back to Lake Turcot. We thought she'd keep to herself, live quiet, stop killing men off by drowning in the lake. After the first time, we thought she'd keep the good ways. But then, after the second drowning, we knew that we were dealing with something much more serious. She was haywire, out of control. She messed with evil, laughed at the old women's advice, and dressed like a man. She got herself into some half-forgotten medicine, studied ways we shouldn't talk about. Some say she kept the finger of a child in her pocket and a powder of unborn rabbits in a leather thong around her neck. She laid the heart of an owl on her tongue so she could see at night, and went out, hunting, not even in her own body. We know for sure because the next morning, in the snow or dust, we followed the tracks of her bare feet and saw where they changed, where the claws sprang out, the pad broadened and pressed into the dirt. By night we heard her chuffing cough, the bear cough. By day her silence and the wide grin she threw to bring down our guard made us frightened. Some thought that Fleur Pillager should be driven off the reservation, but not a single person who spoke like this had the nerve. And finally, when people were just about to get together and throw her out, she left on her own and didn't come back all summer. That's what this story is about.

During that summer, when she lived a few miles south in Argus, things happened. She almost destroyed that town.

*   *   *

WHEN she got down to Argus in the year of 1920, it was just a small grid of six streets on either side of the railroad depot. There were two elevators, one central, the other a few miles west. Two stores competed for the trade of the three hundred citizens, and three churches quarreled with one another for their souls. There was a frame building for Lutherans, a heavy brick one for Episcopalians, and a long narrow shingled Catholic church. This last had a tall slender steeple, twice as high as any building or tree.

No doubt, across the low, flat wheat, watching from the road as she came near Argus on foot, Fleur saw that steeple rise, a shadow thin as a needle. Maybe in that raw space it drew her the way a lone tree draws lightning. Maybe, in the end, the Catholics are to blame. For if she hadn't seen that sign of pride, that slim prayer, that marker, maybe she would have kept walking.

But Fleur Pillager turned, and the first place she went once she came into town was to the back door of the priest's residence attached to the landmark church. She didn't go there for a handout, although she got that, but to ask for work. She got that, too, or the town got her. It's hard to tell which came out worse, her or the men or the town, although the upshot of it all was that Fleur lived.

The four men who worked at the butcher's had carved up about a thousand carcasses between them, maybe half of that steers and the other half pigs, sheep, and game animals like deer, elk, and bear. That's not even mentioning the chickens, which were beyond counting. Pete Kozka owned the place, and employed Lily Veddar, Tor Grunewald, and my stepfather, Dutch James, who had brought my mother down from the reservation the year before she disappointed him by dying. Dutch took me out of school to take her place. I kept house half the time and worked the other in the butcher shop, sweeping floors, putting sawdust down, running a hambone across the street to a customer's bean pot or a package of sausage to the corner. I was a good one to have around because until they needed me, I was invisible. I blended into the stained brown walls, a skinny, big-nosed girl with staring eyes. Because I could fade into a corner or squeeze beneath a shelf, I knew everything, what the men said when no one was around, and what they did to Fleur.

Kozka's Meats served farmers for a fifty-mile area, both to slaughter, for it had a stock pen and chute, and to cure the meat by smoking it or spicing it in sausage. The storage locker was a marvel, made of many thicknesses of brick, earth insulation, and Minnesota timber, lined inside with sawdust and vast blocks of ice cut from Lake Turcot, hauled down from home each winter by horse and sledge.

A ramshackle board building, part-slaughterhouse, part store, was fixed to the low, thick square of the lockers. That's where Fleur worked. Kozka hired her for her strength. She could lift a haunch or carry a pole of sausages without stumbling, and she soon learned cutting from Pete's wife, a string-thin blonde who chain-smoked and handled the razor-sharp knives with nerveless precision, slicing close to her stained fingers. Fleur and Fritzie Kozka worked afternoons, wrapping their cuts in paper, and Fleur hauled the packages to the lockers. The meat was left outside the heavy oak doors that were only opened at 5:00 each afternoon, before the men ate supper.

Sometimes Dutch, Tor, and Lily ate at the lockers, and when they did I stayed too, cleaned floors, restoked the fires in the front smokehouses, while the men sat around the squat cast-iron stove spearing slats of herring onto hardtack bread. They played long games of poker or cribbage on a board made from the planed end of a salt crate. They talked and I listened, although there wasn't much to hear since almost nothing ever happened in Argus. Tor was married, Dutch had lost my mother, and Lily read circulars. They mainly discussed about the auctions to come, equipment, or women.

Every so often, Pete Kozka came out front to make a whist, leaving Fritzie to smoke cigarettes and fry raised doughnuts in the back room. He sat and played a few rounds but kept his thoughts to himself. Fritzie did not tolerate him talking behind her back, and the one book he read was the New Testament. If he said something, it concerned weather or a surplus of sheep stomachs, a ham that smoked green or the markets for corn and wheat. He had a good-luck talisman, the opal-white lens of a cow's eye. Playing cards, he rubbed it between his fingers. That soft sound and the slap of cards was about the only conversation.

Fleur finally gave them a subject.

Her cheeks were wide and flat, her hands large, chapped, muscular. Fleur's shoulders were broad as beams, her hips fishlike, slippery, narrow. An old green dress clung to her waist, worn thin where she sat. Her braids were thick like the tails of animals, and swung against her when she moved, deliberately, slowly in her work, held in and half-tamed, but only half. I could tell, but the others never saw. They never looked into her sly brown eyes or noticed her teeth, strong and curved and very white. Her legs were bare, and since she padded around in beadwork moccasins they never saw that her fifth toes were missing. They never knew she'd drowned. They were blinded, they were stupid, they only saw her in the flesh.

And yet it wasn't just that she was a Chippewa, or even that she was a woman, it wasn't that she was good-looking or even that she was alone that made their brains hum. It was how she played cards.

Women didn't usually play with men, so the evening that Fleur drew a chair up to the men's table without being so much as asked, there was a shock of surprise.

"What's this," said Lily. He was fat, with a snake's cold pale eyes and precious skin, smooth and lily-white, which is how he got his name. Lily had a dog, a stumpy mean little bull of a thing with a belly drum-tight from eating pork rinds. The dog liked to play cards just like Lily, and straddled his barrel thighs through games of stud, rum poker, vingt-un. The dog snapped at Fleur's arm that first night, but cringed back, its snarl frozen, when she took her place.

"I thought," she said, her voice soft and stroking, "you might deal me in."

There was a space between the heavy bin of spiced flour and the wall where I just fit. I hunkered down there, kept my eyes open, saw her black hair swing over the chair, her feet solid on the wood floor. I couldn't see up on the table where the cards slapped down, so after they were deep in their game I raised myself up in the shadows, and crouched on a sill of wood.

I watched Fleur's hands stack and ruffle, divide the cards, spill them to each player in a blur, rake them up and shuffle again. Tor, short and scrappy, shut one eye and squinted the other at Fleur. Dutch screwed his lips around a wet cigar.

"Gotta see a man," he mumbled, getting up to go out back to the privy. The others broke, put their cards down, and Fleur sat alone in the lamplight that glowed in a sheen across the push of her breasts. I watched her closely, then she paid me a beam of notice for the first time. She turned, looked straight at me, and grinned the white wolf grin a Pillager turns on its victims, except that she wasn't after me.

"Pauline there," she said, "how much money you got?"

We'd all been paid for the week that day. Eight cents was in my pocket.

"Stake me," she said, holding out her long fingers. I put the coins in her palm and then I melted back to nothing, part of the walls and tables. It was a long time before I understood that the men would not have seen me no matter what I did, how I moved. I wasn't anything like Fleur. My dress hung loose and my back was already curved, an old woman's. Work had roughened me, reading made my eyes sore, caring for my mother before she died had hardened my face. I was not much to look at, so they never saw me.

When the men came back and sat around the table, they had drawn together. They shot each other small glances, stuck their tongues in their cheeks, burst out laughing at odd moments, to rattle Fleur. But she never minded. They played their vingt-un, staying even as Fleur slowly gained. Those pennies I had given her drew nickels and attracted dimes until there was a small pile in front of her.

Then she hooked them with five-card draw, nothing wild. She dealt, discarded, drew, and then she sighed and her cards gave a little shiver. Tor's eyes gleamed, and Dutch straightened in his seat.

"I'll pay to see that hand," said Lily Veddar.

Fleur showed, and she had nothing there, nothing at all.

Tor's thin smile cracked open, and he threw his hand in too.

"Well, we know one thing," he said, leaning back in his chair, "the squaw can't bluff."

With that I lowered myself into a mound of swept sawdust and slept. I woke up during the night, but none of them had moved yet, so I couldn't either. Still later, the men must have gone out again, or Fritzie come out to break the game, because I was lifted, soothed, cradled in a woman's arms and rocked so quiet that I kept my eyes shut while Fleur rolled me into a closet of grimy ledgers, oiled paper, balls of string, and thick files that fit beneath me like a mattress.

The game went on after work the next evening. I got my eight cents back five times over, and Fleur kept the rest of the dollar she'd won for a stake. This time they didn't play so late, but they played regular, and then kept going at it night after night. They played poker now, or variations, for one week straight, and each time Fleur won exactly one dollar, no more and no less, too consistent for luck.

By this time, Lily and the other men were so lit with suspense that they got Pete to join the game with them. They concentrated, the fat dog sitting tense in Lily Veddar's lap, Tor suspicious, Dutch stroking his huge square brow, Pete steady. It wasn't that Fleur won that hooked them in so, because she lost hands too. It was rather that she never had a freak hand or even anything above a straight. She only took on her low cards, which didn't sit right. By chance, Fleur should have gotten a full or flush by now. The irritating thing was she beat with pairs and never bluffed, because she couldn't and still she ended up each night with exactly one dollar. Lily couldn't believe, first of all, that a woman could be smart enough to play cards, but even if she was, that she would then be stupid enough to cheat for a dollar a night. By day I watched him turn the problem over, his hard white face dull, small fingers probing at his knuckles, until he finally thought he had Fleur figured out as a bit-time player, caution her game. Raising the stakes would throw her.

More than anything now, he wanted Fleur to come away with something but a dollar. Two bits less or ten more, the sum didn't matter, just so he broke her streak.

Night after night she played, won her dollar, and left to stay in a place that just Fritzie and I knew about. Fleur bathed in the slaughtering tub, then slept in the unused brick smokehouse behind the lockers, a windowless place tarred on the inside with scorched fats. When I brushed against her skin I noticed that she smelled of the walls, rich and woody, slightly burnt. Since that night she put me in the closet I was no longer afraid of her, but followed her close, stayed with her, became her moving shadow that the men never noticed, the shadow that could have saved her.

AUGUST, the month that bears fruit, closed around the shop, and Pete and Fritzie left for Minnesota to escape the heat. Night by night, running, Fleur had won thirty dollars, but only Pete's presence had kept Lily at bay. But Pete was gone now, and one payday, with the heat so bad no one could move but Fleur, the men sat and played and waited while she finished work. The cards sweat, limp in their fingers, the table was slick with grease, and even the walls were warm to the touch. The air was motionless. Fleur was in the next room boiling heads.

Her green dress, drenched, wrapped her like a transparent sheet. A skin of lakeweed. Black snarls of veining clung to her arms. Her braids were loose, half-unraveled, tied behind her neck in a thick loop. She stood in steam, turning skulls through a vat with a wooden paddle. When scraps boiled to the surface, she bent with a round tin sieve and scooped them out. She'd filled two dishpans.

"Ain't that enough now?" called Lily. "We're waiting." The stump of a dog trembled in his lap, alive with rage. It never smelled me or noticed me above Fleur's smoky skin. The air was heavy in my corner, and pressed me down. Fleur sat with them.

"Now what do you say?" Lily asked the dog. It barked. That was the signal for the real game to start.

"Let's up the ante," said Lily, who had been stalking this night all month. He had a roll of money in his pocket. Fleur had five bills in her dress. The men had each saved their full pay.

"Ante a dollar then," said Fleur, and pitched hers in. She lost, but they let her scrape along, cent by cent. And then she won some. She played unevenly, as if chance was all she had. She reeled them in. The game went on. The dog was stiff now, poised on Lily's knees, a ball of vicious muscle with its yellow eyes slit in concentration. It gave advice, seemed to sniff the lay of Fleur's cards, twitched and nudged. Fleur was up, then down, saved by a scratch. Tor dealt seven cards, three down. The pot grew, round by round, until it held all the money. Nobody folded. Then it all rode on one last card and they went silent. Fleur picked hers up and blew a long breath. The heat lowered like a bell. Her card shook, but she stayed in.

Lily smiled and took the dog's head tenderly between his palms.

"Say, Fatso," he said, crooning the words, "you reckon that girl's bluffing?"

The dog whined and Lily laughed. "Me too," he said, "let's show." He swept his bills and coins into the pot and then they turned their cards over.

Lily looked once, looked again, then he squeezed the dog up like a fist of dough and slammed it on the table.

Fleur threw her arms out and drew the money over, grinning that same wolf grin that she'd used on me, the grin that had them. She jammed the bills in her dress, scooped the coins up in waxed white paper that she tied with string.

"Let's go another round," said Lily, his voice choked with burrs. But

Fleur opened her mouth and yawned, then walked out back to gather slops for the one big hog that was waiting in the stock pen to be killed.

The men sat still as rocks, their hands spread on the oiled wood table. Dutch had chewed his cigar to damp shreds, Tor's eye was dull. Lily's gaze was the only one to follow Fleur. I didn't move. I felt them gathering, saw my stepfather's veins, the ones in his forehead that stood out in anger. The dog had rolled off the table and curled in a knot below the counter, where none of the men could touch it.

Lily rose and stepped out back to the closet of ledgers where Pete kept his private stock. He brought back a bottle, uncorked and tipped it between his fingers. The lump in his throat moved, then he passed it on. They drank, quickly felt the whiskey's fire, and planned with their eyes things they couldn't say out loud.

When they left, I followed. I hid out back in the clutter of broken boards and chicken crates beside the stock pen, where they waited. Fleur could not be seen at first, and then the moon broke and showed her, slipping cautiously along the rough board chute with a bucket in her hand. Her hair fell, wild and coarse, to her waist, and her dress was a floating patch in the dark. She made a pig-calling sound, rang the tin pail lightly against the wood, froze suspiciously. But too late. In the sound of the ring Lily moved, fat and nimble, stepped right behind Fleur and put out his creamy hands. At his first touch, she whirled and doused him with the bucket of sour slops. He pushed her against the big fence and the package of coins split, went clinking and jumping, winked against the wood. Fleur rolled over once and vanished in the yard.

The moon fell behind a curtain of ragged clouds, and Lily followed into the dark muck. But he tripped, pitched over the huge flank of the pig, who lay mired to the snout, heavily snoring. I sprang out of the weeds and climbed the side of the pen, stuck like glue. I saw the sow rise to her neat, knobby knees, gain her balance, and sway, curious, as Lily stumbled forward. Fleur had backed into the angle of rough wood just beyond, and when Lily tried to jostle past, the sow tipped up on her hind legs and struck, quick and hard as a snake. She plunged her head into Lily's thick side and snatched a mouthful of his shirt. She lunged again, caught him lower, so that he grunted in pained surprise. He seemed to ponder, breathing deep. Then he launched his huge body in a swimmer's dive.

The sow screamed as his body smacked over hers. She rolled, striking out with her knife-sharp hooves, and Lily gathered himself upon her, took her foot-long face by the ears and scraped her snout and cheeks against the trestles of the pen. He hurled the sow's tight skull against an iron post, but instead of knocking her dead, he merely woke her from her dream.

She reared, shrieked, drew him with her so that they posed standing upright. They bowed jerkily to each other, as if to begin. Then his arms swung and flailed. She sank her black fangs into his shoulder, clasping him, dancing him forward and backward through the pen. Their steps picked up pace, went wild. The two dipped as one, box-stepped, tripped each other. She ran her split foot through his hair. He grabbed her kinked tail. They went down and came up, the same shape and then the same color, until the men couldn't tell one from the other in that light and Fleur was able to launch herself over the gates, swing down, hit gravel.

The men saw, yelled, and chased her at a dead run to the smokehouse. And Lily too, once the sow gave up in disgust and freed him. That is where I should have gone to Fleur, saved her, thrown myself on Dutch. But I went stiff with fear and couldn't unlatch myself from the trestles or move at all. I closed my eyes and put my head in my arms, tried to hide, so there is nothing to describe but what I couldn't block out. Fleur's hoarse breath, so loud it filled me, her cry in the old language, and my name repeated over and over among the words.

THE heat was still dense the next morning when I came back to work. Fleur was gone but the men were there, slack-faced, hung over. Lily was paler and softer than ever, as if his flesh had steamed on his bones. They smoked, took pulls off a bottle. It wasn't noon yet. I worked awhile, waiting shop and sharpening steel. But I was sick, I was smothered, I was sweating so hard that my hands slipped on the knives, and I wiped my fingers clean of the greasy touch of the customers' coins. Lily opened his mouth and roared once, not in anger. There was no meaning to the sound. His boxer dog, sprawled limp beside his foot, never lifted its head. Nor did the other men.

They didn't notice when I stepped outside, hoping for a clear breath. And then I forgot them because I knew that we were all balanced, ready to tip, to fly, to be crushed as soon as the weather broke. The sky was so low that I felt the weight of it like a yoke. Clouds hung down, witch teats, a tornado's green-brown cones, and as I watched one flicked out and became a delicate probing thumb. Even as I picked up my heels and ran back inside, the wind blew suddenly, cold, and then came rain.

Inside, the men had disappeared already and the whole place was trembling as if a huge hand was pinched at the rafters, shaking it. I ran straight through, screaming for Dutch or for any of them, and then I stopped at the heavy doors of the lockers, where they had surely taken shelter. I stood there a moment. Everything went still. Then I heard a cry building in the wind, faint at first, a whistle and then a shrill scream that tore through the walls and gathered around me, spoke plain so I under-stood that I should move, put my arms out, and slam down the great iron bar that fit across the hasp and lock.

Outside, the wind was stronger, like a hand held against me. I strug-gled forward. The bushes tossed, the awnings flapped off storefronts, the rails of porches rattled. The odd cloud became a fat snout that nosed along the earth and sniffled, jabbed, picked at things, sucked them up, blew them apart, rooted around as if it was following a certain scent, then stopped behind me at the butcher shop and bored down like a drill.

I went flying, landed somewhere in a ball. When I opened my eyes and looked, stranger things were happening.

A herd of cattle flew through the air like giant birds, dropping dung, their mouths opened in stunned bellows. A candle, still lighted, blew past, and tables, napkins, garden tools, a whole school of drifting eyeglasses, jackets on hangers, hams, a checkerboard, a lampshade, and at last the sow from behind the lockers, on the run, her hooves a blur, set free, swooping, diving, screaming as everything in Argus fell apart and got turned upside down, smashed, and thoroughly wrecked.

DAYS passed before the town went looking for the men. They were bach-elors, after all, except for Tor, whose wife had suffered a blow to the head that made her forgetful. Everyone was occupied with digging out, in high relief because even though the Catholic steeple had been torn off like a peaked cap and sent across five fields, those huddled in the cellar were unhurt. Walls had fallen, windows were demolished, but the stores were intact and so were the bankers and shop owners who had taken refuge in their safes or beneath their cash registers. It was a fair-minded disaster, no one could be said to have suffered much more than the next, at least not until Fritzie and Pete came home.

Of all the businesses in Argus, Kozka's Meats had suffered worst. The boards of the front building had been split to kindling, piled in a huge pyramid, and the shop equipment was blasted far and wide. Pete paced off the distance the iron bathtub had been flung—a hundred feet. The glass candy case went fifty, and landed without so much as a cracked pane. There were other surprises as well, for the back rooms where Fritzie and Pete lived were undisturbed. Fritzie said the dust still coated her china figures, and upon her kitchen table, in the ashtray, perched the last cigarette she'd put out in haste. She lit it up and finished it, looking through the window. From there, she could see that the old smokehouse Fleur had slept in was crushed to a reddish sand and the stockpens were completely torn apart, the rails stacked helter-skelter. Fritzie asked for Fleur. People shrugged. Then she asked about the others and, suddenly, the town understood that three men were missing.

There was a rally of help, a gathering of shovels and volunteers. We passed boards from hand to hand, stacked them, uncovered what lay beneath the pile of jagged splinters. The lockers, full of the meat that was Pete and Fritzie's investment, slowly came into sight, still intact. When enough room was made for a man to stand on the roof, there were calls, a general urge to hack through and see what lay below. But Fritzie shouted that she wouldn't allow it because the meat would spoil. And so the work continued, board by board, until at last the heavy oak doors of the freezer were revealed and people pressed to the entry. Everyone wanted to be the first, but since it was my stepfather lost, I was let go in when Pete and Fritzie wedged through into the sudden icy air.

Pete scraped a match on his boot, lit the lamp Fritzie held, and then the three of us stood still in its circle. Light glared off the skinned and hanging carcasses, the crates of wrapped sausages, the bright and cloudy blocks of lake ice, pure as winter. The cold bit into us, pleasant at first, then numbing. We must have stood there a couple of minutes before we saw the men, or more rightly, the humps of fur, the iced and shaggy hides they wore, the bearskins they had taken down and wrapped around themselves. We stepped closer and tilted the lantern beneath the flaps of fur into their faces. The dog was there, perched among them, heavy as a doorstop. The three had hunched around a barrel where the game was still laid out, and a dead lantern and an empty bottle too. But they had thrown down their last hands and hunkered tight, clutching one another, knuckles raw from beating at the door they had also attacked with hooks. Frost stars gleamed off their eyelashes and the stubble of their beards. Their faces were set in concentration, mouths open as if to speak some careful thought, some agreement they'd come to in each other's arms.

POWER travels in the bloodlines, handed out before birth. It comes down through the hands, which in the Pillagers were strong and knotted, big, spidery, and rough, with sensitive fingertips good at dealing cards. It comes through the eyes, too, belligerent, darkest brown, the eyes of those in the bear clan, impolite as they gaze directly at a person.

In my dreams, I look straight back at Fleur, at the men. I am no longer the watcher on the dark sill, the skinny girl.

The blood draws us back, as if it runs through a vein of earth. I've come home and, except for talking to my cousins, live a quiet life. Fleur lives quiet, too, down on Lake Turcot with her boat. Some say she's married to the waterman, Misshepeshu, or that she's living in shame with white men or windigos, or that she's killed them all. I'm about the only one here who ever goes to visit her. Last winter, I went to help out in her cabin when she bore the child, whose green eyes and skin the color of an old penny made more talk, as no one could decide if the child was mixed blood or what, fathered in a smokehouse, or by a man with brass scales, or by the lake. The girl is bold, smiling in her sleep, as if she knows what people wonder, as if she hears the old men talk, turning the story over. It comes up different every time and has no ending, no beginning. They get the middle wrong, too. They only know that they don't know anything.

Toads and Diamonds

CHARLES PERRAULT

*One frustration for practicing witches, when it comes to fairy tales,
is that only the bad magic users are called witches—the good ones
are called "fairies." It's true in "Toads and Diamonds," as well. Still,
the magical Miss Manners in this subtle-as-a-rock-to-the-head tale
makes for a fun story of empowerment, no matter what you call her.*

THERE was once upon a time a widow who had two daughters.
The eldest was so much like her in the face and humour that
whoever looked upon the daughter saw the mother. They were both so
disagreeable and so proud that there was no living with them.

The youngest, who was the very picture of her father for courtesy
and sweetness of temper, was withal one of the most beautiful girls ever
seen. As people naturally love their own likeness, this mother even doted
on her eldest daughter, and at the same time had a horrible aversion for
the youngest—she made her eat in the kitchen and work continually.

Among other things, this poor child was forced twice a day to draw
water above a mile and a half off the house, and bring home a pitcher
full of it. One day, as she was at this fountain, there came to her a poor
woman, who begged of her to let her drink.

'Oh! ay, with all my heart, Goody,' said this pretty little girl; and
rinsing immediately the pitcher, she took up some water from the clearest
place of the fountain, and gave it to her, holding up the pitcher all the
while, that she might drink the easier.

The good woman having drunk, said to her:

'You are so very pretty, my dear, so good and so mannerly, that I
cannot help giving you a gift.' For this was a fairy, who had taken the
form of a poor country-woman, to see how far the civility and good

manners of this pretty girl would go. "I will give you for gift,' continued the Fairy, 'that, at every word you speak, there shall come out of your mouth either a flower or a jewel.'

When this pretty girl came home her mother scolded at her for staying so long at the fountain.

'I beg your pardon, mamma,' said the poor girl, 'for not making more haste.'

And in speaking these words there came out of her mouth two roses, two pearls, and two diamonds.

'What is it I see there?' said her mother, quite astonished. 'I think I see pearls and diamonds come out of the girl's mouth! How happens this, child?'

This was the first time she ever called her child.

The poor creature told her frankly all the matter, not without dropping out infinite numbers of diamonds.

'In good faith,' cried the mother, 'I must send my child thither. Come hither, Fanny; look what comes out of thy sister's mouth when she speaks. Wouldst not thou be glad, my dear, to have the same gift given to thee? Thou hast nothing else to do but go and draw water out of the fountain, and when a certain poor woman asks you to let her drink, to give it her very civilly.'

'It would be a very fine sight indeed,' said this ill-bred minx, 'to see me go draw water.'

'You shall go, hussey!' said the mother; 'and this minute.'

So away she went, but grumbling all the way, taking with her the best silver tankard in the house.

She was no sooner at the fountain than she saw coming out of the wood a lady most gloriously dressed, who came up to her, and asked to drink. This was, you must know, the very fairy who appeared to her sister, but had now taken the air and dress of a princess, to see how far this girl's rudeness would go.

'Am I come hither,' said the proud, saucy slut, 'to serve you with water, pray? I suppose the silver tankard was brought purely for your ladyship, was it? However, you may drink out of it, if you have a fancy.'

'You are not over and above mannerly,' answered the Fairy, without putting herself in a passion. 'Well, then, since you have so little breeding, and are so disobliging, I give you for gift that at every word you speak there shall come out of your mouth a snake or a toad.'

So soon as her mother saw her coming she cried out:

'Well, daughter?'

'Well, mother?' answered the pert hussey, throwing out of her mouth two vipers and two toads.

'Oh! mercy,' cried the mother; 'what is it I see? Oh! it is that wretch her sister who has occasioned all this; but she shall pay for it'; and immediately she ran to beat her. The poor child fled away from her, and went to hide herself in the forest, not far from thence.

The King's son, then on his return from hunting, met her, and seeing her so very pretty, asked her what she did there alone and why she cried.

'Alas! sir, my mamma has turned me out of doors.'

The King's son, who saw five or six pearls and as many diamonds come out of her mouth, desired her to tell him how that happened. She hereupon told him the whole story; and so the King's son fell in love with her, and, considering with himself that such a gift was worth more than any marriage portion, conducted her to the palace of the King his father, and there married her.

As for her sister, she made herself so much hated that her own mother turned her off; and the miserable wretch, having wandered about a good while without finding anybody to take her in, went to a corner of the wood, and there died.

A Pair of Eyes; or, Modern Magic

Louisa May Alcott

If you've read Louisa May Alcott's somewhat autobiographical novel
Little Women—*or seen a movie adaptation of it—you know that
Jo, the character modeled on Louisa, earns a living writing sensational pulp fiction until her professor friend sets her straight. Louisa
was drawing from her own life experiences as a pulp writer. Here
is one of Louisa May Alcott's works of sensational fiction.*

Part I

I was disappointed—the great actress had not given me what I wanted
and my picture must still remain unfinished for want of a pair of eyes.
I knew what they should be, saw them clearly in my fancy, but though
they haunted me by night and day I could not paint them, could not find
a model who would represent the aspect I desired, could not describe it
to any one, and though I looked into every face I met, and visited afflicted
humanity in many shapes, I could find no eyes that visibly presented the
vacant yet not unmeaning stare of Lady Macbeth in her haunted sleep.
It fretted me almost beyond endurance to be delayed in my work so near
its completion, for months of thought and labor had been bestowed upon
it; the few who had seen it in its imperfect state had elated me with
commendation, whose critical sincerity I knew the worth of; and the
many not admitted were impatient for a sight of that which others
praised, and to which the memory of former successes lent an interest
beyond mere curiosity. All was done, and well done, except the eyes; the
dimly lighted chamber, the listening attendants, the ghostly figure with
wan face framed in hair, that streamed shadowy and long against white
draperies, and whiter arms, whose gesture told that the parted lips were
uttering that mournful cry—

"Here's the smell of blood still!
All the perfumes of Arabia will not
Sweeten this little hand—"

The eyes alone baffled me, and for want of these my work waited, and my last success was yet unwon.

I was in a curious mood that night, weary yet restless, eager yet impotent to seize the object of my search, and full of haunting images that would not stay to be reproduced. My friend was absorbed in the play, which no longer possessed any charm for me, and leaning back in my seat I fell into a listless reverie, still harping on the one idea of my life; for impetuous and resolute in all things, I had given myself body and soul to the profession I had chosen and followed through many vicissitudes for fifteen years. Art was wife, child, friend, food and fire to me; the pursuit of fame as a reward for my long labor was the object for which I lived, the hope which gave me courage to press on over every obstacle, sacrifice and suffering, for the word "defeat" was not in my vocabulary. Sitting thus, alone, though in a crowd, I slowly became aware of a disturbing influence whose power invaded my momentary isolation, and soon took shape in the uncomfortable conviction that someone was looking at me. Every one has felt this, and at another time I should have cared little for it, but just then I was laboring under a sense of injury, for of all the myriad eyes about me none would give me the expression I longed for; and unreasonable as it was, the thought that I was watched annoyed me like a silent insult. I sent a searching look through the boxes on either hand, swept the remoter groups with a powerful glass, and scanned the sea of heads below, but met no answering glance; all faces were turned stageward, all minds seemed intent upon the tragic scenes enacting there.

Failing to discover any visible cause for my fancy, I tried to amuse myself with the play, but having seen it many times and being in an ill-humor with the heroine of the hour, my thoughts soon wandered, and though still apparently an interested auditor, I heard nothing, saw nothing, for the instant my mind became abstracted the same uncanny sensation returned. A vague consciousness that some stronger nature was covertly exerting its power upon my own; I smiled as this whim first suggested itself, but it rapidly grew upon me, and a curious feeling of impotent resistance took possession of me, for I was indignant without knowing why, and longed to rebel against—I knew not what. Again I looked far and wide, met several inquiring glances from near neighbors, but none that answered my demand by any betrayal of especial interest or malicious pleasure. Baffled, yet not satisfied, I turned to myself, thinking to find the cause of my disgust there, but did not succeed. I seldom drank wine, had not worked intently that day, and except the picture had no anxiety to harass me; yet without any physical or mental cause that I could discover, every nerve seemed jangled out of tune, my temples beat, my breath came short, and the air seemed feverishly close, though I had not perceived it until then. I did not understand this mood and with an impatient gesture took the playbill from my friend's knee, gathered it into my hand and fanned myself like a petulant woman, I suspect, for Louis turned and surveyed me with surprise as he asked:

"What is it, Max; you seem annoyed?"

"I am, but absurd as it is, I don't know why, except a foolish fancy that someone whom I do not see is looking at me and wishes me to look at him."

Louis laughed—"Of course there is, aren't you used to it yet? And are you so modest as not to know that many eyes take stolen glances at the rising artist, whose ghosts and goblins make their hair stand on end so charmingly? I had the mortification to discover some time ago that, young and comely as I take the liberty of thinking myself, the upturned lorgnettes are not levelled at me, but at the stern-faced, black-bearded gentleman beside me, for he looks particularly moody and interesting tonight."

"Bah! I just wish I could inspire some of those starers with gratitude enough to set them walking in their sleep for my benefit and their own future glory. Your suggestion has proved a dead failure, the woman there cannot give me what I want, the picture will never get done, and the whole affair will go to the deuce for want of a pair of eyes."

I rose to go as I spoke, and there they were behind me!

What sort of expression my face assumed I cannot tell, for I forgot time and place, and might have committed some absurdity if Louis had not pulled me down with a look that made me aware that I was staring with an utter disregard of common courtesy.

"Who are those people? Do you know them?" I demanded in a vehement whisper.

"Yes, but put down that glass and sit still or I'll call an usher to put you out," he answered, scandalized at my energetic demonstrations.

"Good! then introduce me—now at once—Come on," and I rose again, to be again arrested.

"Are you possessed to-night? You have visited so many fever wards and madhouses in your search that you've unsettled your own wits, Max. What whim has got into your brain now? And why do you want to know those people in such haste?"

"Your suggestion has not proved failure, a woman can give me what I want, the picture will be finished, and nothing will go to the deuce, for I've found the eyes—now be obliging and help me to secure them."

Louis stared at me as if he seriously began to think me a little mad, but restrained the explosive remark that rose to his lips and answered hastily, as several persons looked round as if our whispering annoyed them.

"I'll take you in there after the play if you must go, so for heaven's sake behave like a gentleman till then, and let me enjoy myself in peace."

I nodded composedly, he returned to his tragedy and shading my eyes with my hand, I took a critical survey, feeling more and more assured that my long search was at last ended. Three persons occupied the box, a well-dressed elderly lady dozing behind her fan, a lad leaning over the front absorbed in the play, and a young lady looking straight before her with the aspect I had waited for with such impatience. This figure I scrutinized with the eye of an artist which took in every accessory of outline, ornament and hue.

Framed in darkest hair, rose a face delicately cut, but cold and colorless as that of any statue in the vestibule without. The lips were slightly parted with the long slow breaths that came and went, the forehead was femininely broad and low, the brows straight and black, and underneath them the mysterious eyes fixed on vacancy, full of that weird regard so hard to counterfeit, so impossible to describe; for though absent, it was not expressionless, and through its steadfast shine a troubled meaning wandered, as if soul and body could not be utterly divorced by any effort of the will. She seemed unconscious of the scene about her, for the fixture of her glance never changed, and nothing about her stirred but the jewel on her bosom, whose changeful glitter seemed to vary as it rose and fell. Emboldened by this apparent absorption, I prolonged my scrutiny and scanned this countenance as I had never done a woman's face before.

During this examination I had forgotten myself in her, feeling only a strong desire to draw nearer and dive deeper into those two dark wells that seemed so tranquil yet so fathomless, and in the act of trying to fix shape, color and expression in my memory, I lost them all; for a storm of applause broke the attentive hush as the curtain fell, and like one startled from sleep a flash of intelligence lit up the eyes, then a white hand was passed across them, and long downcast lashes hid them from my sight.

Louis stood up, gave himself a comprehensive survey, and walked out, saying, with a nod,

"Now, Max, put on your gloves, shake the hair out of your eyes, assume your best 'deportment,' and come and take an observation which may immortalize your name."

Knocking over a chair in my haste, I followed close upon his heels, as he tapped at the next door; the lad opened it, bowed to my conductor, glanced at me and strolled away, while we passed in. The elderly lady was awake, now, and received us graciously; the younger was leaning on her hand, the plumy fan held between her and the glare of the great chandelier as she watched the moving throng below.

"Agatha, here is Mr. Yorke and a friend whom he wishes to present to you," said the old lady, with a shade of deference in her manner which betrayed the companion, not the friend.

Agatha turned, gave Louis her hand, with a slow smile dawning on her lip, and looked up at me as if the fact of my advent had no particular interest for her, and my appearance promised no great pleasure.

"Miss Eure, my friend Max Erdmann yearned to be made happy by a five minutes audience, and I ventured to bring him without sending an *avant courier* to prepare the way. Am I forgiven?" with which half daring, half apologetic introduction, Louis turned to the chaperone and began to rattle.

Miss Eure bowed, swept the waves of silk from the chair beside her, and I sat down with a bold request waiting at my lips till an auspicious moment came, having resolved not to exert myself for nothing. As we discussed the usual topics suggested by the time and place, I looked often into the face before me and soon found it difficult to look away again, for it was a constant surprise to me. The absent mood had passed and with it the frost seemed to have melted from mien and manner, leaving a living woman in the statue's place. I had thought her melancholy, but her lips were dressed in smiles, and frequent peals of low-toned laughter parted them like pleasant music; I had thought her pale, but in either cheek now bloomed a color deep and clear as any tint my palette could have given; I had thought her shy and proud at first, but with each moment her manner warmed, her speech grew franker and her whole figure seemed to glow and brighten as if a brilliant lamp were lit behind the pale shade she had worn before. But the eyes were the greatest surprise of all—I had fancied them dark, and found them the light, sensitive gray belonging to highly nervous temperaments. They were remarkable eyes; for though softly fringed with shadowy lashes they were not mild, but fiery and keen, with many lights and shadows in them as the pupils dilated, and the irids shone with a transparent lustre which varied with her varying words, and proved the existence of an ardent, imperious nature underneath the seeming snow.

They exercised a curious fascination over me and kept my own obedient to their will, although scarce conscious of it at the time and believing mine to be the controlling power. Wherein the charm lay I cannot tell; it was not the influence of a womanly presence alone, for fairer faces had smiled at me in vain; yet as I sat there I felt a pleasant quietude creep over me, I knew my voice had fallen to a lower key, my eye softened from its wonted cold indifference, my manner grown smooth and my demeanor changed to one almost as courtly as my friend's, who well deserved his soubriquet of "Louis the Debonnair."

"It is because my long fret is over," I thought, and having something to gain, exerted myself to please so successfully that, soon emboldened by her gracious mood and the flattering compliments bestowed upon my earlier works, I ventured to tell my present strait and the daring hope I had conceived that she would help me through it. How I made this blunt request I cannot tell, but remember that it slipped over my tongue as smoothly as if I had meditated upon it for a week. I glanced over my shoulder as I spoke, fearing Louis might mar all with apology or reproof; but he was absorbed in the comely duenna, who was blushing like a girl at the half playful, half serious devotion he paid all womankind; and reassured, I waited, wondering how Miss Eure would receive my request. Very quietly; for with no change but a peculiar dropping of the lids, as if her eyes sometimes played the traitor to her will, she answered, smilingly,

"It is I who receive the honor, sir, not you, for genius possesses the privileges of royalty, and may claim subjects everywhere, sure that its choice ennobles and its power extends beyond the narrow bounds of custom, time and place. When shall I serve you, Mr. Erdmann?"

At any other time I should have felt surprised both at her and at myself; but just then, in the ardor of the propitious moment, I thought only of my work, and with many thanks for her great kindness left the day to her, secretly hoping she would name an early one. She sat silent an instant, then seemed to come to some determination, for when she spoke a shadow of mingled pain and patience swept across her face as if her resolve had cost her some sacrifice of pride or feeling.

"It is but right to tell you that I may not always have it in my power to give you the expression you desire to catch, for the eyes you honor by wishing to perpetuate are not strong and often fail me for a time. I have been utterly blind once and may be again, yet have no present cause to fear it, and if you can come to me on such days as they will serve your purpose, I shall be most glad to do my best for you. Another reason makes me bold to ask this favor of you, I cannot always summon this absent mood, and should certainly fail in a strange place; but in my own home, with all familiar things about me, I can more easily fall into one of my deep reveries and forget time by the hour together. Will this arrangement cause much inconvenience or delay? A room shall be prepared for you—kept inviolate as long as you desire it—and every facility my house affords is at your service, for I feel much interest in the work which is to add another success to your life."

She spoke regretfully at first, but ended with a cordial glance as if she had forgotten herself in giving pleasure to another. I felt that it must have cost her an effort to confess that such a dire affliction had ever darkened her youth and might still return to sadden her prime; this pity mingled with my expressions of gratitude for the unexpected interest she bestowed upon my work, and in a few words the arrangement was made, the day and hour fixed, and a great load off my mind. What the afterpiece was I never knew; Miss Eure stayed to please her young companion, Louis stayed to please himself, and I remained because I had not energy enough to go away. For, leaning where I first sat down, I still looked and listened with a dreamy sort of satisfaction to Miss Eure's low voice, as with downcast eyes, still shaded by her fan, she spoke enthusiastically and well of art (the one interesting theme to me) in a manner which proved that she had read and studied more than her modesty allowed her to acknowledge.

We parted like old friends at her carriage door, and as I walked away with Louis in the cool night air I felt like one who had been asleep in a close room, for I was both languid and drowsy, though a curious under-current of excitement still stirred my blood and tingled along my nerves. "A theatre is no place for me," I decided, and anxious to forget myself said aloud:

"Tell me all you know about that woman."

"What woman, Max?"

"Miss Agatha Eure, the owner of the eyes."

"Aha! smitten at last! That ever I should live to see our Benedict the victim of love at first sight!"

"Have done with your nonsense, and answer my question. I don't ask from mere curiosity, but that I may have some idea how to bear myself at these promised sittings; for it will never do to ask after her papa if she has none, to pay my respects to the old lady as her mother if she is only the duenna, or joke with the lad if he is the heir apparent."

"Do you mean to say that you asked her to sit to you?" cried Louis, falling back a step and staring at me with undisguised astonishment.

"Yes, why not?"

"Why, man, Agatha Eure is the haughtiest piece of humanity ever concocted, and I, with all my daring, never ventured to ask more than an occasional dance with her, and feel myself especially favored that she deigns to bow to me, and lets me pick up her gloves or carry her bouquet as a mark of supreme condescension. What witchcraft did you bring to bear upon her? and how did she grant your audacious request?"

"Agreed to it at once."

"Like an empress conferring knighthood, I fancy."

"Not at all. More like a pretty woman receiving a compliment to her beauty—though she is not pretty, by the way."

Louis indulged himself in the long, low whistle, which seems the only adequate expression for masculine surprise. I enjoyed his amazement, it was my turn to laugh now, and I did so, as I said:

"You are always railing at me for my avoidance of all womankind, but you see I have not lost the art of pleasing, for I won your haughty Agatha to my will in fifteen minutes, and am not only to paint her hand-some eyes, but to do it at her own house, by her own request. I am beginning to find that, after years of effort, I have mounted a few more rounds of the social ladder than I was aware of, and may now confer as well as receive favors; for she seemed to think me the benefactor, and I rather enjoyed the novelty of the thing. Now tell your story of 'the haughtiest piece of humanity' ever known. I like her the better for that trait."

Louis nodded his head, and regarded the moon with an aspect of immense wisdom, as he replied:

"I understand it now; it all comes back to me, and my accusation holds good, only the love at first sight is on the other side. You shall have your story, but it may leave the picture in the lurch if it causes you to fly off, as you usually see fit to do when a woman's name is linked with your own. You never saw Miss Eure before; but what you say reminds me that she has seen you, for one day last autumn, as I was driving with her and old madame—a mark of uncommon favor, mind you—we saw you striding along, with your hat over your eyes, looking very much like a comet streaming down the street. It was crowded, and as you waited at the crossing you spoke to Jack Mellot, and while talking pulled off your hat and tumbled your hair about, in your usual fashion, when very earnest. We were blockaded by cars and coaches for a moment, so Miss Eure had a fine opportunity to feast her eyes upon you, 'though you are not pretty, by the way.' She asked your name, and when I told her she gushed out into a charming little stream of interest in your daubs, and her delight at seeing their creator; all of which was not agreeable to me, for I considered myself much the finer work of art of the two. Just then you caught up a shabby child with a big basket, took them across, under our horses' noses, with never a word for me, though I called to you, and, diving into the crowd, disappeared. 'I like that,' said Miss Eure; and as we drove on she asked questions, which I answered in a truly Christian manner, doing you no harm, old lad; for I told all you had fought through, with the courage of a stout-hearted man, all you had borne with the patience of a woman, and what a grand future lay open to you, if you chose to accept and use it, making quite a fascinating little romance of it, I assure you. There the matter dropped. I forgot it till this minute, but it accounts for the ease with which you gained your first suit, and is prophetic of like success in a second and more serious one. She is young, well-born, lovely to those who love her, and has a fortune and position which will lift you at once to the topmost round of the long ladder you've been climbing all these years. I wish you joy, Max."

"Thank you. I've no time for lovemaking, and want no fortune but that which I earn for myself. I am already married to a fairer wife than Miss Eure, so you may win and wear the lofty lady yourself."

Louis gave a comical groan.

"I've tried that, and failed; for she is too cold to be warmed by any flame of mine, though she is wonderfully attractive when she likes, and I hover about her even now like an infatuated moth, who beats his head against the glass and never reaches the light within. No; you must thankfully accept the good the gods bestow. Let Art be your Leah, but Agatha your Rachel. And so, good-night!"

"Stay and tell me one thing—is she an orphan?"

"Yes; the last of a fine old race, with few relatives and few friends, for death has deprived her of the first, and her own choice of the last. The lady you saw with her plays propriety in her establishment; the lad is Mrs. Snow's son, and fills the role of *cavaliere-servente*; for Miss Eure is a Diana toward men in general, and leads a quietly luxurious life among her books, pencils and music, reading and studying all manner of things few women of two-and-twenty care to know. But she has the wit to see that a woman's mission is to be charming, and when she has sufficient motive for the exertion she fulfils that mission most successfully, as I know to my sorrow. Now let me off, and be for ever grateful for the good turn I have done you to-night, both in urging you to go to the theatre and helping you to your wish when you got there."

We parted merrily, but his words lingered in my memory, and half unconsciously exerted a new influence over me, for they flattered the three ruling passions that make or mar the fortunes of us all—pride, ambition and self-love. I wanted power, fame and ease, and all seemed waiting for me, not in the dim future but the actual present, if my friend's belief was as to be relied upon; and remembering all I had seen and heard that night, I felt that it was not utterly without foundation. I pleased myself for an idle hour in dreaming dreams of what might be; finding that amusement began to grow dangerously attractive, I demolished my castles in the air with the last whiff of my meerschaum, and fell asleep, echoing my own words:

"Art is my wife, I will have no other!"

Punctual to the moment I went to my appointment, and while waiting an answer to my ring took an exterior survey of Miss Eure's house. One of an imposing granite block, it stood in a West End square, with every sign of unostentatious opulence about it. I was very susceptible to all influences, either painful or pleasant, and as I stood there the bland atmosphere that surrounded me seemed most attractive; for my solitary life had been plain and poor, with little time for ease, and few ornaments to give it grace. Now I seemed to have won the right to enjoy both if I would; I no longer felt out of place there, and with this feeling came the wish to try the sunny side of life, and see if its genial gifts would prove more inspiring than the sterner masters I had been serving so long.

The door opened in the middle of my reverie, and I was led through an anteroom, lined with warm-hued pictures, to a large apartment, which had been converted into an impromptu studio by someone who understood all the requisites for such a place. The picture, my easel and other necessaries had preceded me, and I thought to have spent a good hour in arranging matters. All was done, however, with a skill that surprised me; the shaded windows, the carefully-arranged brushes, the proper colors already on the palette, the easel and picture placed as they should be, and a deep curtain hung behind a small dais, where I fancied my model was to sit. The room was empty as I entered, and with the brief message, "Miss Eure will be down directly," the man noiselessly departed.

I stood and looked about me with great satisfaction, thinking, "I cannot fail to work well surrounded by such agreeable sights and sounds." The house was very still, for the turmoil of the city was subdued to a murmur, like the far-off music of the sea; a soft gloom filled the room, divided by one strong ray that fell athwart my picture, gifting it with warmth and light. Through a half-open door I saw the green vista of a conservatory, full of fine blendings of color, and wafts of many odors blown to me by the west wind rustling through orange trees and slender palms; while the only sound that broke the silence was the voice of a flame-colored foreign bird, singing a plaintive little strain like a sorrowful lament. I liked this scene, and, standing in the doorway, was content to look, listen and enjoy, forgetful of time, till a slight stir made me turn and for a moment look straight before me with a startled aspect. It seemed as if my picture had left its frame; for, standing on the narrow dais, clearly defined against the dark background, stood the living likeness of the figure I had painted, the same white folds falling from neck to ankle, the same shadowy hair, and slender hands locked together, as if wrung in slow despair; and fixed full upon my own the weird, unseeing eyes, which made the face a pale mask, through which the haunted spirit spoke eloquently, with its sleepless anguish and remorse.

"Good morning, Miss Eure; how shall I thank you?" I began, but stopped abruptly, for without speaking she waved me towards the easel with a gesture which seemed to say, "Prove your gratitude by industry."

"Very good," thought I, "if she likes the theatrical style she shall have it. It is evident she has studied her part and will play it well, I will do the same, and as Louis recommends, take the good the gods send me while I may."

Without more ado I took my place and fell to work; but, though never more eager to get on, with each moment that I passed I found my interest in the picture grow less and less intent, and with every glance at my model found that it was more and more difficult to look away. Beautiful she was not, but the wild and woeful figure seemed to attract me as no Hebe, Venus or sweet-faced Psyche had ever done. My hand moved slower and slower, the painted face grew dimmer and dimmer, my glances lingered longer and longer, and presently palette and brushes rested on my knee, as I leaned back in the deep chair and gave myself up to an uninterrupted stare. I knew that it was rude, knew that it was as a trespass on Miss Eure's kindness as well as a breach of good manners, but I could not help it, for my eyes seemed beyond my control, and though I momentarily expected to see her color rise and hear some warning of the lapse of time, I never looked away, and soon forgot to imagine her feelings in the mysterious confusion of my own.

I was first conscious of a terrible fear that I ought to speak or move, which seemed impossible, for my eyelids began to be weighed down by a delicious drowsiness in spite of all my efforts to keep them open. Everything grew misty, and the beating of my heart sounded like the rapid, irregular roll of a muffled drum; then a strange weight seemed to oppress and cause me to sigh long and deeply. But soon the act of breathing appeared to grow unnecessary, for a sensation of wonderful airiness came over me, and I felt as if I could float away like a thistledown. Presently every sense seemed to fall asleep, and in the act of dropping both palette and brush I drifted away into a sea of blissful repose, where nothing disturbed me but a fragmentary dream that came and went like a lingering gleam of consciousness through the new experience which had befallen me.

I seemed to be still in the quiet room, still leaning in the deep chair with half-closed eyes, still watching the white figure before me, but that had changed. I saw a smile break over the lips, something like triumph flash into the eyes, sudden color flush the cheeks, and the rigid hands lifted to gather up and put the long hair back; then with noiseless steps it came nearer and nearer till it stood beside me. For awhile it paused there mute and intent, I felt the eager gaze searching my face, but it caused no displeasure; for I seemed to be looking down at myself, as if soul and body had parted company and I was gifted with a double life. Suddenly the vision laid a light hand on my wrist and touched my temples, while a shade of anxiety seemed to flit across its face as it turned and vanished. A dreamy wonder regarding its return woke within me, then my sleep deepened into utter oblivion, for how long I cannot tell. A pungent odor seemed to recall me to the same half wakeful state. I dimly saw a woman's arm holding a glittering object before me, when the fragrance came; an unseen hand stirred my hair with the grateful drip of water, and once there came a touch like the pressure of lips upon my forehead, soft and warm, but gone in an instant. These new sensations grew rapidly more and more defined; I clearly saw a bracelet on the arm and read the Arabic characters engraved upon the golden coins that formed it; I heard the rustle of garments, the hurried breathing of some near presence, and felt the cool sweep of a hand passing to and fro across my forehead. At this point my thoughts began to shape themselves into words, which came slowly and seemed strange to me as I searched for and connected them, then a heavy sigh rose and broke at my lips, and the sound of my own voice woke me, drowsily echoing the last words I had spoken:

"Good morning, Miss Eure; how shall I thank you?"

To my great surprise the well-remembered voice answered quietly:

"Good morning, Mr. Erdmann; will you have some lunch before you begin?"

How I opened my eyes and got upon my feet was never clear to me, but the first object I saw was Miss Eure coming towards me with a glass in her hand. My expression must have been dazed and imbecile in the extreme, for to add to my bewilderment the tragic robes had disappeared, the dishevelled hair was gathered in shining coils under a Venetian net of silk and gold, a white embroidered wrapper replaced the muslins Lady Macbeth had worn, and a countenance half playful, half anxious, now smiled where I had last seen so sorrowful an aspect. The fear of having committed some great absurdity and endangered my success brought me right with a little shock of returning thought. I collected myself, gave a look about the room, a dizzy bow to her, and put my hand to my head with a vague idea that something was wrong there. In doing this I discovered that my hair was wet, which slight fact caused me to exclaim abruptly:

"Miss Eure, what have I been doing? Have I had a fit? been asleep? or do you deal in magic and rock your guests off into oblivion without a moment's warning?"

Standing before me with uplifted eyes, she answered, smiling:

"No, none of these have happened to you; the air from the Indian plants in the conservatory was too powerful, I think; you were a little faint, but closing the door and opening a window has restored you, and a glass of wine will perfect the cure, I hope."

She was offering the glass as she spoke. I took it but forgot to thank her, for on the arm extended to me was the bracelet never seen so near by my waking eyes, yet as familiar as if my vision had come again. Something struck me disagreeably, and I spoke out with my usual bluntness.

"I never fainted in my life, and have an impression that people do not dream when they swoon. Now I did, and so vivid was it that I still remember the characters engraved on the trinket you wear, for that played a prominent part in my vision. Shall I describe them as proof of it, Miss Eure?"

Her arm dropped at her side and her eyes fell for a moment as I spoke; then she glanced up unchanged, saying as she seated herself and motioned me to do the same:

"No, rather tell the dream, and taste these grapes while you amuse me."

I sat down and obeyed her. She listened attentively, and when I ended explained the mystery in the simplest manner.

"You are right in the first part of your story. I did yield to a whim which seized me when I saw your picture, and came down *en costume,* hoping to help you by keeping up the illusion. You began, as canvas and brushes prove; I stood motionless till you turned pale and regarded me with a strange expression; at first I thought it might be inspiration, as your friend Yorke would say, but presently you dropped everything out of your hands and fell back in your chair. I took the liberty of treating you like a woman, for I bathed your temples and wielded my vinaigrette most energetically till you revived and began to talk of 'Rachel, art, castles in the air, and your wife Lady Macbeth'; then I slipped away and modernized myself, ordered some refreshments for you, and waited till you wished me 'Good-morning.' "

She was laughing so infectiously that I could not resist joining her and accepting her belief, for curious as the whole affair seemed to me I could account for it in no other way. She was winningly kind, and urged me not to resume my task, but I was secretly disgusted with myself for such a display of weakness, and finding her hesitation caused solely by fears for me, I persisted, and seating her, painted as I had never done before. Every sense seemed unwontedly acute, and hand and eye obeyed me with a docility they seldom showed. Miss Eure sat where I placed her, silent and intent, but her face did not wear the tragic aspect it had worn before, though she tried to recall it. This no longer troubled me, for the memory of the vanished face was more clearly before me than her own, and with but few and hasty glances at my model, I reproduced it with a speed and skill that filled me with delight. The striking of a clock reminded me that I had far exceeded the specified time, and that even a woman's patience has limits; so concealing my regret at losing so auspicious a mood, I laid down my brush, leaving my work unfinished, yet glad to know I had the right to come again, and complete it in a place and presence which proved so inspiring.

Miss Eure would not look at it till it was all done, saying in reply to my thanks for the pleasant studio she had given me—"I was not quite unselfish in that, and owe you an apology for venturing to meddle with your property; but it gave me real satisfaction to arrange these things, and restore this room to the aspect it wore three years ago. I, too, was an artist then, and dreamed aspiring dreams here, but was arrested on the threshold of my career by loss of sight; and hard as it seemed then to give up all my longings, I see now that it was better so, for a few years later it would have killed me. I have learned to desire for others what I can never hope for myself, and try to find pleasure in their success, unembittered by regrets for my own defeat. Let this explain my readiness to help you, my interest in your work and my best wishes for your present happiness and future fame."

The look of resignation, which accompanied her words, touched me more than a flood of complaints, and the thought of all she had lost woke such sympathy and pity in my frosty heart, that I involuntarily pressed the hand that could never wield a brush again. Then for the first time I saw those keen eyes soften and grow dim with unshed tears; this gave them the one charm they needed to be beautiful as well as penetrating, and as they met my own, so womanly sweet and grateful, I felt that one might love her while that mood remained. But it passed as rapidly as it came, and when we parted in the anteroom the cold, quiet lady bowed me out, and the tender-faced girl was gone.

I never told Louis all the incidents of that first sitting, but began my story where the real interest ended; and Miss Eure was equally silent, through forgetfulness or for some good reason of her own. I went several times again, yet though the conservatory door stood open I felt no ill effects from the Indian plants that still bloomed there, dreamed no more dreams, and Miss Eure no more enacted the somnambulist. I found an indefinable charm in that pleasant room, a curious interest in studying its mistress, who always met me with a smile, and parted with a look of unfeigned regret. Louis rallied me upon my absorption, but it caused me no uneasiness, for it was not love that led me there, and Miss Eure knew it. I never had forgotten our conversation on that first night, and with every interview the truth of my friend's suspicions grew more and more apparent to me. Agatha Eure was a strong-willed, imperious woman, used to command all about her and see her last wish gratified; but now she was conscious of a presence she could not command, a wish she dare not utter, and, though her womanly pride sealed her lips, her eyes often traitorously betrayed the longing of her heart. She was sincere in her love for art, and behind that interest in that concealed, even from herself, her love for the artist; but the most indomitable passion given humanity cannot long be hidden. Agatha soon felt her weakness, and vainly struggled to subdue it. I soon knew my power, and owned its subtle charm, though I disdained to use it.

The picture was finished, exhibited and won me all, and more than I had dared to hope; for rumor served me a good turn, and whispers of Miss Eure's part in my success added zest to public curiosity and warmth to public praise. I enjoyed the little stir it caused, found admiration a sweet draught after a laborious year, and felt real gratitude to the woman who had helped me win it. If my work had proved a failure I should have forgotten her, and been an humbler, happier man; it did not, and she became a part of my success. Her name was often spoken in the same breath with mine, her image was kept before me by no exertion of my own, till the memories it brought with it grew familiar as old friends, and slowly ripened into a purpose which, being born of ambition and not love, bore bitter fruit, and wrought out its own retribution for a sin against myself and her.

The more I won the more I demanded, the higher I climbed the more eager I became; and, at last, seeing how much I could gain by a single step, resolved to take it, even though I knew it to be a false one. Other men married for the furtherance of their ambitions, why should not I? Years ago I had given up love of home for love of fame, and the woman who might have made me what I should be had meekly yielded all, wished me a happy future, and faded from my world, leaving me only a bitter memory, a veiled picture and a quiet grave my feet never visited but once. Miss Eure loved me, sympathised in my aims, understood my tastes; she could give all I asked to complete the purpose of my life, and lift me at once and for ever from the hard lot I had struggled with for thirty years. One word would win the miracle, why should I hesitate to utter it?

I did not long—for three months from the day I first entered that shadowy room I stood there intent on asking her to be my wife. As I waited I lived again the strange hour once passed there, and felt as if it had been the beginning of another dream whose awakening was yet to come. I asked myself if the hard healthful reality was not better than such feverish visions, however brilliant, and the voice that is never silent when we interrogate it with sincerity answered, "Yes." "No matter, I choose to dream, so let the phantom of a wife come to me here as the phantom of a lover came to me so long ago." As I uttered these defiant words aloud, like a visible reply, Agatha appeared upon the threshold of the door. I knew she had heard me—for again I saw the soft-eyed, tender girl, and opened my arms to her without a word. She came at once, and clinging to me with unwonted tears upon her cheek, unwonted fervor in her voice, touched my forehead, as she had done in that earlier dream, whispering like one still doubtful of her happiness—

"Oh, Max! be kind to me, for in all the world I have only you to love."

I promised, and broke that promise in less than a year.

PART II

We were married quietly, went away till the nine days gossip was over, spent our honeymoon as that absurd month is usually spent, and came back to town with the first autumnal frosts; Agatha regretting that I was no longer entirely her own, I secretly thanking heaven that I might drop the lover, and begin my work again, for I was an imprisoned creature in that atmosphere of "love in idleness," though my bonds were only a pair of loving arms. Madame Snow and son departed, we settled ourselves in the fine house and then endowed with every worldly blessing, I looked about me, believing myself master of my fate, but found I was its slave.

If Agatha could have joined me in my work we might have been happy; if she could have solaced herself with other pleasures and left me to my own, we might have been content; if she had loved me less, we might have gone our separate ways, and yet been friends like many another pair, but I soon found that her affection was of that exacting nature which promises but little peace unless met by one as warm. I had nothing but regard to give her, for it was not in her power to stir a deeper passion in me; I told her this before our marriage, told her I was a cold, hard man, rapt in a single purpose; but what woman believes such confessions while her heart still beats fast with the memory of her betrothal? She said everything was possible to love, and prophesied a speedy change; I knew it would not come, but having given my warning left the rest to time. I hoped to lead a quiet life and prove that adverse circumstances, not the want of power, had kept me from excelling in the profession I had chosen; but to my infinite discomfort Agatha turned jealous of my art, for finding the mistress dearer than the wife, she tried to wean me from it, and seemed to feel that having given me love, wealth and ease, I should ask no more, but play the obedient subject to a generous queen. I rebelled against this, told her that one-half my time should be hers, the other belonged to me, and I would so employ it that it should bring honor to the name I had given her. But, Agatha was not used to seeing her will thwarted or her pleasure sacrificed to another, and soon felt that though I scrupulously fulfilled my promise, the one task was irksome, the other all absorbing; that though she had her husband at her side his heart was in his studio, and the hours spent with her were often the most listless in his day. Then began that sorrowful experience old as Adam's reproaches to Eve; we both did wrong, and neither repented; both were self-willed, sharp tongued and proud, and before six months of wedded life had passed we had known many of those scenes which so belittle character and lessen self-respect.

Agatha's love lived through all, and had I answered its appeals by patience, self-denial and genial friendship, if no warmer tie could exist, I might have spared her an early death, and myself from years of bitterest remorse; but I did not. Then her forbearance ended and my subtle punishment began.

"Away again to-night, Max? You have been shut up all day, and I hoped to have you to myself this evening. Hear how the storm rages without, see how cheery I have made all within for you, so put your hat away and stay, for this hour belongs to me, and I claim it."

Agatha took me prisoner as she spoke, and pointed to the cosy nest she had prepared for me. The room was bright and still; the lamp shone clear; the fire glowed; warm-hued curtains muffled the war of gust and sleet without; books, music, a wide-armed seat and a woman's wistful face invited me; but none of these things could satisfy me just then, and though I drew my wife nearer, smoothed her shining hair, and kissed the reproachful lips, I did not yield.

"You must let me go, Agatha, for the great German artist is here, I had rather give a year of life than miss this meeting with him. I have devoted many evenings to you, and though this hour is yours I shall venture to take it, and offer you a morning call instead. Here are novels, new songs, an instrument, embroidery and a dog, who can never offend by moody silence or unpalatable conversation—what more can a contented woman ask, surely not an absentminded husband?"

"Yes, just that and nothing more, for she loves him, and he can supply a want that none of these things can. See how pretty I have tried to make myself for you alone; stay, Max, and make me happy."

"Dear, I shall find my pretty wife to-morrow, but the great painter will be gone; let me go, Agatha, and make me happy."

She drew herself from my arm, saying with a flash of the eye—"Max, you are a tyrant!"

"Am I? then you made me so with too much devotion."

"Ah, if you loved me as I loved there would be no selfishness on your part, no reproaches on mine. What shall I do to make myself dearer, Max?"

"Give me more liberty."

"Then I should lose you entirely, and lead the life of a widow. Oh, Max, this is hard, this is bitter, to give all and receive nothing in return."

She spoke passionately, and the truth of her reproach stung me, for I answered with that coldness that always wounded her.

"Do you count an honest name, sincere regard and much gratitude as nothing? I have given you these, and ask only peace and freedom in return. I desire to do justice to you and to myself, but I am not like you, never can be, and you must not hope it. You say love is all-powerful, prove it upon me, I am willing to be the fondest of husbands if I can; teach me, win me in spite of myself, and make me what you will; but leave me a little time to live and labor for that which is dearer to me than your faulty lord and master can ever be to you."

"Shall I do this?" and her face kindled as she put the question.

"Yes, here is an amusement for you, use what arts you will, make your love irresistible, soften my hard nature, convert me into your shadow, subdue me till I come at your call like a pet dog, and when you make your presence more powerful than painting I will own that you have won your will and made your theory good."

I was smiling as I spoke, for the twelve labors of Hercules seemed less impossible than this, but Agatha watched me with her glittering eyes; and answered slowly—

"I will do it. Now go, and enjoy your liberty while you may, but remember when I have conquered that you dared me to it, and keep your part of the compact. Promise this." She offered me her hand with a strange expression—I took it, said good-night, and hurried away, still smiling at the curious challenge given and accepted.

Agatha told me to enjoy my liberty, and I tried to do so that very night, but failed most signally, for I had not been an hour in the brilliant company gathered to meet the celebrated guest before I found it impossible to banish the thought of my solitary wife. I had left her often, yet never felt disturbed by more than a passing twinge of that uncomfortable bosom friend called conscience; but now the interest of the hour seemed lessened by regret, for through varying conversation held with those about me, mingling with the fine music that I heard, looking at me from every woman's face, and thrusting itself into my mind at every turn, came a vague, disturbing self-reproach, which slowly deepened to a strong anxiety. My attention wandered, words seemed to desert me, fancy to be frostbound, and even in the presence of the great man I had so ardently desired to see I could neither enjoy his society nor play my own part well. More than once I found myself listening for Agatha's voice; more than once I looked behind me expecting to see her figure, and more than once I resolved to go, with no desire to meet her.

"It is an acute fit of what women call nervousness; I will not yield to it," I thought, and plunged into the gayest group I saw, supped, talked, sang a song, and broke down; told a witty story, and spoiled it; laughed and tried to bear myself like the lightest-hearted guest in the rooms; but it would not do, for stronger and stronger grew the strange longing to go home, and soon it became uncontrollable. A foreboding fear that something had happened oppressed me, and suddenly leaving the festival at its height I drove home as if life and death depended on the saving of a second. Like one pursuing or pursued I rode, eager only to be there; yet when I stood on my own threshold I asked myself wonderingly, "Why such haste?" and stole in ashamed at my early return. The storm beat without, but within all was serene and still, and with noiseless steps I went up to the room where I had left my wife, pausing a moment at the half open door to collect myself, lest she should see the disorder of both mind and mien. Looking in I saw her sitting with neither book nor work beside her, and after a momentary glance began to think my anxiety had not been causeless, for she sat erect and motionless as an inanimate figure of intense thought; her eyes were fixed, face colorless, with an expression of iron determination, as if every energy of mind and body were wrought up to the achievement of a single purpose. There was something in the rigid attitude and stern aspect of this familiar shape that filled me with dismay, and found vent in the abrupt exclamation,

"Agatha, what is it?"

She sprang up like a steel spring when the pressure is removed, saw me, and struck her hands together with a wild gesture of surprise, alarm or pleasure, which I could not tell, for in the act she dropped into her seat white and breathless as if smitten with sudden death. Unspeakably shocked, I bestirred myself till she recovered, and though pale and spent, as if with some past exertion, soon seemed quite herself again.

"Agatha, what were you thinking of when I came in?" I asked, as she sat leaning against me with half closed eyes and a faint smile on her lips, as if the unwonted caresses I bestowed upon her were more soothing than any cordial I could give. Without stirring she replied,

"Of you, Max. I was longing for you, with heart and soul and will.

You told me to win you in spite of yourself; and I was sending my love to find and bring you home. Did it reach you? did it lead you back and make you glad to come?"

A peculiar chill ran through me as I listened, though her voice was quieter, her manner gentler than usual as she spoke. She seemed to have such faith in her tender fancy, such assurance of its efficacy, and such a near approach to certain knowledge of its success, that I disliked the thought of continuing the topic, and answered cheerfully,

"My own conscience brought me home, dear; for, discovering that I had left my peace of mind behind me, I came back to find it. If your task is to cost a scene like this it will do more harm than good to both of us, so keep your love from such uncanny wanderings through time and space, and win me with less dangerous arts."

She smiled her strange smile, folded my hand in her own, and answered with soft exultation in her voice,

"It will not happen so again, Max; but I am glad, most glad you came, for it proves I have some power over this wayward heart of yours, where I shall knock until it opens wide and takes me in."

The events of that night made a deep impression on me, for from that night my life was changed. Agatha left me entirely free, never asked my presence, never upbraided me for long absences or silences when together. She seemed to find happiness in her belief that she should yet subdue me, and though I smiled at this in my indifference, there was something half pleasant, half pathetic in the thought of this proud woman leaving all warmer affections for my negligent friendship, the sight of this young wife laboring to win her husband's heart. At first I tried to be all she asked, but soon relapsed into my former life, and finding no reproaches followed, believed I should enjoy it as never before—but I did not. As weeks passed I slowly became conscious that some new power had taken possession of me, swaying my whole nature to its will; a power alien yet sovereign. Fitfully it worked, coming upon me when least desired, enforcing its commands regardless of time, place or mood; mysterious yet irresistible in its strength, this mental tyrant led me at all hours, in all stages of anxiety, repugnance and rebellion, from all pleasures or employments, straight to Agatha. If I sat at my easel the sudden summons came, and wondering at myself I obeyed it, to find her busied in some cheerful occupation, with apparently no thought or wish for me. If I left home I often paused abruptly in my walk or drive, turned and hurried back, simply because I could not resist the impulse that controlled me. If she went away I seldom failed to follow, and found no peace till I was at her side again. I grew moody and restless, slept ill, dreamed wild dreams, and often woke and wandered aimlessly, as if sent upon an unknown errand. I could not fix my mind upon my work; a spell seemed to have benumbed imagination and robbed both brain and hand of power to conceive and skill to execute.

At first I fancied this was only the reaction of entire freedom after long captivity, but I soon found I was bound to a more exacting mistress than my wife had ever been. Then I suspected that it was only the perversity of human nature, and that having gained my wish it grew valueless, and I longed for that which I had lost; but it was not this, for distasteful as my present life had become, the other seemed still more so when I recalled it. For a time I believed that Agatha might be right, that I was really learning to love her, and this unquiet mood was the awakening of that passion which comes swift and strong when it comes to such as I. If I had never loved I might have clung to this belief, but the memory of that earlier affection, so genial, entire and sweet, proved that the present fancy was only a delusion; for searching deeply into myself to discover the truth of this, I found that Agatha was no dearer, and to my own dismay detected a covert dread lurking there, harmless and vague, but threatening to deepen into aversion or resentment for some unknown offence; and while I accused myself of an unjust and ungenerous weakness, I shrank from the thought of her, even while I sought her with the assiduity but not the ardor of a lover.

Long I pondered over this inexplicable state of mind, but found no solution of it; for I would not own, either to myself or Agatha, that the shadow of her prophecy had come to pass, though its substance was still wanting. She sometimes looked inquiringly into my face with those strange eyes of hers, sometimes chid me with a mocking smile when she found me sitting idly before my easel without a line or tint given though hours had passed; and often, when driven by that blind impulse I sought her anxiously among her friends, she would glance at those about her, saying, with a touch of triumph in her mien, "Am I not an enviable wife to have inspired such devotion in this grave husband?" Once, remembering her former words, I asked her playfully if she still "sent her love to find and bring me home?" but she only shook her head and answered, sadly,

"Oh, no; my love was burdensome to you, so I have rocked it to sleep and laid it where it will not trouble you again."

At last I decided that some undetected physical infirmity caused my disquiet, for years of labor and privation might well have worn the delicate machinery of heart or brain, and this warning suggested the wisdom of consulting medical skill in time. This thought grew as month after month increased my mental malady and began to tell upon my hitherto unbroken health. I wondered if Agatha knew how listless, hollow-eyed and wan I had grown; but she never spoke of it, and an unconquerable reserve kept me from uttering a complaint to her.

One day I resolved to bear it no longer, and hurried away to an old friend in whose skill and discretion I had entire faith. He was out, and while I waited I took up a book that lay among the medical works upon his table. I read a page, then a chapter, turning leaf after leaf with a rapid hand, devouring paragraph after paragraph with an eager eye. An hour passed, still I read on. Dr. L—— did not come, but I did not think of that, and when I laid down the book I no longer needed him, for in that hour I had discovered a new world, had seen the diagnosis of my symptoms set forth in unmistakable terms, and found the key to the mystery in the one word—Magnetism. This was years ago, before spirits had begun their labors for good or ill, before ether and hashish had gifted humanity with eternities of bliss in a second, and while Mesmer's mystical discoveries were studied only by the scientific or philosophical few. I knew nothing of these things, for my whole life had led another way, and no child could be more ignorant of the workings or extent of this wonderful power. There was Indian blood in my veins, and superstition lurked there still; consequently the knowledge that I was a victim of this occult magic came upon me like an awful revelation, and filled me with a storm of wrath, disgust and dread.

Like an enchanted spirit who has found the incantation that will free it from subjection, I rejoiced with a grim satisfaction even while I cursed myself for my long blindness, and with no thought for anything but instant accusation on my part, instant confession and atonement on hers, I went straight home, straight into Agatha's presence, and there, in words as brief as bitter, told her that her reign was over. All that was sternest, hottest and most unforgiving ruled me then, and like fire to fire roused a spirit equally strong and high. I might have subdued her by juster and more generous words, but remembering the humiliation of my secret slavery I forgot my own offence in hers, and set no curb on tongue or temper, letting the storm she had raised fall upon her with the suddenness of an unwonted, unexpected outburst.

As I spoke her face changed from its first dismay to a defiant calmness that made it hard as rock and cold as ice, while all expression seemed concentrated in her eye, which burned on me with an unwavering light. There was no excitement in her manner, no sign of fear, or shame, or grief in her mien, and when she answered me her voice was untremulous and clear as when I heard it first.

"Have you done? Then hear me: I knew you long before you dreamed that such a woman as Agatha Eure existed. I was solitary, and longed to be sincerely loved. I was rich, yet I could not buy what is unpurchasable; I was young, yet I could not make my youth sweet with affection; for nowhere did I see the friend whose nature was akin to mine until you passed before me, and I felt at once, 'There is the one I seek!' I never yet desired that I did not possess the coveted object, and believed I should not fail now. Years ago I learned the mysterious gift I was endowed with, and fostered it; for, unblessed with beauty, I hoped its silent magic might draw others near enough to see, under this cold exterior, the woman's nature waiting there. The first night you saw me I yielded to an irresistible longing to attract your eye, and for a moment see the face I had learned to love looking into mine. You know how well I succeeded—you know your own lips asked the favor I was so glad to give, and your own will led you to me. That day I made another trial of my skill and succeeded beyond my hopes, but dared not repeat it, for your strong nature was not easily subdued, it was too perilous a game for me to play, and I resolved that no delusion should make you mine. I would have a free gift or none. You offered me your hand, and believing that it held a loving heart, I took it, to find that heart barred against me, and another woman's name engraved upon its door. Was this a glad discovery for a wife to make? Do you wonder she reproached you when she saw her hopes turn to ashes, and could no longer conceal from herself that she was only a stepping-stone to lift an ambitious man to a position which she could not share? You think me weak and wicked; look back upon the year nearly done and ask yourself if many young wives have such a record of neglect, despised love, unavailing sacrifices, long suffering patience and deepening despair? I had been reading the tear-stained pages of this record when you bid me win you if I could; and with a bitter sense of the fitness of such a punishment, I resolved to do it, still cherishing a hope that some spark of affection might be found. I soon saw the vanity of such a hope, and this hard truth goaded me to redouble my efforts till I had entirely subjugated that arrogant spirit of yours, and made myself master where I would so gladly have been a loving subject. Do you think I have not suffered? have not wept bitter tears in secret, and been wrung by sharper anguish than you have ever known? If you had given any sign of affection, shown any wish to return to me, any shadow of regret for the wrong you had done me, I would have broken my wand like Prospero, and used no magic but the pardon of a faithful heart. You did not, and it has come to this. Before you condemn me, remember that you dared me to do it—that you bid me make my presence more powerful than Art—bid me convert you to my shadow, and subdue you till you came like a pet dog at my call. Have I not obeyed you? Have I not kept my part of the compact? Now keep yours."

There was something terrible in hearing words whose truth wounded while they fell, uttered in a voice whose concentrated passion made its tones distinct and deep, as if an accusing spirit read them from that book whose dread records never are effaced. My hot blood cooled, my harsh mood softened, and though it still burned, my resentment sank lower, for, remembering the little life to be, I wrestled with myself, and won humility enough to say, with regretful energy:

"Forgive me, Agatha, and let this sad past sleep. I have wronged you, but I believed I sinned no more than many another man who, finding love dead, hoped to feed his hunger with friendship and ambition. I never thought of such an act till I saw affection in your face; that tempted me, and I tried to repay all you gave me by the offer of the hand you mutely asked. It was a bargain often made in this strange world of ours, often repented as we repent now. Shall we abide by it, and by mutual forbearance recover mutual peace? or shall I leave you free, to make life sweeter with a better man, and find myself poor and honest as when we met?"

Something in my words stung her; and regarding me with the same baleful aspect, she lifted her slender hand, so wasted since I made it mine, that the single ornament it wore dropped into her palm, and holding it up, she said, as if prompted by the evil genius that lies hidden in every heart:

"I will do neither. I have outlived my love, but pride still remains;

and I will not do as you have done, take cold friendship or selfish ambition to fill an empty heart; I will not be pitied as an injured woman,
or pointed at as one who staked all on a man's faith and lost; I will have
atonement for my long-suffering—you owe me this, and I claim it. Hence-
forth you are the slave of the ring, and when I command you must obey,
for I possess a charm you cannot defy. It is too late to ask for pity,
pardon, liberty or happier life; law and gospel joined us, and as yet law
and gospel cannot put us asunder. You have brought this fate upon yourself, accept it, submit to it, for I have bought you with my wealth, I hold
you with my mystic art, and body and soul, Max Erdmann, you are
mine!"

I knew it was all over then, for a woman never flings such taunts in
her husband's teeth till patience, hope and love are gone. A desperate
purpose sprung up within me as I listened, yet I delayed a moment before
I uttered it, with a last desire to spare us both.

"Agatha, do you mean that I am to lead the life I have been leading
for three months—a life of spiritual slavery worse than any torment of
the flesh?"

"I do."

"Are you implacable? and will you rob me of all self-control, all
peace, all energy, all hope of gaining that for which I have paid so costly
a price?"

"I will."

"Take back all you have given me, take my good name, my few
friends, my hard-earned success; leave me stripped of every earthly blessing, but free me from this unnatural subjection, which is more terrible to
me than death!"

"I will not!"

"Then your own harsh decree drives me from you, for I will break
the bond that holds me, I will go out of this house and never cross its
threshold while I live—never look into the face which has wrought me
all this ill. There is no law, human or divine, that can give you a right
to usurp the mastery of another will, and if it costs life and reason I will
not submit to it."

"Go when and where you choose, put land and sea between us, break
what ties you may, there is one you cannot dissolve, and when I summon
you, in spite of all resistance, you must come."

"I swear I will not!"

I spoke out of a blind and bitter passion, but I kept my oath. How her eyes glittered as she lifted up that small pale hand of hers, pointed with an ominous gesture to the ring, and answered:

"Try it."

As she spoke like a sullen echo came the crash of the heavy picture that hung before us. It bore Lady Macbeth's name, but it was a painted image of my wife. I shuddered as I saw it fall, for to my superstitious fancy it seemed a fateful incident; but Agatha laughed a low metallic laugh that made me cold to hear, and whispered like a sibyl:

"Accept the omen; that is a symbol of the Art you worship so idol-atrously that a woman's heart was sacrificed for its sake. See where it lies in ruins at your feet, never to bring you honor, happiness or peace; for I speak the living truth when I tell you that your ambitious hopes will vanish the cloud now rising like a veil between us, and the memory of this year will haunt you day and night, till the remorse you painted shall be written upon heart, and face, and life. Now go!"

Her swift words and forceful gesture seemed to banish me for ever, and, like one walking in his sleep, I left her there, a stern, still figure, with its shattered image at its feet.

That instant I departed, but not far—for as yet I could not clearly see which way duty led me. I made no confidante, asked no sympathy or help, told no one of my purpose, but resolving to take no decisive step rashly, I went away to a country house of Agatha's, just beyond the city, as I had once done before when busied on a work that needed solitude and quiet, so that if gossip rose it might be harmless to us both. Then I sat down and thought. Submit I would not, desert her utterly I could not, but I dared defy her, and I did; for as if some viewless spirit whispered the suggestion in my ear, I determined to oppose my will to hers, to use her weapons if I could, and teach her to be merciful through suffering like my own. She had confessed my power to draw her to me, in spite of coldness, poverty and all lack of the attractive graces women love; that clue inspired me with hope. I got books and pored over them till their meaning grew clear to me; I sought out learned men and gathered help from their wisdom; I gave myself to the task with indomitable zeal, for I was struggling for the liberty that alone made life worth possessing. The world believed me painting mimic woes, but I was living through a fear-fully real one; friends fancied me busied with the mechanism of material bodies, but I was prying into the mysteries of human souls; and many envied my luxurious leisure in that leafy nest, while I was leading the life of a doomed convict, for as I kept my sinful vow so Agatha kept hers.

She never wrote, or sent, or came, but day and night she called me—day and night I resisted, saved only by the desperate means I used—means that made my own servant think me mad. I bid him lock me in my chamber; I dashed out at all hours to walk fast and far away into the lonely forest; I drowned consciousness in wine; I drugged myself with opiates, and when the crisis had passed, woke spent but victorious. All arts I tried, and slowly found that in this conflict of opposing wills my own grew stronger with each success, the other lost power with each defeat. I never wished to harm my wife, never called her, never sent a baneful thought or desire along that mental telegraph which stretched and thrilled between us; I only longed to free myself, and in this struggle weeks passed, yet neither won a signal victory, for neither proud heart knew the beauty of self-conquest and the power of submission.

One night I went up to the lonely tower that crowned the house, to watch the equinoctial storm that made a Pandemonium of the elements without. Rain streamed as if a second deluge was at hand; whirlwinds tore down the valley; the river chafed and foamed with an angry dash, and the city lights shone dimly through the flying mist as I watched them from my lofty room. The tumult suited me, for my own mood was stormy, dark and bitter, and when the cheerful fire invited me to bask before it I sat there wrapped in reveries as gloomy as the night. Presently the well-known premonition came with its sudden thrill through blood and nerves, and with a revengeful strength never felt before I gathered up my energies for the trial, as I waited some more urgent summons. None came, but in its place a sense of power flashed over me, a swift exultation dilated within me, time seemed to pause, the present rolled away, and nothing but an isolated memory remained, for fixing my thoughts on Agatha, I gave myself up to the dominant spirit that possessed me. I sat motionless, yet I willed to see her. Vivid as the flames that framed it, a picture started from the red embers, and clearly as if my bodily eye rested on it, I saw the well-known room, I saw my wife lying in a deep chair, wan and wasted as if with suffering of soul and body, I saw her grope with outstretched hands, and turn her head with eyes whose long lashes never lifted from the cheek where they lay so dark and still, and through the veil that seemed to wrap my senses I heard my own voice, strange and broken, whispering:

"God forgive me, she is blind!"

For a moment, the vision wandered mistily before me, then grew steady, and I saw her steal like a wraith across the lighted room, so dark to her; saw her bend over a little white nest my own hands placed there, and lift some precious burden in her feeble arms; saw her grope painfully back again, and sitting by that other fire—not solitary like my own—lay her pale cheek to that baby cheek and seem to murmur some lullaby that mother-love had taught her. Over my heart strong and sudden gushed a warmth never known before, and again, strange and broken through the veil that wrapped my senses, came my own voice whispering:

"God be thanked, she is not utterly alone!"

As if my breath dissolved it, the picture faded; but I willed again and another rose—my studio, dim with dust, damp with long disuse, dark with evening gloom—for one flickering lamp made the white shapes ghostly, and the pictured faces smile or frown with fitful vividness. There was no semblance of my old self there, but in the heart of the desolation and the darkness Agatha stood alone, with outstretched arms and an imploring face, full of a love and longing so intense that with a welcoming gesture and a cry that echoed through the room, I answered that mute appeal:

"Come to me! come to me!"

A gust thundered at the window, and rain fell like stormy tears, but nothing else replied; as the bright brands dropped the flames died out, and with it that sad picture of my deserted home. I longed to stir but could not, for I had called up a power I could not lay, the servant ruled the master now, and like one fastened by a spell I still sat leaning forward intent upon a single thought. Slowly from the gray embers smouldering on the hearth a third scene rose behind the smoke wreaths, changeful, dim and strange. Again my former home, again my wife, but this time standing on the threshold of the door I had sworn never to cross again. I saw the wafture of the cloak gathered about her, saw the rain beat on her shelterless head, and followed that slight figure through the deserted streets, over the long bridge where the lamps flickered in the wind, along the leafy road, up the wide steps and in at the door whose closing echo startled me to consciousness that my pulses were beating with a mad rapidity, that a cold dew stood upon my forehead, that every sense was supernaturally alert, and that all were fixed upon one point with a breathless intensity that made that little span of time as fearful as the moment when one hangs poised in air above a chasm in the grasp of nightmare. Suddenly I sprang erect, for through the uproar of the elements without, the awesome hush within, I heard steps ascending, and stood waiting in a speechless agony to see what shape would enter there.

One by one the steady footfalls echoed on my ear, one by one they seemed to bring the climax of some blind conflict nearer, one by one they knelled a human life away, for as the door swung open Agatha fell down before me, storm-beaten, haggard, spent, but loving still, for with a faint attempt to fold her hands submissively, she whispered:

"You have conquered, I am here!" and with that act grew still for ever, as with a great shock I woke to see what I had done.

Ten years have passed since then. I sit on that same hearth a feeble, white-haired man, and beside me, the one companion I shall ever know, my little son—dumb, blind and imbecile. I lavish tender names upcn him, but receive no sweet sound in reply; I gather him close to my desolate heart, but meet no answering caress; I look with yearning glance, but see only those haunting eyes, with no gleam of recognition to warm them, no ray of intellect to inspire them, no change to deepen their sightless beauty; and this fair body moulded with the Divine sculptor's gentlest grace is always here before me, an embodied grief that wrings my heart with its pathetic innocence, its dumb reproach. This is the visible punishment for my sin, but there is an unseen retribution heavier than human judgment could inflict, subtler than human malice could conceive, for with a power made more omnipotent by death Agatha still calls me. God knows I am willing now, that I long with all the passion of desire, the anguish of despair to go to her, and He knows that the one tie that holds me is this aimless little life, this duty that I dare not neglect, this long atonement that I make. Day and night I listen to the voice that whispers to me through the silence of these years; day and night I answer with a yearning cry from the depths of a contrite spirit; day and night I cherish the one sustaining hope that Death, the great consoler, will soon free both father and son from the inevitable doom a broken law has laid upon them; for then I know that somewhere in the long hereafter my remorse-ful soul will find her, and with its poor offering of penitence and love fall down before her, humbly saying:

"You have conquered, I am here!"

Exorcism

RAY BRADBURY

Just how worried would the average small town get if one of their little old ladies started practicing witchcraft? This wonderfully humorous slice of magic and Americana, as well as yet another revenge fantasy, takes a look.

SHE came out of the bathroom putting iodine on her finger where she had almost lopped it off cutting herself a chunk of coconut cake. Just then the mailman came up the porch steps, opened the door, and walked in. The door slammed. Elmira Brown jumped a foot.

"Sam!" she cried. She waved her iodined finger on the air to cool it. "I'm still not used to my husband being a postman. Every time you just walk in, it scares the life out of me!"

Sam Brown stood there with the mail pouch half empty, scratching his head. He looked back out the door as if a fog had suddenly rolled in on a calm sweet summer morn.

"Sam, you're home early," she said.

"Can't stay," he said in a puzzled voice.

"Spit it out, what's wrong?" She came over and looked into his face.

"Maybe nothing, maybe lots. I just delivered some mail to Clara Goodwater up the street. . . ."

"Clara Goodwater!"

"Now don't get your dander up. Books it was, from the Johnson-Smith Company, Racine, Wisconsin. Title of one book . . . let's see now." He screwed up his face, then unscrewed it. "*Albertus Magnus*—that's it. 'Being the approved, verified, sympathetic and natural Egyptian Secrets or . . .'" He peered at the ceiling to summon the lettering. "'White and Black Art for Man and Beast, Revealing the Forbidden Knowledge and Mysteries of Ancient Philosophers'!"

"Clara Goodwater's you say?"

"Walking along, I had a good chance to peek at the front pages, no harm in that. 'Hidden Secrets of Life Unveiled by that celebrated Student, Philosopher, Chemist, Naturalist, Psychomist, Astrologer, Alchemist, Metallurgist, Sorcerer, Explanator of the Mysteries of Wizards and Witchcraft, together with recondite views of numerous Arts and Sciences—Obscure, Plain, Practical, etcetera.' There! By God, I got a head like a box Brownie. Got the words, even if I haven't got the sense."

Elmira stood looking at her iodined finger as if it were pointed at her by a stranger.

"Clara Goodwater," she murmured.

"Looked me right in the eye as I handed it over, said, 'Going to be a witch, first-class, no doubt. Get my diploma in no time. Set up business. Hex crowds and individuals, old and young, big and small.' Then she kinda laughed, put her nose in that book, and went in."

Elmira stared at a bruise on her arm, carefully tongued a loose tooth in her jaw.

A door slammed. Tom Spaulding, kneeling on Elmira Brown's front lawn, looked up. He had been wandering about the neighborhood, seeing how the ants were doing here or there, and had found a particularly good hill with a big hole in which all kinds of fiery bright pismires were tumbling about scissoring the air and wildly carrying little packets of dead grasshopper and infinitesimal bird down into the earth. Now here was something else: Mrs. Brown, swaying on the edge of her porch as if she'd just found out the world was falling through space at sixty trillion miles a second. Behind her was Mr. Brown, who didn't know the miles per second and probably wouldn't care if he did know.

"You, Tom!" said Mrs. Brown. "I need moral support and the equivalent of the blood of the Lamb with me. Come along!"

And off she rushed, squashing ants and kicking tops off dandelions and trotting big spiky holes in flower beds as she cut across yards.

Tom knelt a moment longer studying Mrs. Brown's shoulder blades and spine as she toppled down the street. He read the bones and they were eloquent of melodrama and adventure, a thing he did not ordinarily connect with ladies, even though Mrs. Brown had the remnants of a pirate's mustache. A moment later he was in tandem with her.

"Mrs. Brown, you sure look mad!"

"You don't know what mad *is,* boy!"

"Watch out!" cried Tom.

Mrs. Elmira Brown fell right over an iron dog lying asleep there on the green grass.

"Mrs. Brown!"

"You see?" Mrs. Brown sat there. "Clara Goodwater did this to me! Magic!"

"Magic?"

"Never mind, boy. Here's the steps. You go first and kick any invisible strings out of the way. Ring that doorbell, but pull your finger off quick, the juice'll burn you to a cinder!"

Tom did not touch the bell.

"Clara Goodwater!" Mrs. Brown flicked the bell button with her iodined finger.

Far away in the cool dim empty rooms of the big old house, a silver bell tinkled and faded.

Tom listened. Still farther away there was a stir of mouselike running. A shadow, perhaps a blowing curtain, moved in a distant parlor.

"Hello," said a quiet voice.

And quite suddenly Mrs. Goodwater was there, fresh as a stick of peppermint, behind the screen.

"Why, hello there, Tom, Elmira. What—"

"Don't rush me! We came over about your practicing to be a full-fledged witch!"

Mrs. Goodwater smiled. "Your husband's not only a mailman, but a guardian of the law. Got a nose out to *here!*"

"He didn't look at no mail."

"He's ten minutes between houses laughing at post cards and trying on mail-order shoes."

"It ain't what he seen; it's what you yourself told him about the books you got."

"Just a joke. 'Going to be a witch!' I said, and bang! Off gallops Sam, like I'd flung lightning at him. I declare there can't be one wrinkle in that man's brain."

"You talked about your magic other places yesterday—"

"You must mean the Sandwich Club. . . ."

"To which I pointedly was *not* invited."

"Why, lady, we thought that was your regular day with your grandma."

"I can always have another Grandma day, if people'd only ask me places."

"All there was to it at the Sandwich Club was me sitting there with a ham and pickle sandwich, and I said right out loud, 'At last I'm going to get my witch's diploma. Been studying for years!' "

"That's what come back to me over the phone!"

"Ain't modern inventions wonderful!" said Mrs. Goodwater.

"Considering you been president of the Honeysuckle Ladies Lodge since the Civil War, it seems, I'll put it to you bang on the nose. Have you used witchcraft all these years to spell the ladies and win the ayes-have-it?"

"Do you doubt it for a moment, lady?" said Mrs. Goodwater.

"Election's tomorrow again, and all I want to know is, you running for another term—and ain't you ashamed?"

"Yes to the first question and no to the second. Lady, look here, I bought those books for my boy cousin, Raoul. He's just ten and goes around looking in hats for rabbits. I told him there's about as much chance finding rabbits in hats as brains in heads of certain people I could name, but look he does and so I got these gifts for him."

"Wouldn't believe you on a stack of Bibles."

"God's truth, anyway. I love to fun about the witch thing. The ladies all yodeled when I explained about my dark powers. Wish you'd been there."

"I'll be there tomorrow to fight you with a cross of gold and all the powers of good I can organize behind me," said Elmira. "Right now, tell me how much other magic junk you got in your house."

Mrs. Goodwater pointed to a sidetable inside the door.

"I been buying all kinds of magic herbs. Smell funny and make Raoul happy. That little sack of stuff, that's called thesis rue, and this is sabisse root and that there's ebon herbs; here's black sulphur, and this they claim is bone dust."

"Bone dust!" Elmira skipped back and kicked Tom's ankle. Tom yelped.

"And here's wormwood and fern leaves so you can freeze shotguns and fly like a bat in your dreams, it says in Chapter X of the little book here. I think it's fine for growing boys' heads to think about things like this. Now, from the look on your face you don't believe Raoul exists. Well, I'll give you his Springfield address."

"Yes," said Elmira, "and the day I write him you'll take the Spring-field bus and go to General Delivery and get my letter and write back to me in a boy's hand. I know you!"

"Mrs. Brown, speak up—you want to be president of the Honey-suckle Ladies Lodge, right? You run every year now for ten years. You nominate yourself. And always wind up getting *one* vote. Yours. Elmira, if the ladies wanted you they'd landslide you in. But from where I stand looking up the mountain, ain't so much as one pebble come rattling down save yours. Tell you what, I'll nominate and vote for you myself come noon tomorrow, how's that?"

"Damned for sure, then," said Elmira. "Last year I got a deathly cold right at election time; couldn't get out and campaign back-fence-to-back-fence. Year before that, broke my leg. Mighty strange." She squinted darkly at the lady behind the screen. "That's not all. Last month I cut my fingers six times, bruised my knee ten times, fell off my back porch twice, you hear—twice! I broke a window, dropped four dishes, one vase worth a dollar forty-nine at Bixby's, and I'm billing you for every dropped dish from now on in my house and environs!"

"I'll be poor by Christmas," said Mrs. Goodwater. She opened the screen door and came out suddenly and let the door slam. "Elmira Brown, how old are you?"

"You probably got it written in one of your black books. Thirty-five!"

"Well, when I think of thirty-five years of your life . . ." Mrs. Good-water pursed her lips and blinked her eyes, counting. "That's about twelve thousand seven hundred and seventy-five days, or counting three of them per day, twelve thousand-odd commotions, twelve thousand much-ados and twelve thousand calamities. It's a full rich life you lead, Elmira Brown. Shake hands!"

"Get away!" Elmira fended her off.

"Why, lady, you're only the second most clumsy woman in Green Town, Illinois. You can't sit down without playing the chair like an ac-cordion. You can't stand up but what you kick the cat. You can't trot across an open meadow without falling into a well. Your life has been one long decline, Elmira Alice Brown, so why not admit it?"

"It wasn't clumsiness that caused my calamities, but you being within a mile of me at those times when I dropped a pot of beans or juiced my finger in the electric socket at home."

"Lady, in a town this size, *everybody's* within a mile of someone at one time or other in the day."

"You admit being around then?"

"I admit being born here, yes, but I'd give anything right now to have been born in Kenosha or Zion. Elmira, go to your dentist and see what he can do about that serpent's tongue in there."

"Oh!" said Elmira. "Oh, oh, oh!"

"You've pushed me too far. I wasn't interested in witchcraft, but I think I'll just look into this business. Listen here! You're invisible right now. While you stood there I put a spell on you. You're clean out of sight."

"You didn't!"

"Course," admitted the witch, "I never *could* see you, lady."

Elmira pulled out her pocket mirror. "There I am!" She peered closer and gasped. She reached up like someone tuning a harp and plucked a single thread. She held it up, Exhibit A. "I never had a gray hair in my life till this second!"

The witch smiled charmingly. "Put it in a jar of still water, be an angleworm come morning. Oh, Elmira, look at yourself at last, won't you? All these years, blaming others for your own mallet feet and floaty ways! You ever read Shakespeare? There's little stage directions in there: *Alarums and Excursions.* That's you, Elmira. Alarums and Excursions! Now get home before I feel the bumps on your head and predict gas at night for you! Shoo!"

She waved her hands in the air as if Elmira were a cloud of things. "My, the flies are thick this summer!" she said.

She went inside and hooked the door.

"The line is drawn, Mrs. Goodwater," Elmira said, folding her arms. "I'll give you one last chance. Withdraw from the candidacy of the Honeysuckle Lodge or face me face-to-face tomorrow when I run for office and wrest it from you in a fair fight. I'll bring Tom here with me. An innocent good boy. And innocence and good will win the day."

"I wouldn't count on me being innocent, Mrs. Brown," said the boy. "My mother says—"

"Shut up, Tom, good's good! You'll be there on my right hand, boy."

"Yes'm," said Tom.

"If, that is," said Elmira, "I can live through the night with this lady making wax dummies of me—shoving rusty needles through the very heart and soul of them. If you find a great big fig in my bed all shriveled up come sunrise, Tom, you'll know who picked the fruit in the vineyard. And look to see Mrs. Goodwater president till she's a hundred and ninety-five years old."

"Why, lady," said Mrs. Goodwater, "I'm three hundred and five *now*. Used to call me SHE in the old days." She poked her fingers at the street. "Abracadabra-zimmity-ZAM! How's *that?*"

Elmira ran down off the porch.

"Tomorrow!" she cried.

"Till then, lady!" said Mrs. Goodwater.

Tom followed Elmira, shrugging and kicking ants off the sidewalk as he went.

Running across a driveway, Elmira screamed.

"Mrs. Brown!" cried Tom.

A car backing out of a garage ran right over Elmira's right big toe.

MRS. Elmira Brown's foot hurt her in the middle of the night, so she got up and went down to the kitchen and ate some cold chicken and made a neat, painfully accurate list of things. First, illnesses in the past year. Three colds, four mild attacks of indigestion, one seizure of bloat, arthritis, lumbago, what she imagined to be gout, a severe bronchial cough, incipient asthma, and spots on her arms, plus an abscessed semicircular canal which made her reel like a drunken moth some days, backache, head pains, and nausea. Cost of medicine: *ninety-eight dollars and seventy-eight cents.*

Secondly, things broken in the house during the twelve months just past: two lamps, six vases, ten dishes, one soup tureen, two windows, one chair, one sofa cushion, six glasses, and one crystal chandelier prism. Total cost: *twelve dollars and ten cents.*

Thirdly, her pains this very night. Her toe hurt from being run over. Her stomach was upset. Her back was stiff, her legs were pulsing with agony. Her eyeballs felt like wads of blazing cotton. Her tongue tasted like a dust mop. Her ears were belling and ringing away. Cost? She debated, going back to bed.

Ten thousand dollars in personal suffering.

"Try to settle this out of court!" she said half aloud.

"Eh?" said her husband, awake.

She lay down in bed. "I simply refuse to die."

"Beg pardon?" he said.

"I won't die!" she said, staring at the ceiling.

"That's what I always claimed," said her husband, and turned over to snore.

IN the morning, Mrs. Elmira Brown was up early and down to the library and then to the drugstore and back to the house where she was busy mixing all kinds of chemicals when her husband, Sam, came home with an empty mail pouch at noon.

"Lunch's in the icebox." Elmira stirred a green-looking porridge in a large glass.

"Good Lord, what's that?" asked her husband. "Looks like a milk shake been left out in the sun for forty years. Got kind of a fungus on it."

"Fight magic with magic."

"You goin' to *drink that?*"

"Just before I go up into the Honeysuckle Ladies Lodge for the big doings."

Samuel Brown sniffed the concoction. "Take my advice. Get up those steps first, *then* drink it. What's in it?"

"Snow from angels' wings, well, really menthol, to cool hell's fires that burn you, it says in this book I got at the library. The juice of a fresh grape off the vine, for thinking clear sweet thoughts in the face of dark visions, it says. Also red rhubarb, cream of tartar, white sugar, white of eggs, spring water and clover buds with the strength of the good earth in them. Oh, I could go on all day. It's here in the list, good against bad, white against black. I can't lose!"

"Oh, you'll win, all right," said her husband. "But will you *know* it?"

"Think good thoughts. I'm on my way to get Tom for my charm."

"Poor boy," said her husband. "Innocent, like you say, and about to be torn limb from limb, bargain-basement day at the Honeysuckle Lodge."

"Tom'll survive," said Elmira, and, taking the bubbling concoction with her, hid inside a Quaker Oats box with the lid on, went out the door without catching her dress or snagging her new ninety-eight-cent stockings. Realizing this, she was smug all the way to Tom's house where he waited for her in his white summer suit as she had instructed.

"Phew!" said Tom. "What you got in that box?"

"Destiny," said Elmira.

"I sure hope so," said Tom, walking about two paces ahead of her.

THE Honeysuckle Ladies Lodge was full of ladies looking in each other's mirrors and tugging at their skirts and asking to be sure their slips weren't showing.

At one o'clock Mrs. Elmira Brown came up the steps with a boy in white clothes. He was holding his nose and screwing up one eye so he could only half see where he was going. Mrs. Brown looked at the crowd and then at the Quaker Oats box and opened the top and looked in and gasped, and put the top back on without drinking any of that stuff in there. She moved inside the hall and with her moved a rustling as of taffeta, all the ladies whispering in a tide after her.

She sat down in back with Tom, and Tom looked more miserable than ever. The one eye he had open looked at the crowd of ladies and shut up for good. Sitting there, Elmira got the potion out and drank it slowly down.

At one-thirty, the president, Mrs. Goodwater, banged the gavel and all but two dozen of the ladies quit talking.

"Ladies," she called out over the summer sea of silks and laces, capped here and there with white or gray, "it's election time. But before we start, I believe Mrs. Elmira Brown, wife of our eminent graphologist—"

A titter ran through the room.

"What's graphologist?" Elmira elbowed Tom twice.

"I don't know," whispered Tom fiercely, eyes shut, feeling that elbow come out of darkness at him.

"—wife, as I say, of our eminent handwriting expert, Samuel Brown . . . (more laughter) . . . of the U.S. Postal Service," continued Mrs. Goodwater. "Mrs. Brown wants to give us some opinions. Mrs. Brown?"

Elmira stood up. Her chair fell over backward and snapped shut like a bear trap on itself. She jumped an inch off the floor and teetered on her heels, which gave off cracking sounds like they would fall to dust any moment. "I got plenty to say," she said, holding the empty Quaker Oats box in one hand with a Bible. She grabbed Tom with the other and plowed forward, hitting several people's elbows and muttering to them, "Watch what you're doing! Careful, you!" to reach the platform, turn, and knock a glass of water dripping over the table. She gave Mrs. Goodwater another bristly scowl when this happened and let her mop it up with a tiny handkerchief. Then with a secret look of triumph, Elmira drew forth the empty philter glass and held it up, displaying it for Mrs. Goodwater and whispering, "You know what was in this? It's inside me, now, lady. The charmed circle surrounds me. No knife can cleave, no hatchet break through."

The ladies, all talking, did not hear.

Mrs. Goodwater nodded, held up her hands, and there was silence.

Elmira held tight to Tom's hand. Tom kept his eyes shut, wincing.

"Ladies," Elmira said, "I sympathize with you. I know what you've been through these last ten years. I know why you voted for Mrs. Goodwater here. You've got boys, girls, and men to feed. You've got budgets to follow. You couldn't afford to have your milk sour, your bread fall, or your cakes as flat as wheels. You didn't want mumps, chicken pox, and whooping cough in your house all in three weeks. You didn't want your husband crashing his car or electrocuting himself on the high-tension wires outside town. But now all of that's over. You can come out in the open now. No more heartburns or backaches, because I've brought the good word and we're going to exorcise this witch we've got here!"

Everybody looked around but didn't see any witch.

"I mean your *president!*" cried Elmira.

"*Me!*" Mrs. Goodwater waved at everyone.

"Today," breathed Elmira, holding on to the desk for support, "I went to the library. I looked up counteractions. How to get rid of people who take advantage of others, how to make witches leave off and go. And I found a way to fight for all our rights. I can feel the power growing. I got the magic of all kinds of good roots and chemicals in me. I got . . ." She paused and swayed. She blinked once. "I got cream of tartar and . . . I got . . . white hawkweed and milk soured in the light of the moon and . . ." She stopped and thought for a moment. She shut her mouth and a tiny sound came from deep inside her and worked up through to come out the corner of her lips. She closed her eyes for a moment to see where the strength was.

"Mrs. Brown, you feelin' all right?" asked Mrs. Goodwater.

"Feelin' fine!" said Mrs. Brown slowly. "I put in some pulverized carrots and parsley root, cut fine; juniper berry . . ."

Again she paused as if a voice had said STOP to her and she looked out across all those faces.

The room, she noticed, was beginning to turn slowly, first from left to right, then right to left.

"Rosemary roots and crowfoot flower . . ." she said rather dimly. She let go of Tom's hand. Tom opened one eye and looked at her.

"Bay leaves, nasturtium petals . . ." she said.

"Maybe you better sit down," said Mrs. Goodwater.

One lady at the side went and opened a window.

"Dry betel nuts, lavender and crab-apple seed," said Mrs. Brown and stopped. "Quick now, let's have the election. Got to have the votes. I'll tabulate."

"No hurry, Elmira," said Mrs. Goodwater.

"Yes, there is." Elmira took a deep trembling breath. "Remember, ladies, no more fear. Do like you always wanted to do. Vote for me, and . . ." The room was moving again, up and down. "Honesty in government. All those in favor of Mrs. Goodwater for president say 'Aye.' "

"Aye," said the whole room.

"All those in favor of Mrs. Elmira Brown?" said Elmira in a faint voice.

She swallowed.

After a moment she spoke, alone.

"Aye," she said.

She stood stunned on the rostrum.

A silence filled the room from wall to wall. In that silence Mrs. Elmira Brown made a croaking sound. She put her hand on her throat. She turned and looked dimly at Mrs. Goodwater, who now very casually drew forth from her purse a small wax doll in which were a number of rusted thumbtacks.

"Tom," said Elmira, "show me the way to the ladies' room."

"Yes'm."

They began to walk and then hurry and then run. Elmira ran on ahead, through the crowd, down the aisle. . . . She reached the door and started left.

"No, Elmira, right, right!" cried Mrs. Goodwater.

Elmira turned left and vanished.

There was a noise like coal down a chute.

"Elmira!"

The ladies ran around like a girls' basketball team, colliding with each other.

Only Mrs. Goodwater made a straight line.

She found Tom looking down the stairwell, his hands clenched to the banister.

"Forty steps!" he moaned. "Forty steps to the ground!"

LATER on and for months and years after it was told how like an inebriate Elmira Brown negotiated those steps touching every one on her long way down. It was claimed that when she began the fall she was sick to unconsciousness and that this made her skeleton rubber, so she kind of rolled rather than ricocheted. She landed at the bottom, blinking and feeling better, having left whatever it was that had made her uneasy all along the way. True, she was so badly bruised she looked like a tattooed lady. But, no, not a wrist was sprained or an ankle twisted. She held her head funny for three days, kind of peering out of the sides of her eyeballs instead of turning to look. But the important thing was Mrs. Goodwater at the bottom of the steps, pillowing Elmira's head on her lap and dropping tears on her as the ladies gathered hysterically.

"Elmira, I promise, Elmira, I swear, if you just live, if you don't die, you hear me, Elmira, listen! I'll use my magic for nothing but good from now on. No more black, nothing but white magic. The rest of your life, if I have my way, no more falling over iron dogs, tripping on sills, cutting fingers, or dropping downstairs for you! Elysium, Elmira, Elysium, I promise! If you just live! Look, I'm pulling the tacks out of the doll! Elmira, speak to me! Speak now and sit up! And come upstairs for another vote. President, I promise, president of the Honeysuckle Ladies Lodge, by acclamation, won't we, ladies?"

At this all the ladies cried so hard they had to lean on each other.

Tom, upstairs, thought this meant death down there.

He was halfway down when he met the ladies coming back up, looking like they had just wandered out of a dynamite explosion.

"Get out of the way, boy!"

First came Mrs. Goodwater, laughing and crying.

Next came Mrs. Elmira Brown, doing the same.

And after the two of them came all the one hundred twenty-three members of the lodge, not knowing if they'd just returned from a funeral or were on their way to a ball.

He watched them pass and shook his head.

"Don't need me no more," he said. "No more at all."

So he tiptoed down the stairs before they missed him, holding tight to the rail all the way.

Nightside

MERCEDES LACKEY

Modern witches don't have very many powerful role models, but Mercedes Lackey's Diana Tregarde character, in her continuing fight against evil forces, is one of them. Despite only appearing in three horror novels and a handful of short stories, this character's popularity does not seem to wane. "Nightside," an early version of the story that would later become Children of the Night, *gives you an example of this witch/Guardian's—and her author's—lasting appeal.*

IT was early spring, but the wind held no hint of verdancy, not even the promise of it—it was chill and odorless, and there were ghosts of dead leaves skittering before it. A few of them jittered into the pool of weak yellow light cast by the aging streetlamp—a converted gaslight that was a relic of the previous century. It was old and tired, its pea-green paint flaking away; as weary as this neighborhood, which was older still. Across the street loomed an ancient church, its congregation dwindled over the years to a handful of little old women and men who appeared like scrawny blackbirds every Sunday, and then scattered back to the shabby houses that stood to either side of it until Sunday should come again. On the side of the street that the lamp tried (and failed) to illuminate, was the cemetery.

Like the neighborhood, it was very old—in this case, fifty years shy of being classified as "Colonial." There were few empty gravesites now, and most of those belonged to the same little old ladies and men that had lived and would die here. It was protected from vandals by a thorny hedge as well as a ten-foot wrought-iron fence. Within its confines, as seen through the leafless branches of the hedge, granite cenotaphs and enormous Victorian monuments bulked shapelessly against the bare sliver of a waning moon.

The church across the street was dark and silent; the houses up and down the block showed few lights, if any. There was no reason for anyone of this neighborhood to be out in the night.

So the young woman waiting beneath the lamp-post seemed that much more out-of-place.

Nor could she be considered a typical resident of this neighborhood by any stretch of the imagination—for one thing, she was young; perhaps in her mid-twenties, but no more. Her clothing was neat but casual, too casual for someone visiting an elderly relative. She wore dark, knee-high boots, old, soft jeans tucked into their tops, and a thin windbreaker open at the front to show a leotard beneath. Her attire was far too light to be any real protection against the bite of the wind, yet she seemed unaware of the cold. Her hair was long, down to her waist, and straight—in the uncertain light of the lamp it was an indeterminate shadow, and it fell down her back like a waterfall. Her eyes were large and oddly slanted, but not Oriental; catlike, rather. Even the way she held herself was feline; poised, expectant—a graceful tension like a dancer's or a hunting predator's. She was not watching for something—no, her eyes were unfocused with concentration. She was *listening*.

A soft whistle, barely audible, carried down the street on the chill wind. The tune was of a piece with the neighborhood—old and time-worn.

Many of the residents would have smiled in recollection to hear "Lili Marlene" again.

The tension left the girl as she swung around the lamp-post by one hand to face the direction of the whistle. She waved, and a welcoming smile warmed her eyes.

The whistler stepped into the edge of the circle of light. He, too, was dusky of eye and hair—and heartbreakingly handsome. He wore only dark jeans and a black turtleneck, no coat at all—but like the young woman, he didn't seem to notice the cold. There was an impish glint in his eyes as he finished the tune with a flourish.

"A flair for the dramatic, Diana, *mon cherie?*" he said mockingly. "Would that you were here for the same purpose as the lovely Lili! Alas, I fear my luck cannot be so good . . ."

She laughed. His eyes warmed at the throaty chuckle. "Andre," she chided, "don't you ever think of anything else?"

"Am I not a son of the City of Light? I must uphold her reputation, *mais non?*" The young woman raised an ironic brow. He shrugged. "Ah well—since it is you who seek me, I fear I must be all business. A pity. Well, what lures you to my side this unseasonable night? What horror has *mademoiselle* Tregarde unearthed this time?"

Diana Tregarde sobered instantly, the laughter fleeing her eyes. "I'm afraid you picked the right word this time, Andre. It *is* a horror. The trouble is, I don't know what kind."

"Say on. I wait in breathless anticipation." His expression was mocking as he leaned against the lamp-post, and he feigned a yawn.

Diana scowled at him and her eyes darkened with anger. He raised an eyebrow of his own. "If this weren't so serious," she threatened, "I'd be tempted to pop you one—Andre, people are dying out there. There's a 'Ripper' loose in New York."

He shrugged, and shifted restlessly from one foot to the other. "So? This is new? Tell me when there is *not!* That sort of criminal is as common to the city as a rat. Let your police earn their salaries and capture him."

Her expression hardened. She folded her arms tightly across the thin nylon of her windbreaker; her lips tightened a little. "Use your head, Andre! If this was an ordinary slasher-killer, would *I* be involved?"

He examined his fingernails with care. "And what is it that makes it *extraordinaire,* eh?"

"The victims had no souls."

"I was not aware," he replied wryly, "that the dead possessed such things anymore."

She growled under her breath, and tossed her head impatiently, and the wind caught her hair and whipped it around her throat. "You are *deliberately* being difficult! I have half a mind—"

It finally seemed to penetrate the young man's mind that she was truly angry—and truly frightened, though she was doing her best to conceal the fact; his expression became contrite. "Forgive me, *cherie*. I *am* being recalcitrant."

"You're being a pain in the ass," she replied acidly. "Would I have come to you if I wasn't already out of my depth?"

"Well—" he admitted. "No. But—this business of souls, *cherie,* how can you determine such a thing? I find it most difficult to believe."

She shivered, and her eyes went brooding. "So did I. Trust me, my friend, I know what I'm talking about. There isn't a shred of doubt in my mind. There are at least six victims who no longer exist in *any* fashion anymore."

The young man finally evidenced alarm. "But—how?" he said, bewildered. "How is such a thing possible?"

She shook her head violently, clenching her hands on the arms of her jacket as if by doing so she could protect herself from an unseen—but not unfelt—danger. "I don't know, I don't know! It seems incredible even now—I keep thinking it's a nightmare, but—Andre, it's real, it's not my imagination—" Her voice rose a little with each word, and Andre's sharp eyes rested for a moment on her trembling hands.

"Eh bien," he sighed, "I believe you. So there is something about that devours souls—and mutilates bodies as well, since you mentioned a 'Ripper' persona?"

She nodded.

"Was the devouring before or after the mutilation?"

"Before, I think—it's not easy to judge." She shivered in a way that had nothing to do with the cold.

"And you came into this how?"

"Whatever it is, it took the friend of a friend; I—happened to be there to see the body afterwards, and I knew immediately there was something wrong. When I unshielded and used the Sight—"

"Bad." He made it a statement.

"Worse. I—I can't describe what it felt like. There were still residual emotions, things left behind when—" Her jaw clenched. "Then when I started checking further I found out about the other five victims—that what I had discovered was no fluke. Andre, whatever it is, it has to be stopped." She laughed again, but this time there was no humor in it. "After all, you could say stopping it is in my job description."

He nodded soberly. "And so you become involved. Well enough, if you must hunt this thing, so must I." He became all business. "Tell me of the history. When, and where, and who does it take?"

She bit her lip. " 'Where'—there's no pattern. 'Who' seems to be mostly a matter of opportunity; the only clue is that the victims were always out on the street and entirely alone, there were no witnesses whatsoever, so the thing needs total privacy and apparently can't strike where it will. And 'when'—is moon-dark."

"Bad." He shook his head. "I have no clue at the moment. The *loup-garou* I know, and others, but I know nothing that hunts beneath the dark moon."

She grimaced. "You think I do? That's why I need your help; you're sensitive enough to feel something out of the ordinary, and you can watch and hunt undetected. I can't. And I'm not sure I *want* to go trolling for this thing alone—without knowing what it is, I could end up as a late-night snack for it. But if that's what I have to do, I will."

Anger blazed up in his face like a cold fire. "You go hunting alone for this creature over my dead body!"

"That's a little redundant, isn't it?" Her smile was weak, but genuine again.

"Pah!" he dismissed her attempt at humor with a wave of his hand. "Tomorrow is the first night of moon-dark; *I* shall go a-hunting. Do *you* remain at home, else I shall be most wroth with you. I know where to find you, should I learn anything of note."

"You ought to—" Diana began, but she spoke to the empty air.

THE next night was warmer, and Diana had gone to bed with her windows open to drive out some of the stale odors the long winter had left in her apartment. Not that the air of New York City was exactly fresh—but it was better than what the heating system kept recycling through the building. She didn't particularly like leaving her defenses open while she slept, but the lingering memory of Katy Rourk's fish wafting through the halls as she came in from shopping had decided her. Better exhaust fumes than burned haddock.

She hadn't had an easy time falling asleep, and when she finally managed to do so, tossed restlessly, her dreams uneasy and readily broken——as by the sound of someone in the room.

Before the intruder crossed even half the distance between the window and her bed, she was wide awake, and moving. She threw herself out of bed, somersaulted across her bedroom, and wound up crouched beside the door, one hand on the light switch, the other holding a polished dagger she'd taken from beneath her pillow.

As the lights came on, she saw Andre standing in the center of the bedroom, blinking in surprise, wearing a sheepish grin.

Relief made her knees go weak. "Andre, you *idiot!*" She tried to control her tone, but her voice was shrill and cracked a little. "You could have been *killed!*"

He spread his hands wide in a placating gesture. "Now, Diana—"

" 'Now Diana' my eye!" she growled. "Even *you* would have a hard time getting around a severed spine!" She stood up slowly, shaking from head to toe with released tension.

"I didn't wish to wake you," he said, crestfallen.

She closed her eyes and took several long, deep, calming breaths; focusing on a mantra, moving herself back into stillness until she knew she would be able to reply without screaming at him.

"Don't," she said carefully, "Ever. Do. That. Again." She punctuated the last word by driving the dagger she held into the doorframe.

"*Certainement, ma petite,*" he replied, his eyes widening a little as he began to calculate how fast she'd moved. "The next time I come in your window when you sleep, I shall blow a trumpet first."

"You'd be a *lot* safer. *I'd* be a lot happier," she said crossly, pulling the dagger loose with a snap of her wrist. She palmed the light switch and dimmed the lamps down to where they would be comfortable to his light-sensitive eyes, then crossed the room, the plush brown carpet warm and soft under her bare feet. She bent slightly, and put the silver-plated dagger back under her pillow. Then with a sigh she folded her long legs beneath her to sit on her rumpled bed. This was the first time Andre had ever caught her asleep, and she was irritated far beyond what her disturbed dreams warranted. She was somewhat obsessed with her privacy and with keeping her night-boundaries unbreached—she and Andre were off-and-on lovers, but she'd never let him stay any length of time.

He approached the antique wooden bed slowly. "*Cherie,* this was no idle visit—"

"I should bloody well hope not!" she interrupted, trying to soothe her jangled nerves by combing the tangles out of her hair with her fingers.

"—I have seen your killer."

She froze.

"It is nothing I have ever seen or heard of before."

She clenched her hands on the strand of hair they held, ignoring the pull. "Go on—"

"It—no, *he*—I could not detect until he made his first kill tonight. I found him then, found him just before he took his hunting-shape, or I never would have discovered him at all; for when he is in that shape there is nothing about him that *I* could sense that marked him as different. So ordinary—a man, an Oriental; Japanese, I think, and like many others— not young, not old; not fat, not thin. So unremarkable as to be invisible. I followed him—he was so normal I found it difficult to believe what my own eyes had seen a moment before; then, not ten minutes later, he found yet another victim and—fed again."

He closed his eyes, his face thoughtful. "As I said, I have never seen or heard of his like, yet—yet there was something familiar about him. I cannot even tell you what it was, and yet it was familiar."

"You said you saw him attack—*how*, Andre?" She leaned forward, her face tight with urgency as the bed creaked a little beneath her.

"The second quarry was—the—is it 'bag lady' you say?" At her nod he continued. "He smiled at her—just smiled, that was all. She froze like the frightened rabbit. Then he—changed—into dark, dark smoke; only smoke, nothing more. The smoke enveloped the old woman until I could see her no longer. Then—he fed. I—I can understand your feelings now, *cherie*. It was—nothing to the eye, but—what I felt *within*—"

"Now you see," she said gravely.

"*Mais oui,* and you have no more argument from me. This thing is abomination, and must be ended."

"The question is—" She grimaced.

"How? I have given some thought to this. One cannot fight smoke. But in his hunting form—I think perhaps he is vulnerable to physical measures. As you say, even *I* would have difficulty in dealing with a severed spine or crushed brain. I think maybe it would be the same for him. Have you the courage to play the wounded bird, *ma petite?*" He sat beside her on the edge of the bed and regarded her with solemn and worried eyes.

She considered that for a moment. "Play bait while you wait for him to move in? It sounds like the best plan to me—it wouldn't be the first time I've done that, and I'm not exactly helpless, you know," she replied, twisting a strand of hair around her fingers.

"I think you have finally proved that to me tonight!" There was a hint of laughter in his eyes again, as well as chagrin. "I shall never again make the mistake of thinking you to be a fragile flower. *Bien.* Is tomorrow night too soon for you?"

"Tonight wouldn't be too soon," she stated flatly.

"Except that he has already gone to lair, having fed twice." He took one of her hands, freeing it from the lock of hair she had twisted about it. "No, we rest—I know where he is to be found, and tomorrow night we face him at full strength." Abruptly he grinned. "*Cherie,* I have read one of your books—"

She winced, and closed her eyes in a grimace. "Oh Lord—I was afraid you'd ferret out one of my pseudonyms. You're as bad as the Elephant's Child when it comes to 'satiable curiosity.' "

"It was hardly difficult to guess the author when she used one of my favorite expressions for the title—and then described me so very intimately not three pages from the beginning."

Her expression was woeful. "Oh *no!* Not *that* one!"

He shook an admonishing finger at her. "I do not think it kind, to make me the villain, and all because I told you I spent a good deal of the Regency in London."

"But—but—Andre, these things follow *formulas,* I didn't really have a choice—anybody French in a Regency romance *has* to be either an expatriate aristocrat or a villain—" She bit her lip and looked pleadingly at him. "—I needed a villain and I didn't have a clue—I was in the middle of that phony medium thing *and* I had a deadline—and—" Her words thinned down to a whisper, "—to tell you the truth, I didn't think you'd ever find out. You—you aren't angry, are you?"

He lifted the hair away from her shoulder, cupped his hand beneath her chin and moved close beside her. "I *think* I may possibly be induced to forgive you—"

The near-chuckle in his voice told her she hadn't offended him. Reassured by that, she looked up at him, slyly. "Oh?"

"You could—" He slid her gown off her shoulder a little, and ran an inquisitive finger from the tip of her shoulder blade to just behind her ear "—write another, and let me play the hero—"

"Have you any—suggestions?" she replied, finding it difficult to reply when his mouth followed where his finger had been.

"In that 'Burning Passions' series, perhaps?"

She pushed him away, laughing. "The soft-core porn for housewives? Andre, you can't be serious!"

"Never more." He pulled her back. "Think of how enjoyable the research would be—"

She grabbed his hand again before it could resume its explorations. "Aren't we supposed to be resting?"

He stopped for a moment, and his face and eyes were deadly serious. "*Cherie,* we must face this thing at strength. You need sleep—and to relax. Can you think of any better way to relax body and spirit than—"

"No," she admitted. "I always sleep like a rock when you get done with me."

"Well then. And I—I have needs; I have not tended to those needs for too long, if I am to have full strength, and I should not care to meet this creature at less than that."

"Excuses, excuses—" She briefly contemplated getting up long enough to take care of the lights—then decided a little waste of energy was worth it, and extinguished them with a thought. "C'mere, you—let's do some research."

He laughed deep in his throat as they reached for one another with the same eager hunger.

SHE woke late the next morning—so late that in a half hour it would have been "afternoon"—and lay quietly for a long, contented moment before wriggling out of the tumble of bedclothes and Andre. No fear of waking him—he wouldn't rouse until the sun went down. She arranged him a bit more comfortably and tucked him in, thinking that he looked absurdly young with his hair all rumpled and those long, dark lashes of his lying against his cheek—he looked much better this morning, now that she was in a position to pay attention. Last night he'd been pretty pale and hungry-thin. She shook her head over him. Someday his gallantry was going to get him into trouble. "Idiot—" she whispered, touching his forehead, "—all you ever have to do is *ask*—"

But there were other things to take care of—and to think of. A fight to get ready for; and she had a premonition it wasn't going to be an easy one.

So she showered and changed into a leotard, and took herself into her barren studio at the back of the apartment to run through her *katas* three times—once slow, twice at full speed—and then into some *Tai Chi* exercises to rebalance everything. She followed that with a half hour of meditation, then cast a circle and charged herself with all of the Power she thought she could safely carry.

Without knowing what it was she was to face, that was all she could do, really—that, and have a really good dinner—

She showered and changed again into a bright red sweatsuit and was just finishing dinner when the sun set and Andre strolled into the white-painted kitchen, shirtless, and blinking sleepily.

She gulped the last bite of her liver and waggled her fingers at him. "If you want a shower, you'd better get a fast one—I want to get in place before he comes out for the night."

He sighed happily over the prospect of a hot shower. "The perfect way to start one's—day. *Petite,* you may have difficulty in dislodging me now that you have let me stay overnight—"

She showed her teeth. "Don't count your chickens, kiddo. I can be very nasty!"

"Ma petite—I—" He suddenly sobered, and looked at her with haunted eyes.

She saw his expression and abruptly stopped teasing. "Andre—please don't say it—I can't give you any better answer now than I could when you first asked—if I—cared for you as more than a friend."

He sighed again, less happily. "Then I will say no more, because you wish it—but—what of this notion—would you permit me to stay with you? No more than that. I could be of some use to you, I think, and I would take nothing from you that you did not offer first. I do not like it that you are so much alone. It did not matter when we first met, but you are collecting powerful enemies, *cherie.*"

"I—" She wouldn't look at him, but only at her hands, clenched white-knuckled on the table.

"Unless there are others—" he prompted, hesitantly.

"No—no, there isn't anyone but you." She sat in silence for a moment, then glanced back up at him with one eyebrow lifted sardonically. "You *do* rather spoil a girl for anyone else's attentions."

He was genuinely startled. *"Mille pardons, cherie,"* he stuttered, "I—I did not know—"

She managed a feeble chuckle. "Oh Andre, you idiot—I *like* being spoiled! I don't get many things that are just for me—" she sighed, then gave in to his pleading eyes. "All right then, move in if you want—"

"It is what *you* want that concerns me."

"I want," she said, very softly. "Just—the commitment—don't ask for it. I've got responsibilities as well as Power, you know that; I—can't see how to balance them with what you offered before—"

"Enough," he silenced her with a wave of his hand. "The words are unsaid, we will speak of this no more unless you wish it. I seek the embrace of warm water—"

She turned her mind to the dangers ahead, resolutely pushing the dangers *he* represented into the back of her mind. "And I will go bail the car out of the garage."

HE waited until he was belted in on the passenger's side of the car to comment on her outfit. "I did not know you planned to race him, Diana," he said with a quirk of one corner of his mouth.

"Urban camouflage," she replied, dodging two taxis and a kamikaze panel truck. "Joggers are everywhere, and they run at night a lot in deserted neighborhoods. Cops won't wonder about me or try to stop me, and our boy won't be surprised to see me alone. One of his other victims was out running. His boyfriend thought he'd had a heart attack. Poor thing. He wasn't one of us, so I didn't enlighten him. There are some things it's better the survivors don't know."

"*Oui.* Left here, *cherie.*"

The traffic thinned down to a trickle, then to nothing. There are odd little islands in New York at night; places as deserted as the loneliest country road. The area where Andre directed her was one such; by day it was small warehouses, one floor factories, an odd store or two. None of them had enough business to warrant running second or third shifts, and the neighborhood had not been gentrified yet, so no one actually lived here. There were a handful of night-watchmen, perhaps, but most of these places depended on locks, burglar-alarms, and dogs that were released at night to keep out intruders.

"There—" Andre pointed at a building that appeared to be home to several small manufactories. "He took the smoke-form and went to roost in the elevator control house at the top. That is why I did not advise going against him by day."

"Is he there now?" Diana peered up through the glare of sodium-vapor lights, but couldn't make out the top of the building.

Andre closed his eyes, a frown of concentration creasing his forehead. "No," he said after a moment. "I think he has gone hunting."

She repressed a shiver. "Then it's time to play bait."

Diana found a parking space marked dimly with the legend "President"—she thought it unlikely it would be wanted within the next few hours. It was deep in the shadow of the building Andre had pointed out, and her car was dead-black; with any luck, cops coming by wouldn't even notice it was there and start to wonder.

She hopped out, locking her door behind her, looking now exactly like the lone jogger she was pretending to be, and set off at an easy pace. She did not look back.

If absolutely necessary, she knew she'd be able to keep this up for hours. She decided to take all the north-south streets first, then weave back along the east-west. Before the first hour was up she was wishing she'd dared bring a "walk-thing"—every street was like every other street; blank brick walls broken by dusty, barred windows and metal doors, alleys with only the occasional dumpster visible, refuse blowing along the gutters. She was bored; her nervousness had worn off, and she was lonely. She ran from light to darkness, from darkness to light, and saw and heard nothing but the occasional rat.

Then he struck, just when she was beginning to get a little careless. Careless enough not to see him arrive.

One moment there was nothing, the next, he was before her, waiting halfway down the block. She knew it was him—he was exactly as Andre had described him, a nondescript Oriental man in a dark windbreaker and slacks. He was tall for an Oriental—taller than she by several inches. His appearance nearly startled her into stopping—then she remembered that she was supposed to be an innocent jogger, and resumed her steady trot.

She knew he meant her to see him, he was standing directly beneath the streetlight and right in the middle of the sidewalk. She would have to swerve out of her path to avoid him.

She started to do just that, ignoring him as any real jogger would have—when he raised his head and smiled at her.

She was stopped dead in her tracks by the purest terror she had ever felt in her life. She froze, as all of his other victims must have—unable to think, unable to cry out, unable to run. Her legs had gone numb, and nothing existed for her but that terrible smile and those hard, black eyes that had no bottom—

Then the smile vanished, and the eyes flinched away. Diana could move again, and staggered back against the brick wall of the building behind her, her breath coming in harsh pants, the brick rough and comforting in its reality beneath her hands.

"Diana?" It was Andre's voice behind her.

"I'm—all right—" she said, not at all sure that she really was.

Andre strode silently past her, face grim and purposeful. The man seemed to sense his purpose, and smiled again—

But Andre never faltered for even the barest moment.

The smile wavered and faded; the man fell back a step or two, surprised that his weapon had failed him—

Then he scowled, and pulled something out of the sleeve of his windbreaker; and to Diana's surprise, charged straight for Andre, his sneakered feet scuffing on the cement—

And something suddenly blurring about his right hand. As it connected with Andre's upraised left arm, Diana realized what it was—almost too late.

"Andre—he has nunchuks—they're *wood*," she cried out urgently as Andre grunted in unexpected pain. "He can *kill* you with them! Get the *hell* out of here!"

Andre needed no second warning. In the blink of an eye, he was gone.

Leaving Diana to face the creature alone.

She dropped into guard-stance as he regarded her thoughtfully, still making no sound, not even of heavy breathing. In a moment he seemed to make up his mind, and came for her.

At least he didn't smile again in that terrible way—perhaps the weapon was only effective once.

She hoped fervently he wouldn't try again—as an empath, she was doubly-vulnerable to a weapon forged of fear.

They circled each other warily, like two cats preparing to fight—then Diana thought she saw an opening—and took it.

And quickly came to the conclusion that she was overmatched, as he sent her tumbling with a badly bruised shin. The next few moments reinforced that conclusion—as he continued scatheless while she picked up injury after painful injury.

She was a brown-belt in karate—but he was a black-belt in kung-fu, and the contest was a pathetically uneven match. She knew before very long that he was toying with her—and while he still swung the wooden nunchuks, Andre did not dare move in close enough to help.

She realized (as fear dried her mouth, she grew more and more winded, and she searched frantically for a means of escape) that she was as good as dead.

If only she could get those damn chucks away from him!

And as she ducked and stumbled against the curb, narrowly avoiding the strike he made at her, an idea came to her. He knew from her moves—as she knew from his—that she was no amateur. He would never expect an amateur's move from her—something truly stupid and suicidal—

So the next time he swung at her, she stood her ground. As the 'chuk came at her she took one step forward, smashing his nose with the heel of her right hand and lifting her left to intercept the flying baton.

As it connected with her left hand with a sickening crunch, she whirled and folded her entire body around hand and weapon, and went limp, carrying it away from him.

She collapsed in a heap at his feet, hand afire with pain, eyes blurring with it, and waited for either death or salvation.

And salvation in the form of Andre rose behind her attacker. With one *savate* kick he broke the man's back; Diana could hear it cracking like green wood—and before her assailant could collapse, a second double-handed blow sent him crashing into the brick wall, head crushed like an eggshell.

Diana struggled to her feet, and waited for some arcane transformation.

Nothing.

She staggered to the corpse, face flat and expressionless—a sign she was suppressing pain and shock with utterly implacable iron will. Andre began to move forward as if to stop her, then backed off again at the look in her eyes.

She bent slightly, just enough to touch the shoulder of the body with her good hand—and released the Power.

Andre pulled her back to safety as the corpse exploded into flame, burning as if it had been soaked in oil. She watched the flames for one moment, wooden-faced; then abruptly collapsed.

Andre caught her easily before she could hurt herself further, lifting her in his arms as if she weighed no more than a kitten. "*Ma pauvre petite,*" he murmured, heading back towards the car at a swift but silent run, "It is the hospital for you, I think—"

"Saint—Francis—" she gasped, every step jarring her hand and bringing tears of pain to her eyes, "One of us—is on the night-staff—Dr. Crane—"

"*Bien,*" he replied. "Now be silent—"

"But—how are you—"

"In your car, foolish one. I have the keys you left in it."

"But—"

"I can drive."

"But—"

"*And* I have a license. Will you be silent?"

"How?" she said, disobeying him.

"Night school," he replied succinctly, reaching the car, putting her briefly on her feet to unlock the passenger-side door, then lifting her into it. "You are not the only one who knows of urban camouflage."

This time she did not reply—mostly because she had fainted from pain.

THE emergency room was empty—for which Andre was very grateful. His invocation of Dr. Crane brought a thin, bearded young man around to the tiny examining cubicle in record time.

"Good godalmighty! What did you tangle with, a bus?" he exclaimed, when stripping the sweatsuit jacket and pants revealed that there was little of Diana that was not battered and black-and-blue.

Andre wrinkled his nose at the acrid antiseptic odors around them, and replied shortly. "No. Your 'Ripper.' "

The startled gaze the doctor fastened on him revealed that Andre had scored. "Who—won?" he asked at last.

"We did. I do not think he will prey upon anyone again."

The doctor's eyes closed briefly; Andre read prayerful thankfulness on his face as he sighed with relief. Then he returned to business. "You must be Andre, right? Anything I can supply?"

Andre laughed at the hesitation in his voice. "Fear not, your blood supply is quite safe, and I am unharmed. It is Diana who needs you."

The relief on the doctor's face made Andre laugh again.

Dr. Crane ignored him. "Right," he said, turning to the work *he* knew best.

SHE was lightheaded and groggy with the Demerol Dr. Crane had given her as Andre deftly stripped her and tucked her into her bed; she'd dozed all the way home in the car.

"I just wish I knew *what* that thing was—" she said inconsequentially, as he arranged her arm in its light Fiberglas cast a little more comfortably. "—I won't be happy until I *know*—"

"Then you are about to be happy, *cherie,* for I have had the brainstorm—" Andre ducked into the living room and emerged with a dusty leather-bound book. "Remember I said there was something familiar about it? Now I think I know what it was." He consulted the index, and turned pages rapidly—found the place he sought, and read for a few moments. "As I thought—listen. 'The *gaki*—also known as the Japanese vampire—also takes its nourishment only from the living. There are many kinds of *gaki,* extracting their sustenance from a wide variety of sources. The most harmless are the "perfume" and "music" *gaki*—and they are by far the most common. Far deadlier are those that require blood, flesh—or souls.' "

"Souls?"

"Just so. 'To feed, or when at rest, they take their normal form of a dense cloud of dark smoke. At other times, like the *kitsune,* they take on the form of a human being. Unlike the *kitsune,* however, there is no way to distinguish them in this form from any other human. In the smoke form, they are invulnerable—in the human form, however, they can be killed; but to permanently destroy them, the body must be burned—preferably in conjunction with or solely by Power.' I said there was something familiar about it—it seems to have been a kind of distant cousin." Andre's mouth smiled, but his eyes reflected only a long-abiding bitterness.

"There is *no way* you have any relationship with that—thing!" she said forcefully. "It had no more honor, heart, or soul than a rabid beast!"

"I—I thank you, *cherie,*" he said, slowly, the warmth returning to his eyes. "There are not many who would think as you do."

"Their own closed-minded stupidity."

"To change the subject—what was it made you burn it as you did? I would have abandoned it. It seemed dead enough."

"I don't know—it just seemed the thing to do," she yawned. "Sometimes my instincts just work . . . right. . . ."

Suddenly her eyes seemed too leaden to keep open.

"Like they did with you. . . ." She fought against exhaustion and the drug, trying to keep both at bay.

But without success. Sleep claimed her for its own.

He watched her for the rest of the night, until the leaden lethargy of his own limbs told him dawn was near. He had already decided not to share her bed, lest any movement on his part cause her pain—instead, he made up a pallet on the floor beside her.

He stood over her broodingly while he in his turn fought slumber, and touched her face gently. "Well—" he whispered, holding off torpor far deeper and heavier than hers could ever be—while she was mortal. "You are not aware to hear, so I may say what I will and you cannot forbid. Dream; sleep and dream—I shall see you safe—my only love."

And he took his place beside her, to lie motionless until night should come again.

The Witch

ANTON CHEKHOV

In his own hangdog way, Russian author Anton Chekhov relates the pitfalls of a common theme in witch literature—the beautiful but perilous witch wife.

IT was approaching nightfall. The sexton, Savely Gykin, was lying in his huge bed in the hut adjoining the church. He was not asleep, though it was his habit to go to sleep at the same time as the hens. His coarse red hair peeped from under one end of the greasy patchwork quilt, made up of colored rags, while his big unwashed feet stuck out from the other. He was listening. His hut adjoined the wall that encircled the church and the solitary window in it looked out upon the open country. And out there a regular battle was going on. It was hard to say who was being wiped off the face of the earth, and for the sake of whose destruction nature was being churned up into such a ferment; but, judging from the unceasing malignant roar, someone was getting it very hot. A victorious force was in full chase over the fields, storming in the forest and on the church roof, battering spitefully with its fists upon the windows, raging and tearing, while something vanquished was howling and wailing. . . . A plaintive lament sobbed at the window, on the roof, or in the stove. It sounded not like a call for help, but like a cry of misery, a consciousness that it was too late, that there was no salvation. The snowdrifts were covered with a thin coating of ice; tears quivered on them and on the trees; a dark slush of mud and melting snow flowed along the roads and paths. In short, it was thawing, but through the dark night the heavens failed to see it, and flung flakes of fresh snow upon the melting earth at a terrific rate. And the wind staggered like a drunkard. It would not let the snow settle on the ground, and whirled it round in the darkness at random.

Savely listened to all this din and frowned. The fact was that he knew, or at any rate suspected, what all this racket outside the window was tending to and whose handiwork it was.

"I know!" he muttered, shaking his finger menacingly under the bed-clothes; "I know all about it."

On a stool by the window sat the sexton's wife, Raissa Nilovna. A tin lamp standing on another stool, as though timid and distrustful of its powers, shed a dim and flickering light on her broad shoulders, on the handsome, tempting-looking contours of her person, and on her thick plait, which reached to the floor.

She was making sacks out of coarse hempen stuff. Her hands moved nimbly, while her whole body, her eyes, her eyebrows, her full lips, her white neck were as still as though they were asleep, absorbed in the mo-notonous, mechanical toil. Only from time to time she raised her head to rest her weary neck, glanced for a moment towards the window, be-yond which the snowstorm was raging, and bent again over her sacking. No desire, no joy, no grief, nothing was expressed by her handsome face with its turned-up nose and its dimples. So a beautiful fountain expresses nothing when it is not playing.

But at last she had finished a sack. She flung it aside, and, stretching luxuriously, rested her motionless, lack-lustre eyes on the window. The panes were swimming with drops like tears, and white with short-lived snowflakes which fell on the window, glanced at Raissa, and melted. . . .

"Come to bed!" growled the sexton. Raissa remained mute. But sud-denly her eyelashes flickered and there was a gleam of attention in her eye. Savely, all the time watching her expression from under the quilt, put out his head and asked:

"What is it?"

"Nothing. . . . I fancy someone's coming," she answered quietly.

The sexton flung the quilt off with his arms and legs, knelt up in bed, and looked blankly at his wife. The timid light of the lamp illuminated his hirsute, pock-marked countenance and glided over his rough matted hair.

"Do you hear?" asked his wife.

Through the monotonous roar of the storm he caught a scarcely au-dible thin and jingling monotone like the shrill note of a gnat when it wants to settle on one's cheek and is angry at being prevented.

"It's the post," muttered Savely, squatting on his heels.

Two miles from the church ran the posting road. In windy weather, when the wind was blowing from the road to the church, the inmates of the hut caught the sound of bells.

"Lord! Fancy people wanting to drive about in such weather," sighed Raissa.

"It's government work. You've to go whether you like or not."

The murmur hung in the air and died away.

"It has driven by," said Savely, getting into bed.

But before he had time to cover himself up with the bedclothes he heard a distinct sound of the bell. The sexton looked anxiously at his wife, leapt out of bed and walked, waddling, to and fro by the stove. The bell went on ringing for a little, then died away again as though it had ceased.

"I don't hear it," said the sexton, stopping and looking at his wife with his eyes screwed up.

But at that moment the wind rapped on the window and with it floated a shrill jingling note. Savely turned pale, cleared his throat, and flopped about the floor with his bare feet again.

"The postman is lost in the storm," he wheezed out glancing malignantly at his wife. "Do you hear? The postman has lost his way! . . . I . . . I know! Do you suppose I . . . don't understand?" he muttered. "I know all about it, curse you!"

"What do you know?" Raissa asked quietly, keeping her eyes fixed on the window.

"I know that it's all your doing, you she-devil! Your doing, damn you! This snowstorm and the post going wrong, you've done it all—you!"

"You're mad, you silly," his wife answered calmly.

"I've been watching you for a long time past and I've seen it. From the first day I married you I noticed that you'd bitch's blood in you!"

"Tfoo!" said Raissa, surprised, shrugging her shoulders and crossing herself. "Cross yourself, you fool!"

"A witch is a witch," Savely pronounced in a hollow, tearful voice, hurriedly blowing his nose on the hem of his shirt; "though you are my wife, though you are of a clerical family, I'd say what you are even at *confession.* . . . Why, God have mercy upon us! Last year on the Eve of the Prophet Daniel and the Three Young Men there was a snowstorm, and what happened then? The mechanic came in to warm himself. Then on St. Alexey's Day the ice broke on the river and the district policeman turned up, and he was chatting with you all night . . . the damned brute! And when he came out in the morning and I looked at him, he had rings under his eyes and his cheeks were hollow! Eh? During the August fast there were two storms and each time the huntsman turned up. I saw it all, damn him! Oh, she is redder than a crab now, aha!"

"You didn't see anything."

"Didn't I! And this winter before Christmas on the Day of the Ten Martyrs of Crete, when the storm lasted for a whole day and night—do you remember?—the marshal's clerk was lost, and turned up here, the hound. . . . *Tfoo!* To be tempted by the clerk! It was worth upsetting God's weather for him! A drivelling scribbler, not a foot from the ground, pimples all over his mug and his neck awry! If he were good-looking, anyway—but he, *tfoo!* he is as ugly as Satan!"

The sexton took breath, wiped his lips and listened. The bell was not to be heard, but the wind banged on the roof, and again there came a tinkle in the darkness.

"And it's the same thing now!" Savely went on. "It's not for nothing the postman is lost! Blast my eyes if the postman isn't looking for you! Oh, the devil is a good hand at his work; he is a fine one to help! He will turn him round and round and bring him here. I know, I see! You can't conceal it, you devil's bauble, you heathen wanton! As soon as the storm began I knew what you were up to."

"Here's a fool!" smiled his wife. "Why, do you suppose, you thick-head, that I make the storm?"

"H'm! . . . Grin away! Whether it's your doing or not, I only know that when your blood's on fire there's sure to be bad weather, and when there's bad weather there's bound to be some crazy fellow turning up here. It happens so every time! So it must be you!"

To be more impressive the sexton put his finger to his forehead, closed his left eye, and said in a singsong voice:

"Oh, the madness! oh, the unclean Judas! If you really are a human being and not a witch, you ought to think what if he is not the mechanic, or the clerk, or the huntsman, but the devil in their form! Ah! You'd better think of that!"

"Why, you are stupid, Savely," said his wife, looking at him compassionately. "When father was alive and living here, all sorts of people used to come to him to be cured of the ague: from the village, and the hamlets, and the Armenian settlement. They came almost every day, and no one called them devils. But if anyone once a year comes in bad weather to warm himself, you wonder at it, you silly, and take all sorts of notions into your head at once."

His wife's logic touched Savely. He stood with his bare feet wide apart, bent his head, and pondered. He was not firmly convinced yet of the truth of his suspicions, and his wife's genuine and unconcerned tone quite disconcerted him. Yet after a moment's thought he wagged his head and said:

"It's not as though they were old men or bandy-legged cripples; it's always young men who want to come for the night . . . Why is that? And if they only wanted to warm themselves—But they are up to mischief. No, woman; there's no creature in this world as cunning as your female sort! Of real brains you've not an ounce, less than a starling, but for devilish slyness—oo-oo-oo! The Queen of Heaven protect us! There is the postman's bell! When the storm was only beginning I knew all that was in your mind. That's your witchery, you spider!"

"Why do you keep on at me, you heathen?" His wife lost her patience at last. "Why do you keep sticking to it like pitch?"

"I stick to it because if anything—God forbid—happens to-night . . . do you hear? . . . if anything happens to-night, I'll go straight off to-morrow morning to Father Nikodim and tell him all about it. 'Father Nikodim,' I shall say, 'graciously excuse me, but she is a witch.' 'Why so?' 'H'm! do you want to know why?' 'Certainly. . . .' And I shall tell him. And woe to you, woman! Not only at the dread Seat of Judgment, but in your earthly life you'll be punished, too! It's not for nothing there are prayers in the breviary against your kind!"

Suddenly there was a knock at the window, so loud and unusual that Savely turned pale and almost dropped backwards with fright. His wife jumped up, and she, too, turned pale.

"For God's sake, let us come in and get warm!" they heard in a trembling deep bass. "Who lives here? For mercy's sake! We've lost our way."

"Who are you?" asked Raissa, afraid to look at the window.

"The post," answered a second voice.

"You've succeeded with your devil's tricks," said Savely with a wave of his hand. "No mistake; I am right! Well, you'd better look out!"

The sexton jumped on to the bed in two skips, stretched himself on the feather mattress, and sniffing angrily, turned with his face to the wall. Soon he felt a draught of cold air on his back. The door creaked and the tall figure of a man, plastered over with snow from head to foot, appeared in the doorway. Behind him could be seen a second figure as white.

"Am I to bring in the bags?" asked the second in a hoarse bass voice.

"You can't leave them there." Saying this, the first figure began untying his hood, but gave it up, and pulling it off impatiently with his cap, angrily flung it near the stove. Then taking off his greatcoat, he threw that down beside it, and, without saying good-evening, began pacing up and down the hut.

He was a fair-haired, young postman wearing a shabby uniform and black rusty-looking high boots. After warming himself by walking to and fro, he sat down at the table, stretched out his muddy feet towards the sacks and leaned his chin on his fist. His pale face, reddened in places by the cold, still bore vivid traces of the pain and terror he had just been through. Though distorted by anger and bearing traces of recent suffering, physical and moral, it was handsome in spite of the melting snow on the eyebrows, moustaches, and short beard.

"It's a dog's life!" muttered the postman, looking round the walls and seeming hardly able to believe that he was in the warmth. "We were nearly lost! If it had not been for your light, I don't know what would have happened. Goodness only knows when it will all be over! There's no end to this dog's life! Where have we come?" he asked, dropping his voice and raising his eyes to the sexton's wife.

"To the Gulyaevsky Hill on General Kalinovsky's estate," she answered, startled and blushing.

"Do you hear, Stepan?" The postman turned to the driver, who was wedged in the doorway with a huge mail-bag on his shoulders. "We've got to Gulyaevsky Hill."

"Yes . . . we're a long way out." Jerking out these words like a hoarse sigh, the driver went out and soon after returned with another bag, then went out once more and this time brought the postman's sword on a big belt, of the pattern of that long flat blade with which Judith is portrayed by the bedside of Holofernes in cheap woodcuts. Laying the bags along the wall, he went out into the outer room, sat down there and lighted his pipe.

"Perhaps you'd like some tea after your journey?" Raissa inquired.

"How can we sit drinking tea?" said the postman, frowning. "We must make haste and get warm, and then set off, or we shall be late for the mail train. We'll stay ten minutes and then get on our way. Only be so good as to show us the way."

"What an infliction it is, this weather!" sighed Raissa.

"H'm, yes. . . . Who may you be?"

"We? We live here, by the church. . . . We belong to the clergy. . . . There lies my husband. Savely, get up and say good-evening! This used to be a separate parish till eighteen months ago. Of course, when the gentry lived here there were more people, and it was worthwhile to have the services. But now the gentry have gone, and I need not tell you there's nothing for the clergy to live on. The nearest village is Markovka, and that's over three miles away. Savely is on the retired list now, and has got the watchman's job; he has to look after the church. . . ."

And the postman was immediately informed that if Savely were to go to the General's lady and ask her for a letter to the bishop, he would be given a good berth. "But he doesn't go to the General's lady because he is lazy and afraid of people. We belong to the clergy all the same . . ." added Raissa.

"What do you live on?" asked the postman.

"There's a kitchen garden and a meadow belonging to the church. Only we don't get much from that," sighed Raissa. "The old skinflint, Father Nikodim, from the next village celebrates here on St. Nicolas' Day in the winter and on St. Nicolas' Day in the summer, and for that he takes almost all the crops for himself. There's no one to stick up for us!"

"You are lying," Savely growled hoarsely. "Father Nikodim is a saintly soul, a luminary of the Church; and if he does take it, it's the regulation!"

"You've a cross one!" said the postman, with a grin. "Have you been married long?"

"It was three years ago the last Sunday before Lent. My father was sexton here in the old days, and when the time came for him to die, he went to the Consistory and asked them to send some unmarried man to marry me that I might keep the place. So I married him."

"Aha, so you killed two birds with one stone!" said the postman, looking at Savely's back. "Got wife and job together."

Savely wriggled his leg impatiently and moved closer to the wall. The postman moved away from the table, stretched, and sat down on the mail-bag. After a moment's thought he squeezed the bags with his hands, shifted his sword to the other side, and lay down with one foot touching the floor.

"It's a dog's life," he muttered, putting his hands behind his head and closing his eyes. "I wouldn't wish a wild Tatar such a life."

Soon everything was still. Nothing was audible except the sniffing of Savely and the slow, even breathing of the sleeping postman, who uttered a deep prolonged "h-h-h" at every breath. From time to time there was a sound like a creaking wheel in his throat, and his twitching foot rustled against the bag.

Savely fidgeted under the quilt and looked round slowly. His wife was sitting on the stool, and with her hands pressed against her cheeks was gazing at the postman's face. Her face was immovable, like the face of some one frightened and astonished.

"Well, what are you gaping at?" Savely whispered angrily.

"What is it to you? Lie down!" answered his wife without taking her eyes off the flaxen head.

Savely angrily puffed all the air out of his chest and turned abruptly to the wall. Three minutes later he turned over restlessly again, knelt up on the bed, and with his hands on the pillow looked askance at his wife. She was still sitting motionless, staring at the visitor. Her cheeks were pale and her eyes were glowing with a strange fire. The sexton cleared his throat, crawled on his stomach off the bed, and going up to the postman, put a handkerchief over his face.

"What's that for?" asked his wife.

"To keep the light out of his eyes."

"Then put out the light!"

Savely looked distrustfully at his wife, put out his lips towards the lamp, but at once thought better of it and clasped his hands.

"Isn't that devilish cunning?" he exclaimed. "Ah! Is there any creature slyer than womenkind?"

"Ah, you long-skirted devil!" hissed his wife, frowning with vexation. "You wait a bit!"

And settling herself more comfortably, she stared at the postman again.

It did not matter to her that his face was covered. She was not so much interested in his face as in his whole appearance, in the novelty of this man. His chest was broad and powerful, his hands were slender and well formed, and his graceful, muscular legs were much comelier than Savely's stumps. There could be no comparison, in fact.

"Though I am a long-skirted devil," Savely said after a brief interval, "they've no business to sleep here. . . . It's government work; we shall have to answer for keeping them. If you carry the letters, carry them, you can't go to sleep. . . . Hey! you!" Savely shouted into the outer room. "You, driver. What's your name? Shall I show you the way? Get up; postmen mustn't sleep!"

And Savely, thoroughly roused, ran up to the postman and tugged him by the sleeve.

"Hey, your honour, if you must go, go; and if you don't, it's not the thing. . . . Sleeping won't do."

The postman jumped up, sat down, looked with blank eyes round the hut, and lay down again.

"But when are you going?" Savely pattered away. "That's what the post is for—to get there in good time, do you hear? I'll take you."

The postman opened his eyes. Warmed and relaxed by his first sweet sleep, and not yet quite awake, he saw as through a mist the white neck and the immovable, alluring eyes of the sexton's wife. He closed his eyes and smiled as though he had been dreaming it all.

"Come, how can you go in such weather!" he heard a soft feminine voice; "you ought to have a sound sleep and it would do you good!"

"And what about the post?" said Savely anxiously. "Who's going to take the post? Are you going to take it, pray, you?"

The postman opened his eyes again, looked at the play of the dimples on Raissa's face, remembered where he was, and understood Savely. The thought that he had to go out into the cold darkness sent a chill shudder all down him, and he winced.

"I might sleep another five minutes," he said, yawning. "I shall be late, anyway. . . ."

"We might be just in time," came a voice from the outer room. "All days are not alike; the train may be late for a bit of luck."

The postman got up, and stretching lazily began putting on his coat. Savely positively neighed with delight when he saw his visitors were getting ready to go.

"Give us a hand," the driver shouted to him as he lifted up a mail-bag.

The sexton ran out and helped him drag the post-bags into the yard. The postman began undoing the knot in his hood. The sexton's wife gazed into his eyes, and seemed trying to look right into his soul.

"You ought to have a cup of tea . . ." she said.

"I wouldn't say no . . . but, you see, they're getting ready," he assented. "We are late, anyway."

"Do stay," she whispered, dropping her eyes and touching him by the sleeve.

The postman got the knot undone at last and flung the hood over his elbow, hesitating. He felt it comfortable standing by Raissa.

"What a . . . neck you've got! . . ." And he touched her neck with two fingers. Seeing that she did not resist, he stroked her neck and shoulders.

"I say, you are . . ."

"You'd better stay . . . have some tea."

"Where are you putting it?" The driver's voice could be heard outside. "Lay it crossways."

"You'd better stay . . . Hark how the wind howls."

And the postman, not yet quite awake, not yet quite able to shake off the intoxicating sleep of youth and fatigue, was suddenly overwhelmed by a desire for the sake of which mail-bags, postal trains . . . and all things in the world, are forgotten. He glanced at the door in a frightened way, as though he wanted to escape or hide himself, seized Raissa round the waist, and was just bending over the lamp to put out the light, when he heard the tramp of boots in the outer room, and the driver appeared in the doorway.

Savely peeped in over his shoulder. The postman dropped his hands quickly and stood still as though irresolute.

"It's all ready," said the driver. The postman stood still for a moment, resolutely threw up his head as though waking up completely, and followed the driver out. Raissa was left alone.

"Come, get in and show us the way!" she heard.

One bell sounded languidly, then another, and the jingling notes in a long delicate chain floated away from the hut.

When little by little they had died away, Raissa got up and nervously paced to and fro. At first she was pale, then she flushed all over. Her face was contorted with hate, her breathing was tremulous, her eyes gleamed with wild, savage anger, and, pacing up and down as in a cage, she looked like a tigress menaced with red-hot iron. For a moment she stood still and looked at her abode. Almost half of the room was filled up by the bed, which stretched the length of the whole wall and consisted of a dirty feather-bed, coarse grey pillows, a quilt, and nameless rags of various sorts. The bed was a shapeless ugly mass which suggested the shock of hair that always stood up on Savely's head whenever it occurred to him to oil it. From the bed to the door that led into the cold outer room stretched the dark stove surrounded by pots and hanging clouts. Everything, including the absent Savely himself, was dirty, greasy, and smutty to the last degree, so that it was strange to see a woman's white neck and delicate skin in such surroundings.

Raissa ran up to the bed, stretched out her hands as though she wanted to fling it all about, stamp it underfoot, and tear it to shreds. But then, as though frightened by contact with the dirt, she leapt back and began pacing up and down again.

When Savely returned two hours later, worn out and covered with snow, she was undressed and in bed. Her eyes were closed, but from the slight tremor that ran over her face he guessed that she was not asleep. On his way home he had vowed inwardly to wait till next day and not to touch her, but he could not resist a biting taunt at her.

"Your witchery was all in vain: he's gone off," he said, grinning with malignant joy.

His wife remained mute, but her chin quivered. Savely undressed slowly, clambered over his wife, and lay down next to the wall.

"Tomorrow I'll let Father Nikodim know what sort of wife you are!" he muttered, curling himself up.

Raissa turned her face to him and her eyes gleamed.

"The job's enough for you, and you can look for a wife in the forest, blast you!" she said. "I am no wife for you, a clumsy lout, a slug-a-bed, God forgive me!"

"Come, come . . . go to sleep!"

"How miserable I am!" sobbed his wife. "If it weren't for you, I might have married a merchant or some gentleman! If it weren't for you, I should love my husband now! And you haven't been buried in the snow, you haven't been frozen on the highroad, you Herod!"

Raissa cried for a long time. At last she drew a deep sigh and was still. The storm still raged without. Something wailed in the stove, in the chimney, outside the walls, and it seemed to Savely that the wailing was within him, in his ears. This evening had completely confirmed him in his suspicions about his wife. He no longer doubted that his wife, with the aid of the Evil One, controlled the winds and the post sledges. But to add to his grief, this mysteriousness, this supernatural, weird power gave the woman beside him a peculiar, incomprehensible charm of which he had not been conscious before. The fact that in his stupidity he unconsciously threw a poetic glamour over her made her seem, as it were, whiter, sleeker, more unapproachable.

"Witch!" he muttered indignantly. "*Tfoo,* horrid creature!"

Yet, waiting till she was quiet and began breathing evenly, he touched her head with his finger . . . held her thick plait in his hand for a minute. She did not feel it. Then he grew bolder and stroked her neck.

"Leave off!" she shouted, and prodded him on the nose with her elbow with such violence that he saw stars before his eyes.

The pain in his nose was soon over, but the torture in his heart remained.

Parsley, Sage, Rosemary, and Thyme:
The Nature Witch

And then there's the witch next door, usually not a frightening figure at all, often someone who gets her (or his) powers from bonding with nature itself. Despite Wicca being one of the fastest growing religions in the United States, these stories aren't as plentiful. Maybe it's because people think there isn't as much drama without a battle of good and evil, or at least of the sexes. Maybe it's because people see no thrill in a quiet magic that works by natural means.

Then again, check out Emily Brontë, or Rosemary Edghill.

Some people might just be wrong. . . .

The Witches' Creed

DOREEN VALIENTE

This poem presents a thorough introduction to the basics of modern neopaganism, from the number of Sabbats and Esbats to the faces of the God and Goddess, an example of how even after her death in 1999, Doreen Valiente keeps on teaching.

Hear now the words of the witches,
The secrets we hid in the night,
When dark was our destiny's pathway,
That now we bring forth into light.

Mysterious water and fire,
The earth and the wide-ranging air,
By hidden quintessence we know them,
And will and keep silent and dare.

The birth and rebirth of all nature,
The passing of winter and spring,
We share with the life universal,
Rejoice in the magical ring.

Four times in the year the Great Sabbat
Returns, and the witches are seen
At Lammas and Candlemas dancing,
On May Eve and old Hallowe'en.

When day-time and night-time are equal,
When sun is at greatest and least,

The four Lesser Sabbats are summoned,
Again witches gather in feast.

Thirteen silver moons in a year are,
Thirteen is the coven's array.
Thirteen times at Esbat make merry,
For each golden year and a day.

The power was passed down the ages,
Each time between woman and man,
Each century unto the other,
Ere time and the ages began.

When drawn is the magical circle,
By sword or athame of power,
Its compass between the two worlds lies,
In Land of the Shades for that hour.

This world has no right then to know it,
And world of beyond will tell naught.
The oldest of Gods are invoked there,
The Great Work of magic is wrought.

For two are the mystical pillars,
That stand at the gate of the shrine,
And two are the powers of nature,
The forms and the forces divine.

The dark and the light in succession,
The opposites each unto each,
Shown forth as a God and a Goddess:
Of this did our ancestors teach.

By night he's the wild wind's rider,
The Horn'd One, the Lord of the
    Shades.
By day he's the King of the Woodland,
The dweller in green forest glades.

She is youthful or old as she pleases,
She sails the torn clouds in her barque,
The bright silver lady of midnight,
The crone who weaves spells in the
    dark.

The master and mistress of magic,
They dwell in the deeps of the mind,
Immortal and ever-renewing,
With power to free or to bind.

So drink the good wine to the Old
    Gods,
And dance and make love in their
    praise,
Till Elphame's fair land shall receive us
In peace at the end of our days.

And Do What You Will be the
    challenge,
So be it in Love that harms none,
For this is the only commandment.
By Magic of old, be it done!

The Sorcerer's Apprentice

BROTHERS GRIMM

Admit it—your first thought was of Mickey Mouse from Fantasia. *But this particular fairy tale, along with referencing the magic of certain herbs and berries, also works as a metaphor for the power of reading.*

A man found himself in need of a helper for his workshop, and one day as he was walking along the outskirts of a little hamlet he met a boy with a bundle slung over his shoulder. Stopping him, the man said, "Good morning, my lad. I am looking for an apprentice. Have you a master?"

"No," said the boy, "I have just this morning said good-bye to my mother and am now off to find myself a trade."

"Good," said the man. "You look as though you might be just the lad I need. But wait, do you know anything about reading and writing?"

"Oh yes!" said the boy.

"Too bad!" said the man. "You won't do after all. I have no use for anyone who can read and write."

"Pardon me?" said the boy. "If it was *reading* and *writing* you were talking about, I misunderstood you. I thought you asked if I knew anything about *eating* and *fighting*—those two things I am able to do well, but as to reading and writing that is something I know nothing about."

"Well!" cried the man. "Then you are just the fellow I want. Come with me to my workshop, and I will show you what to do."

The boy, however, had had his wits about him. He could read and write well enough and had only pretended to be a fool. Wondering why a man should prefer to have an unschooled helper, he thought to himself, "I smell a rat. There is something strange about this, and I had better keep my eyes and ears open."

While he was pondering over this, his new master was leading him into the heart of a deep forest. Here in a small clearing stood a house and, as soon as they entered it, the boy could see that this was no ordinary workshop.

At one end of a big room was a huge hearth with a copper cauldron hanging in it; at the other end was a small alcove lined with many big books. A mortar and pestle stood on a bench; bottles and sieves, measuring scales and oddly-shaped glassware were strewn about on the table.

Well! It did not take the clever young apprentice very long to realize that he was working for a magician or sorcerer of some kind and so, although he pretended to be quite stupid, he kept his eyes and ears open, and tried to learn all he could.

"Sorcery—that is a trade I would dearly love to master!" said the boy to himself. "A mouthful of good chants and charms would never come amiss to a poor fellow like me, and with them I might even be able to do some good in the world."

There were many things the boy had to do. Sometimes he was ordered to stir the evil-smelling broths which bubbled in the big copper cauldron; at other times he had to grind up herbs and berries—and other things too gruesome to mention—in the big mortar and pestle. It was also his task to sweep up the workshop, to keep the fire burning in the big hearth, and to gather the strange materials needed by the man for the broths and brews he was always mixing.

This went on day after day, week after week, and month after month, until the boy was almost beside himself with curiosity. He was most curious about the thick heavy books in the alcove. How often he had wondered about them, and how many times had he been tempted to take a peep between their covers! But, remembering that he was not supposed to know how to read or write, he had been wise enough never to show the least interest in them. At last there came a day when he made up his mind to see what was in them, no matter what the risk.

"I'll try it before another day dawns," he thought.

That night he waited until the sorcerer was sound asleep and was snoring loudly in his bedchamber; then, creeping out of his straw couch, the boy took a light into the corner of the alcove and began paging through one of the heavy volumes. What was written in them has never been told, but they were conjuring books, each and every one of them; and from that time on, the boy read in them silently, secretly, for an hour or two, night after night. In this way he learned many magic tricks: chants and charms and countercharms; recipes for philters and potions, for broths and brews and witches' stews; signs mystic and cabalistic, and other helpful spells of many kinds. All these he memorized carefully, and it was not long before he sometimes was able to figure out what kind of charms his master was working, what brand of potion he was mixing, what sort of stews he was brewing. And what kind of charms and potions and stews were they? Alas, they were all wicked ones! Now the boy knew that he was not working for an ordinary magician, but for a cruel, dangerous sorcerer. And because of this, the boy made a plan, a bold one.

He went on with his nightly studies until his head was swarming with magic recipes and incantations. He even had time to work at them in the daytime, for the sorcerer sometimes left the workshop for hours—working harm and havoc on mortals, no doubt. At such times the boy would try out a few bits of his newly learned wisdom. He began with simple things, such as changing the cat into a bee and back to a cat again, making a viper out of the poker, an imp out of the broom, and so on. Sometimes he was successful, often he was not; so he said to himself, "The time is not yet ripe."

One day, after the sorcerer had again gone forth on one of his mysterious trips, the boy hurried through his work, and had just settled himself in the dingy alcove with one of the conjuring books on his knees, when the master returned unexpectedly. The boy, thinking fast, pointed smilingly at one of the pictures, after which he quietly closed the book and went on with his work as though nothing were amiss.

But the sorcerer was not deceived.

"If the wretch can read," he thought, "he may learn how to outwit me. And I can't send him off with a beating and a 'bad speed to you', either—doubtless he knows too much already and will reveal all my fine mean tricks, and then I can't have any more sport working mischief on man and beast."

He acted quickly.

With one leap he rushed at the boy, who in turn made a spring for the door.

"Stop!" cried the sorcerer. "You shall not escape me!"

He was about to grab the boy by the collar when the quick-witted lad mumbled a powerful incantation by which he changed himself into a bird—and—Wootsch!—he had flown into the woods.

The sorcerer, not to be outdone, shouted a charm, thus changing himself into a larger bird—and Whoosh!—he was after the little one.

With a new incantation the boy made himself into a fish—and Whish!—he was swimming across a big pond.

But the master was equal to this, for, with a few words he made himself into a fish too, a big one, and swam after the little one.

At this the boy changed himself into a still bigger fish but the magician, by a master stroke, turned himself into a tiny kernel of grain and rolled into a small crack in a stone where the fish couldn't touch him.

Quickly the boy changed himself into a rooster, and—Peck! Peck! Peck!—with his sharp beak he snapped at the kernel of grain and ate it up.

That was the end of the wicked sorcerer, and the boy became the owner of the magic workshop. And wasn't it fine that all the powers and ingredients which had been used for evil by the sorcerer were now in the hands of a boy who would use them only for the good of man and beast?

The Humming of Stars and Bees and Waves

Anita Endrezze

This poetic short story celebrates the cycles of life—and death—in ways that few "wicked witch" tales have ever considered.

Long ago, there was a spirit woman and her name was *Yomumuli*.* She made the earth:

the rippling grasses gone swaying into the wind
the scarlet mountains floating in clouds of tiny blue birds.

And the day was divided into astonished animal faces, and the night was a fountainhead of stars and the slumber of river turtles.

Since that time, the papery husks of stars have fallen into the seas and mothers have grown older. Rosa is a woman who talks to herself. Although she doesn't remember the first creation, she does remember the birth of her only child, a son named Natchez.

She made the people and put them in a village. And in the middle of the village was a Talking Tree that hummed like bees.

(When Natchez was little, Rosa talked to the coyotes and ravens and flowers. But now she is old and can't see very well.

I wonder, she thinks, if my dreams can tell me how to make my eyes better. She knows that her tribe believes in dreams, but since she's half-

---

*Note: *Yomumuli* means "enchanted bee" in Yaqui.

Yaqui, she doesn't know if the dreams believe in her. Still, she begs for
a dream that would speak healing words.)

The tree spoke a sacred language. No one could understand. Not the
youngest. Not the wisest or bravest or strongest. Not even the oldest.

(Rosa wakes one morning and remembers a dream that tells her to enter
a cave. Grandmother Spider Woman tells her to bring cedar, tobacco,
and corn. No walkie-talkie. No flashlight. No strings or bread crumbs to
mark the path. Just blind faith.

And so, when the moon is yellow and the mist low under the dark
apples . . . when the fields are gold and dry with rows of stars shining on
the tassels . . . when the horizon is lilac and the mountains to the west
are blue-black, Rosa ties the bag with the offerings around her waist and
hikes up the trail to the old caves. The caves are usually there, but legends
have it that they sometimes disappear. Rose is not sure what to expect,
so she mutters to herself as she walks.

The back of her neck is hot and sticky, even though the air is cooling
and rising from the valley. The trail gets steeper and narrows to one foot
in front of the other. She puts one hand on her knee in order to propel
herself forward on the steepest parts and prays the rest of her will follow.

"Damn stupid thing to do," she mumbles. She's a little worried about
bears, even though one of her husbands had been a bear spirit. That's
how she saw her men: this one, a bull, that one a St. Bernard. At least
talking would scare away a bear now; she is too old for such foolishness.

Finally, she rounds the curve of the mountain. Her heart is beating
fast. The cave opens in front of her like a huge toothless mouth. She can
feel the cold, musty air push out toward her. The floor of the cave is
rough, littered with angular rocks.

She's a small woman with bony knees and with one shoulder slightly
higher than the other, but her skin is surprisingly smooth for her age and
her hair is still thick. She waits until her heart calms down, then pretty
soon, it's getting dark outside. She might as well go in.

I hope I know what I'm doing, she thinks. She walks with her hands
stuck out in front of her. She can hear water rushing to her left: a swift
stream. "Don't let me die in here," she prays.)

When *Yomumuli* returned from her creating, she shook off the images of
shimmering feathers and jungle greens and small monkey faces and loos-

ened her fingers from speckled granite and purple-spiked sea urchins and
brushed off the coral sands from her memory and listened to her children.

They were worried: they had been given something sacred and had not
understood it. Some argued that the holy is never understood.

(Rosa listens. The stream has a voice and it chants: *earthbowl* and *dusk-
womb*. The walls have a voice that says: *terra-cotta hands* and *eyes of
clay*.

Rosa feels the presence of tiny spider women, sitting with their spin-
dly legs crossed. Minerals drip drip, funnels of teeth-like spikes, vaginal
and wet. The spider women unlid their thousand eyes and reach out,
sticky fingerlings, silken threads slivering the cracks of deeper darkness.
The threads anchor on Rosa, the outworlder. The voices are those from
the void: *terra marina, terra noche*. In Rosa's ears, she hears the bullroar
and raw rushing out of a water drum.

My own body is full of minerals, she thinks, and thousands of her
cells echo the stratification of the earth. She isn't lost.)

Yomumuli puts her cheek to the Talking Tree and listens to the humming
voice.

(Rosa is a stone woman. She is a stone fish swimming through a river of
turquoise. A half-blind fish, finny and leaping, to the rhythm of a sha-
dowless current.

When she was a young woman, she liked men. She still likes men,
but none of them will look at her. When she was young, she needed a
cane to walk sometimes. Her sight was good; now it's cloudy in one eye,
and life's so lame that she doesn't need a cane.

Often, life is beyond understanding to her. There's more than blood
in her veins now. There's a longing for more life, more stories, more
kisses.

She remembers her own grandmother who lived alone for forty-six
years after her husband died, celebrating his birthday with flowers in
front of the silver-framed photo, and yearly visits to the cemetery. Now
Natchez has a baby and Rosa sleeps alone, her husband of thirty years
dead for some time. She remembers his nightly whispers to her before

they fell asleep. One of his favorite sayings was: "Life has no guaran-
tees.")

Yomumuli heard what the tree was saying. She turned to look at her
people and spoke, shrugging a cloud from her shoulder: I'll tell you what
the tree says, but you must promise to believe me!

(Rosa trips and falls to her knee. There's blood and a sharp pain. "Shit,"
she moans. She feels old, old as the clay shards in the lap of earth, old
as the curled fetus shapes in red clay graves, skin wrinkled over thin ribs
and around, faces of grief. *Terra recepta Corpus terra.*

"I'm not crazy," she repeats to herself. "I'm here for a reason. I know
what I need, to see, but not how to do it."

Inching forward, her knee throbbing, she feels the walls narrowing.
The stream widens into a pool: she can hear the stillness in the center
and the rushing out near her feet.

The spider women throw a ball of moony webs up into the air and
a soft light fills the cave's inner heart.

"So, now what do I do?" asks Rosa.

"Do you believe in us?" click the spider women.)

Of course! of course! And so the people listened: the tree told the animals
how to live . . . that the deer should eat grass and the puma eat the deer.
Then it spoke about the future when men from a far country will come
and everything will change. There will be new laws and new death and
a great metal snake with smoke plumes will race across the land. When
the people heard this, they became afraid.

(Being half-Yaqui isn't easy, Rosa thinks. You have to believe that trees
and rocks and birds talk and you have to have faith in glass-walled elevators and voices that are transmitted from space. Then there's panty
hose that assumes your shape and dreams that struggle to shape your
awareness.

Long ago, Rosa got real tired of shape-changing: being Indian with
Indians and white with whites. As she got older, she became less afraid
and howled like a coyote in heat whenever she damn well felt like it.
From the ceiling of the cave, tree roots hang down in a gnarled nest. The
cave seems to be breathing.

"I believe," whispers Rosa.)

Some didn't believe *Yomumuli*. So she left, with her favorite river rolled up under her arm, walking north, her feet like two dark thunderclouds.

(Rosa thinks about her white mothers, their names rolling off her tongue like pearls: Jean, Ann, Yohana, Marija, Barbara, Ana, Margareta, Elizabeth, Sussie, Giuliana, Anna, Orsola, Felicita. And her Indian mothers: Estefana, Charlotta, Empimenia, and others whose names were lost, unwritten, but remembered in a certain flash of eyes. Names of grandmothers who still sing in the blood.

Rosa feels Grandmothers' eyes all around her. She sees with their eyes. She sees the pond, its water clear as air. The elements are transmutable.)

And some of the people went to live in the sea, their whale songs tubular and roiling, boom-echo and deep in the interior seas of their throats, longing and sounding all in a moaning song, floating up to the spume moon.

(Rosa turns to the cave walls. Clay. She pulls a chunk out and rolls it in her hands, forming a ball. Little clay baby. Cave naval, lodestar, and motherlode. She pinches it into a rough bowl. With her thumbs she shapes it, smooths it.

Quickly, she fills the bowl with pond water. A sip. It tastes like metal and semen and breast milk. It is sour and sweet and musty and white and black and red and yellow.)

And some became flying fish, ringing the waves, sparkling, and others became the singers of the sea, with their long hair and rainbow skin. They say if you're lost at sea, these creatures will help you because they remember the time when we were all one.

(Rosa unties her bag of offerings and puts the tobacco in the bowl. The cedar chips to the right, the corn to the left. Fumbling a bit, she pulls out a book of matches and carefully lights the tobacco. A thin hand-like shape of smoke rises.

She thanks her family. She thanks her guardian spirits. She thanks her own strength. She thanks the creator.

The Grandmothers sing: *ebb and return, web and wheel, smoke and water, the void has wings, we sing and reel. Spinner and spinal songs, spiraling symphonic and symbiotic, sightless but full of visions: we Grandmothers, we dreamers.*

The singing stops and Rosa gathers the strands of webs into a little ball. She puts it into her weak eye. The tobacco has burnt itself out. She lights the cedar chips. No fire, but sweet and piercing. Then she scatters the corn on the floor.

Her insight is blooming. It is becoming a way of seeing.

Sparkling eyes, whirlwinds of nerves. A visible cortex. Quartz quadrants. Four corners of wind and gates into seeing. She crosses the earth, she crosses the sky.)

And some of the people descended into the earth and became jointed: jet-black or red. These little ant people who live in the sand will also help you if you are lost.

(She took the clay bowl and pressed it back into the cave wall.)

For they also remember the time when we were all one.

(Rosa stands and feels the darkness fall around her, but she can see. Her white moon-eye, her shedded-snake-skin-eye, her winter-worn-leaf-eye: gone the thickening curtain, gone into the thoughts of the spider women. In and spin. Filaments of eyes.

There are cedar trees floating in the air and the faces of those she has loved waver delicately in front of her. She is seeing with her heart.

She feels the pain burning away. It's the pain of learning to let go. *Que serà, serà.* Sierra Rosa is the name of the daughter she never had. *Let go.* Her husband's hands hugging her in the morning. *Let go.* Her little son saying, "I'll always stay with you." *Let go.* Herself thinking: I never want another friend; they all leave or die and it hurts too much. *Let go. Let go.*

Her eye is clear. There is no division between the worlds of seeing and believing.

Rosa is ready to leave. She knows there is confusion outside and the noise of cars honking in the night. But there are also stars with no room for self-pity. Rosa ties a lace on her Reeboks and turns around.)

Those who stayed in the village grew taller and taught their children how to face the future.

(She walks quickly toward the cave entrance, which has a lesser denseness of dark. Then she sees the moon seeping out of the fat wheat heads. It's full and yellow.

In the valley, she hears the cottonwoods shaking under the force of their water-filled roots. The bees are sleeping, dreaming of heavy black clouds booming over gold-white fields and sheet-lightning flashing into a hot and crinkly air.

And the ravens are dreaming of circling in a chickory-blue sky. Twirly seeds of yellow star-bursts fall in floating circles to the earth. Rosa feels the circles growing inside her, as if she were a tree of immense dawns.

Taking a deep breath, she smiles to herself, thinking of her son and her new granddaughter. "I'm not useless," she says firmly, "and I'm not alone."

As she brushes the dirt from her clothes, she spares one last look at the cave. Its darkness, its blindness, had terrified her. It was the blindness of death, the conception of nothing.

Now she begins the way back. In the distance, the sky is luminous with the lights of the city, a city that may turn into thin air, for it also remembers the time when we were one.

And the people who live there are like enchanted trees, with bones for branches and eyes for leaves. If they listen, they can hear the humming of stars and bees and waves.

These are my ancestors, my future.

Witchcraft was hung, in History

EMILY DICKINSON

Emily Dickinson makes it clear in such poems as "Some keep the Sabbath going to Church" (#324) that, in another time and place, she may well have become a nature-worshipping pagan herself. For her own time and place, she worked a different kind of magic in her poetry.

Witchcraft was hung, in History,
But History and I
Find all the Witchcraft that we need
Around us, every Day—

The Spell

DAVID GERROLD

This story could have fit in the "Empowerment" section, as it is something of a revenge fantasy. But it also illustrates how magic can work not with fireworks and levitation but by natural means—an often repeated theme among modern practitioners.

M Y next-door neighbors have six children. This is not enough reason to hate them, but it's a good start.

The smallest one, Tali, is ambulatory, but still preverbal. She is not a problem. She can stay. We will leave her name off the eviction notice.

Next up is Nolan. He has been retarded at the age of three for four years now. Nolan is an interesting social experiment. What do you get if you allow a child to raise himself without any parental involvement at all?

He breaks things. He takes things. He denies accountability. He starts fires. He blames other children. He screams. He goes into other people's yards, and he climbs up onto the roofs of houses—usually his own, but occasionally the roof of a neighbor as well. He throws things over the fence into my yard, oftentimes aiming for the pool. A half-eaten Taco Bell burrito must be retrieved within the first thirty minutes or you can plan on having the filter cleaned again.

Wait, there's someone at the door—

(on paper the pauses don't show)

—it was Nolan. I can't even write this down without one of the little monsters knocking on the door. They have been sent to bedevil me.

Next up are Jason and Jabed, hovering somewhere in age between eleven and juvenile hall. Jason and Jabed are the coming attractions for Nolan's adolescence. They specialize in noise and attitude. They have no manners. They have no courtesy. They have no conception of consideration for others.

My life was quiet and peaceful once. I work at home. I take my time to think things out. I sit in my office and think and write. I sit in my living room and read and listen to classical music; Bach, Vivaldi, occasionally a Shostakovitch string quartet—nothing too strenuous. I open all the doors and all the windows, and the cross breeze keeps the house pleasant and sweet-smelling. I would love to be able to do that again. Last year, I paid six thousand dollars to install a 12,000 BTU air conditioner on the roof so I could close all the doors and windows and still keep working. The noise from the fan drowns out the softer strains of Debussy.

In the afternoon, they play touch football and baseball across three lawns. Mine is in the middle. Even the judicious planting of large amounts of purple Wandering Jew has not deterred them. They leap over it . . . sometimes. They scream, they shout, they claim the ball in midair. "It's mine—mine!" Their voices are atonal and dissonant, precisely mistuned to jar with whatever music is on the turntable.

In the evenings, they play basketball in the back yard. I used to go to bed at eleven. But they play basketball until one in the ayem, shouting and jabbering. The basketball hoop is opposite my bedroom window. It serves as the perfect acoustic focus aimed at my headboard. I am not making this up. A specialist in theatrical sound systems came out to my house, took some measurements, and ran them through the computer.

Jabed and Jason like to climb roofs, too. Last January, they climbed up on the roof of the auto parts store behind the alley, and plugged up its storm drains, just for the fun of it. When the big rains came in February, the water puddled on the roof. The weight of the water brought the whole ceiling crashing in, causing over a half-million dollars worth of damage to the store. The police refused to arrest the boys because of insufficient evidence. In August, they were accused of stealing 120 dollars from a neighbor's wallet and spent the night in juvenile hall. The next day, they were swimming at the same neighbor's house. How do they get away with it? What magic are they working?

Then there's Vanessa. She's another sweetheart. I think she's eighteen. She takes care of the kids while Mom's at work. No, check that. She's *supposed* to take care of the kids while Mom's at work. What she does is have parties. One of her friends once took forty bucks from mom's purse—but Mom and Dad blamed every other child on the street for the theft, and when the truth came out, didn't bother to apologize.

I'm not the only one who feels this way. The neighbor on the other side of Hell House has developed an ulcer. The neighbors across the street have put their house up for sale. Half the parents on the block have forbidden their children to play with the demonic brood. This is validation. It's not me. It's *them*.

Mom and Dad. Lyn and Bryce. He's a former minister, she's a former cheerleader who never aspired to anything more than the right shade of blonde. She hasn't yet noticed that her tits are working their way south and her ass is spreading faster than the crabgrass on their lawn. I gave up on my lawn this year. There's no point in it while the crabgrass sod farm next door is so aggressive.

Their philosophy of childrearing is nonexistent. They daydream their way through life, drifting from one day to the next, oblivious to the fact that they are loathed by all of their neighbors. No, check that. They are loathed by all of the neighbors who live close enough to know who they are.

Oh—I almost skipped Damien. He's the one I like. He moved out and went to college four hundred miles away. We only see him on holidays. He has manners and courtesy and is obviously a changeling, not a real part of the family. He wants to major in art. Maybe he's gay. I hope so. I'd like to see the look on their faces when he comes home with a boyfriend. Idle fantasies of revenge are rapidly becoming an obsession over here.

I like to believe I'm smarter than they are; but I still haven't been able to plot the perfect crime—one that would allow me to chop their bones into fragments, burn their house down, and salt the earth into toxic uninhabitability, without anyone ever suspecting that I was the agent responsible. In some matters, anonymity is preferable to acknowledgment. Revenge is one of them.

It bothers me, because I am supposed to be a specialist in revenge. Writers, as a class, are the research-and-development team for the whole human race in the domain of revenge. We ennoble it, we glorify it; we earn our livings inventing wonderful and exotic ways to justify the delicious deed of puncturing the pompous who make our lives miserable. We create virtual daydreams for the masses in which the mighty are humiliated for their misdeeds of oppression against those who are still climbing the evolutionary ladder. It is our job to tend the flames of mythic vision, creating the cultural context in which the arrogant are accurately mirrored and drawn, so that all will know who they are. It is our job to prepare the ground so that the thieves of joy can be reduced to craven, whimpering, pitiful objects of scorn and abuse.

And . . . the fact that I remain unable to find a way to drive these people screaming from their house frustrates me beyond words, because it implies that I am not yet a master of my trade. If anyone should be able to envision a suitable revenge here, it should be me. Through a delightfully Machiavellian bit of timing, innuendo, and legal maneuvering, I once engineered the enforced exit off the Paramount lot of a particularly leechsome lawyer; studio security officers arrived with boxes, and physically escorted him off the premises—so abusing a few troublesome neighbors should be easy. Shouldn't it?

The problem is Grandma. Theirs, not mine. Grandma is a space-case. Not of this world. She exists in her own reality of hydrangeas and luncheons and Cadillacs. Life is pleasant, life is good, there are no problems. Let's all be nice to each other and everything will work out fine. She sees and hears only what she chooses to. Grandma owns the house and Mom and Dad and all the little Mansons live in it rent-free. They couldn't afford to live in this neighborhood otherwise. There is no way they're ever going to move out. Ever try to pull a tick off a dog? Grandma is the problem—

(narrative interrupted again)

—that one used up the rest of my evening. While I admit that it gave me no small amount of satisfaction to see three police cars pulled up in front of *that* house, it did not bring me any joy. I appreciate the validation, I do not appreciate losing half a day of working time.

This time, Jason was chasing Damien with a knife, threatening him. Damien socked him with a frying pan in self-defense. Damien got arrested. He'll end up with a charge of child abuse on his record. These people have a way of getting *other* people in trouble, and coming out unscathed themselves. It's a talent.

PART TWO:
That was six months ago.

The day after I wrote that, I ran into my friend, Sara McNealy. Sara is a witch.

I had stopped in at Dangerous Visions bookstore in Sherman Oaks to deliver my monthly box of books that I would rather not have in the house and to select a few volumes in return that would enhance my bookshelves. Given the fact that most publishers seem to have given up the publication of real books in favor of the production of commodity products, the task of reinvigorating the sleeping sense of wonder becomes harder and harder every year. Nothing destroys a person's enjoyment of a subject as fast as becoming obsessive about it. Never mind.

Sara was standing at the counter, chatting with Lydia Marano, the store owner. There were two other customers in the back of the store, browsing through the nonreaders' section, looking for the latest *Star Trek* novel.

Sara doesn't look like a witch. She does not have flaming red hair. She does not have green eyes. She does not dress in flowing capes with unicorn embroidery.

Sara is short, not quite dumpy but almost, and she has little tight black curls framing her pie-shaped face. She is given to flowery dresses and little round spectacles, that look like windows into her dark gray eyes. She looks like a yenta-in-training, but without the guilt attached. She is obscenely calm and unruffled.

Sara never talks about the goddess, she is not given to feminist rhetoric, and she rarely reads fiction. She created her own job, managing the computers for a major theatrical booking-chain. She is the first stop for technical support for a very small and very exclusive group of science-fiction, fantasy, and horror writers. She is equally conversant with nanotechnology, transhuman chickens, selfish genes, undisturbed universes, dancing Wu-Li masters, motorcycle maintenance (with or without the zen), virology (both human and silicon strains), paleontology, biblical history, and several mutant strains of Buddhist discourse. She can quote from Sun Tzu's *Art of War* as easily as from *The Watchmen*.

She does not cast spells herself. She works only as a consultant, serving as the midwife at the spellcasting sessions of others. She was telling Lydia, behind the counter, about her experiences breaking up a fannish coven, trying to grow hair on Patrick Stewart. "Finally, I just flat out told them, 'Witchcraft is potent stuff. Every spell you cast uses up part of your life force. If you assume that every spell you cast takes a year off your life expectancy, you don't do it casually. You save it for things that matter.' "

I looked up from the copy of *Locus* I was browsing through. They hadn't reviewed a book of mine in years—not since I'd requested that the reviewers read the books before writing about them. "Hey, Sara, didn't you say there were ways to rebuild your life force?"

"Oh, yes." She smiled sweetly as she said it. "Creativity. Haven't you ever noticed that a disproportionate share of conductors, writers, musicians, directors, et al, live well into their 90s? The act of creation is very powerful. When you bring something into existence out of nothing, it become a focus for energy. If you create positive energy, you get invigorated. If you create negative energy, you diminish yourself. You can't afford the luxury of nastiness."

"You're right, *I* can't—but what if you don't have a choice in the matter?"

"You *always* have a choice," she said.

"You don't know my next-door neighbors."

She raised an eyebrow at me. A raised eyebrow from Sara McNealy is enough to curdle milk.

I refused to be intimidated. "My next-door neighbors are destroying my life," I said. "They're noisy and intrusive. They've upset my whole life. My writing is suffering. And I can't afford to move."

Sara scratched her nose. "Negativism starts by blaming the other person. It's a way of avoiding personal responsibility."

"I'm not avoiding personal responsibility," I said. "I just don't know what to do."

"What result do you want to produce?" Sara asked.

"I want them to move away. Very far away."

She nodded. She was thinking. Lydia studied us both. Sara was turning over ideas in her mind. She said, "You could invite an evil spirit to move in with them. But that's dangerous. Sometimes the spirit decides it would rather move in with *you*."

"No, no spirits, thank you. Is there some other way?"

"Are you willing to pay the price—time off your life?"

"I'll earn it back with increased writing time. Won't I?"

Sara didn't answer that. At the same moment, we both noticed that there were suddenly other customers waiting—*and listening*. Sara put down the copy of *Chaos Theory* she had been browsing through and drew me carefully aside, leaving Lydia to ring up another large royalty for Stephen King.

"Listen to me," Sara said softly. "Witchcraft is a very specialized form of magic—you're trying to control the physical universe with experiential forces. That means that you need to create a specific context and appropriate symbology with which to control those forces. I prefer to do it with symbolic magic, rather than calling on spirits. Sometimes when no spirit responds to your call, new ones are created out of nothingness, and that can be extremely dangerous. Young spirits are . . . well, they're like kittens and puppies. They leave puddles."

"Can't I just animate the life force of their property or something?"

"It doesn't work that way." She frowned. "You're going to have to give me the whole story if you want me to advise you."

I took Sara by the arm and led her to the specialty coffee shop next door. She had hazelnut coffee with bay leaves. I had fruit tea. I can't stomach caffeine. I told her about the Partridge Family from hell; I didn't leave anything out. I even told her about Princess, the unfettered cocker spaniel who never missed a chance to run up onto my porch and bark *into* my house.

Sara listened intently to the whole story without comment. Her dark eyes looked sorrowful. I could understand why she was such a good witch. Most of it was good listening. When I finished, she said, "You have a great deal of negative energy bound up in these people. That's a very expensive burden you are carrying. It needs to be released." She made a decision. "I'll help you."

"How much will it cost?" I asked.

She shook her head. "Witches don't work for money. Prostitutes do. Witches take . . . *favors.*"

"Okay, I'll read your manuscript," I said with real resignation.

"Sorry, I have no interest in writing a novel."

"Thank God."

"Don't worry," she said. "I don't want your soul. Writer's souls are usually very small anyway, and not good eating. Too much gristle." She reached over and patted my hand warmly. "We'll talk about your first-born later, all right?"

I assumed she was joking.

*   *   *

PART Three:

Sara showed up at 7:00, carrying two shopping bags.

"Ahh," I said, thinking I was being funny. "Did you bring the right eye of a left-handed newt? The first menstrual blood of the seventh virginal daughter?"

"This is California," she said. "There are no virgins. I brought pasta, mushrooms, bell peppers, tomato sauce, olives, garlic bread, salad, and a bottle of wine. Let's eat first, then we'll plan. Did you get the Cherry Garcia like I asked?"

"Of course, I did." I took the bags from her. "But I really have to say I miss the old traditions of witchcraft."

"Do you want to dance naked around a bonfire at midnight?"

"Not particularly."

"Neither do I. Open the wine."

After dinner, we cleared the table and spread out our plans. "First of all," Sara said, "you have to decide what power you want to invoke. Who are you calling on to do the deed?" She handed me a printout. "You don't want to invoke the powers of Satan, whatever you do. Dealing with demons is also dangerous; for the most part, the demons are only facets of Satan anyway. You don't want to do anything that puts your immortal soul in danger. I'm just showing you this to give you some sense of what you're going to be dealing with.

"Lower down, you have the lesser spirits and the spirits of the dead. Also not recommended. Spirits usually have their own agendas. They're very hard to control, and almost never grant requests. Spirits are deranged."

I scanned the lists with very little interest, then passed her back the printout. "Let's stick to white magic, okay?"

'Right." She passed me another set of pages. "See, the thing is, you have to invoke *some* power to energize the spell. Otherwise, it's like a new Corvette, all shiny and beautiful, but without an engine it isn't going anywhere."

"Yeah, I just hate it when that happens."

She ignored my flippant interjection. "The problem with Western magic is that as a result of the pernicious influence of Christian theology, Westernized magic has anthropomorphized everything; we've given personalities to supernatural forces. It gives them *attitude*. It makes them impossible to deal with. But when we go back to the Eastern disciplines, we're operating in a whole other context. The truth is that the flows of paranormal influence are directly linked to the yin-yang flow of solidity and nothingness, of creation and destruction, of beingness and nonbeing. Real magic happens when you align yourself with the flows of chaos and order. When you ride the avalanche, you need only a nudge to steer it. If you want to have a profound effect on the course of events in the physical universe, without running the risk of a serious causal backwash of energy, you have to create spells that are in harmony with what the universe already wants to do. From what you've been telling me, it seems to me that the universe already *wants* to do something about these people next door. All you need to do is give it a focus."

I wasn't sure I understood anything of what she said, but I nodded as if I did.

Sara wasn't fooled. "Listen to me. Remember what I said about negative energy? You can't afford it. You are a fountain of creative power. You can't risk having your spring contaminated. You have to act now before you are permanently polluted. But whatever you do—you have to make sure that you don't do *greater* harm to yourself."

"What are you recommending?" I asked. She sounded so serious.

"Think of the peacock," she said.

"Pretty. Loud. Pretty loud." I free-associated.

"Do you know what a peacock eats?"

I shook my head.

"It eats the poisonous berries. It thrives on all the toxics that other birds won't touch. And it turns them into beautiful peacock feathers. That's the peacock—it takes nastiness and turns it into beauty. That's your job. Find a way to take all the stuff about your neighbors and turn it into something useful and rewarding and enlightening."

"A nice bonfire is the first thing that comes to mind. We could dance naked around it."

"It's time to stop being silly," Sara said. "You asked for my help. That's why I'm here. What kind of spell do you want to cast and what power do you want to invoke?"

"I want a spell that's quiet and unobtrusive. Inconspicuous. It shouldn't call attention to itself. No fireworks. No explosions. No ectoplasm, no manifestations, no mysterious cold spots. Just something that makes them *go away*."

"That's the best kind," Sara said.

I was looking at the list. "Let's invoke the power of the universe," I said.

"Huh?"

I pointed at the organization chart. "Look, all the power flows from the top. Let's go to the source. Let's call upon the universe to activate the spell."

Sara thought about it. "It might be overkill."

"There's no such thing as overkill," I said. "Dead is dead."

"How big an impact crater are you willing to live with?" she asked. "Remember, your house is well within the blast radius."

"We're going for gentleness, aren't we?"

"Gentleness is not delivered with a firehose," Sara said.

"Good point. We'll have to be careful."

"There could be side effects. You're probably going to get hit with some of them. Are you sure you want to do this?"

I nodded. A thought had been lurking at the back of my mind for three days. Ever since Sara had first begun coaching me. Now it was ready to blossom forth as a full-blown idea. I handed her my notes. 43 ideas. 42 of them had been crossed off. Only one remained.

Sara looked at it. She frowned. She narrowed her eyes. Her eyebrows squinched together. Her lips pursed. All of the separate parts of her face squinched up for a second, then relaxed, morphlike, into a big happy grin. "I think you may have a real talent in this area," she said.

She took her pen and double-underlined my note. *Love-bomb the bastards!*

PART FOUR:

At a quarter to midnight, we began. I went out to the backyard and flipped off every circuit breaker. There was no electrical power at all to the house. There would be no contaminating fields of magnetic resonance. The computers had all been unplugged. The batteries had been removed from every radio and flashlight.

Sara gave me a diagram, and I began to lay out a complex pattern of 39 votive candles. As I went around the room, lighting them, I recited a simple prayer of absolution. "May this light give me guidance. Help me align myself with the flows of universal power."

When I finished, I began unwinding a long yellow cord around the room, putting a loop around each candle as I strung a spiral pattern leading to an empty plate in the center. I sat down at the outside of the spiral and held the other end of the cord. I began winding it around the fingers of my left hand. The power would flow from my heart to the empty plate. And back again.

I looked to Sara. She nodded. I hadn't forgotten anything.

"Hello," I said.

I waited a moment. If the universe was listening, it hadn't given me any evidence. But then again, the universe never gives evidence of its involvement. It's just there—the ultimate in passive aggressive.

I took three deep breaths. I closed my eyes and took three more. I waited until I thought I could see the candle flames through my closed eyelids. Then I waited until I was certain we were no longer alone.

"Hello," I repeated. "Thank you. I apologize for any intrusion this action of mine might represent. I only wish to serve the flows of the universe, not to impede them. And I hope that the universe will let me be a part of its grander plans."

I waited. This time I got the feeling that some*thing* was waiting for me.

"My neighbors," I said. "The people who live in the house next door. Particularly Bryce, Lyn, Vanessa, Jabed, Jason, and Nolan. I believe that they have been impeding the natural rise toward godliness. Perhaps it is through no fault of their own. Perhaps it is because they have been seduced by the darker flows of nature. Perhaps there are reasons for which I have no language. Whatever forces are at work, I believe that they are at odds with the natural flow of universal power and goodness."

I glanced over at Sara. She was watching me intently. She nodded and smiled.

"I believe that somehow they have become separated from their own abilities to connect with others and feel compassion. I believe that they are unable to know the effects they have on the people around them. I believe that they do not see the pain they leave in their wake."

With my right hand, I placed a bowl on the empty plate in the center of the room. I poured red wine into the bowl, then I placed a single rose blossom in the wine. "I offer you this gift," I said. "I do so freely and with no thought of personal reward or gain. I ask nothing for myself, nor for anyone close to me. I ask only that you grant my neighbors an opportunity to join our larger purposes, to swim in the flow of universal spirit that heads inevitably toward enlightenment. Please help direct their energies toward goodness and joy."

I bowed my head. "Thank you," I said. "Thank you for listening. Thank you for being here. Thank you for letting me serve you tonight."

And—maybe it was the sudden breeze from the door—but every single candle in the room went out simultaneously.

"Nicely done," said Sara, after a long startled silence. "*Very* nicely done."

EPILOGUE:

The next morning, I felt rather silly for having gone through such a baroque ritual. But I made up my mind to wait a week. Or two. Or even six.

Nothing happened at first.

Then, one horrible weekend, *everything* happened. Lyn and Bryce were out somewhere. Vanessa had invited five hundred close friends to a backyard bash, with 600 decibels of heavy metal rock music and illegal fireworks. Jabed and Jason were sitting on the roof of the garage throwing cherry bombs into the dancers, which triggered a spate of angry gunfire between members of two rival gangs who were trying to crash the party from the alley side of the yard. In the ensuing panic, several automobiles were smashed into each other as people tried to flee—a dead-end street does not lend itself to an orderly evacuation. In the confusion, Nolan found the box of fireworks and managed to light both them *and the house* on fire. By the time the police and fire department arrived, the structure was sending fifty-foot flames into the air and I was hosing down my roof and praying that the overhanging tree wouldn't catch. The fire crew couldn't get through the mass of cars to the fire hydrant, and even if they could have, it wouldn't have done any good because someone had crashed into it, knocking it off, sending a high-pressure fountain spraying high into the air where it made an impressive, but otherwise useless, display of uncontained aquatic energy. They ended up taking one of the units around to the alley side and backing it into my backyard so they could pump the water out of my pool and onto the neighbor's roof. It took them twenty minutes to knock down the blaze, leaving the house a charred and waterlogged mess. By the time they were through, there were over twenty police vehicles on the block, three ambulances, and four news vans.

In the aftermath, four stolen cars were recovered from joy-riding gang-bangers, seventeen people were arrested for possession and dealing of illegal substances, twelve illegal weapons were confiscated, and twenty-six of the party-goers spent the night in jail for being drunk and disorderly. Fourteen outstanding warrants were served for offenses as varied as unpaid parking tickets and felony armed robbery. Vanessa's friends were an assorted lot.

The following Monday, Lyn and Bryce were investigated by the Department of Social Services.

And I called Sara and asked what went wrong.

She told me not to worry. Everything was fine. Just be patient.

She was right. It took a while for everything to get sorted out, but eventually, it did.

The judge ordered three years of family counseling for the whole clan. Vanessa was put on probation, conditional on her remaining in Alcoholics Anonymous. Jabed and Jason were put into a special education program to help them recover from prolongued emotional abuse and also to prevent them from drifting into patterns of juvenile delinquency. Nolan was identified as suffering from a serious learning disability and is now in full-time therapy. Tali is in preschool. Damien is president of the local Gay Students' Union chapter. Grandma had to sell the house to help Lynn and Bryce cover the legal expenses. They all live with her now.

The insurance company leveled the remains of the house and sold the land to the city for use as a pocket park. It wasn't cost effective to rebuild.

To paraphrase my favorite moose, sometimes I don't know my own strength.

For a while, both Sara and I were concerned about the backwash from the spell. We'd love-bombed the entire family, and they were all definitely much better off than they had been before. But Sara was afraid that there would be serious side effects to the spell that might affect both of us. If there have been any, we haven't noticed them yet. But then again, we've been much too busy. Sara's planning to move in with me next month, and I've applied to adopt a little boy. And I expect to get back to my writing Real Soon Now.

The Christmas Witch

ROSEMARY EDGHILL

Rosemary Edghill is best known among readers of witch fiction for the heroine of her "Bast" mystery series—a neopagan character who rivals Mercedes Lackey's Diana Tregarde in popularity. Here, however, she shares a beautiful story of Yuletide roots and traditions for young readers, Wiccan and non-Wiccan alike.

ROWAN liked winter. The weeks after Halloween, when the world turned dark and cold, were special to her. They seemed to be full of magic. Everybody felt it. Houses were decorated with lights and evergreen wreaths. It was as if the air itself were filled with mystery, as if everyone was awaiting the arrival of a special guest.

But everyone else celebrated Christmas, and Rowan's family did not.

"Why don't we have a tree like everyone else?" Rowan asked.

Rowan's family decorated the house with evergreen garlands, holly, and mistletoe, but they did not have a Christmas tree.

"That is not our way," said Rowan's aunt, and explained how the Norse decorated trees in honor of the Aesir and the Vanir, and how Christians had kept on decorating trees even when they had forgotten why.

"Well, why don't we have a menorah?" Rowan asked.

Rowan's family put silver stars in all the windows, but their stars all had five points, not six.

"That is not our way," said Rowan's uncle, and explained how the Jews lit the nine candles at Chanukah to remember a miracle from long ago.

"Well, could we have a crèche, then?" Rowan asked. She liked the angels with their golden hair and the way the animals all gathered together.

"That is not our way," said Rowan's father, and explained how the crèche was so that Christians could celebrate the birth of their god.

"Santa isn't Christian or Jewish," Rowan said. "Why don't we have Santa at our house?" In December, Rowan saw Santas everywhere. There were pictures of him on almost every house. But there were no pictures of Santa at Rowan's house.

"That is not our way," said Ash. "Wait and see." He was Rowan's older brother, and never explained anything.

On the Winter Solstice, the shortest day of the year, Rowan's family would gather together with their friends to celebrate the fact that the days would now become longer. Rowan's family had a big Yule log with thirteen candles, one for each week of winter and for each full moon of the year. They lit the candles when everyone was together. They exchanged gifts with each other, and sang songs like "Welcome, Winter," and ate Yule cake. Rowan got the biggest piece, but she still wasn't happy. She thought they'd left something out.

"I guess Witches are different from everybody else," Rowan said sadly. Rowan's family practiced the ancient earth religion called Wicca, and the Winter Solstice was one of their special days.

"Wait and see," said Rowan's mother, as she tucked her into bed that night.

That night Rowan dreamed of a time long ago, when the first winter came. The grass turned brown, and the leaves fell from the trees. It rained, and then the rain froze and fell as snow, until all the land was white and silver. The skies were dark, and the sun set earlier each day. Everyone was cold and sad, for they did not know if the sun would ever come back.

"What will we do?" asked the First Mother.

"What will we eat?" asked the First Father.

"Will it ever be warm again?" asked the First Boy.

"I will go to look for the sun!" said the First Girl.

She dressed in her warmest clothes and began to walk. She walked all day toward the sun, but the shadows grew long as the day ended and she was no nearer to the sun than she had been when she began. The only green things she could see were the green pine trees and the green holly bushes, and she began to be afraid, for she was lost and all alone in the wide world.

As she stood in the snow, she heard bells. Soon she could see a man walking toward her from the place where the sun set. He had a staff that was garlanded with ribbons and bells. He was dressed all in green, and wore a crown of holly and evergreen. On his back he carried a big sack.

"I am the Winter King," he said to the First Girl. "I have come to tell you that winter will not last forever. Soon you will see the sun rise higher in the sky. Soon green grass will grow and flowers will blossom, and everything will grow warm again."

"I do not believe it!" said the First Girl, looking at the snow. Because this was the first winter, she had never seen spring come.

The Winter King laughed. He swung the sack down off his shoulder and reached into it. "I have brought you a present to brighten these dark days, and as a token of my promise that the grass will grow and the flowers will bloom." And he handed her a beautiful golden ball. When she shook it she heard the chuckling of summer brooks, and the rustling of wind in summer grass.

"Now take me home to your family," the Winter King said, "because I have presents for all of them, too, and a promise that winter will not last forever."

And so the First Girl and the Winter King went to find her family.

AFTER she had dreamed, Rowan woke up. It was the middle of the night. She heard noise in the living room and ran to look.

A man was in the living room, putting gifts wrapped in shiny gold paper beside the Yule log.

He wore green velvet the color of pine trees and holly branches. He had flowing silver hair and a long white beard, and his black boots were so shiny that she could see the streetlights in them. He wore a crown of holly, and standing beside him was a magnificent silver stag, whose coat was as white as snow and whose antlers were as silver as the Moon. It wore a wreath of holly and pine around its neck, and its antlers were decorated with stars.

"I know you!" Rowan exclaimed.

"I am the Winter King," he said, smiling. "And I know you, too."

Her mother came and put an arm around Rowan's shoulders. "The Winter King has many names. Some people say he is Santa Claus, and only brings gifts for good children. We call him Father Winter, and he comes to us at the beginning of winter to bring everyone gifts and to make certain we will all be well until spring comes."

"That is our way!" said Rowan. She was happy. They had a special time in December just like everyone else, and their own special ways. "Witches aren't that different from everybody else," Rowan told her mother proudly.

The Strange People

*Modern witches draw from many sources, not just the Celtic, and of
particular interest to many is Native American shamanism. This
poem reminds us of the shamanic tradition of shape-shifting.*

The antelope are strange people . . .
they are beautiful to look at, and yet
they are tricky. We do not trust them.
They appear and disappear; they are
like shadows on the plains. Because
of their great beauty, young men
sometimes follow the antelope and are
lost forever. Even if those foolish ones
find themselves and return, they are
never again right in their heads.
— PRETTY SHIELD

All night I am the doe, breathing
his name in a frozen field,
the small mist of the word
drifting always before me.

And again he has heard it
and I have gone burning
to meet him, the jacklight
fills my eyes with blue fire;
the heart in my chest
explodes like a hot stone.

Then slung like a sack
in the back of his pick-up,
I wipe the death scum
from my mouth, sit up laughing
and shriek in my speeding grave.

Safely shut in the garage,
when he sharpens his knife
and thinks to have me, like that,
I come toward him,
a lean grey witch,
through the bullets that enter and dissolve.

I sit in his house
drinking coffee till dawn,
and leave as frost reddens on hubcaps,
crawling back into my shadowy body.
All day, asleep in clean grasses,
I dream of the one who could really wound me.

When he comes, more quiet
than the others,
I take him away with me.
On his head
fix the simple, cleft prongs.
I make him come with me to the trees and lie down.

Wind cries like a cat.
The leaves cut where they touch
and we curl from our wet flesh like smoke,
leaving the light of our hunger in the bones
that will burn till dew falls
in the ashes.

When you pass
these grey forms

that flake and shiver in the wind,
Do not touch them, turn back.
Human, frail human,
Lope toward your own dark shelter.

Reunion

Kathryn Ptacek

Kathryn Ptacek is a writer of many faces—suspense, fantasy, horror, romance. Like Gerrold's The Spell, *this story could also fit in the section on empowerment and wish fulfillment. But consider the tools the story's witches use, and the natural means by which their spell manifests, and you'll see that it's also pure nature magic.*

I was enjoying the warmth of the sun upon my head, the sound of waves crashing upon the beach, the gritty feel of the sand beneath my bare toes. The sea gulls wheeled overhead, occasionally swooping down for a tasty tidbit; somewhere a radio played softly in the background. The white sails of boats dotted the blue ocean.

I was growing drowsy and thinking of napping when a loud voice interrupted my sun-induced reverie. I cocked open an eye and saw the source: the woman who had just married into the family a year or so ago.

My husband had talked me into attending his family's late spring reunion at the Jersey shore. I had wanted to stay home and tend my garden. While I'd already planted most everything, there is the matter of maintenance; you see, a garden is crucial to a witch. But my husband convinced me it would be good for me to get out of the house—he's rarely there, since he commutes long hours to New York City; often he travels on company business. He thinks nothing of flying thousands of miles, while I hardly stray from the house.

The loud voice broke into my thoughts again.

The newcomer was holding forth to whomever would listen, and her voice was much too loud for such a relaxing day. I couldn't hear everything she said, although once in a while individual words floated my way.

She wasn't angry; she just had her opinions, and she was determined that everyone would know them, whether they'd asked or not. She approached her husband Michael and his brothers now and pointed at the barbecue, which they were in charge of. Obviously she was unhappy about something she saw there, or perhaps she thought she knew a better way of doing it, and her husband's face was growing redder by the moment as he listened to her. My husband laughed, but Michael shook his head and his lips were pressed tightly together.

Another brother made a dismissive gesture, and realizing she wasn't wanted there at that moment, Sherry—for so she had called herself when we were first introduced; I had not gone to their wedding last year—cornered the teenagers next. From the beginning, the teens had clumped together, bemoaning loudly their fate at having been dragged away from the mall for a weekend. Now they looked bored and uncomfortable as Sherry obviously corrected them on some matter, then began lecturing a dark-haired girl in a skimpy bikini on proper attire, and finally, out of desperation, the teens left to help their fathers. Next she pounced upon the small children—and there were many, for my in-laws have always been prodigious breeders—who up to that minute had been happily engaged in games of tag and Frisbee. Sherry wanted to organize them into regular games, but no one could agree on what kind or who'd be the leader because they all wanted to be it. Minutes later a fistfight broke out between the blonde twins, who were the best natured of children, and one of the children went screaming to his mother.

My husband's sisters had made themselves scarce, and I wondered where they could have disappeared to so quickly and efficiently. Next, Sherry lectured the rest of her new family, including my mother-in-law, who as she lounged on her beach blanket was pretending to be hard of hearing, which she most certainly is not.

It was going to be a long three days. Since she'd driven in with her husband Michael this morning, Sherry hadn't shut up once.

Yes, a very long weekend.

As I watched a miniature crab scuttle across the sand by my toes, I wished then that I had brought some books with me. I had several paperbacks to read, but the books I'd left behind were the ones with spells in them. There are many tomes to study. I have learned much in my life, but there is still much to master. It's not widely known what I do, because there are in our society certain archaic attitudes still in existence. But I did not need to advertise; word of mouth played a goodly part. Sometimes the neighbor women come to me when they don't feel well, or when they want to attract the attention of a man at work, and when they no longer wish the attention of their husbands, and I prepare certain recipes for them.

I do like to be supportive. And it is crucial that I learn new spells and practice them on a regular basis.

Next week, I thought with a yawn. This is my vacation. I'm here to sit in the sun and stare off into the distance and do nothing harder than lift a glass of iced tea to my lips.

Suddenly Sherry spotted me, sprinted over as if she feared I would leap to my feet and flee, and dropped down onto the sand alongside me. In doing so, she knocked over my glass and splashed sand onto my open book. I managed to retrieve the book before the tea drenched it. I wondered if the tiny crab had moved out of her way in time, then I saw one tiny pincher jutting out of the sand at a broken angle.

"Oh, sorry, did I do that? Geez, I'm such a klutz." She tried to grab the overturned tumbler. I was faster.

I murmured something polite.

"What's that you're reading?" she asked and seized my book before I could do anything. "Geez, you read this kind of stuff, honey?" She shook her head at my apparent lack of taste. "I don't read much, y'know, but when I do, I like the gritty stuff, if you know what I mean. You know, realistic. I don't like fantasy much, or that horror stuff."

"I like to read all sorts of things," I admitted.

"Time's too short to read everything, I say. You know that? I mean we only got so many hours in the day, and if you work all day, you don't have much time at home for dumb stuff, you know? And brother, you better believe I work hard. You know, I've got this important job—I just got promoted—" She paused.

I murmured my congratulations. She had been waiting for that. She went on.

"So, I got this promotion, and my boss says to me we really expect big things out of you, Sher—he calls me that, you know—and I says to him that I won't let him down, and you better believe that I won't. I am in charge of operations for a coupla hunnert salesguys, you know, and you had better believe that that's a damned important thing. I mean, if I weren't there the company would come apart at the seams, you know?" She squinted at me. "So, you're like what, a housewife?"

I smiled.

"Geez, I didn't know there were any of those around anymore. I mean, how can you stand to be cooped up in the house all the time day after day and not doing something really important? I mean, I'm not one of those women libbers or whatever, but you gotta get out of the house and do something for yourself, gotta work to keep the cobwebs out of the mind, if you know what I mean. I mean, working keeps you young. You gotta put some meaning in your life, you know? Plus it's nice to get the extra dough. You got kids yet?"

"Not yet."

"Geez, you guys have been married a long time, like seven or eight years or something, right?"

"Or something."

"Geez, I hope nothing's wrong." She paused.

My smile stretched.

"You know, Tommy and his wife over here have been to the fertility clinic I don't know how many times in the past couple of years. It's gonna cost them a fortune to just have the kid, you know. That is, if they can have one. I kept tellin' them they oughta adopt, and Tina just kept bawlin' like some lost calf or something. Tommy just left in a huff; I don't know why. You know, Michael and me are gonna start our family in about a year or two. I'll be thirty then, and we'll be pretty set with our finances and all by then, and then Michael says he'll stay home with the kid. Pretty good, huh? Geez, I couldn't have asked for a better husband. He sure has done a lot better than his brothers—except for your husband, of course. I mean, the others are, well, you couldn't very well call them successful, could you? Bruce is on his, what, fifth or sixth wife now?"

"Second," I corrected.

"Oh. And then there's Will; I heard him and his wife had to declare bankruptcy. What kind of high living were they doing or what?"

"I believe her mother was dying of cancer and had no hospitalization, and that the medical bills just keep mounting up. You know, hospitals and doctors don't like to wait for their money."

"Oh yeah? I thought it was because they got too many new cars or something. Actually, I thought they had this gamblin' problem cause they live so close to Atlantic City and all. They probably went there hoping they'd win a potful so they could pay those bills." Sherry paused to shake her head. She ran a hand through her hair, which was honey-blonde and quite luxurious; her eyes were blue-green and wide-set, and she had that sort of ingenuous face and shapely figure that would motivate men to leap forward and open doors for her and light her cigarette or otherwise fetch for her. Until she opened her mouth, that was. "And Evan, he's a real souse. I never saw anyone enjoy his beer as much as he does, if you know what I mean. You know, honey, I don't go in for alcohol and that sort of thing; I just don't think it's right."

"Evan's had a hard time. His wife left him, taking their two daughters, and a few days later they were killed in a car crash."

"Geez? Really? That's too bad. I dunno. I guess I can understand then. But the others . . . what's their excuses, I mean? The sisters—our sisters-in-law—they're not that much better, you know? I mean Cindy has had two liposuctions already, and the way she keeps gettin' into the cupcakes and potato chips, she's gonna need a third. And Beth's got a real weight problem. Her kids are kinda chunky too. She'd better set a better example for them; you know, kids imitate adults." She nodded again. "Yeah, I got the real pick of the litter—except for your husband, of course."

Blessedly for a moment she fell silent, then she half-turned in my direction.

"The guys are all cute, though, don't you think?"

She meant the brothers, I realized. "Yes, they're all very good-looking. I understand they look much like their father did when he was young. Of course, I didn't know him long before he died."

"Oh yeah, I heard he had some sort of . . . disease, you know." She looked at me knowingly.

"Disease? I thought it was a heart attack that killed him."

"Oh no, I heard he picked up this . . . disease . . . you know . . . from someone not his family."

My fingers, resting in the sand, clenched.

"Geez, I hope none of the brothers take after him, you know, honey? I mean I'd just kill Michael if he did something like that. But I don't know, him and your husband, they're quite the lookers, huh? I just bet you get women crawling all over your husband all the time."

"Not really."

"I'm amazed. Of course, I'll let you know what the women say about your husband and all."

"What?" I asked, a little startled.

"Oh yeah, didn't I tell you, honey? I work at Fosterfields & Sons. You know, he got me my job at the company. When he was out at the wedding last year, I happened to mention that I was looking for work, and he said he knew a position at his company, and the next thing you know I was interviewing for it, and then I got hired. I'm in the office right next to your husband."

My smile froze.

She winked. "So I'll keep a good eye on him for you, honey." She took a deep breath and swiveled her head, scanning for other family members she could move in on. "Geez, here I've been talkin' about everybody in the family and going on and on, and I hope you don't think I'm a, well, you know," she leaned toward me confidentially, "the 'b' word. I don't wanna use it, because it's not the kind of word you use in polite company, if you know what I mean, it not being a very nice word, if you take my meaning."

"Not at all," I said at my diplomatic best. Indeed, I did take her meaning. "Oh, look, Sherry, I think Michael is looking for you."

"Oh yeah? I guess I ought to go. He's just so jealous, you know; hates to have me talking to other guys. I bet he'd just *kill* me if he saw all the times me and your husband get together to talk at the office. Hey, it was real nice chattin' with you. We'll have to do this again, you know." She sprang up and trotted off toward Michael.

"Not on your life," I said aloud after she had gone. I had never met a more obnoxious woman, and what was worse is they didn't live all that far away from us, which meant I would be seeing her again.

In fact, my husband had mentioned something about getting together with Michael and Sherry after the reunion.

And he had helped her get the job at the company. He had never said a word to me.

I stared at the ocean for a moment, then glanced at Sherry. Then with my left hand I smoothed the sand in front of the towel, and with great concentration began making tracings. I was relying on my memory because I didn't have my special books with me. If anyone saw me, they would simply think I was doodling in the sand.

I glanced back up at Sherry. Nothing seemed to have happened. She was still talking away, and now I thought my husband looked fairly entranced by her. But perhaps I was mistaken.

I swept away the old patterns, began knew ones. Minutes went by, and still nothing happened. One sister had left in a huff after Sherry had converged upon their group.

I realized with some frustration that I just couldn't recall the proper spell. If only I had my books. . . . I closed my eyes and tried to visualize the lines upon the pages.

Nothing.

Angrily I kicked my useless paperback away.

A shadow loomed over my patterns, and I looked up, halfway expecting it to be Sherry.

"Actually, I prefer shells," Chloe, Bruce's wife, said as she dropped to her knees and unloaded the delicate shells she had collected in the front of her sweatshirt. "Does the trick just as well, I think."

"I beg your pardon?"

"Shells. I like to use them when I'm engaged in my . . . work . . ." She began laying the shells out in intricate patterns.

I watched as the patterns grew, and I recognized them. I was speechless. I had found a kindred spirit, and here in my husband's family!

"How long have you known?" I finally managed to ask.

"Well, I suspected it for a while, but when I saw your expression when Motormouth was here, and then saw what you were doing in the sand, I knew."

" 'Motormouth.' That's not very kind."

Chloe glanced over at Sherry, who seemed now to be bawling her husband out for some reason. His head hung down slightly, as if he had heard all of this before. "She's a gossip, a nag, a bore—and I'm sure we could find a few more choice words for her."

"The 'b' word."

" 'I don't wanna use it . . .' " Chloe quoted.

" 'It's not the kind of word you use in polite company . . .' "

". . . 'It not being a very nice word . . .' "

" 'If you take my meaning,' " we finished together and then laughed.

"She is indeed that," Chloe said. "I don't know how Michael got involved with her."

"A moment of weakness," I suggested, and we laughed again.

Sherry had moved on to the group of brothers, and it was apparent even from where we sat that she was informing them they were incorrectly barbecuing. Tommy looked thoroughly disgusted, and Evan had opened another beer, and Sherry's husband was standing there with his back to everyone. Two of the sisters were arguing with each other, and a ten-year-old had knocked another down and was kicking sand in his face.

"She's ruining everyone's mood, and this is just the beginning of the reunion. The way things are going we'll all be pissed at each other inside of an hour and heading home by the end of the day. What are we going to do?"

"Well, Chloe, I don't know about you, but I really am having a good time. I admit I didn't want to come, but I'm glad I did. And now that I'm here, I don't want anything to spoil it. Not anything."

We smiled at each other.

"It's a shame I don't have my books here with me," I said. "I've been having a hard time remembering the proper spell."

"Well, I don't have mine with me, either. We could improvise, though," Chloe said, and laid a line of pink shells at a right angle to half of an oyster shell. "I'm sure what we can come up with together would be stronger than one of us alone."

"I'm sure you're right." My fingers moved through the sand. "We can't do anything too terrible. I mean, if she dies, it really will put a damper on the party."

"That's true. Hmm. What about stomach cramps?"

"I thought about that, but . . . no. The others might think it's because of the food, and we wouldn't want that."

"Hmm. You're right. A headache?"

"She'd get sympathy then."

"Can't have that." Chloe tapped her knee with her fingertips. "You know, when we get home, we'll have to swap some recipes. I've got one for a love potion that's the quickest, safest thing I've ever seen."

"I'd like to hear about it. I don't know if you've ever used a poppet before, but I once had occasion to employ a paper one, and it worked beautifully."

The wind had shifted, and now we could hear Sherry's voice more clearly than before. Her tone was becoming increasingly strident, and Michael had just turned and was stomping back to the hotel where we all had rooms for the long weekend. More little kids were wailing, and now some of the teenaged boy cousins had become involved in a shouting match. I noticed that Sherry had a bottle of beer in her hand; it would seem she didn't operate well with alcohol, either.

I looked at Chloe. "I know."

She cocked an eyebrow. "Yeah?"

"Muteness."

We both smiled.

It didn't take long, and before even half an hour had gone by, Sherry's voice began to fail her. She sputtered and choked, although she was never in any danger. She waved a hand in front of her mouth, as if she believed that would make her voice come back, and she tried to talk, but only a squeak came out. She called for Michael, but by then her voice was gone—it would be for the next three days—and when she tried to wave at someone to make them understand she'd gotten an abrupt case of laryngitis, she found they simply stared at her; no one cared that she couldn't talk any longer. Finally, she went off toward the hotel. A few minutes later Michael came out to join the family.

"Time for dinner, ladies," my husband called to us, waving the spatula over his head as if it were a sword triumphant.

"Shall we go?" Chloe said.

"Delighted," I said as I stood and walked back toward the others with my newfound friend. I must, I decided at that moment, have Chloe and Bruce over to dinner when Michael and Sherry came to visit. Chloe would bring her books, and I would have mine at hand and . . . well, imagine what we could do then . . .

I smiled, fully enjoying the reunion now.

The Witch's Daughter

MARY WILKINS FREEMAN

Mary Wilkins Freeman, born on Halloween in 1852, wrote over twenty volumes of short stories, fourteen novels, plays, and poetry. She's best remembered for her ghost stories, which managed to include a touch of carefully veiled feminism. What better writer for witches?

IT was well for old Elma Franklin that Cotton Mather had passed to either the heaven or hell in which he believed; it was well that the Salem witchcraft days were over, although not so long ago, or it would have fared ill with her. As it was, she was shunned, and at the same time cringed to. People feared to fear her. Witches were no longer accused in court, and put to torture and death, but human superstitions die hard. The heads thereof may be cut off, but their noxious bodies of fear and suspicions writhe long. People in that little New England village, which was as stiff and unyielding as its own poplar-trees which sentinelled so many of its houses, knew nothing of that making of horns which averts the evil eye. They shuddered upon their orthodox heights at the idea of the sign of the cross, but many would have fain taken refuge therein for the easing of their unquiet imaginations when they dwelt upon old Elma Franklin. Many a woman whispered to another under promise of strict secrecy that she was sure that Elma bore upon her lean, withered body the witch-sign; many a man, when he told his neighbor of the death of his cow or horse, nodded furtively toward old Elma's dwelling. In truth, old Elma's appearance alone, had it been only a few years ago, would have condemned her. Lean was she, and withered in a hard brown fashion like old leather. Her eyes were of a blue so bright that people said they felt like swooning before their glance; and what right had a woman, so old and wrinkled, with a head of golden hair like a young girl's? Her own hair, too, and she would wear no wig like other decent women of less than her age. And what right had she with that flower-like daughter Daphne?

Young creatures like Daphne are not born of women like Elma Franklin, who must have been old sixteen years agone. Daphne was sixteen. Daphne had a Greek name and Greek beauty. She was very small, but very perfect, and finished like an ivory statue whose sculptor had toiled for his own immortality. Daphne had golden hair like her mother's, but it waved in a fashion past finding out over her little ears, whose tips showed below like the pointed petals of pink roses, and her chin and cheeks curved as clearly as a rose, and her nose made a rapture of her profile, and her neck was long and slowly turning, and her eyes were not blue like her mother's, but sweet and dark, and gently regardant, and her hands were as white and smooth as lilies, whereas hands had never been seen so knotted and wickedly veined as if with unholy clawing as her mother's.

Daphne led, however, as lonely a life as her mother. People were afraid. Dark stories, vile stories, were whispered among that pitiless, bigoted people. Old Elma and Daphne lived alone in their poor little cottage, although in the midst of fertile fields, and they fed on the milk of their two cows, and the eggs of their chickens, and the vegetables of their garden, and the honey of their bees. Old Elma hived them when they swarmed with never any protection for that strange face and those hands of hers, and people said the bees were of an evil breed, and familiars of old Elma's, and durst not sting her. Young men sometimes cast eyes askance at Daphne, but turned away, and old Elma knew the reason why, and she hated them; for hatred prospered in her heart, coming as she did of a strong and fierce race. Elma combed her daughter's wonderful golden locks, and dressed her in fine stuff made of a store which she had in a great carved chest in the garret, and would have had the girl go to meeting where she could be seen and admired; but Daphne went once, and was ever after afraid to venture, because of the black looks cast upon her, which seemed to sear her gentle heart, for the girl was so gentle that she seemed to have no voice of insistence for her own rights. When her mother chid her, saying, with the disappointment of a great love, that she had with her own hands fashioned her wonderful gown of red shot with golden threads and embroidered with silver flowers, and had wrought with fine needlework her lace kerchief and her mitts and her scarf, and that it was a shame that she must needs, with all this goodly apparel, slink beside her own hearth and be seen of no one, the girl only kissed her mother on her leathery brown cheek, and smiled like an angel. Daphne was a maiden of few words, and that would have enticed lovers had it not been for her mother. However, at last came Harry Edgelake, and he was bolder than the rest, and the moment he set eyes upon the girl clad in green with a rose in her hair and a rose at her breast, spinning in a cool shadow at her mother's door, his heart melted, and he swore that he would wed her, came she of a whole witch-tribe. But Harry had more than he recked at first to deal with in the way of opposition. He came of a long line of eminent ministers of the Word, and his grandfather and father still survived, and were of the Cotton Mather strain. Although they talked none, they would, if the good old days had endured, have had old Elma up before the judges; for all the cattle in the precinct, and all the poor crops, and every thunder tempest and lightning stroke, and all strange noises they laid at her door, nodding at each other and whispering.

Therefore when it came to their ears that Harry, who had just come home from Harvard, and was to be, had he a call, a minister of the Word, like themselves, had been seen standing and chatting by the hour beside the witch's daughter as she spun in the shade with her golden head shining out in it like a star, he was sternly reasoned with. And when he heeded not the counsel of his elders, but was seen strolling down lovers' lane with the maid, great stress was laid to bear upon him, and he was sent away to Boston town, and Daphne watched and he came not, and old Elma watched the girl watch in vain, and her evil passions grew; for evil surely dwelt in her heart, as in most human hearts, and she had been sorely dealt with and badgered, and the girl was her one delight of life, and the girl's sorrow was her own magnified into the most cruel torture that a heart can bear and live.

And whether she were a witch or not, much brooding upon the suspicion with which people regarded her had made her uncertain of herself, and she owned a strange book of magic, over which she loved to pore when the cry of the hounds of her kind was in her ears, and she resolved one night, when a month had passed and she knew her daughter to be pining for her lover, that if she were indeed witch as they said, she would use witchcraft.

The moon was at the full, and the wide field behind her cottage, which had been shorn for hay for the cows, glittered like a silver shield, and upon the silver shield were little wheels also like silver woven by spiders for their prey, and strange lights of dew blazed out here and there like stars. And old Elma led her daughter out into the field, and Elma wore a sad-colored gown which made her passing like the passing of a shadow, and Daphne was all in white, which made her passing like that of a moonbeam; and the mother took her daughter by the arm, and she so loved her that she hurt her.

"Mother, you hurt me, you hurt me!" moaned Daphne, and directly the mother's grasp of the little fair arm was as if she touched a newborn babe.

"What aileth thee, sweetheart?" she whispered, but the girl only sobbed gently.

"It is for thy lover, and not a maid in the precinct so fair and good," said the mother, in her fierce old voice.

And Daphne sobbed again, and the mother gathered her in her arms.

"Sweetheart, thy mother will compel love for thee," she whispered, and the girl shrank away in fear, for there was something strange in her mother's voice.

"I want no witchery," she whispered.

"Nay, but this is good witchery, to call true love to true love."

"If love cannot be called else, I want not love at all."

"But, sweetheart, this is not black but white witchery."

"I want none, and besides—"

"Besides?"

The girl said no more, but the mother knew that it was because of her that the lover had fled, and not because of lack of love.

"See, sweetheart," said old Elma, "I know a charm."

"I will have no charm, mother; I tell thee I will have no charm."

"Sweetheart, watch thy mother cross the field from east to west and from north to south, and crisscross like the spiders' webs, and see if thou thinkest it harmful witchcraft."

"I will not, mother," said the girl, but she watched.

And old Elma crossed the field from east to west and from north to south, and crisscrossed like the spiders' webs, and ever after her trailed lines of brighter silver than the dew which lay up the field, until the whole was like a wonderful web, and in the midst shone a great silver light as if the moon had fallen there, although still in the sky.

Then came old Elma to her daughter, and her face in the strange light was fair and young. "Daughter, daughter," said the mother, "but follow the lines of light thy mother's feet have made and come to the central light, and thy lover shall be there."

But the daughter stood in her place, like a white lily whose roots none could stir save to her death. "I follow not, mother," she said. "It would be to his soul's undoing, and better I love his soul and its fair salvation than his body and his heart in this world."

And the mother was silent, for she truly knew not as to the spell whether it concerned the soul's salvation.

But she had still another spell, which she had learned from her strange book. "Then stay, daughter," said old Elma, and straightway she crossed the paths of light which she made, and they vanished, and the meadow became as before, but in the midst old Elma stood, and said strange words under her breath, and waved her arms, while her daughter watched her fearfully. And as she watched, Daphne saw spring up, in the meadow in the space over which her mother's long arms waved, a patch of white lilies, which gave out lights like no lilies of earth, and their wonderful scent came in her face. And her mother hurried back, and in her hurrying was like a black shadow passing over the meadow.

"And go to the patch of lilies, sweetheart," she said, "and in the time which it takes thee to reach them thy lover will have gone over the forests and the waters, and he will meet thee in the lilies."

But Daphne stood firm in her place. "I go not, mother," she said. "It would be to his dear soul's undoing, and better I love his soul and his soul's heaven than I love him and myself."

Then down lay old Elma upon the silver shield of the meadow like a black shadow at her daughter's feet.

"Then is there but one way left, sweetheart," came her voice from among the meadow grasses like the love-song of a stricken mother-bird. "There is but one way, sweet daughter of mine. Step thou over thy mother's body, darling, and cross to the patch of lilies, and I swear to thee, by the Christ and the Cross and all that the meeting-folk hold sacred, that thou shalt have thy lover, and his soul shall not miss heaven, neither his soul nor thine."

"And thine?"

"I am thy mother."

And Daphne stood firm. "Better I love thee, mother," she said, "than heaven on earth with my lover; better I love thee than his weal or mine in this world, better than all save his dear soul."

"I tell thee, sweet, cross my body, and his soul and thy soul shall be safe."

"But thy life on earth, and thy soul?"

"I am thy mother."

"I will not go."

Then came a wail of despair from old Elma at her daughter's feet upon the silver shield of the meadow, and then she was raised up by young Harry Edgelake, and she stood with her leathern old face like an angel's for pure joy and forgetfulness of self. For her daughter stood in her lover's arms and his voice sounded like a song.

"Nothing on earth and nothing in heaven shall part me from thee, who hold my soul dearer than myself, and thy mother dearer than thyself, for, witch or no witch, thy mother has shown me thy angel in the meadow to-night," he said.

Old Elma stood watching them with her face of pure joy, and all the fierceness and the bitter grief of injury received from those whom she had not injured faded from her heart. She forgot the strange book which she had studied, she forgot her power of strange deeds, she forgot herself, and remembered nothing, nothing save her daughter and her love, and such bliss possessed her that she could stand no longer upon the silver shield of the meadow. She sank down slowly as a flower sinks when its time has come before the sun and the wind which have given it life, and she lay still at the feet of her daughter and the youth, and they stooped over her and they knew that she had been no witch, but a great lover.

Shall Earth no more inspire thee

EMILY BRONTË

Yes, I'm really *pretty sure the author of* Wuthering Heights *was neither neopagan nor witch. But considering all the supposed theories offered about her work (Heathcliff and Cathy were related! Bramwell Brontë wrote all his sisters' supposed work!) I'm willing to be proven wrong.*

Shall Earth no more inspire thee,
Thou lonely dreamer now?
Since passion may not fire thee
Shall Nature cease to bow?

Thy mind is ever moving
In regions dark to thee;
Recall its useless roving—
Come back and dwell with me.

I know my mountain breezes
Enchant and soothe thee still—
I know my sunshine pleases
Despite thy wayward will.

When day with evening blending
Sinks from the summer sky,
I've seen thy spirit bending
In fond idolatry.

I've watched thee every hour—
I know my mighty sway—

I know my magic power
To drive thy griefs away.

Few hearts to mortals given
On earth so wildly pine,
Yet none would ask a Heaven
More like the Earth than mine.

Then let my winds caress thee—
Thy comrade let me be—
Since naught beside can bless thee,
Return and dwell with me.

Winter Solstice

Evelyn Vaughn

Evelyn Vaughn's well-received Circle series for the Silhouette Shadows romance line showed yet again that witchcraft and love stories can go together. Winter Solstice *explores the Wiccan mythology of the Oak King and the Holly King's twice-a-year battles for dominion. Evelyn Vaughn also writes as Yvonne Jocks.*

DARKNESS surrounded the isolated cabin—in more ways than one. "This," murmured Ivy, watching her breath mist a cold pane of the cabin window, "is *not* what people mean when they call December a season of magic."

Not that the wintery night beyond didn't have a hushed otherworldliness about it. Snow swirled out of the blackness so quietly, Ivy wasn't sure if she heard its tiny, gritty impact against the glass with her ears . . . or with less mundane senses. Magic, *real* magic, worked like that—so subtle it could hardly be differentiated from coincidence, or imagination, or even delusions.

Chenille-sweatered arms braced against the windowsill, narrow chin pillowed on her arms, Ivy stared at her dark-haired, dark-eyed reflection. Sometimes, even the most devoted of witches found that kind of subtlety frustratingly anticlimactic. Maybe that's why so few potential magic users stayed with the discipline. Nowadays, people wanted the kind of instant pyrotechnics only *movie*-witches produced.

Ivy wasn't looking for laser beams and levitation—but over the last half-year, especially since the Harvest Moon, she'd become so desperate for a little proof, a little reassurance, that she ached for it, *dreamed* about it. That's why she'd driven out here, by herself, on a day when her friends were preparing to party as only pagans could.

"Magical quest, or fool's errand," she sighed, and in her breath's resulting fog she drew a squeaky, five-pointed star with one finger. " 'Only my hair-dresser knows for sure.' "

As the drawing began to weep from its outermost edges, she turned back to the too-old room and faced her only companion for the Winter Solstice.

The gray tabby cat stared back, unblinking and unimpressed, from where she lay on the towel Ivy had laid out. She'd darted into the cabin while Ivy carried in her supplies for her night of vigil. Was the cat a visitor from the fairy realm, here to test Ivy's hospitality? A totem animal, arrived to guide her? Perhaps a future familiar. . . .

Or maybe, just maybe, she was simply a stray cat, mooching for warmth and a handout. One never *could* tell, with magic . . . unless this night went as Ivy hoped. And she had a long night to get through before she found out.

In any case, the temperatures had been dropping all afternoon. Now that a blizzard had moved in, wind howling in a way that could not sound *less* joyous, the cat would stay.

"My dreams couldn't have arranged for me to do this on the *shortest* night of the year, huh?" Ivy asked now, returning to her nylon camp chair by the rusty-grated fire. Lord and Lady, but it was cold. The flame's warmth seemed to extend only as far as its orange glow. *Yes, the weather outside is frightful. . . .*

The cat boosted herself up with her front legs to curl lithely around and chew at the back of one thigh, spread-toed foot high in the air, supremely unimpressed.

Once, Ivy would have laughed at so classic a feline brush-off; now she barely managed a smile. A run of bad luck, from finances to health, had slowly disillusioned her, robbed her of her optimism one disappointment at a time. She'd tried to always do the right thing for so long! But now that she'd reached thirty, with little to show for it, she'd begun to question why. And that wasn't a big leap from questioning all the other intangibles of her life, magic included. Ivy's doctor diagnosed her as clinically depressed. He prescribed antidepressants, which she began to take, and a tranquilizer, which she hadn't touched. As if inspired by her efforts at healing herself, her dreams then gave her even more hopeful instructions—for her magic, anyway. Though almost intangible here on the physical realm, magic could appear *very* dramatic in dreams.

So here Ivy sat, humming Yuletide carols to a stray cat in a dusty, rented cabin. She'd draped the walls with evergreen garlands, like a good little pagan, to symbolize continued life in the midst of winter's cold. The wreath she'd woven, as the storm blew in, represented the turning of the Year Wheel. On the rough-hewn mantle of the fireplace, she'd lit two pillar candles, green for the goddess and red for the god of old. Together, they added a perfume of bayberry and cinnamon to the rich scent of wood smoke and fresh pine. And between them, pillowed on silver-gray silk, lay all her hopes for her sanity, her life path—her magic.

The decorative, double-edged knife had a pewter blade, like a letter opener; it would be used on nothing in this physical realm, and in the astral realm, soft metals worked just fine. Its artist had etched an intricate design of oak-leaves up the blade, to match the carvings of leaves and acorns in its oaken handle. Ivy had never seen so beautiful an athame before buying this one. That she'd dreamed the importance of a cere-monial blade for weeks, with clear instructions for its use, only added to its enchantment. Planning and packing for this witchly version of a vision quest had given her more confidence than she'd felt in months.

This was Yule, after all, the longest night of the year, an ancient holiday from which so many winter traditions evolved. Per her dreams, Ivy intended to spend the night meditating on the true meaning of the Winter Solstice and its returning light. Then—and this, she felt certain, was key—she would take her athame outside to catch the energy of the first rays of the new sun. Somehow, if she did that—and if her dreams really *were* instructions from the astral realm and not side-effects from her serontonin reuptake inhibitor—Ivy would finally gain proof that magic existed, that it worked . . . that it made a difference.

For once and for always, all subtlety aside, she would *know*.

"Okay then—the true meaning of Yule," she said now to the cat, glad to have *someone* to bounce this off of. "Most of the pagans I know equate it with the rebirth of the sun, but some also talk about the myth of the Oak King, who wages heroic battle against the Holly—"

Amidst the storm outside, Ivy heard a thump against the door.

The tabby cat sat up, ready to run. The fire shrank, then stretched. When Ivy turned toward the old cabin's door, away from the fire, her breath misted in the air and warmed her quilted vest to moistness against her cheek.

". . . King," she finished faintly.

For a long moment, she resisted investigating. How *could* there be anybody out on a night like tonight? But it was too cold to risk being wrong. She stood.

The door opened on its own, dragged an arc across the floor toward her. Wind sliced in, hurling shards of frozen crystal and sending her chair skittering across the floor. It tormented the writhing fire and filled the cabin with an unnerving, otherworldly screech.

"I'm a witch," Ivy reminded herself softly, to maintain calm as she watched the door open further. "A stone in the ancient circle. I can handle whatever this night sends."

She would feel more confidence were it not so dark . . . and if she had more faith in magic, of late.

From the swirling, shadowy white emerged a form of black, tall and broad-shouldered. It filled the doorway for a moment. Then it half-staggered, half-fell through the entrance, crumpling across the cold dirt floor. A glaze of ice that had crusted its heavy coat shattered into dagger-like shards.

Magic or no magic—*this* was real.

Quickly, Ivy waded against the wind to the doorway, past the prone black form. She found temporary shelter behind the door. Bracing on it, she pushed—but Nature pushed back. Her hiking boots slipped from beneath her and she fell to her knees on the frozen floor.

The cat, peeking out from its new shelter behind the woodpile, gave no help.

Ivy dragged herself up and, legs straining, puuushed. Slowly the door retreated from her and finally, blessedly, closed against the wind and the worst of the cold . . . and the darkness.

But not all of it.

She latched the door, leaned on it for support. The chaos outside seemed almost silent in contrast to the indoors only moments before. Then she looked at the fallen stranger.

A sense of unreasonable foreboding stilled her—and not because of any extrasensory abilities. Witches watched the news too. Ivy knew the threat that strangers, especially strange men, could pose. But she could ignore a human being's suffering no more than she could have put the cat out into the cold. She pushed past her hesitance to kneel beside the man.

He wore all black—a long, black wool coat, a black ski cap, a black scarf that cowled his face to obscurity. As Ivy unwound the wrappings, more ice crackled off and she wondered how, or if, he could breathe. When she unveiled his pale, handsome face, she saw that his breath had frozen into a thin, frosty crust over his mouth and nose.

She pressed her hands onto the stranger's high cheeks, leaned forward and breathed on him to melt the frost from his closed eyes and downturned lips before carefully, tentatively, wiping it away. The cold of his skin repelled her. She checked the pulse in his throat—was it weak? When she pressed cold fingers to her own neck, for a comparison, she decided it was. Desperation shook her hand.

Was he breathing? Did he have any chance of life at all? The cell phone she'd left in her car would not work this far from a transmitter, even if she risked hiking down the hill for it. And even if she did contact emergency services, could an ambulance get here until the storm broke?

Could the police?

"Useless," Ivy muttered. Never had she been so tempted to simply give up. She felt as though an outer presence were urging her pessimism on.

It's the darkness, she thought then. *The darkness wants me to stop.*

Darker magic, the kind that dangerous magicians and creatures that weren't even human practiced, could work in subtle ways too. And this *was* the darkest night of the year . . . in more ways than one.

Was *that* the true meaning of the Winter Solstice?

Fa la la la la.

Ivy shook off that possibility and the apathy it engendered. Tipping the man's head back, she pinched his nose shut. Then she bent and covered his mouth, his cold lips, with hers and breathed for him. *In with the good air. . . .*

His eyes opened, strong and sad, depthless and dark.

Ivy drew back, startled.

Arched eyebrows lowered. The stranger's now-damp lips moved, producing only a sigh, and his frown grew fiercer.

Ivy leaned closer, straining.

"You're . . . oak," he whispered, seemingly distressed. Then his eyes fell shut again, dark lashes smudging his high, too-pale cheeks.

Ivy raised fingers to her throat, this time feeling for the pendant she always wore, a branching tree within a circle. To her, the tree represented Yggdrasil, the World Tree of Norse mythology, its roots connecting the earth to the underworld and its branches reaching wide into the realm of the spirit. But . . . Yggdrasil was generally thought to be a yew or an ash tree, not an oak.

Was she hunting for hidden meanings where none existed? Now Ivy couldn't tell if she shivered from the cold or from this man's wan vulnerability, from mundane fears about intruders at night or otherworldly fears less easily defined.

As she'd told the cat, Solstice Night also represented the last stand of the Holly King—the god who, by this time of year, reigned over darkness and even death.

"Well don't use this one in your battle," Ivy hissed from where she crouched over the stranger—hardly a standard holiday prayer. Once again she strained the muscles of her legs, arms and back, this time to drag the prone figure nearer the fire. Since he did not appear to be frost-bitten—to her amateur eye, anyway—she chafed his wrists, his face. Trying not to dwell on his dangerously powerful build, she undressed him of his iced, outer layer of clothing so that the fire's warmth would reach him . . .

. . . and she saw that he wore around his neck, on a leather thong, a pentagram overlaid with a tiny, two-headed axe. Despite that he wore the star point up, not point down as Satanists or chic Goths might, Ivy shivered again. These were pagan symbols. Mere coincidence? Or . . . magic?

Her heart drumming louder than a full-moon ritual, she glanced toward the rough fireplace mantle, the fine new athame that must catch the returning sun . . .

She could meditate on the true meaning of the Solstice while fixing something warm for this man to eat—should he regain consciousness—as easily as she could by sitting still. Reassured by his rough but steady breathing and, to be honest, the safety of his continued unconsciousness, Ivy took time for one thing, first. She re-lit the candles that the wind through the open door had blown out. *Then* she turned to her supplies and retrieved a can of stew.

The cat crept out from behind the firewood to investigate this new opportunity.

You're oak, this man had said. Or more likely, of course, *your oak*.

" 'My oak,' " Ivy repeated softly. "Could he have seen my necklace as a symbol of the Oak King?"

The cat, staring expectantly at the can she held, opened and closed her mouth in a silent meow.

"It's an ancient legend of the Winter Solstice," Ivy explained softly, peeling open the pop-top of the can and spooning a little of its contents out for the eager cat before pouring the rest into an aluminum pot. "The forest god has two different aspects—the Oak King and the Holly King. As I remember it, the Oak King stands for light, growth, rebirth. He rules during the waxing year—from Winter Solstice through Midsummer, while the sun gains power. His reign starts tomorrow," she clarified.

Rather, it *would*, if there really were an Oak King. . . .

After some consideration, Ivy returned to her backpack for a few more ingredients. "But at Midsummer, the Holly King kills the Oak King in battle. Then *he* rules, through to the Winter Solstice, during the waning year, until the reborn Oak King defeats him again. The world gets lighter, then it gets darker, then it gets lighter, and so on."

And then it gets darker. And so on. Wasn't Midsummer when things had started going wrong in her own life?

Adding her extra ingredients, then stirring, Ivy hung the pot over the fireplace. She felt jittery, overly alert, as if she could *sense* the dark god of withdrawal and death lurking in the shadows . . . or even standing over her unconscious visitor in black.

Black?

Her gaze slid back to the stranger and her heightened awareness saw more than an intruder. His thick, carefully cut hair was dark brown, not black. Although his face seemed taut, somewhat angry—more likely pained, she thought charitably—he couldn't be much older than her. She noted something of a bruised expression in his otherwise regal features.

Leaning closer, she lay her fingers on the smoothness of his cheek, relieved to feel that this man felt warmer now—and still very real. Lord and Lady, but he was handsome. Handsome enough that even *she* noticed. How long had it been since she'd felt physically attracted to anyone . . . ?

His dark eyes slid open again. His gaze wandered, bewildered, and then focused on her, and she reluctantly reclaimed her hand.

"Hello," she said.

He stared at her, then sat up with surprising strength, ignoring her automatic plea to be still. After wincing only once, he examined his hands, then felt his face. Finally, his gaze returned to Ivy.

"How long have I been here?" he demanded in a crisp, authoritative voice.

"Only a short while. You're very lucky."

"That is a matter of opinion. Who are you?"

Her smile felt tighter than it would have been only a minute earlier, but she might as well alleviate his tension—and thus his threat? "Ivy MacDaraich."

"Ivy." His eyes, hardly welcoming in the first place, narrowed with speculation. "How very appropriate."

Like she'd never heard that before, at this time of year. Considering his pentagram, she altered her season's greeting. "Happy Yule."

"For whom?" He spared her a scathing look before rolling to a crouch. He stood to his full, impressive height, swayed, then steadied himself by force of will. When Ivy moved to help him, he glared at her. Though she still found him attractive, he suddenly became much easier to resist. Score a big zero for Ivy's instincts.

She stood too, then stepped back from the reality of his height over hers. *Regal,* she thought again. Despite that he wore black jeans and a sweater, and modern hiking boots, he could as easily have worn a black cape and armor.

She tried not to picture the Holly King. "You can't go," she said. "There's a terrible storm out."

The man studied her. "Yes," he said, after a moment, then sank into her camp chair without asking. His next words came out so softly, she almost didn't hear. "We were seperated in the storm."

We? "Someone else is out there?"

"It's none of your concern." *That,* she heard.

"But they might need help!"

"I have no doubt that my companion is quite safe," he snapped, without a glimmer of concern. His next words came out soft again, as if spoken to himself. "Safer than I."

He was worried about *his* safety? Ivy hesitated before spooning some stew from the pot, into a camp plate, and held it toward him. "Would you like to eat something? It will warm you."

Instead of accepting the food, the stranger folded his arms. She could see the lines of his muscles even through the layers of his clothing. Noting her confused expression, he raised an eyebrow and said, "After you."

He was not, she thought, being polite. He *was* worried about his safety.

A head shorter than him, did she look that dangerous? "Pretty suspicious, aren't you?"

"I have cause to be."

Ah. Without hesitating further, she blew on a spoonful of stew to cool it, then took a bite. Not bad, she thought. For what it was. Since he continued to watch, she took another bite, chewed, and even swallowed, despite her tight throat. "See? Harmless."

When she held the plate to him again he took it and ate greedily, shuddering slightly—from the shock of its warmth against the cold that had held him, Ivy supposed. Despite herself, and his attitude, she softened toward him. He seemed so tense, brittle even, under the weight of his own suspicions. He looked like he could use a good neck rub—*not* that she was offering. But she did move to the other side of the cabin to dig an extra blanket from her pile of supplies for the poor, prickly misanthrope.

She noticed the tabby cat watching her from behind a box of groceries, pupils large and dark, but carefully did nothing to clue the stranger in on its silent, feline presence. Instead she said, over her shoulder, "I noticed that you're wearing a pent. Am I right in assuming that you follow the old ways?"

She turned back—and gasped. Without her hearing him, her visitor had claimed her athame off the mantle and stepped up behind her. Now he loomed over her, the knife too near to her throat.

Its blade might only be pewter . . . but Ivy's throat was only flesh. She swallowed. Hard.

"Yes," said the dark stranger, his voice almost a purr. "And I honor an ancient god."

Pieces clicked into place, subtly—but unavoidably.

"The . . . Holly King?" She couldn't drag her gaze from the blade. So much for subtlety. . . .

"Your enemy, this night," he prompted.

"I don't have any enemies." She hoped her breathless words proved true. "Not that I know of."

"You're a Wiccan," he accused—pretty much implying that his own brand of paganism wouldn't follow the comforting beliefs of "Harm

None" and "What ye send forth comes back to ye" that her own did. "Yes? One of those love-and-light types, no doubt, who expect nothing but goodness and growth from their magic and their traditions. And you wear the oak."

"It's not an oak, it's a yew. Or an ash. It stands for—"

But when he pressed the tip of her athame to her throat, she let her protest fall to silence.

He said, "Do not pretend ignorance about this night."

"You mean about the Oak King and the . . . ?"

"Holly King," he repeated.

This was *not* what she'd assumed her night of meditating on the meaning of Yule would encompass.

"You . . ." She hated to sound crazy—but with a knife to her throat, what did she have to lose? How much *less* subtle did magic have to get? "Are *you* the Holly King?"

And he said, almost a hiss, "Tonight I am."

It was crazy—and yet, damnably, it made sense. Especially on the metaphysical level. The one thing all pagans had in common, be they Wiccans or Druids, Shamans or Discordians, were the old gods. The Ancient Ones' essence could permeate the pine trees and the snowflakes, the wind and the sky . . . and, sometimes, their followers. Whether viewed as formal pantheons or mere metaphors, pagan gods were as immanent as they were transcendent.

If Zeus could become a swan to have his wicked way with a mortal maiden—if priestesses could "draw down the moon," taking on the essence of a goddess for ritual purposes—then surely the Holly King could co-habit the body of a strong man to. . . .

There went that unsteady foreboding again. To what?

"Why?" demanded Ivy, raising her chin slightly to add another millimeter's distance from her ceremonial blade.

"I tire of your pretense," he warned, as casually as if he held women at knifepoint all the time. "To do battle, of course; the same battle that has darkened each winter throughout millennia. And preferably to win."

"Don't be ridicu—" With the point of the athame, he reminded her to choose her words more carefully. "Magic works *with* nature," she insisted, voice lower. "Not against it. The earth's axis will start to tip back and the sun will gain power starting tomorrow, no matter what happens tonight."

He appeared unimpressed. "That hardly means the *real* light—peace and love, comfort and joy, all those saccharin ideals the Oak King represents—need necessarily return. Not if I prevail."

And that, too, made a horrible sense.

Deal with the knife first, thought Ivy wildly. *Encroaching darkness and despair later.* "Just out of . . . um . . . curiosity. What's any of this got to do with me?"

"You really don't know?" He sounded intrigued, even amused—and still wholly in control of the situation.

"From my take on things, this is between you and Oak King, isn't it?" Maybe the Oak King was the companion he'd been separated from in the storm, the one he'd insisted was safe. She licked her lips. "I don't have any reason to hurt you—I don't *believe* in hurting people. Or gods. And even if I did, I don't have a weapon. So how about you save your strength for the real battle, we call it a truce, and we just get through this night as best we can."

In a smooth movement, the stranger turned and threw her athame into the fireplace. Sparks billowed up around its engraved blade, and the carved hilt immediately began to darken.

"Perhaps," he agreed, turning back to her.

Ivy reached helplessly toward the fire, but she did not dare take a step in that direction. She knew he could stop her.

"That's important to me," she did protest, voice trembling, as she raised her gaze back to this man—this apparent servant of death, of darkness. "It's why I'm here."

"It *was* why you are here," he stressed—and slowly drew a hunting knife from his boot. This blade was obviously of steel, far more deadly than decorative. "Now you are here because of me only. Remember that." And he casually tapped her cheek with the flat of the weapon. The cold of the metal stung. "You are all I have to ward off the boredom of this confinement. But my idea of amusement does not include my death."

Briefly, exhaustion dulled his sharp features, sallowed his cheeks. Then his head snapped straighter, and he glared at Ivy.

She refused to imagine what his idea of amusement *was*. No need to give negative images power by visualizing them. "Would you like some more stew?" she offered instead, her voice a breath away from shaky.

"No." But at least he slid his own knife back into his boot. "I do not want you near the fire."

"But it's *cold*."

He sounded annoyed when he demanded, "What do you expect in December?"

The storm's wail, muffled by the cabin's walls, emphasized their words—and had Ivy wondering, again, if the Oak King were out there. For a moment, she indulged in the fantasy of a golden-haired hero bursting in, defeating the dark stranger, and rescuing her. "Let me at least sit closer."

He turned calm, dark eyes to her. She found herself awaiting the inevitable pause before he spoke. "I would rather you not."

"You already know I'm a love-and-light type of witch." One whose greatest hope for true magic was currently smelting in the fireplace, damn it. She told herself that survival was more important than her ritual . . . but she'd been merely surviving for a half year now. She'd hoped for so much more from this holiday. "Don't you trust me?"

"Of course not. And if you were anything but a fool, you would not have trusted me. You would not have left your door unlocked. You would not have turned your back to me." He looked almost sad as he sank again into the camp chair, his hand dangerously near the hilt protruding from his boot.

She knew for sure, then, that the crushed tranquilizer tablets she'd added to the stew were starting to take effect.

"It is annoying to be trusted by fools," he sighed mournfully. Somehow she didn't think that meant he'd approve of the tranquilizer.

"Why?" she challenged. "Do you feel obliged to meet their expectations?"

He shook his head. "No. They are just so terribly boring to defeat. No fight to them."

Think again, holly boy. But she *was* torn. She did not like being bossed around, even by a god, much less held at knifepoint, robbed of her beautiful athame. She did not intend to play the role of victim. But . . . neither did she want to do anybody, even him, actual harm.

Why add more pain and negativity to the universe?

Instead, she settled onto her sleeping bag, wrapping her sweatered arms around her knees. Maybe she could keep him talking until the tranquilizers kicked in, or until the Oak King showed up—whichever came first. "What's your name, anyway? Assuming you have some identity beyond being the Holly King."

"Duncan," he sighed, eyelids beginning to sink. "Duncan Bercilak. But for tonight, you may call me 'My Lord.'"

Like *that* would happen anytime soon! But surprisingly, a wicked gleam in the stranger's dark eyes seemed to acknowledge that. Darkness apparently had a sense of humor.

"Hasn't it occurred to you, Duncan, that your timing with this little apotheosis sucks? The Holly King is supposed to die tonight."

He frowned, seemingly miffed. "Not if I have anything to do with it."

"And you planned to defeat the Oak King by going out in the middle of a blizzard?" insisted Ivy. "No offense, but I don't get it."

"Perhaps you do not *wish* to 'get it,'" Duncan Bercilak assured her. And, she noticed, he took another spoonful of stew. "Perhaps that is wise."

With her athame gone, she needn't worry about meditating on the meaning of Yule anymore—but Ivy shrugged. "Humor me."

"Even though your knowledge could increase the menace you pose, and my reasons for killing you?" Reading her blank look, he sneered— albeit sleepily. "I already told you that I am the bad guy, Ivy. Stop trusting me for your answers."

"Yeah, well you're the only one here."

"Am I?"

Did he mean the cat? But no, from the intense way he watched her, he did not. "*Me?*"

"You've *never* heard of the Ivy Girl?"

And, like a burst of magic, she realized she had. But as with most magic, this did not truly come out of nowhere. The term, "Ivy Girl," mixed with the smell of the fireplace and the pine boughs, channeled a memory from her early childhood, her grandfather telling her about English harvest festivals. "*Some country folk bind the last sheaf of grain with an ivy vine,*" Grampa had said, explaining why he called her his Ivy Girl. "*It's their superstition that the grain stands for the fallen king, who dies each autumn, and the Ivy stands for a goddess who takes over for him. The Holly Boy and the Ivy Girl, they say.*"

"You think *I'm* the Ivy Girl?" she demanded. "That I'm here to *bind* you or something?"

He visibly stifled a yawn. "Amusing, isn't it? You see why my hopes for victory are so high this year."

"But what about the Oak King?"

His stare clarified things for her. The point of this struggle wasn't whether he fought a man or a woman, Oak or Ivy. The point was that darkness and light met, struggled—and one prevailed. Still . . . *"Me?"*

So much for a god-like blond hero riding to her rescue. She found herself suddenly annoyed with the Oak King for leaving her in this mess—and with the universe for not asking if she was willing to play!

Deal with encroaching darkness and despair first, she reminded herself. *Righteous indignation later.*

But she'd never believed in fighting fire with fire, much less darkness with darkness. "What if I don't *want* to fight you?" she demanded. "What's the penalty for forfeiture?"

"It could be your death," he suggested, far too intrigued, and began to stand from the camp chair. "You *did* accept the benefits happily enough while life was going well for you."

Without any real physical defense, she grabbed her tree pendant for the protection that earth elements—metal and wood—afforded.

Duncan swayed visibly, then braced himself against the mantle. He stared at the plate by his feet, then at her, incredulity mounting. "Damn you! You *did* drug me!"

He kicked the plate at her, but missed in his dizziness. She did not even have to duck.

"I did it even before I knew you were the Holly King, if that helps," she said softly. "I didn't trust you on a mundane level . . . and I thought you could probably use the sleep."

He staggered back, then fell to his knees, his dark, somehow-bruised eyes still fixed on her face. "Damn you. . . ." he whispered, his voice almost as hushed as when he'd first tried speaking.

She waited to feel triumph, but all she felt was a sad relief—and the yawn that struggled to escape her, from her own share of the stew. She had not escaped yet.

"What is the penalty for forfeiture if you *don't* kill me?" she asked, with careful calm.

Duncan still stared at her, shocked, even as his eyes struggled to close. He shuddered, and almost against her will, she extended a hand in his direction.

She would not have touched him, but still he winced away.

"I don't intend to hurt you," she insisted, wincing herself from the accusation in his depthless eyes. "I'm one of those love-and-light witches, remember?"

"There is more than one kind of battle," he gasped, crumpling onto the dirt floor, exhausted. "You are my enemy, this night."

She realized then the full meaning of his bruised expression and why, even at his worst, he had not completely frightened her.

"You're scared," she said, surprised. "Your darkness isn't anything as simple as evil, is it? It's fear, even withdrawal—you're scared to let me close enough to help you, maybe to let anyone close enough. It's distrust. And maybe it's the loss of power—if you let me help you, it might change who you are."

His eyes slid shut as the drug overpowered him, and his breathing fell into a soft, steady rhythm.

"You've been weakened by the very things you stand for," she whispered . . . then yawned.

The cat crept out of its corner, sniffed the plate of stew, then turned with annoyance to Ivy and meowed. Loudly. *She* knew better than to eat that stuff.

"You're right," said Ivy. She herself had not eaten as much of the stew, or the drug, as Duncan Bercilak. But she was smaller. She couldn't count on much time before she, too, became useless. So if she meant to do anything significant to protect herself, now was her chance.

"I don't have to kill him, do I?" she asked the cat, now sniffing the unconscious man. The cat ignored her.

He'd meant to kill *her*, right? Or had he? He'd passed up enough chances. In any case, Ivy wasn't sure she *could* do something like that, neither cut his throat with his own dagger—yuck!—nor drag him back into the snow and leave him to the elements. He'd said himself: there was more than one kind of battle.

She would not defeat darkness by giving into it. But neither would she win by waiting passively for the light to return on its own. Not without helping it along.

"The meaning of Yule?" she suggested to the cat, with a wry smile.

The cat moved back to her towel by the fire and curled into the classic feline-at-rest pose, front legs tucked under, tail wrapped neatly around herself. Her eyes narrowed into satisfied slants.

Decided, Ivy kneeled beside Duncan, drew the long, double-edged dagger from his boot, and gingerly moved it to her own backpack. Then, like any good Ivy Girl, she bound the Holly King with strips of cloth that she tore from her sheets, securing both his wrists and ankles.

Warmth radiated off him, despite lying on a near-frozen floor. He had strong legs, chiseled wrists. This was not *only* the Holly King, after all. This was a man named Duncan Bercilak, who had for whatever reason taken on the job.

Pausing to brush brown hair from his troubled face, she wondered how bad *his* year had been, to drive him this far. But she still tied him. And that, she decided, wiping her hands on her jeans, was as pragmatic and mundane as she meant to get tonight.

Then she swayed—and shivered. She wasn't out of danger yet. Exhaustion blurred her vision, and it was so cold out! To stay with this man would be dangerous. So would be trying to leave in the middle of a still-howling blizzard, to hike a good half mile to her car through the night woods, then to drive while tranquilized.

After a long moment's consideration, she pulled her sleeping bag closer and wrestled Duncan Bercilak's heavy form onto it, off the frozen floor. Then she added her extra blanket and reluctantly lay beside his warmth.

Later on, we'll conspire as we dream by the fire. . . .

It seemed the right thing to do, and not just because she felt so cold.

It seemed the right thing to do in the same, subtle way that magic worked. . . .

WHEN she awoke, Ivy felt blessedly warm, curled against Duncan Bercilak's chest. His arms encircled her protectively in his sleep, and the cat—she realized from the vibration of its purr—cuddled against the back of her legs. The winds had fallen silent, marking the end of the long storm. The fire was nearly dead, and only her Coleman lantern and the two pillar candles—one red, one green—lit the cabin. The morning held that hushed magic that had blessed her Christmas mornings as a child, her Yuletide mornings once she recognized herself as a witch.

She hated to leave such peace and warmth for a long, dark, snowy trek to her car.

Then it occurred to her that *Duncan's arms were around her*, despite her having tied his hands! Holding her breath, she slid from his heavy embrace and slowly sat up . . . then sighed with relief to see that he still slept. Somehow in the night his hands had worked free of their bonds. So much for her job as the Ivy Girl.

She found it even harder to believe that he would kill her now than she had before. Did a handsome face blur her judgement so terribly much . . . or were there stronger powers at work here?

The cat stalked away, then sat with its back to her in silent protest at the disruption to her sleep. Bitter air tingled at Ivy's skin, deprived of Duncan's warmth, as though she weren't wearing layered winter clothing. It burned in her lungs and misted her breath as—deciding not to risk waking Duncan by trying to re-tie him—she crept to her supplies and put on her quilted winter coat, her gloves, her scarf. She didn't dare the noise of repacking her supplies—the only belonging she'd considered ir-replaceable was her athame, and it, she saw, was a pitted, misshapen thing on the dying embers.

Magic might well exist . . . but so much for her chance at finding proof this year, anyway. On an afterthought, Ivy opened the flap of her half-empty backpack and clucked softly to the gray tabby cat. As if it understood, it trotted over, tried her patience with only a moment of cautious exploration, then crawled into the safety of the bag.

Ivy shouldered the pack, checking its pocket for Duncan's dagger, lest he come after her. When she reached the door, she turned and looked back for a final moment. It really might be best for her physical safety if she killed him, or at least bashed him over the head.

As if she could be sure of not killing him if she bashed him over the head, anyway.

But it would not, she thought, be best for the world, to add even one more act of violence to it. When she got to the closest town, she could do her mundane duty by reporting him as an intruder to the police. Per-haps *they* could keep him from harming anyone else. But she would not empower the darkness by hurting him. It might seem stupid, on the phys-ical level. But on deeper levels, magical levels, it felt surprisingly . . . right. Again.

Impulsively, Ivy blew a kiss at the sleeping man. Then she turned, unlatched the door, and swung it open.

Face to face with an older man, his eyes piggy and small over his purple scarf, she screamed.

Only as the man's voice fell silent in surprise did Ivy realize that he'd been chanting, chanting something that she did not quite understand but which her subconscious did, and it made all the fine hairs on her body stand up. He advanced and she retreated, fumbling the dagger from its pocket in her backpack. Behind her she heard noise—

Duncan's squared hand closed hard around her wrist, made her drop the knife as he pulled her against him, trapped her arms with his hands. Then, to her surprise, Bercilak and the newcomer exchanged familiar glances.

"Silas," said Duncan in his clear, authoritative voice. "I thought perhaps you'd deserted me."

"I searched as quickly as I could, Dun—that is, my lord," assured the older man ingratiatingly. Ivy thought he looked guilty. "I searched through the night, despite the storm. You cannot know how frantic I was for your safety."

The man reeked of deceit. More than her fright, Ivy felt amazement that Duncan, who'd seemed intelligent enough, did not see it. Perhaps that was what his distance and apathy had done to this Holly King's instincts.

The stranger, Silas, seemed to sense Ivy's hostility. He searched her face with his piggish eyes. "M'lord," he ventured, "if we might speak for a moment?"

"Granted," said Duncan, as if he truly *were* a king . . . or a god. With a parting glare to Ivy, he set her further into the cabin before releasing her. Then he picked up his dagger and strode out into the darkness of the cold, early morning, his feet crunching in the snow, leaving her alone to contemplate her fate.

Ivy knew she should be afraid . . . but it seemed impossible to fear someone mussed by sleep, someone who had yet to do more to her than threaten and disarm her.

She let the cat out of the backpack. Then she checked her watch—past six a.m. Almost dawn.

"Bring back the light," she said softly, firmly, as she waited. "Bring back the light. Bring back the light. . . ."

It felt better than doing nothing.

"My lord," whispered Silas, outside. "I am surprised you've left her alive this long. Dawn is almost upon us. . . ."

"And as you can see," noted Duncan, more annoyed by the blind fool than usual, "I still live."

"But she remains a threat. She cannot allow the Solstice to arrive without defeating you. *It is foreordained!* One of you *must* vanquish—"

Duncan glared the older, weaker man into silence. Sadly, it was temporary.

"Ah," said Silas now, more ingratiating than ever. He'd played his role in the Holly King's reign thus far, but . . . "If you do not wish to distress yourself by doing the deed—"

Duncan allowed his face to show his contempt at the assumed insult. "Silas," he corrected, "I am no schoolboy to be softened by a night with a pacifistic white-lighter. You would not deny me my pleasure, would you?"

Silas smiled, obviously relieved by this show of authority. "No, m'lord. I would not."

Duncan sighed. After preparing for this moment for so long, he found himself wishing the danger, the uncertainty, were over. Soon, now. Soon. "I only wish I had time for more creativity . . . but you are right. Daylight presses."

When he strode back into the dugout, the woman named Ivy MacDaraich looked up and smiled at him. *Smiled!* "Are the stars out?" she asked. "Now that the storm's passed, I mean?"

He stared at her, incredulous. He knew the power of the Oak King's representatives as well as anyone, and still she amazed him. How frightened would most pretty young women be, alone in a cabin with him? How many chances had he given her to destroy him? How many excuses to hate him?

How many opportunities to choose darkness at long last?

Curious, unwilling to waste these last few moments, he strode to stand in front of her. Her eyes widened slightly as she stared up at him, more in curiosity than fear even now. Then, as he bent and covered her mouth with his own, she caught her breath with surprise. Touching a tentative hand to his sweatered chest, she kissed him back.

Their kiss deepened. She smelled of wood smoke, pine, cinnamon, and bayberry. Of Yule.

Drawing back from her, Duncan studied her face for a moment longer, resigning himself to what he must do. Her dazed, sated look ought not have made this more difficult.

"You know, one *can* resist the darkness without denying it," he scolded, almost gently, as he raised a hand to her cheek. "One *can* accept it without embracing it. You should not have trusted me."

"I didn't," she reminded him, voice husky with sleep—and something else. "I just refused to *be* you."

He slid his hand downward, found just the right place on her soft throat with his fingers—yes, there. "So you did."

Her green eyes widened, then fluttered shut. In a moment, she'd crumpled as if boneless to the frozen floor.

The cat she'd thought to have hidden from him arched its back and hissed. Duncan ignored it to crouch beside Ivy MacDaraich. He touched her cheek again, touched the tree pendant she wore around her neck on a leather thong.

Then, retrieving his knife from his boot, Duncan slashed it downward toward her throat. . . .

He strode into the graying morning, crunching through the snow, and raised an eyebrow at his lackey. "Surely you did not doubt me, Silas?"

"Of course not, m'lord," assured Silas, too quickly.

Duncan looked at the dagger in his hand, contemplating. In a sudden moment, he turned and threw it back into the cabin. With a distinct thud, it buried itself into the opposite wall.

He met his companion's surprise with superiority. "We cannot let people think that the Holly King is stingy," he said haughtily. "The next poor wretch who falls upon this place in a snowstorm might be hungry."

Silas stared, startled by the viciousness of Duncan's statement. Then, belatedly, he began to laugh. Amused by the obnoxious man's ignorance, Duncan joined him, and together they hiked downward toward the road and their transportation—and the new year, with its continued possibilities for change in either direction.

In the pocket of his coat, Duncan fingered Ivy's tree-shaped amulet and made plans for the future.

Plans for growth.

Ivy's head hurt. As she became aware of her own existence, sucked deep breaths, the throbbing softened—slightly. Disoriented, she sat up. Dizziness blurred the edges of her sight to a yellow black, and she felt cold . . . so cold.

And . . . alive?

Not that she wasn't grateful, but . . . *why?*

The cat butted its striped head against her hip as Ivy stared out the still-open door. Iron gray expectation was beginning to lighten the winter sky. Perhaps Duncan had left her alive to twist the knife—so to speak. He'd won, hadn't he? He'd not killed her . . . but there was more than one kind of battle. She hadn't "defeated" him, either.

Assuming she'd really been acting in the role of the light, or he in the role of Holly King. Assuming their strange night meant anything on the astral, magic realm at all.

Slowly she stood, shuffled to the doorway, and braced herself against the doorjamb. Occasionally, through snow-draped branches on the path far below the cabin, she caught glimpses of the two men descending the hillside. As the sky lightened, Duncan's hair took on an unexpected, burnished tint.

Behind her, in the cabin, the cat yowled.

She'd survived him. He'd kissed her—the most intense kiss she'd ever known, from god or man—and he'd left her feeling more alive than she'd felt in months. Not that she approved of his behavior, of course! But suddenly, the crisp smell of snow and pine and wood smoke seemed to tingle through her with something akin to . . . joy. She'd guarded against the darkness, hadn't given into it. The worst of it had passed, and now she appreciated what she had more than ever.

"Winter Solstice," she whispered, understanding, and smiled as the eastern horizon brightened. Then she frowned. *Damn*, but she'd wanted to do that spell.

If only the son-of-a-bitch hadn't destroyed her athame.

The cat yowled again. When Ivy turned to look, she saw the tabby sitting purposefully beneath something stuck in the wall. Something that had not been there before. Something that caught the waxing light.

What she felt then was still subtle—no pyrotechnics, no levitation. But it also was very real. *True* magic. She crossed the room to take a closer look, to make sure. Slowly, she pulled Duncan Bercilak's hunting knife out of the wooden wall.

He'd *left* it for her?

That was not the sort of thing the Holly King would do, was it? The Holly King tested, challenged, reigned over a world that slowly became barren and cold. He took away. The god who *gave* was the . . .

She remembered how Duncan Bercilak's hair had glinted in the distance.

When Ivy turned toward the doorway with the knife in her hand, its double-edged blade caught and glowed with the Solstice morning's rising sun.

The Witch

MARY COLERIDGE

Mary Coleridge's relationship to the famed Samuel Taylor Coleridge is light—she's the great-great-granddaughter of his brother. She was also a popular author in her own right, whose melancholy belief in the painful power is mimicked in the power of this poem's forlorn little witch who, once let in, brings her pain with her.

I have walked a great while over the snow,
And I am not tall or strong.
My clothes are wet, and my teeth are set,
And the way was hard and long.
I have wandered over the fruitful earth,
But I never came here before.
Oh, lift me over the threshold, and let me in at the
   door!

The cutting wind is a cruel foe.
I dare not stand in the blast.
My hands are stone, and my voice a groan,
And the worst of death is past.
I am but a little maiden still,
My little white feet are sore.
Oh, lift me over the threshold, and let me in at the
   door!

Her voice was the voice that women have,
Who plead for their heart's desire.
She came—she came—and the quivering flame

Sank and died in the fire.
It never was lit again on my hearth
Since I hurried across the floor,
To lift her over the threshold, and let her in at the door.

The Very Strange House Next Door

SHIRLEY JACKSON

Maybe it's because of "The Lottery" that so many scholars only look at Shirley Jackson's dark work. This lesser-known story, a companion piece to Mary Poppins*–like "Family Magician," presents a far more delightful look at the topic while still commenting on our tendency toward witch hunts.*

I don't gossip. If there is anything in this world I loathe, it is gossip. A week or so ago in the store, Dora Powers started to tell me that nasty rumor about the Harris boy again, and I came right out and said to her if she repeated one more word of that story to me I wouldn't speak to her for the rest of my life, and I haven't. It's been a week, and not one word have I said to Dora Powers, and that's what I think of gossip. Tom Harris has always been too easy on that boy anyway; the young fellow needs a good whipping, and he'd stop all this ranting around, and I've said so to Tom Harris a hundred times or more.

If I didn't get so mad when I think about that house next door, I'd almost have to laugh, seeing people in town standing in the store and on corners and dropping their voices to talk about fairies and leprechauns, when every living one of them knows there isn't any such thing and never has been, and them just racking their brains to find new tales to tell. I don't hold with gossip, as I say, even if it's about leprechauns and fairies, and it's my held opinion that Jane Dollar is getting feeble in the mind. The Dollars weren't ever noted for keeping their senses right up to the end, anyway, and Jane's no older than her mother was when she sent a cake to the bake sale and forgot to put the eggs in it. Some said she did it on purpose to get even with the ladies for not asking her to take a booth, but most just said the old lady had lost track of things, and I dare say she could have looked out and seen fairies in her garden if it ever came into her mind. When the Dollars get that age, they'll tell anything, and that's right where Jane Dollar is now, give or take six months.

My name is Addie Spinner, and I live down on Main Street, the last house but one. There's just one house after mine, and then Main Street kind of runs off into the woods—Spinner's Thicket, they call the woods, on account of my grandfather building the first house in the village. Before the crazy people moved in, the house past mine belonged to the Bartons, but they moved away because he got a job in the city, and high time, too, after them living off her sister and her husband for upward of a year.

Well, after the Bartons finally moved out—owing everyone in town, if you want my guess—it wasn't long before the crazy people moved in, and I knew they were crazy right off when I saw that furniture. I already knew they were young folks, and probably not married long, because I saw them when they came to look at the house. Then when I saw the furniture go in I knew there was going to be trouble between me and her.

The moving van got to the house about eight in the morning. Of course, I always have my dishes done and my house swept up long before that, so I took my mending for the poor out on the side porch and really got caught up on a lot I'd been letting slide. It was a hot day, so I just fixed myself a salad for my lunch, and the side porch is a nice cool place to sit and eat on a hot day, so I never missed a thing going into that house.

First, there were the chairs, all modern, with no proper legs and seats, and I always say that a woman who buys herself that flyaway kind of furniture has no proper feeling for her house—for one thing, it's too easy to clean around those little thin legs; you can't get a floor well-swept without a lot of hard work. Then, she had a lot of low tables, and you can't fool me with them—when you see those little low tables, you can always tell there's going to be a lot of drinking liquor going on in that house; those little tables are made for people who give cocktail parties and need a lot of places to put glasses down. Hattie Martin, she has one of those low tables, and the way Martin drinks is a crime. Then, when I saw the barrels going in next door, I was sure. No one just married has that many dishes without a lot of cocktail glasses, and you can't tell me any different.

When I went down to the store later, after they were all moved in, I met Jane Dollar, and I told her about the drinking that was going to go on next door, and she said she wasn't a bit surprised, because the people had a maid. Not someone to come one day a week and do the heavy cleaning—a maid. Lived in the house and everything. I said I hadn't noticed any maid, and Jane said most things if I hadn't noticed them she wouldn't believe they existed in this world, but the Wests' maid was sure enough; she'd been in the store not ten minutes earlier buying a chicken. We didn't think she'd rightly have time enough to cook a chicken before suppertime, but then we decided that probably the chicken was for tomorrow, and tonight the Wests were planning on going over to the inn for dinner and the maid could fix herself an egg or something. Jane did say that one trouble with having a maid—Jane never had a maid in her life, and I wouldn't speak to her if she did—was that you never had anything left over. No matter what you planned, you had to get new meat every day.

I looked around for the maid on my way home. The quickest way to get to my house from the store is to take the path that cuts across the back garden of the house next door, and even though I don't use it generally—you don't meet neighbors to pass the time of day with, going along a back path—I thought I'd better be hurrying a little to fix my own supper, so I cut across the Wests' back garden. West, that was their name, and what the maid was called I don't know, because Jane hadn't been able to find out. It was a good thing I did take the path, because there was the maid, right out there in the garden, down on her hands and knees, digging.

"Good evening," I said just as polite as I could. "It's kind of damp to be down on the ground."

"I don't mind," she said. "I like things that grow."

I must say she was a pleasant-speaking woman, although too old, I'd think, for domestic work. The poor thing must have been in sad straits to hire out, and yet here she was just as jolly and round as an apple. I thought maybe she was an old aunt or something, and they took this way of keeping her, so I said, still very polite, "I see you just moved in today?"

"Yes," she said, not really telling me much.

"The family's name is West?"

"Yes."

"You might be Mrs. West's mother?"

"No."

"An aunt, possibly?"

"No."

"Not related at all?"

"No."

"You're just the maid?" I thought afterward that she might not like it mentioned, but once it was out I couldn't take it back.

"Yes." She answered pleasant enough, I will say that for her.

"The work is hard, I expect?"

"No."

"Just the two of them to care for?"

"Yes."

"I'd say you wouldn't like it much."

"It's not bad," she said. "I use magic a lot, of course."

"Magic?" I said. "Does that get your work done sooner?"

"Indeed it does," she said with not so much as a smile or a wink. "You wouldn't think, would you, that right now I'm down on my hands and knees making dinner for my family?"

"No," I said. "I wouldn't think that."

"See?" she said. "Here's our dinner." And she showed me an acorn, I swear she did, with a mushroom and a scrap of grass in it.

"It hardly looks like enough to go around," I said, kind of backing away.

She laughed at me, kneeling there on the ground with her acorn, and said, "If there's any left over, I'll bring you a dish; you'll find it wonderfully filling."

"But what about your chicken?" I said; I was well along the path away from her, and I did want to know why she got the chicken if she didn't think they were going to eat it.

"Oh, that," she said. "That's for my cat."

Well, who buys a whole chicken for a cat, that shouldn't have chicken bones anyway? Like I told Jane over the phone as soon as I got home, Mr. Honeywell down at the store ought to refuse to sell it to her, or at least make her take something more fitting, like ground meat, even though neither of us believed for a minute that the cat was really going to get the chicken, or that she even had a cat, come to think of it; crazy people will say anything that comes into their heads.

*   *   *

I KNOW for a fact that no one next door ate chicken that night, though; my kitchen window overlooks their dining room if I stand on a chair, and what they ate for dinner was something steaming in a big brown bowl. I had to laugh, thinking about that acorn, because that was just what the bowl looked like—a big acorn. Probably that was what put the notion in her head. And, sure enough, later she brought over a dish of it and left it on my back steps, me not wanting to open the door late at night with a crazy lady outside, and like I told Jane, I certainly wasn't going to eat any outlandish concoction made by a crazy lady. But I kind of stirred it around with the end of a spoon, and it smelled all right. It had mushrooms in it and beans, but I couldn't tell what else, and Jane and I decided that probably we were right the first time and the chicken was for tomorrow.

I had to promise Jane I'd try to get a look inside to see how they set out that fancy furniture, so next morning I brought back their bowl and marched right up to the front door—mostly around town we go in and out back doors but being as they were new and especially since I wasn't sure how you went about calling when people had a maid, I used the front—and gave a knock. I had gotten up early to make a batch of dough-nuts, so I'd have something to put in the bowl when I took it back, so I knew that the people next door were up and about because I saw him leaving for work at seven-thirty. He must have worked in the city, to have to get off so early. Jane thinks he's in an office, because she saw him going toward the depot, and he wasn't running; people who work in offices don't have to get in on the dot, Jane said, although how she would know I couldn't tell you.

It was little Mrs. West who opened the door, and I must say she looked agreeable enough. I thought with the maid to bring her breakfast and all, she might still be lying in bed, the way they do, but she was all dressed in a pink housedress and was wide awake. She didn't ask me in right away, so I kind of moved a little toward the door, and then she stepped back and said wouldn't I come in, and I must say, funny as that furniture is, she had it fixed up nice, with green curtains on the windows. I couldn't tell from my house what the pattern was on those curtains, but once I was inside I could see it was a pattern of green leaves kind of woven in, and the rug, which of course I had seen when they brought it in, was green, too. Some of those big boxes that went in must have held books, because there were a lot of books all put away in bookcases, and before I had a chance to think I said, "My, you must have worked all night to get everything arranged so quick. I didn't see your lights on, though."

"Mallie did it," she said.

"Mallie being the maid?"

She kind of smiled, and then she said, "She's more like a godmother than a maid, really."

I do hate to seem curious, so I just said, "Mallie must keep herself pretty busy. Yesterday she was out digging your garden."

"Yes." It was hard to glean anything out of these people, with their short answers.

"I brought you some doughnuts," I said.

"Thank you." She put the bowl down on one of those little tables—Jane thinks they must hide the wine, because there wasn't a sight of any such thing that I could see—and then she said, "We'll offer them to the cat."

Well, I can tell you I didn't much care for that. "You must have quite a hungry cat," I said to her.

"Yes," she said. "I don't know what we'd do without him. He's Mallie's cat, of course."

"I haven't seen him," I said. If we were going to talk about cats, I figured I could hold my own, having had one cat or another for a matter of sixty years, although it hardly seemed a sensible subject for two ladies to chat over. Like I told Jane, there was a lot she ought to be wanting to know about the village and the people in it and who to go to for hardware and whatnot—I know for a fact I've put a dozen people off Tom Harris' hardware store since he charged me seventeen cents for a pound of nails—and I was just the person to set her straight on the town. But she was going on about the cat. "—fond of children," she was saying.

"I expect he's company for Mallie," I said.

"Well, he helps her, you know," she said, and then I began to think maybe she was crazy, too.

"And how does the cat help Mallie?"

"With her magic."

"I see," I said, and I started to say goodbye fast, figuring to get home to the telephone, because people around the village certainly ought to be hearing about what was going on. But before I could get to the door, the maid came out of the kitchen and said good morning to me, real polite, and then the maid said to Mrs. West that she was putting together the curtains for the front bedroom, and would Mrs. West like to decide on the pattern? And while I just stood there with my jaw hanging, she held out a handful of cobwebs—and I never did see anyone before or since who was able to hold a cobweb pulled out neat, or anyone who would want to, for that matter—and she had a blue jay's feather and a curl of blue ribbon, and she asked me how I liked her curtains.

Well, that did for me, and I got out of there and ran all the way to Jane's house, and, of course, she never believed me. She walked me home just so she could get a look at the outside of the house, and I will be everlastingly shaken if they hadn't gone and put up curtains in that front bedroom, soft white net with a design of blue that Jane said looked like a blue jay's feather. Jane said they were the prettiest curtains she ever saw, but they gave me the shivers every time I looked at them.

It wasn't two days after that I began finding things. Little things, and even some inside my own house. Once there was a basket of grapes on my back steps, and I swear those grapes were never grown around our village. For one thing, they shone like they were covered with silver dust, and smelled like some foreign perfume. I threw them in the garbage, but I kept a little embroidered handkerchief I found on the table in my front hall, and I've got it still in my dresser drawer.

Once I found a colored thimble on the fence post, and once my cat, Samantha, that I've had for eleven years and more, came in wearing a little green collar and spat at me when I took it off. One day I found a leaf basket on my kitchen table filled with hazelnuts, and it made me downright shaking mad to think of someone's coming in and out of my house without so much as asking, and me never seeing them come or go.

Things like that never happened before the crazy people moved into the house next door, and I was telling Mrs. Acton so, down on the corner one morning, when young Mrs. O'Neil came by and told us that when she was in the store with her baby she met Mallie the maid. The baby was crying because he was having a time with his teething, and Mallie gave him a little green candy to bite on. We thought Mrs. O'Neil was crazy herself to let her baby have candy that came from that family, and said so, and I told them about the drinking that went on, and the furniture getting arranged in the dark, and the digging in the garden, and Mrs. Acton said she certainly hoped they weren't going to think that just because they had a garden they had any claim to be in the Garden Club.

Mrs. Acton is president of the Garden Club. Jane says I ought to be president, if things were done right, on account of having the oldest garden in town, but Mrs. Acton's husband is the doctor, and I don't know what people thought he might do to them when they were sick if Mrs. Acton didn't get to be president. Anyway, you'd think Mrs. Acton had some say about who got into the Garden Club and who didn't, but I had to admit that in this case we'd all vote with her, even though Mrs. O'Neil did tell us the next day that she didn't think the people could be all crazy, because the baby's tooth came through that night with no more trouble.

Do you know, all this time that maid came into the store every day, and every day she bought one chicken. Nothing else. Jane took to dropping in the store when she saw the maid going along, and she says the maid never bought but one chicken a day. Once Jane got her nerve up and said to the maid that they must be fond of chicken, and the maid looked straight at her and told her right to her face that they were vegetarians.

"All but the cat, I suppose," Jane said, being pretty nervy when she gets her nerve up.

"Yes," the maid said, "all but the cat."

We finally decided that he must bring food home from the city, although why Mr. Honeywell's store wasn't good enough for them, I couldn't tell you. After the baby's tooth was better, Tom O'Neil took them over a batch of fresh-picked sweet corn, and they must have liked that, because they sent the baby a furry blue blanket that was so soft that young Mrs. O'Neil said the baby never needed another, winter or summer, and after being so sickly, that baby began to grow and got so healthy, you wouldn't know it was the same one, even though the O'Neils never should have accepted presents from strangers, not knowing whether the wool might be clean or not.

Then I found out they were dancing next door. Night after night after night, dancing. Sometimes I'd lie there awake until ten, eleven o'clock, listening to that heathen music and wishing I could get up the nerve to go over and give them a piece of my mind. It wasn't so much the noise keeping me from sleeping—I will say the music was soft and kind of like a lullaby—but people haven't got any right to live like that. Folks should go to bed at a sensible hour and get up at a sensible hour and spend their days doing good deeds and housework. A wife ought to cook dinner for her husband—and not out of cans from the city, either—and she ought to run over next door sometimes with a home-baked cake to pass the time of day and keep up with the news. And most of all a wife ought to go to the store herself, where she can meet her neighbors, and not just send the maid.

EVERY morning I'd go out and find fairy rings on the grass, and anyone around here will tell you that means an early winter, and here next door they hadn't even thought to get in coal. I watched every day for Adams and his truck, because I knew for a fact that cellar was empty of coal; all I had to do was lean down a little when I was in my garden and I could see right into the cellar, just as swept and clear as though they planned to treat their guests in there. Jane thought they were the kind who went off on a trip somewhere in the winter, shirking responsibilities for facing the snow with their neighbors. The cellar was all you could see, though. They had those green curtains pulled so tight against the windows that even right up close there wasn't a chink to look through from outside, and them inside dancing away. I do wish I could have nerved myself to go right up to that front door and knock some night.

Now, Mary Corn thought I ought to. "You got a right, Addie," she told me one day in the store. "You got every right in the world to make them quiet down at night. You're the nearest neighbor they got, and it's the right thing to do. Tell them they're making a name for themselves around the village."

Well, I couldn't nerve myself, and that's the gracious truth. Every now and then I'd see little Mrs. West walking in the garden, or Mallie the maid coming out of the woods with a basket—gathering acorns, never a doubt of it—but I never so much as nodded my head at them. Down at the store I had to tell Mary Corn that I couldn't do it. "They're foreigners, that's why," I said. "Foreigners of some kind. They don't rightly seem to understand what a person says—it's like they're always answering some other question you didn't ask."

"If they're foreigners," Dora Powers put in, being at the store to pick up some sugar to frost a cake, "it stands to reason there's something wrong to bring them here."

"Well, I won't call on foreigners," Mary said.

"You can't treat them the same as you'd treat regular people," I said. "I went inside the house, remember, although not, as you might say, to pay a call."

So then I had to tell them all over again about the furniture and the drinking—and it stands to reason that anyone who dances all night is going to be drinking, too—and my good doughnuts from my grandmother's recipe going to the cat. And Dora, she thought they were up to no good in the village. Mary said she didn't know anyone who was going to call, not being sure they were proper, and then we had to stop talking because in came Mallie the maid for her chicken.

You would have thought I was the chairman of a committee or something, the way Dora and Mary kept nudging me and winking that I should go over and speak to her, but I wasn't going to make a fool of myself twice, I can tell you. Finally Dora saw there was no use pushing me, so she marched over and stood there until the maid turned around and said, "Good morning."

Dora came right out and said, "There's a lot of people around this village, miss, would like to know a few things."

"I imagine so," the maid said.

"We'd like to know what you're doing in our village," Dora said.

"We thought it would be a nice place to live," the maid said. You could see that Dora was caught up short on that, because who picks a place to live because it's nice? People live in our village because they were born here; they don't just come.

I guess Dora knew we were all waiting for her, because she took a big breath and asked, "And how long do you plan on staying?"

"Oh," the maid said. "I don't think we'll stay very long, after all."

"Even if they don't stay," Mary said later, "they can do a lot of harm while they're here, setting a bad example for our young folk. Just for instance, I heard that the Harris boy got picked up again by the state police for driving without a license."

"Tom Harris is too gentle on that boy," I said. "A boy like that needs whipping and not people living in a house right in town showing him how to drink and dance all night."

Jane came in right then, and she had heard that all the children in town had taken to dropping by the house next door to bring dandelions and berries from the woods—and from their own fathers' gardens, too, I'll be bound—and the children were telling around that the cat next door could talk. They said he told them stories.

Well, that just about did for me, you can imagine. Children have too much freedom nowadays, anyway, without getting nonsense like that into their heads. We asked Annie Lee when she came into the store, and she thought somebody ought to call the police, so it could all be stopped before somebody got hurt. She said, suppose one of those kids got a step too far inside that house—how did we know he'd ever get out again? Well, it wasn't too pleasant a thought, I can tell you, but trust Annie Lee to be always looking on the black side. I don't have much dealing with the children as a rule, once they learn they better keep away from my apple trees and my melons, and I can't say I know one from the next, except for the Martin boy I had to call the police on once for stealing a piece of tin from my front yard; but I can't say I relished the notion that that cat had his eyes on them. It's not natural, somehow.

And don't you know it was the very next day that they stole the littlest Acton boy? Not quite three years old, and Mrs. Acton so busy with her Garden Club she let him run along into the woods with his sister, and first thing anyone knew they got him. Jane phoned and told me. She heard from Dora, who had been right in the store when the Acton girl came running in to find her mother and tell her the baby had wandered away in the woods, and Mallie the maid had been digging around not ten feet from where they saw him last. Jane said Mrs. Acton and Dora and Mary Corn and half a dozen others were heading right over to the house next door, and I better get outside fast before I missed something, and if she got there late to let her know everything that happened. I barely got out my own front door, when down the street they came, maybe ten or twelve mothers, marching along so mad they never had time to be scared.

"Come on, Addie," Dora said to me. "They've finally done it this time."

I knew Jane would never forgive me if I hung back, so out I went and up the front walk to the house next door. Mrs. Acton was ready to go right up and knock, because she was so mad, but before she had a chance the door opened and there was Mrs. West and the little boy, smiling all over as if nothing had happened.

"Mallie found him in the woods," Mrs. West said, and Mrs. Acton grabbed the boy away from her; you could tell they had been frightening him by the way he started to cry as soon as he got to his own mother. All he would say was "kitty," and that put a chill down our backs, you can imagine.

Mrs. Acton was so mad she could hardly talk, but she did manage to say, "You keep away from my children, you hear me?" And Mrs. West looked surprised.

"Mallie found him in the woods," she said. "We were going to bring him home."

"We can guess how you were going to bring him home," Dora shouted, and then Annie Lee piped up from well in the back, "Why don't you get out of our town?"

"I guess we will," Mrs. West said. "It's not the way we thought it was going to be."

That was nice, wasn't it? Nothing riles me like people knocking this town, where my grandfather built the first house, and I just spoke up right then and there.

"Foreign ways!" I said. "You're heathen, wicked people, with your dancing and your maid, and the sooner you leave this town, the better it's going to be for you. Because I might as well tell you"—and I shook my finger right at her—"that certain people in this town aren't going to put up with your fancy ways much longer, and you would be well advised—very well advised, I say—to pack up your furniture and your curtains and your maid and cat, and get out of our town before we put you out."

Jane claims she doesn't think I really said it, but all the others were there and can testify I did—all but Mrs. Acton, who never had a good word to say for anybody.

Anyway, right then we found out they had given the little boy something, trying to buy his affection, because Mrs. Acton pried it out of his hand, and he was crying all the time. When she held it out, it was hard to believe, but of course with them there's nothing too low. It was a little gold-colored apple, all shiny and bright, and Mrs. Acton threw it right at the porch floor, as hard as she could, and that little toy shattered into dust. "We don't want anything from you," Mrs. Acton said, and as I told Jane afterward, it was terrible to see the look on Mrs. West's face. For a minute she just stood there looking at us. Then she turned and went back inside and shut the door.

Someone wanted to throw rocks through the windows, but, as I told them, destroying private property is a crime and we might better leave violence to the menfolk, so Mrs. Acton took her little boy home, and I went in and called Jane. Poor Jane; the whole thing had gone off so fast, she hadn't had time to get her corset on.

I hadn't any more than gotten Jane on the phone, when I saw through the hall window that a moving van was right there next door, and the men were starting to carry out that fancy furniture. Jane wasn't surprised when I told her over the phone. "Nobody can get moving that fast," she said. "They were probably planning to slip out with that little boy."

"Or maybe the maid did it with magic," I said, and Jane laughed.

"Listen," she said, "go and see what else is going on—I'll hang on the phone."

There wasn't anything to see, even from my front porch, except the moving van and the furniture coming out; not a sign of Mrs. West or the maid.

"He hasn't come home from the city yet," Jane said. "I can see the street from here. They'll have news for him tonight."

That was how they left. I take a lot of the credit for myself, even though Jane tries to make me mad by saying Mrs. Acton did her share. By that night they were gone, bag and baggage, and Jane and I went over the house with a flashlight to see what damage they had left behind. There wasn't a thing left in that house—not a chicken bone, not an acorn— except for one blue jay's wing upstairs, and that wasn't worth taking home. Jane put it in the incinerator when we came downstairs.

One more thing. My cat, Samantha, had kittens. That may not surprise you, but it sure as judgment surprised me and Samantha, her being over eleven years old and well past her kitten days, the old fool. But you would have laughed to see her dancing around like a young lady cat, just as light-footed and as pleased as if she thought she was doing something no cat ever did before; and those kittens troubled me.

Folks don't dare come right out and say anything to me about my kittens, of course, but they do keep on with that silly talk about fairies and leprechauns. And there's no denying that the kittens are bright yellow, with orange eyes, and much bigger than normal kittens have a right to be. Sometimes I see them all watching me when I go around the kitchen, and it gives me a cold finger down my back. Half the children in town are begging for those kittens—"fairy kittens," they're calling them—but there isn't a grown-up in town would take one.

Jane says there's something downright uncanny about those kittens, but then, I may never speak to her again in all my life. Jane would even gossip about cats, and gossip is one thing I simply cannot endure.

Smoke

Erica Jong

A warning never to consider ourselves too "enlightened" to notice the lurking darkness of fear and prejudice.

Smoke, it is all smoke
in the throat of eternity. . . .
For centuries, the air was full of witches
Whistling up chimneys
on their spiky brooms
cackling or singing more sweetly than Circe,
as they flew over rooftops
blessing & cursing their kind.

We banished & burned them
making them smoke
in the throat of god;
we declared ourselves "enlightened."
"The dark age of horrors is past,"
said my mother to me in 1952,
seven years after our people went up in smoke,
leaving a few teeth, a pile of bones.

The smoke curls and beckons.
It is blue & lavender
& green as the undersea world.
It will take us, too.

O let us not go sheepishly
clinging to our nakedness.

But let us go like witches sucked heavenward
by the Goddess' powerful breath
& whistling, whistling, whistling
on our beautiful brooms.

Acknowledgments

Bradbury, Ray. "Exorcism." Copyright © 1945 by Ray Bradbury. First appeared in *Dandelion Wine*. Reprinted by permission of the author and his agent, Don Congdon Associates, Inc.

Edghill, Rosemary. "The Christmas Witch." Copyright © 2001 by Rosemary Edghill, reprinted by permission of the author.

Ellison, Harlan. "The Goddess in the Ice." Copyright © 1967 by Harlan Ellison. Revised version © 1982 by the Kilimanjaro Corporation Renewed, © 1995 by Harlan Ellison. Reprinted by arrangement with, and permission of, the Author and the Author's agent, Richard Curtis Associates, Inc., New York, New York, USA. All rights reserved.

Elrod, P. N. "The Tea Room Beasts." Copyright © 2000 by P. N. Elrod. Reprinted by permission of the author. First appeared in *Creature Fantastic*, DAW.

Endrezze, Anita. "The Humming of Stars and Bees and Waves." Copyright © 2000 by Anita Endrezze, reprinted by permission of the author. First appeared in *Throwing Fire at the Sun, Water at the Moon* (University of Arizona Press, 2000).

Erdrich, Lousie. "Fleur." Copyright © 1994 by Louise Erdrich. Reprinted by permission of the author and her agents, The Wylie Agency, Inc.

Erdrich, Louise. "The Strange People." Copyright © 1984 by Louise Erdrich. Reprinted by permission of the author and her agents, The Wylie Agency, Inc.

Gerrold, David. "The Spell." Copyright © 1993 by David Gerrold, reprinted by permission of the author.

Jackson, Shirley. "The Very Strange House Next Door." From *Just an Ordinary Day: The Uncollected Stories*, by Shirley Jackson. Copyright © 1997 by The Estate of Shirley Jackson. Used by permission of Bantam Books, a division of Random House, Inc.

Jong, Erica. "Figure of the Witch." Copyright © 1981, 1991 by Erica Mann Jong. All rights reserved. Used by arrangement with the poet.

Jong, Erica. "Smoke." Copyright © 1981, 1991 by Erica Mann Jong. All rights reserved. Used by arrangement with the poet.